'A book that consistently operates on many levels of meaning, its apparent simplicity, in fact, part of a rich fabric of symbol, echo and allusion...Okri loves paradox, one of the striking affinities he has with Blake, and uses words to point at the hidden, the space where the sacred lives and breathes...The intrusion of humanity's inhumanity anchors the metaphysical lyricism of the book, creatively chills its enchanted air, reminds us that all the best fairy tales hold a mirror up to the darkness of the world...But it is the imaginative generosity and peculiar purity of the writing that continually touch the heart. Here is a prose with a tender tread, alive to human frailty...[Okri] seduces the reader with a rapt recounting of the infinite within the particular' *Observer*

'The language of [Okri's] story is simple, courtly, timeless, childlike, beautiful...What he has created, however, is a unique and beguiling world of his own imagining' *Sunday Herald*

'Building phrase upon rich phrase, Okri sweeps across the whole of the mythical world he creates, yet manages, too, to hold before the reader's gaze, steadily, moment by moment, each small fragment of this reality...Welling up through this book is a sense of the sheer mystery of life, of story, of beginnings and endings...Each phrase is pregnant with possibility and magic' *London Magazine*

'Each sentence is like a magical capsule breaking open with a burst of coloured light' *Books Quarterly*

'Okri's prose carries off a remarkably difficult balancing act in which reality is transfigured into a prose that aspires to be poetry...like many of Okri's books it's hard to describe because of the rich, dreamlike, almost hallucinatory prose' *The Sunday Times* (Scottish edition)

'This is quite, s[...]y we are all so speci[...]

'Readers who loved *The Famished Road*, which won the Booker Prize, will fall on it avidly...Okri's is an art that sometimes communicates before it is understood. It echoes the Bible in it conundrums. It rhymes like Shakespeare in its couplets. It often evokes Judaism's Book of Life. And like the New Testament, it advocates that salvation stems from pure love' *Scotsman*

'This long-awaited novel from the author of *The Famished Road* is a bewitching story, at once old-fashioned fairy tale and modern exploration of human experience...Lyrical and intensely imaginative' *Good Book Guide*

'This most simple of plots belies the extraordinary messages and hidden meanings waiting to be extracted from Okri's text...a profound philosophical meditation...this book pushes the experience of reading far beyond any usual boundaries ... passionate, moving and intense' *Scotland on Sunday*

'*Starbook* is the book [Okri] has waited all his life to write, the completion of a story his mother began to tell him as a child...Okri considers the infection and destruction of a culture in such a way that it becomes clearly the province of art and not of history books to do so' *Yorkshire Post*

'At the centre of this novel – as it has been in many of [Okri's] novels – is the noble attempt to find the Good, the starting engine for recovery and progress, and the role of the artist, the storyteller, and the imagination in the process' *Glasgow Herald*

'Part mythical romance, part an exploration of freedom and regeneration, this is a rich tale with complex themes' *Psychologies*

'Visionary, utopian and magical' *Western Daily Press*

'As ever with Okri, there are passages of incredible beauty' *Financial Times*

Ben Okri has published eight novels, including *The Famished Road*, for which he won the Booker Prize. He has also written collections of poetry, short stories and essays, and his work has been translated into more than twenty languages. He is a Fellow of the Royal Society of Literature and he has been awarded the OBE as well as numerous international prizes, including the Commonwealth Writers Prize for Africa, the Aga Khan Prize for Fiction and the Chianti Rufino-Antico Fattore. He is a Vice-President of the English Centre of International PEN and was presented with a Crystal Award by the World Economic Forum. He was born in Nigeria and lives in London.

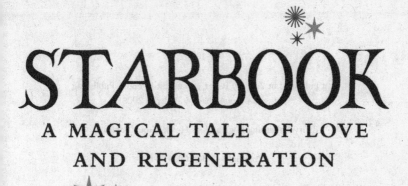

STARBOOK

A MAGICAL TALE OF LOVE
AND REGENERATION

BEN OKRI

RIDER

LONDON · SYDNEY · AUCKLAND · JOHANNESBURG

7 9 10 8

First published in 2007 by Rider, an imprint of Ebury Publishing
This edition published by Rider in 2008

Ebury Publishing is a Random House Group company

Copyright © Ben Okri 2007

Ben Okri has asserted his right to be identified as the author of this Work in
accordance with the Copyright, Designs and Patents Act 1988

The Random House Group Limited Reg. No. 954009

Addresses for companies within the Random House Group can be found at

www.randomhouse.co.uk

A CIP catalogue record for this book is available from the British Library

ISBN 978-1-846-04081-8

To buy books by your favourite authors and register for offers visit

www.randomhouse.co.uk

The Random House Group Limited supports The Forest Stewardship
Council® (FSC®), the leading international forest-certification organisation.
Our books carrying the FSC label are printed on FSC®-certified paper.
FSC is the only forest-certification scheme supported by the leading
environmental organisations, including Greenpeace. Our
paper procurement policy can be found at
www.randomhouse.co.uk/environment

Printed and bound in Great Britain by Clays Ltd, St Ives plc

In memory of my father, Silver Okri, 1928–1998
With gratitude for the magic foundation

Acknowledgements

I wish to express my special thanks to the Marsh Agency,
To Paul Marsh, Camilla Ferrier and Jessica Woollard for their tenacity;
To Judith Kendra for her vision, and to all at Rider Books;
To Rosemary Clunie and the ongoing alchemy.

Contents

Contents

Book One

THE
PRINCE

CHAPTER ONE

This is a story my mother began to tell me when I was a child. The rest I gleaned from the book of life among the stars, in which all things are known.

In the heart of the kingdom there was a place where the earth was dark and sweet to taste. Anything that was planted grew in rich profusion. The village was built in the shape of a magnificent circle. And in the centre of the circle stood the palace of the king. Four rivers met in the forest around the village. The shrinehouse was at the edge of the village and the path that ran past it led to the outside world. The forest was dense about the village, and it seemed that those in the heart of the kingdom lived in a magic dream, an oasis of huts and good harvests in the midst of an enveloping world of trees.

There is an ancient saying in the village that my mother used to tell me. They say that it is not who you are that makes the world respect you, but what power it is that stands behind you. It is not you that the world sees, but that power. The village was small but, behind it, all around it, stood the power and the majesty of the dense forest. At night the forest was dark and rich with magic and enchantment. In the day it was lovely and of a sunlit green, and a haunting barely audible music could be heard from its earth. Gifted children often said that they could hear the trees singing charmed melodies. On certain nights, when the moon was full and white like the perfect egg at the beginning of creation, the wise ones claimed that the trees whispered stories in the abundant darkness. Those stories, they said, took form and wandered about the world and one day would take on a life of their own. The people of the village very rarely went into the forest because it was so powerful, so unpredictable, like the immeasurable mythology of an unknown god.

Long ago, in the time when the imagination ruled the world, there was a prince in this kingdom who grew up in the serenity of all things. He was my mother's ancestor, and he alone of all the people in that village loved playing in the forest. He was very handsome and fair and bright and the elders suspected that he was a child of heaven, one of those children from another place, who was not destined to live long. He was never so happy as when he played alone in the forest or by the river. He was a favourite of the mermaids and the mysterious girls of the forest and he took them flowers and things he had made and he played music to the spirits of the river. Because he was a child of heaven, he was left alone to do as he pleased, so long as he did not express a wish to die.

He was a surprise to the royal family. The soothsayers at his birth predicted for him an unusual life. He will be a king and a slave, they said. He will be sold like a goat, treated like an animal, he will fight in a war, he will suffer like a great sinner, he will live like a god, and will know freedom more than the freest of men. The most puzzling thing the soothsayers said, however, was that he would die young in his old age or that he would die old in his youth.

The elders expected him to be sickly. He never was. They didn't know whether to groom him for kingship. He showed no interest. Politics and royal duties bored him. He seemed to much prefer working with the common people in the farms, harvesting corn, teasing the maidens, building huts for the frail old women of the village, splitting firewood, and piping music around the edges of the kingdom, as if he were haunted by a sad beauty that fringed the limits of the world. It touched the hearts of the elders to see his fragile body bent to such difficult tasks he set himself, or to see his fading presence dissipate itself in the lovely music that he teased out in the dappled shadowy realm of the myth-infested forests that was his second home. What were they going to do about this royal vagabond, this noble tramp who so swayed the hearts of the women and the elders, who fascinated the young, who moved the heart of the kingdom like a string instrument plucked to perfection by a dying master? It was like watching a strange game of life and death being played out before the eyes of everyone.

No one dared offer him their daughters for fear that he would early desert them for the land of death that he seemed to find so sweet. And yet all the maidens loved him passionately, mutely, dreamily, from a distance. When he spoke to them with his soft and confident and thrilling voice, they became petrified with an unmasterable enchantment. And when he touched them, it was like being scalded by something sublime, and some maidens were known to cry out suddenly, others to suffer great pain and agony, and many became unwell afterwards and shivered in love fevers undiagnosed for weeks. Later, one maiden whom he played with and wrestled into the river fell profoundly ill, lost her senses to incomprehensible love ravings, and died, when least expected, of a kind of fatal happiness. Some said, in malice, that a curse hovered over our young hero, and that one day . . .

CHAPTER TWO

And so time passed as he grew up in mystery. In accordance with the rites instituted by the ancient traditions of the royal family, our young hero was initiated into the deep mysteries of the tribe, and of royalty. He underwent seven initiations, most of which took place when he wasn't aware of them. There were the mysteries of the hidden order that showed his place among the stars, the sands, the gods, the ancestors. There were the mysteries that revealed to him his place in the royal tradition, revealed the terrors of kingship, the dread that attends noble blood, the fire that follows the line of his birth, the madness he must overcome as a gift of his birth, and the greatness of heart he must cultivate in the midst of the tangled threads of a strong destiny.

These initiations took place at night, in the forest. He witnessed the raising of the ancestral spirits in their fearful splendour, and spent seven nights in the company of the illustrious and the infamous dead of all times and all places, so that all the great and most wicked and most loving deeds of men and women would never be a stranger to him.

These initiations into the mysteries began in him an unsuspected transformation. He became more silent, and yet more open. His utterances, though perfectly clear, were completely opaque. His voice changed and took on tones that were at once deep, surprising and gentle. Sometimes he seemed hard, cold, remote; and other times joyful, rich with love, basking in wonderment. He became an enigma to the village, but was a bigger enigma to himself. He didn't know who he was any more.

And so he spent more time in the forest, around the river, in the hills, listening to the birds, searching for God to give him the answers to the questions that the initiations had awoken in him like thunderous bells, or drums.

The royal family began to fear that the initiations had done him more harm than good. Instead of making a bigger man of him, they had, it seemed, made him more vulnerable, more unstable. They feared he was going mad. Or that, worse, he might take his own life, in an attempt to return to heaven. So they decided that what he needed was a wife.

CHAPTER THREE

He didn't need a wife. He needed time. No one thought to leave him alone so that he could come round in his own way. They fretted over him and troubled him with their fears and projections. They made him the concern and the problem and the focus of the kingdom. They interfered with every aspect of his life. They gave him no space to grow into his own man. They robbed him of space and time. They spied on him everywhere he went. They reported his every move. They misunderstood his every gesture and utterance. They magnified his silence. They distorted his stillness. They suspected his prayers. They saw sinister aspects to his complete innocence.

And so, unwittingly, they drove him further and further away from the kingdom.

He began to roam, to explore the deep forests, in unconscious attempts to escape the prying eyes that gave him no peace. If they hadn't worried over him so much, and made him seek escape, what happened would never have happened; and, mysteriously, the world would have been smaller for it. Destiny conceals strange illuminations in the suffering life visits on us. The tale of fate is entangled with mysteries. Dare one say such and such shouldn't have happened? History is replete with monstrosities that shouldn't have happened. But they did. And we are what we are because they did. And history's bizarre seeding has not yet yielded all of its harvest. Who knows what events will mean in the fullness of time? Our hero ran away from the prison of his royal role into something much worse. Who is to say why, or what its purpose and ultimate meaning was? In the presence of great things glimpsed in the book of life one can only be silent and humble. The ultimate meaning of history is beyond the mortal mind. All one can say is that this happened. Make of it what you will. Our hero went searching for God in the hills, and one day came upon a maiden by the river, with a bucket of water on her head. She was returning to the farms. And he took her for a sign.

She was not, at first, beautiful. She became very beautiful later on. She was, at that time, quite plain, quite odd in the face, like a work of art in formation, verging on ugly, but rich with the potential of many different kinds of harmonies emerging from the early stages of the manifestation of a personality. There was something about her that was rare, special, hidden, waiting. Something fine, clear, like a cloudy uncertain dawn that, to the trained eye, already hints at an especially brilliant day.

Our hero didn't fall in love with her at first sight. Nor did she notice him. She was like a swan in infancy, all clumsy, out of colour, perplexed, seeing things all wrong. How unpromising excellent things are in their youth. How awkward true beauty seems in its early stages. Who could tell that a butterfly would emerge from such a mess of matter that is a caterpillar? She was such a creature, all at sixes and sevens, at odds with her own unique spirit growing within her. And yet her eyes, how clearly they revealed the presence of diamonds within. Except that the young all have clear eyes. But hers had a touch of heaven. He didn't notice. He saw her as a sign.

CHAPTER FOUR

He called to her from his hiding place, and she started, and fell. He was silent. She looked about her, and saw nothing. She got up and fetched more water from the river. As she was leaving he called her again, and she jumped. It seemed to her that the spirits of the land were addressing her. Or that she had heard the goddess of the sea. This was a sign for her that she was about to die, as a mark of special favour.

'But I have not lived yet,' she said out aloud, as if pleading for clemency.

'You will live now,' he said, enjoying this game of destiny.

'What am I to do?'

'Answer my three questions then you can live.'

She put down the bucket, and then fell on her knees.

'I am ready,' she said, with tears in her voice.

He laughed to himself in his hiding place among the wild flowers on the border of his kingdom.

'First,' he said, in his strange disguised voice, 'where does the river end?'

'In the wisdom of God,' she replied, humbly.

He was startled by the answer. He stayed silent a while. The wind blew enchantments over them. The river yielded the lights of the sky. Spirits converged at the river's edge to witness a special moment in time. Unborn children hovered over that potent space above her head. Invisible story-tellers held their breaths. Those who wander in dreams paused there, to drink in the mood of magic.

'Second,' he said, more sternly, 'where does all our suffering end?'

'In the happiness that lies beyond all things,' she replied, as if in a trance.

He caught his breath. For the first time in his life he knew that deep inside agony there is a sweetness that is beyond compare. Only those who venture into such a dark find such a light. Deep in the pain is beauty from the high mountains of the sublime. How can it be? What fruit would give bitterness and reserve such impossible richness in its core, in its seed that is tough as diamond? The world's puzzle shone around him. The river shone with gold and silver showers from the sun. Is the air so rich with the vitality that makes new life? He breathed in enchantments, and the air he breathed changed the initiated man within into something rested, settled, and forming, as an angel crystallises into a child. Dreamers all around, lingering in that ancient mood, felt the happy sunlight above their houses. Spirits were in a mood of delight. Time converged here. Such lovely moments pipe an eternal happiness all over the world, through all time, wherever it is needed, and can be reached, by the fortunate, or those who know.

He spoke like an oracle now, except not giving, but asking. He said:

'And finally, what are we all seeking?'

'The kingdom,' she replied, 'which we are in already, which we have got, and which is our home.'

The answer seemed so appropriate that he was astonished. He fell into a deep silence in which he was borne by the wind and the fragrance of mysterious flowers into a dim realm where, for a moment, he glimpsed a strange white horse with a golden horn in the middle of its forehead.

When his mind cleared he saw that the girl was rising from her prayerful position, and he felt he had to say something while the mystery still held. He noticed though that there was a mist rising from the river. It was a white mist, like a shroud, or an unusual cloud, and some of its skeins seemed to float across towards the girl, obscuring her. He was suddenly afraid. Seized with a sense of immensity he had never felt before, and having the presence of mind to break through it, he said:

'Come back here the same time tomorrow. Come alone.'

The mist around her briefly cleared, and he saw her nodding. Then before he could think what else to do or say, she got up, snatched her bucket, and disappeared into the forest.

CHAPTER FIVE

He left his hiding place and wandered the woods in this new mood of splendour, of faint shining terror, and a joy bordering on madness. What had come over him? He was addressing love songs to the birds and the trees, wrestling playfully with spirits in the air, laughing at dreams that floated past him, making jokes at wood sprites that he saw dancing in yellow clearings. The whole sky had become a love mood wherein he saw everything more clearly. Everything made sense. Everything was simple. And in the kingdom he saw himself everywhere, with all the people in the world, all as one.

He wandered in this state, dreaming of the girl he had just seen, who was so clear to him in his mind that she seemed to accompany him. And he spoke to her, and sang, and laughed at the rich silence of her replies; and he remained spellbound by her liquid luminous eyes and her pale awkward face.

The elders found him in this state, and fearing him to be unhinged they grappled with him and were surprised that he offered no resistance. They carried him home on their shoulders to the royal palace. He re-entered the village a different person, and saw it all anew, as if he were waking up from a deep sleep that had lasted all his life.

CHAPTER SIX

In the palace the first thing he noticed were the slaves. Then he became aware of the numerous servants. Then he saw the many wives of his father. Then he saw his father. It was strange. He thought: who are all these people?

'Are you well, my son?' his father asked.

He stared at the imposing, fleshy, big and powerful face of his father, the king. He stared into the big, wise and sensuous eyes, at once alert and lazy, at once dangerous and complacent. The king did not smile. He never remembered his father as ever having smiled. Laughing, yes; but never smiling. He smiled at his father. The elders who were present nodded sagely at this interesting development. Then they were baffled when he put his arms round his father's neck and held him in a deep unrequited embrace.

'I only asked you if you are well, my son,' the king said, embarrassed. 'There is no need for all this demonstration. Remember who you are. You are a prince, and the future king. Now control yourself.'

He didn't. He stayed hugging his father, breathing in the strong essences and smells of his body, smells rich and potent with the personality of the king, his power, his strength, his unyielding force, his compact radiance, his awesome build, the herbs and potions of his personal and spiritual fortification. The son held on to the father as on to a great tree, a mighty legend. The son held on even when the father threw up his hands in royal exasperation. Then the father, the king, began to laugh. It was a wonderful laughter, and it rocked the kingdom.

And all the elders began laughing too, and they held hands and spontaneously formed a circle and they danced, singing praise-songs around the son and his father, the prince and the king. And still the son held on to the might of the man, to the splendour of the father, feeling the king's great laughter shaking his tender frame and reordering forces within him that were misaligned, and filling him with energies, with wisdom, with unknown powers, with the spiritual strength of kingship, and with a love he could not express to his son but which was there in the embarrassment of laughter.

Then suddenly the son disengaged from the father, and said:

'Father, I am not well. I saw a maiden today who touched my heart. I don't know who she is or where she comes from. I am not well and I am too well because of her.'

Then abruptly he left the presence of the king. Silence fell over the elders. The king was perplexed by what his son had said, and his odd behaviour. He sensed something sinister. He feared that enemies had bewitched his son, or cast a spell on him, or twisted his mind with the vision of woman. He feared bewitchment more than wars. Armies can fight armies; but how do you fight bewitchment?

'My son has been bewitched,' he said out loud. 'Keep an eye on him. Follow his movements. And find out who this maiden is that has clouded the mind of the prince.'

The elders bowed. Instructions were given, and put into motion. The forest became the home of spies.

CHAPTER SEVEN

An intuition made him take a convoluted route that confused the spies watching him from behind every tree. The next day he returned to his hiding place in the far boundary of the kingdom and waited for the maiden to appear. He arrived long before the appointed time. He hadn't slept all night, or so he thought.

He felt he hadn't slept because he spent all night wandering through the world looking for a maiden who bore his heart in her womb. His heart grew in her like a child. She was pregnant with his heart for a long time, for a year, for ten years, for a generation, for a hundred and two years. His heart grew bigger and bigger in her, and she grew bigger and bigger to accommodate the growth of his heart in her womb. He never knew when she would give birth to his heart and he lost her and searched for her the world over and couldn't find her. His father, the king, told him that the world in which he searched for her was his heart, and that she was the mother of the world, and that his search was over when it began but he didn't know it. He was nonetheless unconsoled and was still searching when he awoke into a sleepless state that left him unrested and bewildered.

The birds played, the flowers breathed out their fragrances, the river ran on into the heart of God, the sky was clear and sent down fine spangles of diamonds, and dreams floated past, and the forest sang, and the spirits danced in the air, and the future hovered over him, and the sun passed the shadows it cast at the appointed hour, and still the maiden didn't appear.

He waited till strange women came to the river and fetched water and laughed and played and went away. He waited till the noonday sun changed its colour and its flashing swords cut down on the earth and water. He slept while he waited and many voices spoke around him and wizards danced above him and sorcerers chanted over his sleeping form. When he awoke it was evening. And she still hadn't appeared.

He went home with a heavy heart and didn't notice the trees in the forest or the cats that eyed him or the spies that watched him. It was only when he got to the village that he saw a group of men and women that he had never seen before. They were from a different land. They were fetching wood and they were downcast and the men looked brave and the women looked unhappy. So he went among them and asked who they were. The leader among them, a burly man, with a warrior's mien, said:

'We are men and women captured in war. We are slaves of your kingdom. We do your dirty work till our people can pay our ransom.'

'What are slaves?' the young prince asked.

'The lowest of the low,' the warrior replied.

'What does that mean?'

'Mean, sir? It means we are nothing. We have no freedom. We do whatever you tell us to do. You can kill us whenever you want. Our people don't know where we are. We are here by force. We don't want to be here. We want to be in our villages, with our own families, and our people.'

'So why don't you just go?' the prince asked, amazed.

'Because they will kill us if we try. We are slaves, sir. Captured people.'

'What are you doing?'

'We are digging latrines.'

'How long have you been here?'

'Not long for a free man, but too long for a slave.'

The prince was about to ask another question when the elders descended on him and led him away. He protested.

'Your highness, you can't talk to those people.'

'Why not?'

'They are animals.'

'Animals? They are not animals. They are human beings,' the prince said, astonished.

'They are slaves, your highness, and a prince cannot talk with slaves.'

'Why not?'

'Because it is forbidden.'

'By who?'

'The laws of the kingdom.'

'The laws? Who made the laws?'

'The Wise Ones.'

'Which Wise Ones?'

'From long ago.'

'Then they must have been fools, or monsters.'

'Your highness, they were your ancestors.'

'I am ashamed to have such ancestors.'

The elders were silent and took his remarks as further proof that he was either deranged or bewitched, as the wise king had said.

CHAPTER EIGHT

He left the elders and went straight to his father and made an unusual request. His father, the king, heard him out without blinking. When he had finished, the king stared at his son for a long time. Then he laughed. It was not the same laughter as the last time. It was a troubled laughter.

He summoned the elders. When they were gathered the king asked his son to repeat his request. The prince, calm, innocent and sad with love, said:

'If I am to be future king I want to know what good and what evils we have done as a people.'

There was a deep silence among the elders. Then they began to murmur in great perplexity. Their murmurings turned into discussions and then into arguments. They argued among themselves about what were evils and what were good. They argued furiously. The prince watched them in amazement. He heard mention of tortures, floggings, murders, wars, rapes, burning of villages, outcasts, banishments. Then he thought he hadn't heard them right. Some elders said they were not evils but necessities, matters of justified war, acts of defence needed to protect the kingdom. The king became impatient.

'Are you going to answer my son, or what?' he bellowed.

There was another silence. The elders stared at the prince. The prince stared at them. Then, quite suddenly, the king began laughing again; and the elders, taking their cue, relieved, laughed as well.

What a fearful laughter it was, this peculiar laughter of the custodians and the elders. It was a laughter the prince had never heard or seen before. It was a laughter threaded with dark energies. It almost made him ill. The king, noticing that his son had turned pale, stopped laughing. Then gradually silence descended upon the elders.

'You have not replied to my request,' the young prince said, eventually.

The senior among the elders stepped forward, prostrated himself majestically, and said:

'We as a people have only done good. We have done no evil. The bad things it appears we have done were for good reasons. We are a good people, with a clean conscience. You should be assured, your highness, that as a future king your hands and the hands of your ancestors are clean.'

'What about the slaves?'

'Dear prince,' said the senior custodian, 'there are no slaves in the kingdom.'

'What?'

'It is best for a prince not to know the good or the necessary evil done in the realm. That is our job. Yours, in time, is to rule with good hands.'

'How can my hands be clean if there is wickedness done in my name?'

'Done in the name of the kingdom, dear prince. Your hands will always be clean.'

The custodian smiled benignly.

'So there are no slaves in the kingdom?'

'Yes.'

'Yes there are or yes there are none?'

'No.'

The prince was exasperated. He turned to the king, his father. The king was grim and mute. He offered no support. He merely listened. He watched his son.

Suddenly the prince bolted from the chamber and was gone before the custodians and elders could react. Not long afterwards a commotion was heard in the palace corridors. Guards and soldiers made loud noises. There was much shouting, and a clashing of weapons. Then voices bellowing. The prince reappeared in the hall of custodians, leading seven of the slaves he had spoken to earlier.

'You can't bring slaves in here!' the elders shouted, almost as one.

'What slaves?' the prince replied. 'These are men captured in war.'

'And some are criminals, sold by their own people,' said the senior of the custodians. 'Some are murderers, running away from justice. And some are dogs in disguise, animals and beasts to their own kind. We make them work. We do them no harm. They feed, they can marry, and they can earn their freedom. They are not slaves.'

'I want them freed!' cried the prince.

'Don't get involved in these matters, your highness. Keep your hands clean. Don't enquire too much into affairs of the kingdom. Things are more complicated than they seem. There are no chains on these people. They are almost free. We have an ancient understanding between villages and kingdoms. These threads are too entangled to unravel in a day.'

The prince was silent. The custodian gave a sign for the slaves to be removed. Soldiers came in and led them away.

'What else is there that I must not know?'

'Many things.'

'Like what?'

The head custodian paused. He turned helplessly to the king. The king nodded.

'Outcasts. The burial of kings with their servants and wives. Low castes who work in the dark, never seen, never allowed to marry above . . .'

On and on the custodian went, pouring out the practices of the land from time immemorial, the good and the bad. But first the bad, for that was the theme of the day. It was a worrying list. It included peculiar things like days when no animal, insect, bird or living thing is killed. Days of laughter. Nights of story-telling. The special day of the spirits. The day of the long-haired babies. The festivities for the lower caste, when all the villages stage dances and rituals for them and bring gifts and food, and perform for all outcasts, beggars and rejects. Then there were the leprous left out in the hills. The night of the dead, when ancestors are honoured. The flogging of thieves. The exile of adulterers. The banishment of cowards, traitors, murderers. The rigorously reasoned laws. The list went on, for hours, till the young prince began to hallucinate. Then he fell down in exhaustion and over-wrought emotion.

That night the king went to the prince's bedroom and watched him sleeping. The king sat and stared at his son for hours as he slept. At dawn the king left. He was silent most of the next day. Silent and thoughtful.

CHAPTER NINE

Not long after the king left, the prince awoke. And he remembered the maiden. And, without eating, taking only the swiftest bath and some water to drink and a few fruits, he hurried off into the forest to his hiding place beside the river.

The world had changed. The air was cooler. The shimmer on the water was more muted. The prince waited in a state bordering on illness. He waited in a mildly hallucinated condition and he drifted off and thought he saw the king above him, staring at him. He thought he saw the king by the river, gazing into the water at scenes of the future unfolding before him.

Then seven maidens appeared from out of the river, attired in splendid white robes. Three of them had musical instruments he had never seen before, of shining metal, gleaming like polished silver in the sun. The maidens, with hands linked, danced on the surface of the river, laughing and singing. Then as they danced they rose in the air, like a ring of diamonds, a circle of angels, and then they came back down again, and landed on the shore.

There was one among them who was the most beautiful, who was the princess of them all. She had eyes that shone like moonlight. She had a face that was clear in its beauty and happy sadness, skin that was smooth, and she walked elegantly. The other maidens clustered about her and made a seat for her of flowers they picked from the shores of the river. She lay languidly on the bed of flowers. Then one of the maidens struck up an instrument and they all began playing the most haunting music. The princess among them began to sing:

'Who knows why we wait,
For love comes to us like gentle fate.
It hides along the river of time
And gives off the fragrance of thyme.
To love is to suffer is what they say;
But to suffer sweetly is better than to decay.
This life is not a river under the sky.
Many things must happen, who knows why.'

And so she sang and when she came to the end she began to hum and the others hummed and giggled and soon silence fell over them as the light made their beauty shine so brightly by the river. They were silent as they stared into the air. Then the princess among them said:

'Oh, but we are so happy today, and all is well in the kingdom, and so let us prophesy a little under this gentle breeze.'

'O yes,' cried one, 'let us prophesy a little.'

'Who shall begin?'

'You will?' the maidens said in chorus to the princess.

'All right,' she replied.

She picked up a white flower, spun its stalk between her palms, and sent it whirling into the air, and it turned, spinning, and sailed away in the breeze, down the river. Then she began, saying:

'I speak backwards and forwards and sideways and inside out, and always speak the truth. There will be a marriage between a prince and an outcast, a prince and a slave, and a magic line will be conceived. The prince will become a slave before his son is born. There will be sweetness made out of the blood and suffering of men and women. Music will come from their bones, which the whole world will dance to, and fall in love through. Suffering like a curse will fall on the land. The sea will swallow up thousands of the men of the soil. There will be darkness over its sky for two hundred years. Then light will return. The world will be upside down. White will be black, and black white. Good will be evil, and evil good. And stones will give off more love than the hearts of men. And freedom will be in chains for a thousand thousand moons. And women will curse the day they were born and men will long for death to come. And the ways of God will work through all this, making all things better. Out of fire comes the purest gold. Only the flesh dies, but nothing grows old. Songs of fishes that taste the flesh of men, songs of chains that bind the flesh of men, songs of the whip and the cane, sweetness from such pain, beauty from such horror, immortality from the terror. Such are the ways of gods in stone, of spirit in bone, of love in the dust, of magic in rust. Love by the river, lightning in the heart, time will quiver, man and magic will never part.'

Then silence in the breeze. Then music in the empty air. Then a circle of maidens dancing in an opposite direction in the bright spaces, the world aglow with the vaporous brilliance of their white robes. A voice singing from the other shore. The king measuring out the good and evil in the land with his strides in the dark. Someone weeping in the forest, weeping and weeping as if the sorrows in the world were too much even for the trees and the earth to bear. And a single flower spinning in the breeze, and falling on the face of the prince as he waited, drifting in an enchanted illness.

He was not so much awoken by the flower as that he became aware that the day had darkened. It seemed as if he had been waiting by the river all his life. The maiden he sought did not appear. He stole back home, without hearing the great weeping in the forest, without noticing the eyes that followed him in the darkness of the woods.

CHAPTER TEN

When he re-entered the village the light was different; a rich blue colour seemed to touch the world everywhere. He wandered to the farms, and saw the women at their work, their children straddling their backs, held securely with broad strips of cloth. He watched the women harvesting the crops. He watched them in the cornfields, the yam fields and the cassava fields. He watched them separate pineapple fruits from their thick green stalks. He saw all the women as his mother. He had no mother. His mother had died early, when he was still a child. He knew her only by stories, by myths and royal legends. And by sighs.

For the first time, he became aware how hard the women worked. He went up to some of them and engaged them in conversation while they worked. They woke early, before dawn, prepared food for the family, swept their yards, cleaned the house, bathed, went to the river to wash clothes, went to the market miles away, returned home, prepared the afternoon meal, washed the utensils, then went to the distant farms again, then to the market to trade. They often came back with heavy bundles on their heads. Then, making several journeys there and back, they fetched water from the wells. They prepared dinner. They attended the meetings of women. Back home they discussed family matters with their husbands and relations. They took part in the social and communal business of the village, and made their contributions to looking after the sick. Then they slept very late at night. They were usually the last ones to sleep in the whole family, and the first to rise. In addition they bore several children, tended them, told them stories, taught them the traditions and legends of the tribe. They supported their husbands in all major undertakings, and were the pillars on which the village, indeed the kingdom rested.

'But you must be slaves!' the prince cried when he learnt how hard the women worked.

The women were offended.

'We are not slaves! We are freeborn women. We are the mothers of the kingdom, upholders of tradition. Without us nothing will work in the land. We are half of the kingdom. Do you not think we are proud of it? The children and all the men depend on us. This is a great thing. We have talked enough and must now return to our work.'

The prince left them and wandered back to the palace, and sought out the elders and the custodians. When they gathered, under the watchful eye of the king, he said:

'If I am to be future king I want to know about the lives of our women. How do we treat our women? Why do they work so hard, from dawn to dusk? And what do we do for them in return?'

The king began laughing again. The elders, taking his cue, laughed with him, but not as enthusiastically as before. They were becoming increasingly troubled by the persistent questioning of the young prince. Never before had any royal asked so many fundamental questions about the kingdom and how it was governed.

'Answer the prince!' bellowed the king, as he shook in laughter.

'We treat our women very well,' replied the chief custodian. 'They have no complaints.'

The prince was astonished at this reply. And before they knew it, he was gone, he had vanished, and returned, not long after, leading a group of women, old and young, into the chamber of elders. As before, soldiers and guards were in commotion; there was shouting. An elder cried:

'You can't bring women into the hall of the custodians!'

But it was too late; the prince had ushered them into the presence of the king. And under his questioning emerged a strange life led by women, one he had never suspected but which seemed so terrifying a burdensome yoke to him that he kept looking around in consternation. Then he gazed about him in utter surprise that everyone thought the lives of women so normal, especially the women themselves, who seemed to make light of what seemed to him so intolerable.

The prince felt he was under a spell, under an enchanted misunderstanding, or that he had come from a different world, as he listened to the catalogue of duties and functions. In a flash he heard them, for the first time. Marriage at an early age. Circumcision. Having children while still being almost children themselves. The lifelong unremitting chores, in illness or in health. Impossible tasks fulfilled every day. Little sleep. And no representation in the council of elders for all their extensive labours. They bore the death of children or husbands, in addition to all their labours, and carried on. They lived through wars and famines, and carried on. They aged quickly, seemed insufficiently loved, had no holidays, but worked and worked at one thing or another, and then died. And were replaced by another wife. And so on. There seemed no end to the catalogue.

The prince was dazed. Did he live in the same space as other people? Had he been in a dream? The king watched him as he listened to the women. Tears formed in the prince's eyes. These were all his mothers, his sisters, his companions, these women. The elders made fun of the women as they spoke of their duties. The elders teased the women about how much they exaggerated, how much they enjoyed their responsibilities, and the power it gave them to have the world so dependent on their diligence. The women laughed and said women had all the power and the leisure. The chief custodian said:

'But, your royal highness, the women have not told you of their benefits. They have special festivals, feast days, cults, mysteries and rituals. They are the ones who choose, in secret, the superior custodians. Don't let them deceive you into thinking that they have no power. Nothing happens in the land that doesn't have their spiritual approval. More than that, they are the secret movers of the kingdom. Men rule by day, women rule by night. Men perform deeds in public, women undo them in private. Men make history, women make legend. Legend lasts longer. Men conquer bodies, women conquer hearts. Hearts feel longer. Men think, women dream. Dreams create the future. Men fight, women bring light. Men think they rule the world, but find the world has turned to water. Women understand that water. Men make laws, women make ways. Men build, women make the building live. Men know death, but women know life. If men make mistakes thousands die, if women make mistakes a whole tribe perishes. The folly of men ends in fighting, the folly of women leads to death. The folly of men is a stupid thing, the folly of women is of historical significance. Men can be stupid and the world will not fall down; but if women are stupid the world comes to an end. The responsibility for women to be wise is truly great. The greatness of a people is a tribute to the wisdom of its women. If a kingdom is hopeless it is because its women are foolish. Show me a kingdom, a village that is collapsing and you will find that its women have been slack. The strength of women is the backbone of the land. God help us if women should fall into lazy ways and get foolish thoughts in their heads and forget their ancient greatness, their powerful responsibilities, for then the kingdom will turn to dust and be scattered to the four winds. A kingdom cannot afford its women to lose themselves, to lose their vision, and have nothing significant to do, and forget how their ancestors held up the world. Sometimes I see visions of a world gone mad because women have abandoned their shrines and lost the wisdom of their goddesses and become wild and too free. Such a world as I saw was a world without sense, without belief, a world of suicides and despair, folly and madness. Such a world is a world already cursed by the departure of the gods. An empty world. So, your royal highness, there are two sides to this. Much labour on the one hand, great invisible power and blessings on the other. It is women who bring happiness to this world, through their mysteries.'

CHAPTER ELEVEN

There was a great silence when the custodian finished. Then, in the silence, the king made a sign. The prince declared himself.

'I want to know about the nature and mystery of women, of mothers,' he said, in a gentle voice.

The king roared with laughter. But the women regarded the prince in silence and looked at one another significantly. The elders and custodians laughed too; and all the way down the corridors, throughout the palace, the servants, the cooks, the handmaidens all laughed because of the echo of the king laughing.

And soon the whole palace and kingdom and forests and rivers were laughing too. But the prince did not laugh, for he was serious. He wanted to share in the suffering of women, their beauty and their secret majesty. Their grace. Their hidden humiliations. And because of his interest he was the first and only man ever to be initiated into the mysteries of women, the nature of mothers, the great cults of the goddesses. The initiation took place that night, in his sleep, in his dreams, in a place where women do their greatest work, deep in the secret consciousness of men and the world. They initiated the prince with the help and the intervention of the spirit of his mother, who was most powerful in the highest court of women, where she carried out great advocacy for the life of her son with the weavers of destiny, and the wonderful angels of fate.

CHAPTER TWELVE

That night the prince asked to be told about his mother, whom he never knew. The king told him about her till he fell asleep and all the rest that he wanted to know he learnt in his dreams; for a goddess came to him in his sleep and took him to the realm of the dead and showed him that his mother was not there. The prince saw many people he did not recognise, people who had recently arrived. He saw a few people who told him they were from his kingdom and that they had died suddenly or of diseases or had been poisoned or murdered. This place of the dead was like that of the living, only it seemed to have no depth and no time. It was not a place, as such, but a realm like life, only that the voices were more real than the bodies.

Then the prince realised that the dead were like people in a dream, but it was a dream they couldn't wake up from, a dream that was like real life. The prince was marvelling at this discovery when the goddess took him to another realm and showed him the book of life, and in the book he saw the life of his mother, and she seemed to come alive and he spoke to her and listened to her a long time in the most blissful experience of his life.

Then he fell into a deeper sleep in which his mother disappeared and in which the women initiated his spirit in their mysteries. He left his room in a sleepwalking state and wandered to a secret shrine near the river and figures in white clothes buried him in the earth, leaving space for him to breathe, and performed rituals over his buried body. Then, still in a sleepwalking state, newly born, newly bathed in the river, and anointed with potent oils and blood and the juices of nocturnal herbs, and having been made to recite certain oaths, and permitted to dwell in the presence of the radiant great mother of all things, the prince returned to his bed and continued the fabulous sleep of his initiation.

CHAPTER THIRTEEN

The prince awoke the next day a different person, but he didn't know how he was different. He felt he had developed an extra faculty, another head, or that his eyes saw things he had never seen or noticed before, as if on loan from the spirits. The world was new to him, and yet ancient and familiar. He understood more things than he had lived; and his being seemed to bristle with the knowledge of countless lives. He seemed to carry within him the wisdom of countless multitudes, a thousand forms of dying, a million ways of living, and an understanding of the simplicity of all things. He felt possessed of the simple certainty that the many ways led to one place, that the many forms were one formless harmony, the thousand histories were all one moment, one breath, one story, and that all suffering, all flesh, all living was just one astonishing tale of illusion in a dream in which the boundaries seemed fixed in the body but limitless beyond the body.

The prince felt himself both light as a bird, free as a dream, and troubled by this shining knowledge that burned in him like a tragedy about to be revealed in the dark by lightning flash.

He told no one of his new condition, but all the women looked upon his face with love, with secret knowledge in the glint of their eyes, with a smile on their faces, as if they were thinking of making love to him in public, there and then, if only decorum would allow it.

In short, he had become beautiful to women in an inexplicable way, a way that had nothing to do with his face, but with a light that shone from him which women felt so powerfully in all their secret places and which made their eyes linger on him. He had that effect too on spirits. Even objects seemed to fall in love with him and fall under his unknowing spell . . .

CHAPTER FOURTEEN

On the third day of his peculiar enlightenment he found himself at his hiding place, on the riverbank, waiting for the maiden to appear. He dimly remembered what it was he sought. He waited now because he had fallen into the condition of waiting for a long-forgotten manifestation. He had almost forgotten when he began waiting. The thing he remembered most was that setting out, finding his place among the reeds, looking out over the river and its shore, and dwelling in shining anticipation for some kind of mystery to appear, were among the most delicious moments of his life. It was for him like going from one dream to another.

It was the first light of day, and the river that never sleeps seemed, in that dawning, to shine, flow and quiver with a beautiful light he had never seen before. How golden and brown and great the river was that morning. White birds, cranes, herons, sunbirds, played on its shores. The prince watched the proud solitary heron as, like an actor on a stage with a majestically melancholic monologue, it strolled to a lonely eminence and brooded nonchalantly over the water. The prince was very fond of herons. He loved their ability to be great and small, visible and invisible, majestic and minor, tall and insignificant. The heron could conceal its own magnificence and appear to be a raggedy creature not worthy of being noticed. It was a royal creature that understood that to survive in the world you must not overly dazzle out your brilliance, otherwise you wouldn't catch true fish, and you would be hunted for your beauty. Only a truly beautiful creature could so conceal its own beauty for a higher purpose.

The prince watched the way the heron walked. With long thin legs it walked with such stealth, such lightness, such humility, as if it didn't want to make the slightest sound, as if it didn't want to displace even the air, as if it didn't want to have any effect at all on reality. It seemed, therefore, not to walk on the ground, but to tread just above it, with a tentativeness that was almost tender. Such a gentle, humble, wise, patient bird. And yet while affecting perfect uninterest in anything at all in the universe, how swiftly, how indirectly it strikes with its beak into the water and, unaffectedly, gobbles down a fish it has so casually caught. And yet what magnificence, what majesty, what grace and power, what a flashing slow white miracle that mesmerises the gaze when it flies low above the water, as if not flying, as if, in fact, almost unable to fly. And yet how it flies — flies with such economy of energy, using all the support of the wind, barely needing to stir its marvellous and awkward wings.

The prince loved the heron so much that he stared at it a long time in a dreaming sort of contemplation. And the heron, so sensitive, so intuitive, knew that it was being watched, and adjusted its body ever so slightly so as to achieve a condition totally lacking in visual interest, designed to bore the eyes, so that the looker might be induced to find something else to look at. But the prince knew this subtle trick of the heron, and wasn't going to be fooled.

And, in love, and fascination with a creature of marvels that didn't want to be noticed so that it could go about its business of making the miraculous ordinary, the prince kept his enraptured but awakened and vigilant gaze on that most cunning of birds. The heron was a test of his concentration, his ability to maintain interest in that which deliberately oozes boredom, deliberately emanates plainness, in order to be successfully invisible, and within that condition, wonderfully happy. The heron was a challenge to the prince. He couldn't take his eyes off this bird that had now made itself so bedraggled, so devoid of interest and stimulation; and yet he had to keep his eyes open with great effort.

He kept his gaze fixed on the heron even when, out of the corner of his eye, he saw a most extraordinary form materialising from the air, or emerging from the earth. The prince was so mesmerised by this double vision that he had the greatest difficulty keeping his eyes on the heron. For, it seemed, the more boring and plain and unappealing to the eye the heron made itself, the harder and purer the prince's concentration had to be. And the purer the prince's concentration was on the heron, the more marvellous was the thing that was forming on the shoreline, out of the corner of his eye. Then, before he knew it, he began to hear things. This was such a severe test for him.

He heard voices, guttural, unreal, thin, reedy, comical, loud, savage, unnatural voices. He heard thunderous drum-rolls and tinkling bells and rattled cowries and cowhorns blaring and rattles shaking and seashells cascading and above, beneath and within the instruments, voices singing, hollering, wailing, in notes piercing and deep, as if a whole world was coming into being out of the myth and mysteries of the river. And while all this was happening, while the shoreline was populating with figures, the prince kept his tender gaze on the white heron. It was truly an epic battle of attention.

The prince felt himself being torn in two, between an overwhelming interest in the magnificent spectacle unfolding on the shore and a complete loyalty and undying fascination with the mysterious heron that stood so humbly, so undramatically in a quiet, barely noticeable section of the shore, standing on decaying reeds, partially concealed by the dreary patch of faded bushes around. And yet, what an unequal contest. How could the poor-looking unmajestic bedraggled heron compete with the epic spectacle which had bloomed with all power on the riverbank? For it seemed that in wavering between the wretched-looking heron and the mighty spectacle, the heron vanished just a little more from reality.

The more attention the prince paid to the great spectacle the more the heron was effaced from the world. It became smaller, it shrank, it became more unattractive and uglier the more the spectacle revealed itself in its wonderful glory. For the spectacle was glorious, was grand, was, indeed, almost monstrous, and fearful. The prince saw, as if in the horror of a dream, the appearance, on the riverbank, of a most fantastic masquerade.

It shone and blazed in rich colours of red and yellows, with black toes, white feet, purple legs, and glittering, flaming materials of orange and gold, of red and violet and green. It was as gigantic as a big tree. The masquerade, with its enormous presence, its branches of fire and flashing lightning, black smoke billowing from its vents, was like the figure of a terrible deity. It was more terrifying than death itself was fabled to be. And it had seven heads.

So mighty was this masquerade that its shadow alone stretched halfway across the river. Its seven heads blocked out the sun. All about its person were things too horrible to behold. For, when the prince paid closer attention, out of the corner of his eye, to the items bristling on the ferocious body of this gigantic masquerade, he saw the writhing forms of dead babies, he saw disembodied heads dangling from golden ropes with their eyes wide open, their tongues sticking out, pulling agonised faces. He saw limbs of bodies, twitching and alive;

feet that kicked and wriggled their toes; fingers that flicked and stuck out and writhed; eyes that stared every which way with wonder and horror at what they saw; nostrils still breathing; lips still jabbering; and hearts that pumped blood interminably, blood that flowed down the horrid raffia and vegetation dress of the grim masquerade.

And the masquerade, mighty as an iroko tree, began dancing like a monster set free from an eternal slavery. It danced a dreadful terrifying dance. It waved its trunk-like arms in the air, in vile exultation. Every step it took made the earth shake and the kingdom tremble. Every time it jumped the land quaked, the riverbed cracked. With its ferocious dance the river heaved as if a storm had been unleashed at the bottom of the world, as if creation itself was being broken down and destroyed and split asunder . . .

CHAPTER FIFTEEN

And all this time the prince struggled to keep his devoted attention fixed on the insignificant-seeming heron.

But it was a difficult struggle, and the heron began to pale into insubstantiality as the masquerade became more awesome, and as its dance began to break down the real world.

And when the masquerade began its utterances, a cacophonic tribe of voices speaking from all over its vast and mighty body, the heron practically dwindled to a point, a dirty white spot, still kept alive by the sheer strength of an unintentional will. The masquerade, now so gigantic that it dwarfed the highest trees around, started to utter intolerable incantations, vile and practical prophecies; and the prince was mesmerised by the dreaded poetry of the fearsome figure. It was a poetry that accompanied its destructive dance. And the poetry, the incantations, was so powerful, so monstrous, that it made the dance more violent. The words unleashed great evil forces in the air of the kingdom. The poetry, when uttered, turned dark and murky in the air, and turned into nightmare forms that populated the riverbank and began to devour everything. The ugly forms that formed from the poetry uttered by the horrid figure remained connected to it through pulsing umbilical cords. And what the forms devoured fed the masquerade's gargantuan appetite.

'Eat, eat, eat the world
Conquer, conquer, conquer the world
Rule, rule, rule the world
I am the king, the king of the world.

Blood, blood, blood in the world
Death, death, death in the world
Enslave, enslave, enslave the world
I am the king, the king of the world.

Take, take, take the world
Destroy, destroy, destroy the world
Hate, hate, hate the world
I am the king, the king of the world.

Unmake, unmake, unmake the world
Evil, evil, evil in the world
Darkness, darkness, darkness in the world
I am the happy happy king of the world.

Dance, dance, dance away this dream
Drink, drink, drink away this stream
Swallow, swallow, swallow the sun
Then I, the king, will be the only one.
Ha Ha Ha Ha Ha; Ha Ha Ha Ha Ha!'

And as the masquerade laughed its ugly laughter, the prince noticed that its dance, grown more ferocious, was actually beginning to destroy the world. Its dance began to break the kingdom's foundations. The land split open and all over, from far away and near by, the prince heard the cries of people falling into a gaping chasm that appeared under their feet. He heard huts and abodes collapsing, he heard voices screaming in an interminable fall, he heard trees crashing down and the forests shrieking.

And the prince momentarily fell into a dream in which the heron stood clear, upright, majestic and bright. The heron stood in the middle of a space full of noble bronze figures; and among the figures was the maiden that he had been waiting for. He knew at once that she came from a family of bronze-casters, sculptors, a tribe of artists, a hidden race that lived away from all other peoples and tribes, so that they could listen to the oracles in the air and create forms in bronze and stone that warned of things to come, or things that haven't been done, or of disturbances to the realm, prophecies and revelations, or just forms that give a secret joy to some unknown self within. Such was the tribe she came from, a tribe that knew and kept the ancient secrets of bronze-casting, of divination through art, of healing through created forms, of the mysteries of creation. They were an underground tribe, who lived and created invisibly, not disdaining others, but knowing that the only way they could serve the land was to live their own way, with their own freedom, following their own magical and fluid laws, guided by constant intuitions and directives of the spirit, in accordance with the needs of the times. Such was the way of the maiden and her people.

He knew now that he was extremely fortunate to have seen her at all the first time, and now he would have to persevere and be very lucky if he was ever going to see her again, and to inspire her love, and win her heart. For he had seen her, and dreamt of her, but she had never seen him, and didn't know that he even existed . . .

CHAPTER SIXTEEN

And all the while, in the dream, the prince saw the radiant beauty of the heron, shining like a diamond in a dying world. And all of a sudden the prince heard a mighty tumult, the wailing and the crashing, and woke from his dream and saw the masquerade in its destruction of the world. At that moment the prince had the absurd notion that the destruction of the world was somehow delayed by keeping his attention on the heron, who, at that moment, had disappeared to a speck.

And only when the masquerade began devouring the trees, eating up the shore, and drinking up the water of the river, drinking it dry, leaving only a deep chasm of a dry riverbed full of skeletons, only when the masquerade had eaten up the bushes, was breathing in all the air, and had begun to break off the sun and to devour it, bringing on night, only when the prince saw the body of the masquerade grow bigger and bigger till it was almost greater than the earth itself, and only when the masquerade was about to devour the prince himself, because of too much attention the prince had paid to it, only then did the prince remember the heron again.

And the prince noticed that the heron had made a very minute movement, the tiniest, subtlest movement. And this movement, small though it was, proved enough for the reality, the mystery and the true luminous hidden magnificence of the heron to be revealed again. And when the prince regained his loyal gaze on the heron, seeing it as a radiant thing in a dying space, the prime living thing in a dead world, only then did the masquerade begin to diminish.

But first the masquerade howled, it raged, it thundered, it leaked blood from all over its vast trunk, and blood and liverish fluids filled the hollow world and flowed into the riverbed and the river became a river of blood. And the sun shone out from all parts of the masquerade. And air leaked from its vents. And the heron became clear and white and stood tall and unveiled, in its unfolding, its true hieratic splendour. And then it pressed up gently its feet, and outstretched, with barely an effort, its wings. And like a king of space, a king of light, it flew above the blood-red river, and in its flight it changed all things. Its humble majesty restored a new attention to the world.

And the masquerade tried to swat the heron, and to snatch it with its thousand hands and devour it with its seven heads. But the masquerade got all mixed up and so confused that it began a war against itself as it became self-entangled trying to kill the white heron sailing along nonchalantly, unaware, it seemed, that anything out of the ordinary was going on.

The prince was fascinated. The heron didn't notice, or didn't seem to see, or register the existence of, the masquerade. And in its not-knowing it caused the greatest damage of all. For the masquerade, wielding its thousand swords, spears, bows and arrows and lethal instruments of war, had unleashed a mighty battle against itself. It had cut off some of its own heads in its attempts to slay the heron; it had blinded itself with its poisoned spears; and had, eventually, pierced its own heart, in the most ferocious battle ever witnessed by human eyes.

What a battle it was, this self-battle of the masquerade. The clash of mighty armies never produced more cries, more anguish, more tragedy, more blood, more agony, or more drama and destruction than the battle of the masquerade against itself, against its many selves. And then, with a sigh that released all the air of the world back into the spaces, the masquerade fell slowly into the blood-filled river. And the sun, freed from its mouth as it drowned, changed and purified the water.

The sun rose in majesty from the far side of the red river, and its light restored the world to itself.

And in the distance, herald of a new dawn, soared the heron, flying gently as a breeze, borne aloft by the gentlest light.

The prince bade it farewell with tears in his eyes.

And still the maiden did not appear.

CHAPTER 17

The prince made his way home through a forest that bristled with prying eyes. When he got back to the village he noticed the silence in the air. He had not heard the silence before, and it puzzled him. He noticed the shadows that hung over the huts and abodes. He hadn't seen them before. He also noticed that between all things, between the trees, between the huts, between the walls and the gates, there were indistinguishable forms, like invisible beings investing the air with wavy shapes, that he had never noticed before. All this troubled him.

Then he saw something new on the faces of the people of the kingdom, the faces of the men, women and children who greeted him on the way to the palace. And what he saw was something that wasn't there before, something that even the people didn't know they had on their faces. It was something akin to the shadow of doom. The prince hurried on, in apprehension.

In the palace he summoned the elders to the presence of the king and asked to be taken to the shrines, to the oracles. He wanted to consult the diviners, the soothsayers. He wanted to be told about the guardian spirits of the kingdom. He wanted to know the disposition of the gods and the mood of the ancestors. He wanted to know the legends and genealogies and the origin of monsters, of shadow forms, of spirits, of evil beings, and of the forces that warred against the welfare of the kingdom. He wanted to know the origin of evil in the world. And the king roared with laughter as he listened to the requests of his son ...

The elders protested at how much the young prince was, with his perfectly reasonable, but slightly unseasonable requests, wasting their time. They should, they said, be deliberating on important matters of state.

'Like what?' roared the king.

'Like collecting taxes ...'

The king bellowed with laughter.

'And what else?'

The elders enumerated items of significant state concern.

'But you never discuss these things at all,' the king said, sternly. 'You squabble endlessly, you exchange wise but useless proverbs, you engage in excellent subtleties of reasoning, you endlessly postpone coming to a decision about anything, you waste the time with slippery words in which your meanings cannot be understood, in which your positions or attitudes cannot be detected, you are always waiting to see which way the wind blows, always protecting your interests and ensuring your continued presence on the council of elders, you spend the time doing profitable business with one another, advancing your privileges, acquiring wives, furthering the interests of your children, families and tribes ... In fact can you remember the last time you came to a collective decision about anything?'

'Many times, your majesty,' cried one elder.

'Name one, then,' replied the king.

There was silence. Then the elders consulted among themselves. They consulted a long time and soon began to squabble in low voices. The king roared with his characteristic laughter, and said:

'You see! The decisions that are taken happen by themselves in the very mouth of the crisis. So don't complain about the request of the prince. He is my heir, and future king. His request is legitimate. Do what he asks.'

The elders turned and stared at the prince. He looked upon them innocently, and noticed that there were signs on their faces that he could not read. They asked for some time in which to prepare themselves, but the prince said it had to be now. There was no time, he said. It was urgent. So they adjourned to the council rooms and they told him, one by one, as in a ritual chorus, the genealogy of monsters, the origin of evil beings, the permutations of dark forms. They took him to the shrines, and consulted the oracles, gained signs about the disposition of the gods and the mood of the ancestors, and were told conflicting myths about the origin of evil in the world.

The oracles were bewildering in what they said. The world is upside-down, has turned on its axis, the people live in a dream, and death has come to wake them up in long lines of ants that walk into the seas. The kingdoms do not look out, do not see. The outside world comes with fire and blinding light, in silence, bearing new words that will destroy old worlds. A dream of chains, a trick that makes people two in magic glasses, young lions raided, villages with nests destroyed, war dances silenced, gods in flames, ancestors forgotten, an earthquake in which the earth does not quake but the people are made dumb for a hundred and forty years, a new sun that rises from the red river in time, and after the exodus of hope and dreams a people made new with the fire of the gods, made new and beautiful and aware and gifted, blessed. But only after the years in the wilderness, and after the songs of the dead, and after the lamentation of flowers, and after the rebirth of rivers, and the reuniting of brothers and sisters across the great seas of life and death.

These things the oracle uttered.

The disposition of the gods was more oblique.

They stand on the edge of burning stars, the heavens are not reflected on earth, darkness comes between their messages and our eyes, lost is the way handed down to you by your wise ancestors who came from elsewhere bringing wisdom and guidance to the new heaven, gone are the gold-makers. Find the masters of the tradition. The gods stand in harmony in the centre of the source, but we have lost the lantern.

The mood of the ancestors was obscure. They spoke, but in a language the diviners could not understand. They sang, but the interpreters could not hear the words, nor could they hear the music.

CHAPTER 18

The prince fell asleep amid all this confusion, and was borne lightly to his bed. That night the dark forms, the shadows over the huts, and the invisible beings in between things came to him. They paid him a visit in his sleep. The ancestors spoke to him in songs and dances that were like words. The gods appeared to him and showed him signs and indications that baffled him. Briefly, in a flash, he was shown the origin of evil in the world. On a higher plane an angel had disobeyed the supreme being; and man, high in the scheme of things, disobeyed too and lost his vigilance, and broke the axis of heaven. And in order to create a higher state for all men, he descended into unreality, preyed on by the disobedient angel and his gang of higher spirits. And the prince saw that evil was ignorance, was darkness, and was confined only to the earth and the lower spheres of the universe.

He saw that evil was related only to mortality and the lowly souls. Beyond the lower spheres the prince saw that all was light. He saw that evil served its function, which was to provide the opposition needed for the light to grow, and keep growing; for there can be no good without evil, no light without darkness, day without night. But the destination of the soul was beyond good and evil, darkness and light, beyond it all. Evil was the ladder by which the difficult ascension was made. Evil was not the only way for the ascension, for the ascension was simpler by grace, goodness, love and natural flight – but evil was the one thing that humanity, in its blindness, was prey to, must overcome, transcend, and turn into light. Evil was a battle or a non-battle which humanity must win and overcome consciously in itself if it is to regain its former place, or find a new place, in heaven.

The prince was shown all this and understood it all in a flash, and much more besides. And what the ancestors said to him in songs, in music and in dances he absorbed but forgot, and would remember much later, in time, when needed, and when events so terrible would spring them out in his mind as his own thoughts, his own deeds.

But that night the visitations he attracted from the evil forms (to see them is to be seen by them), the shadows over things (they go where they must grow), and the ambiguous beings between things (if the space is there they fill up the air; if the space is not light, they grow there in might) – the visitations were so strong that they troubled the prince's sleep.

They occupied the prince's dreams because he was an open soul and gave all things habitation, and was not yet strong enough or fortified enough to resist such inhabitation. For this possession was part of the ritual fortification. First the soul must be infected with that which it will become impervious to; if it survives the attack, the foundation becomes impregnable; if it doesn't, a good person perishes, and has to begin again from where they left off the struggle. So it was with the prince.

CHAPTER 19

The dreams he had were monstrous. The evil forms that visited him and the shadows over things that descended on him and the visions of the night were so terrible that a great unease entered his spirit. His dreams were mixed and confusing; and monsters with teeth all over their bodies appeared beside him and began to eat of his flesh, till only his heart remained. Liverish spirits with snake-like legs and eyes that reflected what they saw and bodies crawling with white worms slid into him and danced and wriggled in his being. A host of evil-looking critters took up occupation in his brain and held long meetings about how to conquer the kingdom of his soul.

And then he saw unspeakable acts of witchcraft and dark cultic activities – power-seekers who ate the brains of newborn babies, women who poisoned their husbands and married their brothers, men who murdered their wives and buried them in farmlands, warriors who beheaded the conquered and danced at night with their skulls under a luminous moon. The prince saw so much evil and he was the home of so many kinds of nightmare beings that he became ill. He fell into a deep illness because of all the evils in the kingdom that he was shown in his dreams. All the hidden evils affected him so powerfully that he slid into a profound sickness that lasted a long time.

Everyone thought he was going to die. He didn't eat. He didn't speak. And he barely stirred from his bed. He seemed unconscious for a long time and when he appeared to be awake he stared at the ceiling or at the sky for long hours without seeming to see anything. They said that his soul had fled from the home of his body and that his eyes longed for some place beyond the sky. He saw no one, recognised no one, not even the king.

They brought people to see him in his chamber, friends, beautiful young princesses whom he had been thought to favour, relations, and comedians. He stared through the friends, was deaf to the entreaties of beauty, and did not so much as register the performances of the funniest people in the kingdom. They brought musicians, who played rousing tunes, with rich rhythmed drumbeats that seduced the feet and fingers to joy and dancing, but he did not so much as betray the slightest pulse of rapture. The musicians played the most tender and bewitching melodies, laced with sadness and poignant sorrow, music so moving that palace officials reported that they saw dogs weeping, but not a tear appeared in the eyes of the prince, nor did a muscle move on his impassive face that had surrendered to the greater melodies of dying.

The king didn't laugh as he used to, and wandered thoughtfully and gloomily through the corridors of the palace. The king was never known to be affected by anything under the sun, be it great disaster, defeat in battles, the death of his children, triumphs in statecraft, prosperity in the land, periods of unexpected happiness, sudden invasions; he would laugh uproariously at crises or victories, setbacks or accomplishments. However, this indomitable king was mysteriously subdued by the inexplicable sickness of his fragile son. The king had never really expected the prince to last long in this world; and had always reconciled himself to the omens that the prince was doomed to early death, being one of the precious visitors that the gods sent down to dwell for a while among the living, to spy on their hearts, and report on their deeds.

The king had expected him to die in childhood, but the prince survived perilous fevers, melancholies, moods, disappearances, and became an adolescent. Then the king expected that early youth would claim the prince unexpectedly, one morning, without warning. But the prince not only thrived but grew strong, and took on challenging tasks, and worked on the farms like the ordinary people of the land. The king found much to laugh at, but none more than the quiet defiance of death that his son had shown every day. And when the prince began to take such a profound interest in the deeper matters of life and the kingdom, the king was delighted, and all things conspired to make him laugh at the mystery of things, for laughter was his way of breathing, of thinking and non-thinking. He had been laughing at life since he was young. But behind his laughter lay a deep and grave soul that saw deeply into the heart of mysteries.

The king pondered much on the strange sickness of his son, and he ruled the kingdom with a slightly abstracted air. His wives found him a trifle mentally preoccupied and his advisers refrained from breaking into his long silences and vacant stares. The king would come and sit for long periods in the prince's chamber and watch his sleeping son. He remembered how, on the day his son was born, the diviners had said the alignment of the stars was especially auspicious and yet enigmatic. It was as if, they said, the heavens couldn't make up their mind whether they were announcing a great occasion or a strange event. There were enigmas among the stars. A white horse was said to have appeared in the village square with a golden horn in the middle of its forehead. A great cry was heard from the oracle and a message was brought to the king which said:

'That which is best will be lost so that that which is greatest can be found.'

The shrines were swarmed by white birds and a rare animal caught in a net was seen staring out with calm eyes near the palace. Some say it was a white tiger. Seven meteors, falling stars, were seen at dusk; and a bright burst of golden light flashed in the middle of the night and alarmed the wise ones of the kingdom. But all around the palace musicians were playing and women were singing their praises and prayers for the newborn prince. The king remembered how favoured his son had been at birth with the love of the people, especially the women. They had an instinct about the prince even before his arrival, as his coming had been whispered to them in their dreams, by their inscrutable goddesses.

The king, listening now to musicians playing gentle airs outside the chamber, reminisced about his own youth, and about the prince's mother, whom he loved and still loved above all others in the world; and thoughts of her filled him with a sweet sorrow that made him laugh tenderly to himself. When she was dying the queen had said to the king:

'This son of ours will need great support on the other side if he is going to fulfil his destiny. I will give him all the support and strength he needs. Tell him to think of me when he is in trouble and I will move heaven to help him. As for you, my love, I am always in your heart, I am your happiness, and so always laugh and never dwell in sorrow about anything. We have been great companions on the path together, and we know the glories of the mountaintop, so be joyful, and be a great king and an even greater man. We will be in dreams together.'

But more characteristic of her were her words:

'My dear,' she said, with a smile, 'the day's harvest has been done. Maybe I'll cook you something special. You'd like that, wouldn't you,' she whispered, and then she was gone.

The king didn't like to think about the death of his wife. Not because of the infinite sadness, but because he didn't believe she was gone. He laughed often because she was there, here, in the palace, all over the kingdom. She had simply taken on a vaster personality and grown in space and time.

But in his son, sleeping or dying of a malaise without a

name, the king found much by which to be troubled. So many prophecies hung on the life of his son. If he dies before a certain age, the kingdom will perish. If the sun doesn't rise from the river at the death of a monster, the prince will perish. If the land doesn't give up its evils and load them in chains on the back of the prince, the kingdom will perish. If the prince is not lost and does not return, the kingdom will perish. If those who are made slaves in the land of white spirits never become free, the kingdom will perish. If the white spirits do not become human beings and purge the world of the evils they have unleashed, the world will perish. If the prince does not fulfil his obscure destiny no one will fulfil their simple destiny, and the land will perish. So many prophecies. If the king stops laughing hope will vanish from the kingdom, and the people will perish. So many responsibilities.

CHAPTER 20

The king loved to watch over sleeping beings. Often he wandered the kingdom at night, watching over his sleeping subjects. He went to the quarters of his guardsmen and watched them sleep in their turn. He loved watching sleeping mothers and their children. He derived much strength from being the protector of those who slept, so defenceless, in his realm. The good and the bad all slept in the same way, under the mercy of immense forces, under the mercy of the ultimate mysteries. Sleeping women in their huts. Sleeping farmers. Sleeping wizards and witches, sleeping magicians, sleeping musicians, sleeping thieves, sleeping traitors, spies, servants, palm-wine tappers, sleeping hunters and fishermen, sleeping children, sleeping babies breathing deeply half the vital air in the world, sleeping men on the verge of death breathing out wisps of the last miracles of life, sleeping women on the edge of death breathing in dreams of their children's futures full of tragedies and gains, sleeping herbalists, sleeping dogs in the village square, sleeping horses that snort suddenly and rear, sleeping lions that can be watched from afar, sleeping flies and sleeping insects, forests sleeping in the dark and breathing out pure energies that balance the earth, sleeping flowers tender and soft, sleeping clouds that wander aloft. The king loved them all. But he loved none more than his sleeping son, who was dying beneath his helpless gaze.

CHAPTER 21

At dawn the king sent abroad for the greatest herbalists that the world had spawned. They arrived in great numbers, with great personalities, with contradictory notions; and they treated the prince with many potions, subjected him to diverse incantations, baths, massages, midnight exposures to special spirits evoked in the sacred forest, but nothing they did helped him get better.

The herbalists changed his diet, altered his sleeping position, drew out sinister objects that had been mysteriously projected into his body – nails, the black tooth of an ageing dog, the claw of a vulture; they twisted the poor prince into contortions, they bent and knotted him, to force out the evil spirits lodged in him; and they prescribed a course of spirit-flogging, which was roundly rejected by the king.

The herbalists made the prince walk backwards in precisely delineated circles, to perplex the evil occupants in him; and they bared him to the harsh rays of the noonday sun and the dim rays of the invisible nocturnal planets, to puzzle and punish his elusive occupants. The herbalists even found their way into his dreams and attempted to do battle with the shadow forms that lurked in the prince's mind; but all they succeeded in doing was making his nightmares worse, and exacerbating his illness, till it became so bad that the prince couldn't even speak.

Some muttered in the court that the prince was being murdered by superstition.

CHAPTER 22

The prince hovered between life and death for many moons. The people of the kingdom heard that their beloved prince was dying and they came in their multitudes to the palace. The women swarmed there in their hundreds. They brought their children with them. They left their farms, their marketplaces, their homes, and they came and sat in silence outside the palace, and kept vigil. They brought lamps which they kept alight all night, and all day, as if the light of the lamps somehow sustained the life of their much-loved prince.

The women brought a splendid variety of food and they made aromatic dishes of great delicacy and had them sent to the palace for the delectation of the prince. And all night, in sundry tongues, in sweet passionate murmurs, they prayed to the gods for the life of the prince. It was reported that the days of their prayers scented the kingdom lightly with the fragrance of roses, and that never did a gentler breeze blow in the land, nor was there such a subdued air over the rivers and forests and mountains of the kingdom.

Men came too, from great distances; they came to pay homage and to show their support for the king in the dark hours of the prince's illness. Famous warriors had set aside their weapons for a brief season, calling a short truce in their wars so as to join in vigil outside the palace. Their rough and brooding mood was made tender by the subdued air of the women murmuring in prayer and entreaty. Nimble dancers, celebrated wrestlers, notorious robbers, legendary criminals, priests of obscure religions, diviners of the forests, shepherds, farmers, hunters, acrobats, magicians, and wandering bards who were called griots, all travelled great and small distances to the palace. They all delegated their important engagements and those that could brought their work with them. The hunters brought gifts of fabulous game they had caught in the abundant forests. The priests led prayers and offered sacrifices for the purification of the land. The dancers performed their mighty dances which were reputed to have powers of healing, powers of regeneration, powers of realigning the broken axis of the world. The wondrous drummers beat out astonishing rhythms on their talking drums, their healing drums, their wailing drums, and their drums of reinvigoration, rhythms that shook the land and retuned the nerves and altered the heartbeat of the kingdom, rhythms that communicated to the spirits and summoned the ancestors in the farthest reaches of the invisible realms of dreams and higher deeds where they reside and where they watch their descendants through a veil thinner than the morning mist and yet farther than remote stars. The celebrated wrestlers staged wrestling contests on the fields outside the village gates; and the children and assembled lamenters watched the ritual contest between the hero of the kingdom's soul and the dreaded illness that threatened to snatch it away.

In silence the assembled ones watched the epic contest between the champion of the prince's life and the champion of death. They were formidable adversaries, and the battle swayed back and forth, sometimes the champion of death appearing to have the upper hand, almost strangling and breaking the back of the champion of the prince's life. And suddenly the audience would cry out, and wail, and shout encouragements, and the champion of the prince's life would recover, and the audience would sigh loudly in relief. This wrestling match went on, day after day, with no clear winner in sight. It followed the course of the prince's illness, ebbing and flowing, rising and falling with what dribbled out about the condition of the prince. On days when he was in a coma the champion of death strode the field alone, boastful and arrogant, cocksure and proud, defiant and challenging all comers, and daring the beaten horizontal form of the champion of the prince's life to rise up and continue the fight.

And the audience booed and hissed and threw ritual objects at the vile figure of the champion of death as he bestrode the stage with his terrifying mien, his huge ugly mask. When the news came through that the prince had stirred from his coma, the champion of the prince's life, with minute movements, in ritual slowness, as if transformed and energised by sleep, rose dramatically from the earth. With courage and unsuspected cunning he resumed a new and ferocious battle with the champion of death, to the rousing and cheering of the reinvigorated audience, whose spirits were swept aloft by the electrifying rhythms of the fortifying drums.

During a lull in the wrestling match the acrobats came on and performed extraordinary feats of juggling, tumbling, balancing, and walking on ropes in the air. They delighted the crowds with their agility and their dignity. The somersaulters amazed with wonderful turns and twists of their bodies, and they performed their feats with a sad and sober air, a ritual air, for it was all meant to empower the spirit of the prince as he fought for life in his dreams. And after the acrobats came the wandering griots.

One after another, in the sombre darkness that fell over the village, these mysterious story-tellers held the crowds and took their minds on fabulous journeys through forests and through the ages, in songs and with powerful dances, with incantations and bewildering impersonations. The audiences gasped as the griots, in their renderings, turned into golden tigers before their eyes, or changed into monsters, or spoke with seven voices echoing out of deep resonating chests. Suddenly the griots changed into giant birds and flew among the women, spreading silent panic, frozen horror, while still narrating their electrifying epics. The griots held the crowds in states of terrifying enchantment as they unfolded and embodied tales of miracles and battles with demons and tales of journeys that tribal heroes made to bring back the secret of immortality.

The notorious robbers and the legendary criminals that came to the great vigil prowled among the audiences with their acolytes and for once used their skills to make sure no crimes were committed and no thefts took place as they all kept vigil for the prince. It seemed the mere presence of these famed figures of crime was enough to deter wrongdoing, much more so than the presence of innumerable soldiers or legally empowered protectors of the realm. No one noticed this, of course, except the people; and no one really asks the opinion of the people, for if they did they might learn that there was a special role for criminals in the land, a role to do with the prevention of crime, as like knows like. And the reputation of the criminals did much to give the vigil a unique air of safety and authenticity, such as the king and the guards alone could not have commanded.

CHAPTER 23

The magicians charmed the children, and delighted the women, as they made objects disappear, swallowed swords to the hilt, made birds fly out of perfect white eggs and caused water to spout out of dry stones held in their hands. The magicians too, in making dead birds suddenly spring to life, in turning wood into cats that leapt into dark freedom, in chanting swords to transform into long stalks with luminous roses, also performed ritual enrichments which charged the air of the palace with a special strength of healing.

The priests led the vast motley gathering in strange prayers and stranger rites; and the magnetic force of the crowd kept on working its attraction throughout the kingdom. Spirits appeared at night among the yellow lanterns and conversed in odd languages with women and men, who understood perfectly well what they said. Spirits spoke to the children and told them stories so vivid that they never forgot them all their lives, stories they would pass on to their children, and which are still being whispered to this day under moonlit skies, in sundry villages, where one credulous child still listens with wide open eyes to tales that the spirits told their ancestors long ago during the vigil for a famous prince. And spirits wandered through the palace, listening to rumours, conspiracies, gossip, plots, lies, confessions and secrets; listening and saying nothing, knowing what was to come; listening, and passing through, like spies for the future.

All manner of men, women, children, spirits, ancestors, beasts and insects converged, from many lands and realms, and camped outside the palace. They had all been drawn there, moved by the gentle spirit of the prince, which they had heard about in the murmured rumours of the world. They had converged, and kept on converging; they chanted, sang, prayed, and dwelt in long silences, holding up their lanterns for the prince, encouraging him to get better, so that the land could be whole again.

CHAPTER 24

The elders were astonished and frightened by the effect that the prince's illness had on the people. They were the guardians of tradition and of history; and in all their years, with all their combined memories, they had never witnessed or known or heard of a more extraordinary display of affection for a prince. The king, of course, can command such adoration, if he is a good and wise king; but a prince is another matter. Besides, they were puzzled at how the prince had managed to become so famous.

The elders thought that they were the controllers and manipulators of fame and reputation. They thought they were the guardians at the gates through which a person's name and deeds are trumpeted to the world. They had not done any such trumpeting for the prince because they were looking forward to reducing his powers when he became king. He seemed such a weak and fragile figure, a perfect candidate, in fact, for royal demotion, for control, for intimidation by tradition. Then the elders intended to make themselves more powerful. Then, eventually, they might get rid of the future king altogether, and the land would forevermore be ruled by them, the council of elders.

All these, of course, were vague whispered notions, dreams, hopes, concealed and hinted at so indirectly, in such convoluted proverbs, that only the most subtle of elders could detect this intangible current of thinking. Visibly, the elders were the very models of loyalty, and the loudest and most passionate defenders of the existing order. It would constitute treason to think otherwise, even for a moment. It was in such an atmosphere that the elders found themselves amazed and trapped by the great love the people bore the prince, people who had never known him, never seen him, and perhaps never would. There is a kind of expressed love which is easy to subvert. When a figure is loved for their deeds, their conquests, their heroism, their goodness, their love of the people, these are easy enough to destroy. Rumours, whispers, lies, distortions, facts revealed, can undo such reputations, such bonds. But there is a kind of love which is felt for apparently no reason, purely because of affinity and kinship, purely because a people can't do otherwise; a love inspired, it seems, by the gods, which it is impossible to fight, distort, destroy or weaken. In fact, the attempts to destroy such loves only strengthen them. And to do nothing allows them to continue to grow at their natural pace, inexorably, till this love becomes a wide and silent adoration.

The elders found themselves confounded by such a magical love. And it left them helpless and rendered them powerless. They were marginalised by it. Suddenly they found they had nothing to do. They felt acutely how primarily useless they were. They found themselves spectators in a grand love story between the people and their prince. They realised how unknown, and how unloved, they were. And, strangely, they resented it. This resentment was new to them. It was a sign that their ancient institution, their place in the scheme of things, was insecure. They felt a new age dawning, and they were not in that new age. The prince's illness was in fact killing them off. They were dying with the prince, with the great tide of love the people felt for him. It did not take the elders long to realise that something had to be done.

CHAPTER 25

The king was moved by the tenderness of his people. He watched from the palace window the great crowds that had gathered from all over the known world to show their support for his family. The ragged women, the fishermen, the market women, the quarrelsome bar owners, the seamstresses, the warriors from distant lands, the one-armed, the one-legged, the crippled, the blind, the mad, the refugees from other kingdoms, the fugitives, the clowns, the fools, the celebrated heroes, the boxers, wrestlers, jugglers, mendicants, the pregnant mothers, the albinos, the runaways, the exiles who had returned home in disguise, the disheartened, the lonely, the old, the dying, the young, the brave, the merchants, the salt-traders, the city-builders, the prophets and visionaries, the adventurers and explorers of remote places, the dreamers, the insomniacs, all who suffered excessive love or anxiety or fear of death, women who sought husbands, men who wanted wives, all those weighed down with too many problems, and perplexed by strife, the hallucinators, the overly superstitious, all kinds and forms and manner of men and women were here, and kept on coming, and converging, as if the illness of the prince were the illness of the world.

The king, who was wise in heart and great in innocence, embraced in his spirit the wonderful and varied crowds that had overrun his palace. He was no stranger to wonders. All his long life he had lived in wonders. All that he saw about him he had in some way helped to bring about; and all things made him laugh, for the wonder he had hidden in them. He knew the hearts of men and women at a glance; he could read their intentions. He knew the inclinations of all the courtiers, the chiefs, the elders, his wives, his children, the servants, the horsemen. He knew the destiny of their thoughts. He knew of the disasters to come, and the great adventures. He knew what the stars foretold in their misalignments, in their chaos. And in all things he found laughter. He found laughter in good as much as in evil. He found laughter in all those who thought they could escape the effects that they set into motion by their hidden deeds and dreams. He laughed at the harvest of good and bad intentions. And he laughed with love in his heart.

The king, who had fathered the new mysteries in the kingdom, who had guarded the secret rites that had been brought to his land by a caravan of magi long ago; the king, who had been initiated as a child into the wonders of the sages from the land of the magic river where stones had been raised into perfect structures for the adoration of the sun; the king had long ago entered and crossed the chambers of death and dwelt among the higher beings who whispered the secret ways in silence all through the timeless moments of an eternal life that shone above the African sands. The king had glimpsed all things in an inward glance; and the world as he saw it, obscure and yet so clear, was a place where the drama of unfolding is staged, for the education of the gods through the evolution of the spirit of the people. And so the king saw the people as the children of his love, as a farmer loves the seeds that will become the fruits and flowers of the kingdom, for the nourishment of the dreams of the great ancestors, and the ultimate enrichment of the stars.

It was with such simplicity of spirit that the king beheld the crowds gathered outside the palace; and he laughed silently at the tender spectacle of the drama of their unfolding, their piety, their love. And the king sent food and blankets out among the gathered peoples; he sent his medicine men to make sure that the ill among them were tended to, that the pregnant women were comfortable and well, that the women who gave birth did so in satisfactory conditions. He sent his court bards among the crowds to bear witness to their expressions; he sent historians to register their reality; and at night, while they slept, he went out among them in simple disguise and watched over their sleeping forms and partook of their dreams and shared their distress. It was a great education for him; and it greatly enriched his laughter.

CHAPTER 26

The prince, however, remained ill. On his favourite bed of hardened clay, he tossed in dreams. He turned in horrors. He awoke while asleep and lived in a separate realm, as if freed from his body, and he got lost in a labyrinth of images and narratives. His sickness was very deep indeed and it snatched him away from his home and dragged him through the forests, past the elders, who were men of teak and thunder. The elders became giants that he encountered everywhere and they blocked his way and always he had to find a way through them in order to continue on his quest. The sickness dragged him through mud, through valleys, across rivers, over mountain ranges, and down into the dark earth. He journeyed with the sickness in a darkened world where there was no moon, only voices. The voices echoed in the dark, as in a giant room. Then he recognised the voices of the elders. His sickness took him deep into the earth and at last he emerged in a grey world, where everything was made of ash, and a pale and sickly light that was no light was spread evenly over everything. There was no one there, in this world. There were no spirits, no shadows, no ancestors, no voices, no laughter. Just a world of ash, and a pale dull sickly even light that was no light. And the prince sat still in that world without shadows and waited patiently for time to turn him into nothing. Or everything.

Book Two

THE MASTER ARTISTS

Part One

CHAPTER ONE

Many are the things to be read in the inscriptions of the world. Many are the facts, dates, times, events; many also are the signs and omens, the symbols and resonances, the secret messages, the hints, the enigmas, the mysteries, and the tantalising flashes of meaning to be sensed in the inscriptions of the world. Many are the faces to be seen in cracks on the wall, in the shapes of clouds, in buckets of water seen at odd angles in a certain frame of mind. Many are the people noticed standing still in a forest, seen as a stick, or at a distance in the dark, that turn into bushes clustered, when a moment before they were women conniving or a group of men plotting evil. Many are the marches of battalions that sail past in cloud formations, massed towards war. Many are the days and evenings when the sun seems to bleed light as if leaking out all the blood spilt in wars and pogroms and genocides and murders and secret evils, bleeding light back into our world for all the wicked deeds that we send up to heaven under the all-seeing eye of the sun.

Many are the times when the moon waxes and seems to quiver in its overflowing hallucinating power, as if it were an oracle bloated with too many prophecies, or a transparent gourd of palm-wine intoxicated with its own excessive magnetic force over the spirits of all liquid things. Many are the moments when the moon speaks a strange tongue to the eye, when it is half eaten by the sun or the dark, when it is red, or too blue, or flecked with diverse images that perplex the mind, or riddled with letters of an obscure alphabet, or cracked, or chewed at the edges by a cosmic mouse, as if at cheese prophetic, or when its face is pitted with signs, or when faces old and strange, the face of one's grandfather, or of a stranger once glimpsed in a crowd, or of a face that betrays an emotion too complex for the human heart to comprehend appears on the moon's visage, above our bewildered superstitious gaze.

Many are the empires that reveal themselves in decay on blotches and stains on stone walls. Many are nations that appear in patches of mud long after the rains have gone. Many are the shapes of divination that show up in coffee stains on white pages, or on tablecloths. The mind sees myriad things in the illusory surfaces of the meaning-transparent, meaning-infested world.

But many are the well-studied forms of divination; the readings of fortunes in the arrangement of leaves at the bottom of the teacup; and angles and configurations of cowries thrown and deciphered by the master's spirit; the flow of the wind and its scattering of the petals of certain flowers at dawn; the tinkling of bells teased by the breeze; the aerial formations of birds of prophecy when summoned by the gods of destiny to speak to lands that will not listen.

Many are the ways the gods speak to us: through dreams, which we misread, which we do not experience clearly, which we forget, which we wrongly interpret, creating more chaos instead of achieving more clarity; dreams that we act on directly, as if they spoke a literal language; dreams that we fear; dreams that perplex and which we get others to explain to us, when the message and key is with us alone.

Many are the ways of seeing the future, glimpsing the past. Some stare into crystal balls, into clear waters of prophecy; some read the fall and placement of kola nut lobes in enamel bowls; some read the shapes and direction of the footprint of herons or chickens or rare birds; some read the past in momentary visions had outside time; some use the Bible or other sacred texts; some resort to sorceries and consult wizards that may or may not know the mystery of the stars; some travel in the minds of tortoises to the beginnings of the race; some fly to the moon on the back of beams of light; some wander deaf amongst angels; some consult the ancient oracles and ponder the incomprehensible messages from the gods, delivered in verse to the sibyls. Some listen to the prophecies that fall from the mouths of babbling children, or the language of crows, or the accidental words that reach them in marketplaces, or pay too much attention to words said to them by strangers or the insane. Such are the perplexities of the ways of man and woman in a world where the past and future do not speak, and where the present has not fully revealed itself to our partial-seeing eyes. And thus we live our days between knowing and unknowing, blind and deaf in a vast panorama of revelations, a perpetual theatre of timeless events where history is as much the future as the past, an infinite living book in which all things are present. We live in these wonders and do not see.

Many are the wonders to be glimpsed in the book of life: the beginnings of the universe, the death of stars, the obscure life of a thief, the rich hidden life of a maiden, the abstracted life of a queen, the last days of a musician leaning against a column, a mysterious flood, the lives of the ancient philosophers, an evening in Atlantis, the afternoon on a normal day in a desert town, the sight of a baby lost in a city of groundnut pyramids, the glorious dream of Alexander, the happy exiled days in the life of my mother, the magical adolescence of my father, and all stories known and unknown, lived and unlived, in the endless chain of universal life.

Many wonders to be glimpsed in this eternal book, and I have chosen this one, and I don't know why.

CHAPTER TWO

On that day, by the river, when she heard the mysterious questions in the wind, the maiden's life changed for ever. Before that day she lived deep in a dream. The world was strange to her. All things were strange to her. It was as if she had come from another constellation, another world, and had found herself marooned on an odd planet where she was completely lost. Her only good fortune, it seemed, was that she was born into a tribe of artists, into a family of gold-shapers, bronze-workers and dreamers.

Her tribe was a nomadic tribe with a place, a land as their hidden centre. They lived in the forests, away from towns and cities. And their lives were entirely dedicated to listening at the oracles and creating sculptures in secret and displaying them at night in the village centre, as a guide and warning of events and troubles and disturbances happening in the land, in the world, in the tribe, in the family, or in the spirit of one man or woman. And so it was not unusual for the tribe to wake up one morning and find a wooden sculpture of a man chained to another man, and wonder what it meant.

These images led to great discussions, interpretations and misinterpretations. They were like dreams made public. Sometimes many years would pass before a famous image mysteriously displayed near the shrine would reveal its true purpose and social meaning, or spiritual value. Then suddenly a familiar image became strange as it began to speak, to reveal what it was warning the tribe of, future events waiting to unfold, hidden events brought gradually to light, past events that take on a new aspect. These images required master interpreters, image-readers, sign-decipherers to help decode them, or their continued mystery bothered and perplexed the tribe. Often they would send for wise men from far away to come and help with the unravelling of the bewildering images that haunted their shrines, uninterpreted. There were few things as intolerable as an uninterpreted image.

How many famines, plagues, wars, earthquakes, abductions, outrages, were minimised because one of the invisible artists of the tribe had felt the overwhelming pressure of a vision, and created an image that freed that vision, displayed it, and had seen it properly interpreted for the larger benefit of the land? There were many; so many, in fact, that the tribe had become legendary. And in their legend they had gained their freedom to live as they felt best, as they felt best able to serve their vision and the goddess of artistic revelation.

They were a unique tribe, and to many they were a rumour, a legend; which is to say that many people did not believe that they really existed. This suited the tribe immensely; it cloaked them with invisibility; it freed them from external restraints; it made them wholesome creators, listeners, makers, guides, revealers, dealers in mysteries, messengers of unknown divinities, travellers between realms, image-bearers, and supreme creators of beauty in the land.

They were free. Not all their creations related to divination, revelations, omens, warnings. They also created images of lamentation, images of jubilation, bronze castings celebrating life in the round, good harvests, a young man hunting, a famous athlete, lovers, mother and child. They created works which were simply beautiful in themselves, works that had no meaning but which gave great pleasure, joy and health to all who gazed upon them. Works that were like sunlight, like rainbows, like lights glinting on the surface of rivers, like the sparkling eyes of a happy child. These works were dreamt up, made in secrecy, and appeared one morning in the most prominent or surprising places in the village.

Sometimes the artists would plant their works outside the house of a chief, or beside the most visited well, or hidden in the forest to be stumbled upon by hunters or travellers or children playing. Sometimes the artists would place the works at the centre of the path leading out of the village, or have them dangling from a tree, or would arrange for a group of children to bear them up and down the square while chanting the line of a song.

The artists were always anonymous. No one ever knew who had created what work of art. This way the dreamer was free to reveal their deepest fears, hopes, visions. The works were debated on often; and, in relation to their power, mystery, beauty or relevance, they were treated as unstated laws to be interpreted, and then acted on.

Some works of art were not found for many years, and were discovered in their hiding places years, even decades, after they had originally been left there; but whenever they were found was the moment when one of their possible meanings was most necessary for the land. Many works have still not been found, and the things they warn of, or draw attention to, still lie sleeping, unseen. Sometimes the works are discovered at the exact time when what they draw attention to is just about to cause havoc to the people; the work thus helps them see what they wouldn't have seen. The finding of works was of great significance to the tribe, as much as the making of them, or their interpretation.

It was such a unique tribe that the maiden came from. Her father was a man of mystery. He appeared to do nothing. No one knew what he did in the community, and yet he prospered enormously. Some say he was a great sorcerer, and could create gold just by thinking it into being, or by living long enough with a stone under his pillow. Some say he traded with spirits. Some claim he was a secret favourite guide to an unknown king. He was often away from home for long periods. No one knew where he went. And yet he knew everything that was going on in the tribe, and in the land. He was a man who spoke little, seldom laughed, and had piercing eyes like those of a hooded eagle. He was believed to be one of the greatest artists in the tribe, and a key guardian of its ancient mysteries.

The maiden's mother was also a strange figure in the tribe. Long and often she would stare at her daughter, and say:

'She is not from here. She will not stay long. When she has

found what she is looking for she will return. We must delay her discovery.'

Delay her discovery: that was the theme of her life.

CHAPTER THREE

Before she heard the questions by the river on that fateful day, the maiden had been shy, awkward, plain, and hard-working. No one remarked her much. She was not beautiful. None of the men had singled her out for love or marriage. She had not inflamed any loins. She was a bit of a burden on her mother, a bit of a worry. She spoke little, and fled when anyone stared at her. She couldn't bear too long the company of others, and seemed lost and lonely. She was always wandering off by herself into the forest, or sitting in isolated places by the river, staring into nothingness, yearning for the happiness that only death or a great love can bring. Hidden in her desolate spot, she was always singing sad songs to herself, absent-mindedly, in a low voice.

Sometimes, alone, a wonderful mood would come over her and she would chuckle and giggle, and run skittering along the shore, performing cartwheels and odd somersaults, playing at being a crab, or a bird. She would talk to the wind, to spirits, to imaginary and immortal friends, confiding her deep unknown yearnings to the air, overcome with an unaccountable joy that made her want to jump out of her skin. In times like that she made up songs and made up the music to go with them. Or she would rush back home to her father's workshop and begin a wood-carving, in secret.

In one such mood, under the inspiration of a dark and powerful happiness, a happiness so profound that if it didn't find something to do it would have driven her mad or made her take her life, under the spell of this tragic happiness, she began the creation of a new wood-carving. This carving she turned into a mould. And from the days and weeks she had spent working in complete secrecy with her father, learning the art of bronze casting, and gold working, she made of this mould a bronze cast of a face so pure, so mysterious, so serene that she herself was surprised at the beauty that had sprung from her own hands. To her mind it was the bust of a queen. Radiant, tranquil, with a fine patterned regal head-dress and sensuous in-turned contemplative eyes, it was a face she had never seen before, not with her eyes or in her dreams, but it was the face of her dangerous youthful happiness. When the bronze casting was completed, using her absent father's authority with the men of the foundry, she hid it among her things, till she could find a use for it.

Every morning, at dawn, she brought it out and looked at it and mooned over it. At night, before she fell asleep, she cradled it and delighted in its mystery. At that time she appeared even stranger to her mother, to whom she was a great burden.

'What am I going to do with you?' her mother would say. 'No man will marry you. You have no beauty. You do not talk. You are strange, as if you come from the land of spirits. You are not lucky. You don't have the art of women, the art of sweetening life. You are too unfriendly. Your eyes see too much; they are too big and frightening. You will grow old and lonely and unloved, the way you are. What shall I do with you?'

'Nothing, mama,' the maiden would say.

Then she would go out, to do some work about the house, or to the well to fetch water, or to the river to wash clothes, or to the forest to wander amid its mysterious hum, or to the square to gaze on the sculpture that had been made public the previous night, which the whole village was talking about.

CHAPTER FOUR

The maiden, without knowing it, and for one so young, was already wise in the ways of bronze, gold and art. As an only child she spent much time watching her father in his secret workshop, as he beat and shaped magic symbols in gold, or in bronze. She watched him at his spells, as he worked the forge of his enchantments, worked like a mysterious sorcerer on wood and iron, with fire, flint and molten things. He worked with spells and incantations, as if he were always busy with the very greatest secrets of life. She watched in silence as her father worked, in his secret workshop, with sparks in the air, with plants and oils. She watched as he made stones and iron rods invisible, just by staring at them. She watched as he made a rose appear on a white table, just by concentrating on that space. Sometimes, when he heard people coming towards their workshop, he would make them hurry out through a secret passage, out into the forest, and spy on those who were trespassing on his dreams. She would watch, in amazement, as gradually the workshop disappeared, became invisible, and a pure white mist, along with a rose fragrance, would envelop the surrounding spaces.

Once, when the horsemen of the king had come to take him away, over some false accusation or other, the maiden gazed on in astonishment as she saw her father vanish from their midst and turn into pure white air. Only a bird was left standing in his place. The soldiers seized the bird; but her father's amused laughter was heard echoing in the forest as they rode away with the captive of their superstition.

The maiden was wise in the ways of art and gold because she grew up in her father's silence. And in the enchantments of his workshop. He explained nothing to her. But when he wanted her to learn something he would cough, look at her in a particular way, and perform the operation slowly. She learnt in silence, and by his trance-making example. She learnt from the mood he created around him. All the great mysteries and manifestations are simple, she learnt, if you know the laws involved. He embodied the laws. Everything he did was steeped in the way. And yet he was so light, so simple, so unassuming that he could be taken for anything you chose. When asked what he was doing, and if he happened to be drinking, in company, in silence, with his companions, he would smile, and might say:

'I'm listening at the oracle.'

It was a favourite phrase of his; and it became a favourite expression of the tribe. They were known as people who listened at the oracle. Whenever others asked a member of the tribe what they were up to they invariably gave that reply, whether they were doing something trivial or not. Many of his expressions had thus entered the language of the tribe. It couldn't be helped. He spoke to deflect: instead he infected. He was mostly silent, and so drew attention to his speech. Everything he said resonated in the land and altered the thought-patterns of the age. Some suspected him of being the perpetrator of most of the works displayed to the tribe, that provoked the greatest reactions, or had the most profound effects. Some claimed they could detect the tone of his spirit in the spirit of certain works. Secretly, he was considered the master-artist and magus of the tribe. The fact that he was the only one who never commented on artworks found in caves or forests, that he never took part in any discussions provoked by the finds, made him more complicit. Surrounded by such mystery, luminous in health, gifted with an awkward ability to seem normal, shining with unstated integrity, respected by the mighty, feared by the great, regarded with awed silence and suspicion, it was not surprising that this man should find attributed to him most of the astounding and monstrous deeds of the tribe, and in the land. And yet there was something untouchable about him. No one could stare long into his eyes. His face, mild and gentle, seemed to resist being looked at; people felt unaccountably blinded by his presence. The maiden grew up in the air of his legend. This alone saved her from complete isolation in the world.

When her father was not there, her world returned to its emptiness, its strangeness. Often she sensed trees, birds, flowers, and forms in the air trying to tell her something. She felt acutely the need to learn the hidden languages of things, to read the secret languages of flowers. She felt that the world had messages for her which she wasn't getting. This made her unusually attentive to the eyes of goats and cats, the speech in the eyes of antelopes, the hinted dialogues of tortoises, the suggestive arrival of birds. She heard hidden meanings in what people said, and sensed the presence of angels in unlikely places. Often she had a sense, while staring into space, daydreaming between duties, that she returned to her real home on a distant star and lived a full life among forgotten loved ones. This perplexed her. Sometimes at night, when she slept, she was the father of a tribe, its wise patriarch, with innumerable children, and they could all fly, and they built things with their minds, and they loved across time and space, and they were masters of stars and galaxies, and they were bigger than giants, larger than the earth, and their heads grazed the outposts of heaven, and their dreams took them to the place of angels, in whose presence they were small. And when the maiden awoke it was with a shock, as she realised that she could not fly, that her body had weight, and that her thoughts were so unfree. She felt like a slave, a prisoner in her body, in her condition. She felt like an exile, like one banished from a home she never knew. And she wept often at dawn at the humiliation of being human, without knowing why; as if she suspected that she ought to be an angel, a being at ease among the stars.

CHAPTER FIVE

And so she was silent. Silent even when the whole tribe was troubled by the new revelation in the square: the great wooden sculpture of three men and a woman bound together by chains at the ankles, in positions of intolerable lamentation and humiliation, and yet rendered with stoic dignity, as if gods had been made the slaves of fools.

The maiden had gone to the square to see the sculpture. Everyone was puzzled by it. No one had any idea what it meant. So profound was its effect that this sculpture seemed to come alive, seemed to appear in the midst of those who talked about it. Words seemed to make it materialise. Slowly, quickly, suddenly, the sculpture was everywhere, in the tribe's mind, in their dreams, in their work, in their play. The sculpture accompanied and haunted their every activity, like a spirit desperately trying to draw attention to its reality, or like a dream or nightmare that can't be shaken off. Or like an impending illness that fills one with unease precisely because the illness itself never arrives and never leaves, just hovers. Or like the hint of death in the midst of silent happiness.

The sculpture accused, haunted, frightened, soothed, troubled, perplexed, annoyed, paralysed, trapped and engulfed them. It was like a curse, an anathema. It was stronger in the mind than in reality. To see it at first is to perceive it, to encompass it merely with the eyes. But afterwards its horror and its mystery grows, like a dreadful infection deep in the body where the hands cannot reach. It grows so in the mind, horrible and mighty, and the monstrous sublimity of it is such that those who have seen it do not know what to do with their heads afterwards. They can't cleanse their minds of the image, they can't open their brains and physically remove the offending vision. They can't wash their heads out. And so they go around obsessed, sleepless, raggy, furious, bad-tempered, displeased, displaced. The world changes for them. They feel the need to die, or do something awful, or make a long journey, or undertake a great spiritual pilgrimage, or, better still, find the cause of the sculpture, why it came into being, understand what it is saying, and do something about it.

But unable to do this the elders began to whisper the unthinkable. They felt the sculpture, in its mysterious power, was becoming so powerful and obsessive and soul-sapping to the tribe that maybe it should be hidden away as a dangerous object, or destroyed, before it destroyed the psychic fabric and spiritual cohesion of the tribe.

Never before had a sculpture or a work had such a profound effect on the people.

The sages suspected that the highest sorcery went into its creation.

The interpreters were bewildered at the too many meanings that the work suggested, and the more they discussed it the more meanings and hints and warnings it threw out. Things got so bad that three interpreters fought over their interpretations of the work, and one of them was killed. It was the first time ever that a man had died because of the impossibility of understanding a work of art of the tribe.

Not long afterwards a woman who screamed at dawn that she understood what the work meant – and that it was a great warning of a most vile anathema that would befall the land – not long afterwards, screaming that it was better to die than to suffer what was to come, the woman committed suicide near the shrine where the work stood in all its ferocious yet sublime power.

Soon everyone for miles around heard about this mysterious work that wreaked havoc on the mind. They came in their multitudes to see it. High-pitched wailings were heard at noon from young girls who fainted in its presence. A man, howling, went mad with grief when he beheld it. A sage tied himself to the sculpture, making himself the fifth figure in the living continuity of the intolerable image. The sage refused to eat till the work was understood, till he understood the work, which meant to understand himself, he said. He died on the fourteenth day, still bound to the infamous and sinister work. The sage had declared that he must not be buried till someone had pierced its mystery. His body rotted alongside the image for a month, spreading disease and illness among the people, till the elders decreed that at least he be buried near the work, near the shrine, or that his body be covered with earth, or burned, to stop further public contamination.

Thus the sculpture which the tribe couldn't seem to do anything about continued its strange destructive work. People came and gathered and stared at it, and camped in front of it, and refused to leave. The sculpture seemed to speak of a great world calamity, a tragedy of vast proportions, so vast, in fact, that it threatened the world. It seemed the world would never be the same again because of the tragedy and intolerable sorrow and noble suffering that the work breathed out in its broken proportions and the agonised shapes that broke the heart and yet still spoke of divine resolution beyond human understanding.

Then, one evening, when a white bird with a yellow flower in its mouth alighted on the crest of the sculpture, all the gathered people began, suddenly, to weep. It happened spontaneously, with an imperceptible change in the atmosphere. It seemed some mysterious light from the sculpture, caused by the presence of the bird, precipitated a mass change in feeling. The weeping went on for hours; it went on all night. The women wept, and the children cried, and the men broke down into loud weeping too, and couldn't be stopped, because of some deep unaccountable sorrow awoken in them by the work. Under the moonlight, with the white bird on the head of one of the figures, it was as though a god were making the work speak to the soul of the people.

This weeping shook the tribe. Someone tried covering up the work with a white cloth, so it couldn't be seen, and yet its power multiplied in rumour, in the minds of those who had seen it. And the sages screamed that it was better to see the work than to be haunted to madness by its magnified power in the mind; for seeing it, they said, somehow soothed the madness it threatened to bring forth.

But one night a group of elders, paying no heed to what the sages said, had the work stolen away. And in its place its absence shone, and caused greater rumours, made more crowds gather, for the space where it used to be became more powerful than ever. The space appeared to retain, in a pure white form, the very image that they sought to remove. In short, the work shone more in its invisible space. People could see the sculpture there in the empty space, even when they had never seen the work before. It was more powerful, majestic, tragic, sublime and heart-breaking in its invisible form than ever it was before. And this power caused that space to become more magnetic than any shrine of the tribe; and multitudes gathered to witness the marvel of the sculpture that wasn't there that they could see shining there in the dark as if it were a living spirit.

CHAPTER SIX

This dreaded apparition, this inexplicable manifestation overwhelmed the town. And every night the space of the invisible sculpture shone brighter, like the moon, and took on a greater form, as if it were being given greater power from the minds of the massed multitudes that came and saw it in its invisible place. Together, as one, the huge crowds brought the absent image alive with their minds and their eyes. Sobbing, fainting, illnesses and wailings abounded. Work slowed down in the village. The square became overrun. Hallucinations flashed among the people; and soon the sculpture began to appear everywhere.

People saw it by the river; people saw it in the sky, sailing past. Farmers saw it in their farms, among the cornstalks. Hunters saw it in the forests, disappearing behind baobab trees. Women saw it at the bottom of wells, when they went to fetch water. By day or night, at noon or at dusk, suddenly there would be a cry, and someone would rush out from a hut shouting that the absent sculpture had appeared near their bed. It became a plague of the mind.

It roamed the countryside. It vanished among the hills. And soon it became a rumour that ran wild in the land, and became real in the dark, as people reported that the image was multiplying. It became not four figures chained to one another, but ten, then twenty, then a hundred. Then it became a whole tribe, then a whole people, then a vast chain of people that stretched all across the plains and forests and savannahs and vanished into the mighty sea and was swallowed by the hallowed waves of the unnamed and feared ocean. And then, after a while, the people didn't see the sculpture any more. It vanished. It died in its space. The space where it was became empty. Its spirit went. No one saw the image any more. And a strange peace returned to the tribe.

CHAPTER SEVEN

The maiden had gone to see the work just before the elders had it removed. She had gone to see the work that was the most significant revelation in art that the tribe had ever known, and she had been so oppressed by it that she couldn't sleep for weeks. There are some works of art that the eyes shouldn't see. There are some works of art so terrible that they should only be seen as a reflection, in a mirror, like the heads of the Medusa. There are some works of art that should be seen only by initiates and strong-souled masters and then kept in silence for generations for their power to be changed by time into the gold of their highest fruition; works that should be described to the young, hinted at, till the people are themselves strong enough for such terrible truths. This work which had caused such upheaval in the tribe was more troubling and mysterious than any of these.

This work which the maiden saw, in the flush of her youth, her awkward, her dreaming years, was instantly intuited by her to be the beginning of the end of a great cycle. She did not know what cycle that was; but she knew that in some way the work signalled the end of a world. The end of her world. The end of the world of what was known. The end of dreams and spirits. The end of the playtime of the tribe. The end of the clear stars and the story-telling moon. The end of the clear easy spaces between the living and the dead. The end of art that can heal sicknesses of the body and mind. The end of myths. The end of a life of story-telling with intervals of deeds. The end of flowers that sing. The end of nakedness. The end of the life of the gods who now will die in their mountains in the empty hearts of the tribes that have turned their eyes, by a destruction, to new and strange horizons. The end of song and the speaking drums, the dancing flutes, the incantatory cymbals. The end of dance that spoke without words of everything under the sun. The end of the sun, and its light, and its power to recharge the spiritual journey of the tribe. The end of meaning in life, or purpose in living. The work the maiden saw filled her, in a flash, with all these intuitions. And, indeed, she could not sleep for weeks afterwards when she set eyes on this work that had so transfixed the strongest minds of the tribe, and broken the spirit of the people in its sublime foreboding.

For it was a work beyond art. It was a disaster of the soul. It was a splitting apart of the mind. It was a breach of the heavens. It was a sign that the gods had somehow abandoned the people. What else could it be, this work, this colossus, of three men and a woman, all of them huge, giants, chained together, heads bowed and broken, all blinded and tragic, as if the greatest humiliation had been heaped on their bodies. And yet how they shone, these beings, as if they were gods, unconquerable even by the vilest suffering. How they shone, unknowing, in their mighty godlike suffering. It seemed like the suffering the gods visited only on the greatest beings, because they are the only ones who can bear it, bear the evils of humanity and still let the light of their sublimity shine through. It seemed like a suffering they bore as a sacrifice and purification for the continued history of humanity on earth. Only the abysmally great can bear such abhorrently great suffering. And the injustice of it, along with the hinted nobility of it, was what so broke the heart of the maiden who saw the work and was never the same again, as if she had been poisoned by a glimpse of her own destiny . . .

CHAPTER EIGHT

The maiden was unable to sleep after her encounter with the work. At night she stared at the moon or the stars and sang lamentations and wept. At dawn she would be found muttering disconnected phrases about suffering and evil, pursued by demons and white spirits of the mind till she drowned at sea amid a chorus of alien hymns. She became obsessed, hounded by the oddest notions, surrounded by children that had been borne to her by a fat servile wife in a blond wig. Her mind opened up into disturbing vistas. Obsession chased her eyes inwards: The sculpture tormented her, accused her; in waking dreams one of the figures was her father. And leaning over her, enchained, bleeding, but not blind, he said:

'My daughter, if God cracks the gourd, God leaks into it. What God breaks, God fills. Nothing is spilt from the sacred vessel that is humanity which is not filled with the sacred spirit of heaven. We break, that we may be blessed. We had a choice in it, but we failed, and we suffer, because we didn't make the choice of power on earth; and we till the earth, like animals, and later, when time has flowed, like blood, back to the kingdom, and after many disasters, wars, suffering, folly, injustice, rage and music, my daughter, afterwards the blood will flow back as the spirit of the highest, changed into the gold of the soul. And history would be a strange dream read in an invisible book among the stars.'

But the maiden didn't understand these bewildering words and raved and muttered at dawn and cried out about the horror of the work. And her father, smiling, ministered unto her healing potions, and played a flute gently above her ears, and uttered tender incantations that soothed her obsessed spirit. She was hard to soothe; and maybe she was evidence that there is an evil when a work succeeds too well. Her father pondered this; pondered the responsibility of master-makers. If what they make creates such troubles and brings such paralysis to the people, mustn't they also be master-healers of the excessive power they have unleashed? How do you heal what must be ruptured in order to grow? The gourd of man must be broken for God to leak in; how do you heal what will, in the monstrosity of time, be in the higher glory of all things? The father contemplated his ailing daughter.

'What ails you, my child?'

'All the evils in the world.'

'How do you know of them so young?'

'I saw them in the work.'

'The work is but a dream shared amongst dreamers.'

'It has awoken us to horrors, but not shown us how to live awakened to horrors. Better to die than to know.'

'You blame the work?'

'Everyone curses the work and its maker for disturbing our dream,' cried the maiden.

The father was astonished, and stayed silent, and stared into the amber of things, the dust and red gold of the mould he saw encasing the light that enters through the wounds of humanity bleeding history on an invisible sea. Silent, the father stayed. Lions roared from the shrine. Death called from the door, and life answered in the wind, like a twin. Stillness became the father. History howled in the forests; trees called out the names of the fallen, the taken, those that will be snatched, and broken; and no one heard the trees, or the names, which vanished, and never were heard again, even in the memory of those who wept for them as rivers weep the moon.

'The maker too was in a dream,' the father said at last, wearily.

'Then curse the dream, if we must wake from it, and see. We cannot bear to see, my father, it makes us mad to see.'

The father stayed silent; the maiden slept. With incantations and words that spoke to her future as she slept, her father strengthened her soul and prepared her for the great difficult destiny to come.

CHAPTER NINE

Everyone in the tribe was an artist. They were born into art, and they were born of art. Art conceived them; art gave birth to them; art nourished them; art helped them grow, sustained their lives, and guided them to the mighty mysteries and to illumination. Art aged them, art devoured them, art made them old. They grew old in art, and they died of art. They were buried in art. And in art they were remembered and immortalised by its continual practice and renewal in the great rituals and initiations of the tribe.

Art was their god and their devil; their destruction and regeneration. All things came from art and fed back into it, as far as the tribe was concerned. Art was their religion, science, dream, temptation, seduction, recreation. Art was their hell and heaven. Every cataclysm or disaster, every crisis, came out of art or was absorbed into it. Plagues were seen as a failure of their art in some way, a failure to listen, to see, to dream, to interpret, to prophesy, to envision, to be silent at the oracles. Famines were seen as a curse from the god of art, in the tribe's failure to create, to anticipate, to adapt, to work, to change, to move on to fruitful places, to be free. Diseases, illnesses, bad fortune, abominations, were all perceived as failures of art, for not being humble enough at the secret shrines of creativity, which creates balance and harmony in the universe.

Their great good fortunes, the beauty of their children, cornucopias, wonderful harvests, fruitful seasons of productivity, happiness and festivities in the tribe were seen as success in the communal practice of their art. For then all doors between heaven and earth, between the ancestors and the present, between spirits and the living, between past and future, between nature and human beings, between dream and living, between man and woman, were open, and no bad things festered because they were unable to emerge, be seen, be freed, released, overcome, transcended.

Their laws were laws of art, the obvious ones and the obscure ones, the known laws and the unknown, the familiar laws and the arcane laws, the exoteric and the esoteric, the public laws and the secret ones, the superficial and the deep. Harmony, balance; disharmony, too, was one of the laws, in the right place, in the right way; and imbalance was a secret law that played its part. Chaos was a deep law, applied judiciously. Order was its obvious counterpart. Asymmetry was a great law, if used with a sense of greater balance.

The tribe did not favour such simple things in its art as order, balance, harmony. These were easy, and had been fully explored for generations. The tribe had advanced to the higher harmony of broken cadencies, discord as beauty, warring elements, violent forms like storms flashing pure lightning of fleeting beauty that cracks the soul asunder till one glimpses illumination. It favoured tactical rawness, indirection, eyes where the navel should be, for the navel is a kind of eye, and the eye is a kind of navel linking us to the known world. It favoured disjointed metaphorical thinking; fusion of unthinkable elements. The greater the discord, the greater the artistry required to bring forth the highest beauty and, paradoxically, the greatest simplicity. The most complex productions must appear simple and clear to the mind, like a portrait, or a line of rhyme, or a famous song that children sing. The works of the greatest masters must be able to speak to the smallest child, or the village idiot.

The tribe's central tenet, unspoken, was that art was the bridge to the creator, and thus to all things, all mysteries on earth or in heaven. Art was their prayer, and their confession, their meditation and their rest, their work and their play, their illness and their cure. They wooed one another with art. In other tribes camels, yams, fame in wrestling, land, were deemed the attractive items in marriage – beauty, strength, prowess, and lineage too; but in this tribe, it was art. The men competed for the hands of the women with their works of art. The works that pleased, that delighted, that surprised, that astonished, that amused the women most tended to incline their choice in marriage. If you weren't a good artist you didn't stand much of a chance of having the kind of wife you wanted. Men too chose their wives by their art; the works that showed the greatest delicacy, patience, love, tenderness, resilience, beauty, strength of spirit, capacity for reconciliation, fruitfulness of invention and conductivity to good dreams tended to win the best husbands. If you weren't a subtle artist you didn't stand much of a chance of having the best husband. When families wanted to bring suitor to encounter prospective wife, they first exchanged the couple's works of art. These works were lived with, slept with, thought about. The inner character of the couples was thus allowed to emerge; great readers of the personality lurking behind a work of art were hired to interpret the tendencies and spirit of the prospective husband or wife.

The tribe believed that nothing revealed a person more than their art. As individuals, there is much they can conceal, mask, or deceive with. In their art everything is there, unveiled, naked. Beauty was therefore not enough in art. For beauty sometimes revealed suicidal inclinations, or a personality troubled, or a mind unstable. Even what is concealed in a work reveals what is absent. Thus coolness may mask and reveal too much passion. Too much passion in a work may reveal too little feeling, or frivolity, or being too easily moved, or a lack of perspective on matters in the greater scheme of things. Size counts for nothing. The small may reveal great ambition. The large may hint at laziness, sloppiness. The small may also point to over-fussiness, a tendency to too much control. The large may reveal plain generosity of spirit, if allied to great care and focus in execution. These matters of reading the soul behind the work were intrinsic to all of the tribe. All were born interpreters, after their own temperaments; but there were those who were specialists at this, and these too, who must be great artists and sages, sat on some of the highest councils of the tribe.

Agriculture, warfare, athletics were all aspects of art, to the tribe. Farms and farming methods were based on firm artistic principles. Warfare was conducted on the greatest artistic principle of maximum effectiveness from minimum effort. In short, winning without fighting, overcoming without warfare. The tribe was the only known tribe that had perfected the art of war. They rarely fought. When they had to fight, they fought spiritually. Artistically. And their victories were never public, or visible. There was no bloodshed. No one felt conquered or overcome. Winning did not bring enemies. Often it seemed as if they had lost. And so they thrived. Warfare was anathema to them, because it reduced the number of artists in the world.

Another great tenet of the tribe was that all men and all women were artists, in one way or another, but did not know it. To be alive was to be a creator, or a co-creator. At least you helped create a destiny. Therefore, with all being artists, humanity was considered to be the greatest work of art that is being created. One way or another, all are contributing to the greatest vision that ever will be, the vision of all above and below, in life and in death, on earth and in heaven. The tribe was therefore fundamentally serene about all things, and lived in the secret freedom of this knowledge, which was more than knowledge.

From birth children were encouraged to create, to make, to dream things, and to be as artists. They therefore had no word for art in their language, it being the all of their all, much as God is to believers, except that to the tribe art was not God, but was one of God's ways of creating the universe. Therefore, to the tribe, vision was primal: the vision of creators, what they dreamt of, their ideal, their hopes, what they bring, the purpose behind, even when purpose is denied. No-purpose was highest, for it implied the artist had submitted to a vision greater than them, of which they were vehicles, conduits, the means by which mysteries came to be. Only a poor artist knows what they have done. The greatest masters say nothing about their works because there is nothing to say, save that it was done, it was seen, it was unseen, it was rendered, it was remembered, carried across, brought here, imperfectly. The less one makes, the more is made.

Imperfection was a great law of the tribe; and so they were

always learning to unlearn. They begin as masters and end as children. They end as babies, innocent and not quite here, rooted in the central place that is not a place, in heaven and on earth at the same time. Sophistication, vigour, brilliance, cleverness, allusion, richness, metaphor, subtlety, wisdom, power, profundity, multiplicity, variety, simplicity, politics, beauty, in a work, were all signs of youth and its greatness. The great masters, however, had nothing. Their works were empty. The world read everything into this emptiness, especially their greatest fears, desires, intuitions and communal prophecies. Sometimes a mighty work of art is a charged empty space on which multitudes converge and witness mass revelations that concur. A space designated by the artist. Like the space which became a form, which was the work that now so obsessed the maiden.

CHAPTER TEN

Everything that happened to the tribe, to the individual, became art, had to become art, if it did not become illness. And so when ill, when obsessed, when they had troubles of the mind, it was designated that they had to create, to create the work of art that would heal them. Other tribes came to this tribe purely for this need: to have works of art created for them that would heal sicknesses in their land that nothing else could heal. But this was especially true for the individual.

There was a work, of some kind or other, that would heal them, or lead to their healing. It could be a carving, an act of cooking, a design of cloth, a new game, a walk by the river, a meditation on a leaf, a song with a magic refrain, a dance with a turn of the body that felt just right, or standing and facing the sun at the best angle, a measured breathing. A good conversation was a work of art. A good argument too. An excellent act of cursing, even. The invention of riddles, parables, word-play, puns, sounds without meaning but with hidden power, an insight, an intuition, a symbol contemplated or invented, a blending of herbs, all these were works of art. Initiation into the mysteries was a great work of spirit art, too. And so, as the maiden lay obsessed by the work that gripped all minds, it became clear that she had to create the art of her own healing.

This was something the tribe much looked forward to: when someone was ill, and they had to create the art of their own cure. This art created was generally one that all paid keen attention to; for it revealed the secret cause or source of the problem. Often it might reveal something about the tribe. Often it might be purely personal, and the result enriched the gossip of the tribe. As with all people who work with matters of the spirit, gossip was almost an art form in the tribe. And rumours were either hints of what will become true, or that which was essentially true, awaiting clarification.

It was soon rumoured that the maiden, daughter of the most enigmatic master of the tribe, was preparing to go into seclusion, for the purpose of vision. Some said she had chosen a cave. There was excitement as to what she would create, and whether she had inherited the mystery of the master's touch. She was the test of the power of his loin, his blood. If she revealed herself average, this would diminish the rich air of myth that surrounded him, which he never encouraged, or even knew, or cared, about. Gossip is thus; one becomes mighty, or nothing, *in absentia* – to one's indifference, but to the unending amusement of the tribe.

CHAPTER ELEVEN

During this time the maiden often followed the path of ants, to see where they led. She kept watch on little snails, and for hours would learn of their destination. Her mother fed her on unripe plantain and fresh spinach and watercress from distant markets. Her mother bathed her like a little girl, and prayed over her, and tempted her with lovely bales of new dyed cloth. Nourishing her daughter, singing to her, beautifying her, watching her wander off towards the river, watching her return, swaying, with a gourd of water on her head, or a basin of washed clothes, or singing gently a sad song to the wind, these moments saddened and gladdened the heart of the mother.

'What will we do with you, my strange child,' her mother would say, sighing to herself.

From birth an odd destiny, told in an enigma, a riddle, had been foretold for her daughter. It was as if an ambiguous star had hovered over the moment of her conception. This was not a child from here. Not from these parts. She is from a star no one has seen yet. And her ancestors are not human. They have faces like the gods. They are huge and mighty like lightning. They travel from one end of the world to another like the light of the moon. They are thousands of years old when they are children. And every now and then they are sent to other places among the stars to suffer and see and to live out a story that has one meaning to the people of that star or planet and another meaning to their own true people. What might seem a life of suffering to the strangers they were born to, might be a brief time in a playground to their own true people. The suffering is felt only if they forget the true meaning of their life, if they forget they are in a playground, a fair, a dream. They suffer much only when they take too seriously the stage on which they are playing a role, and forget that they are free, and are the sons and daughters of gods. They suffer because they forget. No, she is not from here. But she will not leave, as some children do, because of the terrible lives they see. She is of a different kind of star. For most of her life she will live as if lost. Then one day she will wake up, her body will remember something, and she will be comfortable with her life. Then her real life will begin, beyond the sea, and she will be a great voice in the world, bringing the music of a distant star into the narrow spaces of this remote earth. And she will reconcile the people to their forgotten homes.

But who says these things? Who whispers them, in dreams, to the heart of a mother? There are voices in the air, and in the mind, that whisper all over the universe in the heart and dreams of mothers. There are things seen that speak from the invisible future. Messages appear from the book of life. The past is untold, the present is unrolled, the future has been and gone, and whispers in dreams, in signs, and a song. Fortune-tellers of the tribe catch stories of distant stars in a sleep by the shrine when it is the hour of prophecy, when all are creating dreams in the square. How does anything get here? They travel from nowhere. They are always here, where the gods are, in the centre of the heavenly fire that lies hidden in the stone, and the wood, in the flesh of each living child, and the flight of the sunbird. Whispering the way. The way to the home that is in the heart. The heart of the art. The art of the tribe. The tribe of living. The mother listened to all, as she fed, coaxed and nourished her daughter, who prepared to create the art of her own healing.

The mother fed her daughter rich vegetables and the intangible minerals of clear water. The mother fed her daughter on her love. And she watched her daughter grow plainer, stranger, slighter, as if she were becoming a human bird, frail, distracted, puzzled by the mystery of flight, without the knowledge of flying. It was as if she were troubled by an ability to fly that she didn't know of, and yet it was as if she could taste the clouds already.

The mother nourished her daughter and gazed on her as one lost to the dictates of the gods . . .

CHAPTER TWELVE

And enigmas grew about the maiden's heart, and made strange her simple life. The rituals of the tribe became distant to her, and she felt herself becoming evermore a stranger to her land, to her body, to her own life, and didn't know why. Often, at night, she would awaken in the stifling heat of the clay hut, and bring out the doll she had made for herself, and would whisper secrets that she had invented into its delicate ears of fragrant wood. Often she would bring out the bust of the young queen she had sculpted and would address it as herself. She felt, on those nights, that she was a young queen misplaced in the world. She felt that as she was so misplaced, lost to her kingdom, that she might as well be a servant girl. She liked the idea of being either a queen or a servant girl, but she didn't like not knowing who or what she was. So she played the role of the servant girl to the bust of the young queen. She asked, in a whisper, if there was anything her queen wanted; and, in the dark, with little gestures imitating actions in the larger world, she set about obeying and fulfilling the desires of her queen.

On those nights she was both queen and servant girl; and in the role she would fall asleep, and live out many adventures which she did not remember, with people who were very familiar but whom she had never seen before. And then she would awake in perplexity when she found herself on a raised clay bed, in a hot clay abode, in a room entirely strange to her. Then the despair brought on by her encounter with that obsession-making work of art would take hold of her again, like a sickness of the mind.

She would set about her tasks for the day like one divided, broken in two. Half in a dream, half perplexed, she fetched water, helped her mother prepare breakfast, washed clothes, brought in firewood from the forest, cleaned the house with broom and wet cloth, and when her morning's tasks were accomplished she would hurry to her father's workshop to see what the master-artist was doing. And that depended on what he would allow her to witness.

She would sit quietly on the floor, and watch the master work, or pace, or sit staring or suddenly pouncing on some half-dreamt piece of sculpture. Then, in swift sure motions, he would carve greater suggestivity from a figure that a moment ago didn't want to live.

CHAPTER THIRTEEN

Her father's workshop was rich with dreams and deep indigo moods. She was convinced that spirits came there, and that her father created his astonishing works with their help and ministration. How often had she heard him utter to them definite commands, in his stern voice, as to intractable servants. How often had she seen him utter directives and issue orders to this or that portion of empty air, as if to slow-witted attendants that needed everything spelt out for them or they would create havoc from a too literal carrying out of their instructions?

Her father's workshop teemed with such invisible attendants; and while she dozed, in that mood of teak and smoky presences, she often saw them in the transfigured space of the workshop, planing, glazing, polishing, varnishing, casting, carrying and shaping the wooded creations that populated the workshop. She saw them, as she dozed, as rather pleasing, intelligent, bright and humorous-looking beings. They did exactly what they were told to do, the spirits, no more and no less. And they followed instructions to the letter and to the limit. They were always cheerful, in an oddly neutral way. Nothing affected their mood. They seemed peculiarly indestructible, though they were made of pure air and pure light. They worked tirelessly, unendingly, even when her father had shut up the workshop for the day. The work always went on, never stopped; for the spirits were always at the endless artistic tasks which the master had set them.

But when the maiden awoke, she never saw the spirits at all. They seemed, in an instant, tantalisingly, to vanish. All she saw were the multitudinous brooding sculptures that jostled for space in the crammed workshop. The sculptures were everywhere; and they seemed so fiendishly, so mischievously alive. They seemed to breathe out of their wooden mouths. They seemed so to stare, pitilessly, at their surroundings. They seemed to listen, to hear everything, rather intensely. They seemed, more than anything else, to be thinking, and their definite opinions and judgements were almost tangible, like dark wooded dew, in the darkened shadow-filled spaces of the workshop. There were, therefore, many kinds of thoughts, moods, opinions, notions, judgements and mental arguments in that air.

Crowded together, in that workshop, were sculptures of demons with wild eyes and tranquil brows, children with wise adult eyes and ears of antelopes, twins and triplets facing different directions and alternately upside-down and right side up, embossed on huge panels. There were crocodiles, giants, monsters, noble and severe warriors, sages who had pierced the veil of human illusions and gazed with sublime indifference upon all phenomena, kings who were lascivious, cruel, cunning, and lazy-eyed like lions who never need bother to gaze down on the feeble subjects under their reign. There were sculptures of tiny human beings, and half-human creatures of unimaginable beauty, and the radiant forms of gods and goddesses who stood in the shadowed places in an undimmed light of their own astonishing sublimity. There were figures of fools who were lovable, of village idiots, of the mad, of lonely old women, of girls in love, of puzzled law-makers. In short, all manner and permutations of imagined and real beings lived in wood and stone and bronze and they all seemed to breathe and move in the dark spaces of the workshop. One of the maiden's favourite works there was a tortoise so real that it seemed ever so slowly to move; and the mystery of this movement, which she could not disprove to herself, never ceased to fascinate and delight her.

CHAPTER FOURTEEN

Her father was now at his trestle. He was in his work-clothes. His hands moved as if he had seven arms. He worked as if there were three of him. Often she counted her father being in four places at the same time. Planing here, hammering there, stretching the skin of an animal over a wooden shape to fool the eye, or in the shadows, somewhere, rooting around in his secret shrine; always working with spells and incantations that enlarged, charged and transformed the atmosphere of the workshop, and sent her off into dreaming.

What odd dreams she had in her father's workshop. Now she dreamt she was in a ship that tossed on the waves whipped up by the demons of the deep. She was in the ship, in its bowels, in chains, lying upside-down, or sideways, facing the feet of another, who was also chained. Blood on the chains was like rust. Her agony had passed beyond bearing and she was in pain like one dead, floating above the figures lying in opposite directions, head to foot, and foot to head, in the vile-smelling hold of the ship, tossing in the nightmare of demons. Wailing sounded everywhere in the crushed space, and women were dying, calling out the obscure names of their ancestors in languages no one understood. And death and doom was thick in the dream as she floated and saw hundreds of bodies like writhing ebony sculptures bleeding and drowning in the white waves. She howled in the dream, in a white space, and drifted away into eternity, among the stars, where forms in mists of gold led her back down to a land where dead bodies were planted and long green sweet canes grew from their bodies, and at last she saw the sea differently, and returned to her home among the giants of the stars.

What dreams she had, in her father's workshop, as she listened to his sonorous incantations used for the moulding of gold into magic objects.

And then, in the midst of evanescent dreams, she would see the spirits appear in the workshop, as if conjured out of the dark mystic atmosphere.

CHAPTER FIFTEEN

They appeared one by one. The first to appear was the spirit of the forge. He was made of fire, and shone like polished bronze. His face was impassive, impressive, mighty, severe, humourless, and his eyes were full of flames. Upon his appearance, crackles of heat fizzled in the air. He was silent, and awaited his instruction. The maiden's father, uttering further grim incantations, sent him to the forge at the back of the workshop, and immediately the blazing copper would be glowing on the plates and moulds. They would soon become the living busts of kings and queens soon to be dead, or the sacred forms of the almighty father god who created all things from the great word that was brought on golden tablets by the mysterious ancestors of the tribe, who came from somewhere not of this earth, who perished under the seas, and whose legacy had come down to the master, working now, with the secret of the ages, while his daughter slept.

The second spirit to appear was the spirit of making. He had a smiling face and seven hands and three heads and many eyes and was powerful and muscled and lithe and his eyes shone like moonlight. Upon receiving his instructions, with big smiles, and a happy mood, he was amongst the unmade objects, the wood awaiting their dreams, and he began carving from their raw shapes the figures that the master had outlined in their rawness. Among much chipping, hammering and carving, the second spirit was happy.

The third spirit was the spirit of inspiration. It was light as air, luminous, beautiful, mysterious. It kept changing form, and had a pure glow of delight. Its face was turned inwards, and its eyes of purest airy gems shone a clear radiance on all around, transfiguring the rough workshop into a promised land, a paradise of dreams. It seemed as if there were flowers everywhere amongst the stones and shadows, and an open sky visible through the dark rafters of the workshop, and stars in miniature among the ruins of visible forms, and all the gods as one, and all the goddesses as one also. There seemed a gentle song brimming from the heart of form, and music tinkling amongst the tools. The third spirit was a being of pure unfixed magic and enchantment, like a fluid angel, awaiting a simple instruction to turn all things into gold and all living forms into their own paradise and wonder.

The maiden was happy as a happy child at the appearance of the third spirit; and she marvelled at how, upon receiving its instructions from her father, the spirit vanished into the air and became the very glow that shone from all things, as if the great god was revealing itself in all that was.

Her father shone now in majestic splendour, his taut skin seeming to radiate a transforming light through the sweat of his brow and from his three eyes that shone so in the dark light of the workshop.

CHAPTER SIXTEEN

The maiden listened to the work going on in all the spheres of the workshop. She saw the glow of the blazing forge in the distance and the glimmering brilliance of gold flowing into future forms. She heard the steady sound of a head taking shape from the trunk of a dead tree. And she listened to the murmur of her father at his magic work-bench, invoking new forms into being as he worked a living face out of stone.

All over the workshop the spirits were busy. Their hands were everywhere. They went past in silence. They never spoke. They never crashed into anything, or put a foot wrong, never fell, never broke a thing, never ruined a sculpture, and they continually went to her father for further instructions, if their previous task was completed. For they ended a task with the same tranquillity as they began a new one, never tired, never elated, beginning and ending in the same spirit, as if these two phases were the same, or as if they were engaged in one long epic work in which beginning and ending were merely pauses.

How clear, how noble, how magical the spirits were during the magic hour of work, the unforgettable hours of her youth, among mysteries, in her father's dream. She saw them so clearly, and to her mind no further proof was needed. All the whispers and rumours were true. It seemed possible that her father was the invisible master of the great sculpture that had so troubled her. It seemed possible that he was the master of the most magical and subversive sculptures that had perplexed and astonished the people and made the tribe change its location three times in the last twenty years because of the hint of disasters to come. It was possible that her father worked with spirits, that they found the rare and special materials, that they sometimes brought these rare materials from the land of spirits and other times from lands across the great seas where pink humans dwelt in silver cages. It was possible that her father made these spirits work for him in secret at all hours of the day. What else could explain the genius and strangeness of the man? Where did his extraordinary notions and productivity come from, if not from the spirits? She always meant to ask him about this. And on this day, in her sleep, she remembered to do so. And so, waking gently, stirring on the bench, and noticing the spirits vanish into the dark spaces with her awakening and yet carrying on her intention in the face of no evidence, and also risking the wrath of having interrupted her father's profound concentration, she said:

'Father, is it true that you use spirits to do your work?'

There was a long silence as the silence spoke in the workshop. What did the silence say? The silence said: Child, you should not ask questions till you know the answers. Child, questions can never be answered. Child, questions do not ask the questions you really want to ask. Child, ask questions in silence if you want answers in sound. Child, questions disturb the order of things. Child, questions destabilise the world. Child, questions bring answers that would trouble you for ever. Child, questions change the world. Child, questions bring answers we wish we had not brought forth. Do you know what you are doing asking questions, child? Terrors hide in questions, and the end of your happy days, the beginning of the days of knowledge, and the sadness that comes with it, till the day of light, long in the distance, after much suffering is overcome. Child, it is too late to be silent now, and to prolong your happiness, in the years of enchantment, when all was well in the dark groves of childhood, where dreams are as real as rivers.

All these things the silence said, as the maiden listened to the cobwebs increasing in the dark, and the lizards scuttling among the thinking forms of stone heads. Many years passed before the silence was over. Many dreams. She had been raped by a slave-master across the seas; repeatedly, she endured it, at noon, when the house slept. She had borne three children to two slave-masters. She had run away one night and had walked six hundred miles to join a colony of freed slaves. She had grown old telling stories of her magical childhood to incredulous children. She was dying by candlelight. She was with the ancestors, at peace, and joyful at the mysterious understanding of the rich meaning and purpose of her life's suffering and forgotten beauty, before the silence passed and she heard her father, in gentle sonority, answer the question she thought she had asked.

'Do you see spirits?" he said.

The maiden had awoken now. She heard time's gentle flight in the silence; its wings brushed past her face, ageing her tenderly, beginning her long and silent bloom. She could not see the spirits; she could never see the spirits this way, though she was sure they were there.

'I see them when I sleep,' she replied.

'In your dreams?'

There was a mocking smile in her father's interrogation.

Not mocking. Amused. An amused smile in his voice. Are you ready for revelation, child? the air seemed to say after he had spoken.

'Yes, I think in my dreams.'

'So you dream of spirits?'

'Yes, I think so, but they are real, and they are usually here, working for you.'

'But in your dreams.'

'Yes, father, in my dreams, I think so, but they are real.'

'But you are dreaming them.'

'Yes, father.'

'So you are responsible for them.'

'No, father.'

'Why not?'

'Because, father, in the dreams it is you who command them, it is you who they obey.'

'Do I create your dream?'

The father was smiling broadly now in the question. Are you ready to be enlightened, child? the silence seemed to say.

'I don't know, father.'

'You mean you suspect I can do it if I want?'

'It seems to me, my dear father, that you can do anything.'

A profound silence descended on the maiden, like a mantle of calm. A cooling sensation. Did the world change a little? She felt so, but didn't know how, as if an inaudible vowel had altered the spaces in the workshop and transported her across time to a place where only magi lived, among ancient mysteries. Her father suddenly seemed gently transfigured, as if on the verge of becoming invisible, as if he were a work of art himself, whose meaning ever eludes, and which is not seen by most even when looked at intensely by all.

'Your questions and all the questions you will ever ask were answered before you were born, my child. All you have to do is remember, or return.'

'But, my father, you confuse me. How can it be?'

'We of our tribe create out of dreams but we make in broad daylight. Our works have more meaning and more truth than we realise at the time, but it is not meaning or truth that we seek.'

'What do we seek?'

'We seek to serve that which directs us to create. Hence we are somewhat indifferent to what we create, since it serves a purpose higher than we understand. The person who creates is not important, only what they create, what they make. Those who are the best servants of the higher powers have more servants to help them do the work. That is why some have the power of ten while others have only their own power, which is, in the long run, the power of nothing, of dust, of oblivion. Through our works must shine not the power of the person, but the power of the power. True fame should belong to the power which guides us in the dark.'

CHAPTER SEVENTEEN

The father stopped; the maiden had found herself somewhere else. She had been listening to another lesson which was being spoken to her while her father was speaking. It was only through the transported distraction of her father's words that she could hear the other secret words. It was as though her father's voice were a sort of a bridge to another realm, where the real learning is done, a realm of universal knowledge, where masters whisper secrets into the ears of their unknowing pupils as if into the petals of flowers. And when her father stopped, her lesson seemed over. A bizarre joy encompassed her heart. Had she heard a word of what her father said? Only later, much later, in another land, in the fragrance of honeysuckle, on one of the few days of her adult life when she knew true happiness, did she hear what her father said, and more; but she heard it only because she repeated it, as if she were saying it from her own power, to her child, who would one day change the world, invisibly, through the secret power of art.

Deeply her father breathed; deeply the maiden listened. She was back now in the workshop, among shadows, and iroko heads dreaming only of war, and wall geckos scuttling, and cobwebs gathering dust, and eyes that look but do not see, and faces that will carry into the future the only living traces of a tribe vanished from the earth for ever.

She was back now, and listening. Her father did not speak a while. Then he spoke in disconnected fragments, as if repeating words whispered in his mind, words destined for the ears of his daughter, and through his daughter destined for those in the wide world, through time, for whom they would have significance at the special moment that they are encountered. The father, as if in a dream, said:

'We are listeners at the oracle. Some listen, but do not hear. Some hear, but do not listen. Those who hear are touched and changed.'

Then he said:

'Free to be truthful to their dreams.'
Then:
'How they live invisibly.'
Then:
'After the suffering, gold.'
Then:
'When they don't notice, best work is done.'
Then:
'Obscure life of a master.'
Then:
'When they see you hide again.'

CHAPTER EIGHTEEN

And as he spoke, as if he were somewhere else, but also somehow here, the maiden fell under the spell of the strange fragments. They seemed to join, dance and separate in her mind. They seemed also to be words spoken not just by her father but also by the spirits she could no longer see, and by the stone heads and the bronze busts and the figures brooding and breeding in the nocturnal spaces of the workshop.

And the fragments became words crystallised from stars and dreams. She listened as her life changed.

'We do not see what we judge.'
'Conditions change.'
'Now is not now.'
'The winners have lost.'

'Life is a masquerade. What we are seeing is not what is happening.'

'There is a shadow over all victories.'

'It is not here that life is lived. Only where it is felt.'

'All are dreams.'

'It rises and it falls.'

'Only in light can truth be found.'

'Real condition of things do not show.'

'To die is not all.'

'Plant there, reap here.'

'Seek the light that comes from the rose and the cross and the stars and the vanished kingdom under the sea.'

'Prosperity and poverty are not what they seem.'

'Beyond is where it really begins.'

'Slaves are masters in heaven.'

'Whatever happens it is getting better.'

'Then all will be one.'

CHAPTER NINETEEN

The fragments had become whispers now which the maiden barely heard. And then there was a long silence. They say that sorcerers can transport your spirit to distant lands to dwell in dark caves or in the fabulous palace of a non-existent king, while leaving your body behind. These fragments from her father had transported the maiden to many places that would appear to her as dreams. And now, in the silence, she was unsure of the world in which she found herself. She was uncertain even of her father's existence.

She was puzzled. Questions she hadn't asked, and would ask in the years to come, were being answered. Fathers have their way of initiating their children into the long, mysterious journey ahead.

There was a sigh and a smile from the maiden's father in the dark. But was he there? Had he gone? Had he left the sigh and smile behind? The maiden, seeing nothing, waited. She waited for things to be clearer. But the silence seemed to say: Child, nothing gets clearer here, only there. The clearer, the more unclear. Nothing is completed here, only there. Here is incompleteness. Fragments. Unfinished things.

What else was being said? The maiden listened. Then, from out of the dark, with no one there to have uttered them, came the words:

'And still they were haunted by the work.'

And nothing more.

CHAPTER TWENTY

The maiden found herself alone in the workshop, with only the rich mood of her father lingering in the air. Maybe he had never been there. The maiden got up from the chair and made her way home. As she walked down the forest path she breathed in the dark fragrance of the flowers.

There was something in her that was still unwell. But

whatever it was had been deepened, not altered. Yes, she was still haunted by that sculpture. And enigmas grew about her heart, and made strange her simple life.

Time became precious, and new; as if it were over, gone, and all she had was the fragrance of a life vanished for ever in a fading dream.

Part Two

CHAPTER TWENTY-ONE

Meanwhile the tribe's expectation of the work of art the maiden would create to heal the sickness of her spirit continued to press on her. Many were the enquiries directed at her and her father about this self-healing work. It became the subject of rumours, gossip and conversations. It was not unknown for two people to meet in the forest and for one to say:

'Is there any news yet of the work our maiden is supposed to be doing?'

The other might reply:

'No news yet. They say she broods, but does not breed.'

'This is what I heard too. I heard that she wanders about the place talking to herself, looking at the sky, and that she becomes stranger every day. And yet nothing comes from her. Not a dream in wood or stone. An illness that does not produce an art is a bad illness indeed. I fear for her family.'

'In this you are right,' the other would say. 'But it is not surprising. After all, her father is the strangest man in the tribe. Has anyone ever seen his shadow? Do they not say that he works among demons? Was he not seen on the moon some time ago, dancing with spirits who never visit the earth? Does anyone know where he goes to most of the year? Is he amongst us, or does he work for kings, with sorcery? Is he a man like us, or a spy from a strange land of ghosts? Have you ever heard him laugh? And do we know his hand? Do we know his works? Some say he was the one responsible for the sculpture that nearly drove our people mad, the one that has now poisoned the mind of his daughter! Maybe his art is a curse, maybe he curses us; and we all know how powerful he is on the secret council of the tribe! One word from him and we will all have to move from where we are, and change our location, like cattle on the hills. No, I am not surprised that the maiden behaves in a mad manner. Lions with blood in their eyes do not give birth to roosters.'

And these two people might laugh, and the forest would echo their laughter.

'But it is not good for the tribe when there are illnesses and no art.'

'When there are sicknesses that are not fruitful.'

'When there is madness and no magic.'

'When the spirit has troubles, but does not sing.'

'It means that the wells of the tribe become poisoned.'

'The river becomes polluted.'

'The crops give a bad harvest.'

'And the fruits lose their sweetness.'

'One person's sickness without a song makes the whole tribe sick.'

'One person's illness that doesn't give meaning makes the whole tribe ill.'

'One person's madness without a making makes the whole tribe mad.'

'Soon she will infect our dreams.'

'Soon she will make us sick just looking at her.'

'Her failure to heal herself will be catching.'

'The children will get new diseases because of her shadow.'

'The young girls will become infertile because of her bad example.'

'And the daughter of one of our most powerful masters will become an abomination and a curse unto us.'

'The problems of powerful people destroy the land.'

'We must destroy them first before they destroy us.'

'If they don't clear up their own troubles.'

'And give us an art that makes the air good again to breathe.'

'The air is not good now.'

'Because of that maiden.'

'She should create something, before we all die.'

'Or we will have to kill her.'

'Or have her banished from the tribe.'

'Sent into the hills.'

'To join the mad.'

'And all those who are infertile in art.'

'Unable to heal themselves.'

'And heal the tribe.'

'The tribe will not perish because one person is unable to dream.'

'Better if she is not seen.'

'Better if she becomes invisible.'

'And no longer reminds us of what we fear.'

'And what is coming near.'

'The end of our days.'

'And our dreaming ways.'

'Our art and our song.'
'That have lasted long.'
'Our dreams, our freedom.'
'Better than any kingdom.'
'Our vision.'
'Our mission.'
'We will protect them all.'
'That sick maiden will not create our fall.'

And so the two strangers will part. And they would spread their unease through the tribe, as others were doing. And slowly this unease, this gathering expectation worked on her too, and made her malaise worse.

CHAPTER TWENTY-TWO

And so some time before the maiden's life was changed by the encounter at the river, after she had recovered a little from the sleeplessness brought on by her glimpse of the great tragic sculpture, the maiden again found herself overcome with a strange agonised boredom, a peculiar malaise, and a giddy longing in her body.

It was as if about this time some significant event should be happening to her, but wasn't. Her body was full of a ripe rich expectation of an experience beyond her comprehension. Her heart would burst into bizarre palpitations, as if any moment someone she longed for all her life would suddenly appear and take her away to a land of dream.

She became jumpy. She peered into every stranger's face, hoping to recognise someone whom she had never seen, or someone seen too long ago. She waited for a voice, a touch that would wake her into the true enchanted dream of her life.

She fell into a condition akin to stupidity, wandering about in a state of shining and pitiful innocence, a wide-eyed waiting.

In an odd way the same thing was happening to the tribe. It existed in a state of wide-eyed waiting, expecting something momentous to happen without warning. An ennui and restlessness descended on the tribe, like a fatal ailment; a resignation, a boredom, a sense of fatality crept over everything. This was apparent in the listless way that the artisans worked at their masks and carvings, the drowsy manner in which the women wended their ways to the river, the slow atmosphere that hung over the children at play, and the dense breezes bringing heat, forgetfulness, and a sleepwalking quality by day. The tribe also seemed mysteriously to empty out, to become hollowed, and diminished. The sculptures and masks and carvings, the masquerades awaiting their motion and their accoutrement and their spirit possession, hung about the village square empty of power, and drained of significance. Some mysterious thing seemed to be devouring the spirit of the tribe. Some mysterious thing seemed to be devouring the heart and soul of the entire land, for the tribe was the secret heart of the land.

CHAPTER TWENTY-THREE

This new deadly air was never more visible than at the secret council meetings of the hidden masters of the tribe. They met infrequently, but at regular intervals. They convened always in the dead of night. They came without candles or any illumination, and they always wore masks so as not to be recognised by other members, either through their voices or by their faces. Only certain signs and passwords, certain vowel sounds, certain handshakes at the gate of enigmas permitted them entry into the long room of power.

They were chosen anonymously, because of indirect wisdom shown, authority and personal spiritual power made evident in their art; or in a deed accomplished that bordered on the miraculous and which could be repeated, with acceptable variation, as a sign of mastery. Only those who could command spirits, who could make a flower manifest out of empty air, who could enter the dreams of multitudes, who could foresee the future, who had attained a degree of illumination in the great secret mysteries of the tribe, who had battled with evil, who were masters of their art, and who had attained to a sublime impersonality, an inspired indifference and a cosmic sense of humour, only such as these were accepted, initiated, and admitted as hidden masters of the tribe.

Their powers were many and unstated, fluid and invented, in line with the artistic and spiritual needs of the tribe and of the times. It was they who had to go into the seeds of things and read what the future was bringing, or to interpret what the present was saying, or to listen at the oracles of the people's art. It was they who had to attune to the gods, to the ancestors, and to the great heavens, to learn, to avert disasters, to combat evil in the place where it is born, and to replenish the dreams and the breathing of the people. If the quality of masters fell, the tribe was in peril. It had happened before, when an era of low-calibre and brash individuals dominated the council and nearly destroyed the foundations of the tribe. An important lesson was learnt: a people are only as great or as strong as the quality of the secret masters who guide them on their journey through time to their destiny. And this was never so clear as when a people were confronted with a crisis. But there are different sorts of crises: there are visible ones and there are invisible ones. Of the two the invisible crises are the hardest to deal with, and they present the greatest threat to the survival of the people.

It is from invisible dangers that a people most perish. A danger without a name, or a form; a danger that cannot be seen; a danger without a face; a danger that enters a land and destroys it before anyone knows it is there. Then afterwards only a few standing stones, broken shards in the sands and mysterious skulls rolling in the wind give any sign that a vigorous tribe once lived in fertility and joy in a place grown over with trees or made barren by encroaching dust.

To see invisible dangers before they bring destruction is one of the greatest gifts the wise can have. To have their warnings heeded is the good fortune of a people. To believe how that which cannot be seen can bring about the end is the blessing of the heart. Civilisations have not been so fortunate; history is written with their bones and their disappearance.

It was with such a danger, one that didn't seem a danger but a mere malaise, that the tribe and the land as a whole were now confronted, and didn't know it. But the secret masters gathering in anonymity from their diverse places sensed something they didn't know they were sensing.

CHAPTER TWENTY-FOUR

They arrived like ghosts at an appointed hour of the dark. Masters are known by their deeds. They all arrived in silence, without a murmur. Even the old didn't rustle the dark. Degeneracy would come soon and devastate the core of the land, but before then the old clarity and vigour still reigned. Before the age of dust, masters were masters still. Just before the fall, some last splendour survived even in that atmosphere of the last days when the dark and the fireflies fell under the spell of a doom that had crept into the secret heart of the land.

At the last meeting they had sat, these masters, in complete silence, with nothing to say about anything. They drank their harsh alcohol in silence, and chewed their kola nuts and their kaoline as if in a trance. The rituals at the beginning of the proceedings had been listless and seemed irrelevant for the first time in years. Nothing to say. Nothing seen. Nothing thought. Just silence like a poison drunk in the dark. Then at the earliest signs of dawn they all rose and dissipated like shadows back to their homes.

The last time poisoned the next. They had the new habit as malaise. Now, they sat in silence. Old age, wisdom, the vigour of the mature years, time lived in prophecies, skins soaked and cracked in legends, eyes drained by enchantments, hearts that have dwelt in evil as much as in great good, minds that have known what wickedness is, mouths that have lied politically about oracles and distorted the messages of the gods, bones that have worked to the good of the tribe even as they have bent and twisted with prevailing winds, now all these faculties, blended into one spirit of the council at the tribe's heart, were silent, dumb, unable to function. Some sickness had befallen the oracle itself. The well of divinations was poisoned. Slowly, not knowing how, the gods were abandoning a people. Some master twist of fortune was in play.

History, brought down from the heights where the scale of evils past outweighs the good that had been done, history was delivering some strange verdict on the land – a parable, a symbol, a message to future ages, different in meaning when lived through than when examined in the perspective of time. And it was among the council that the enigma of history was first manifest, and no one could read the signs, or interpret the parable that they were living through. Does the feather feel the death of the sun?

Silence, and nothing to say. The masters sat, staring at one another's dark space in the dark. Thinking about nothing. Vacancy in their midst. The desert had arrived in the midst of the forest. Scattered remains of bronze busts emerging from the earth will tell a tale no one can hear. It started here. In the dark.

Then suddenly, as if an invisible point of light had

penetrated the mud walls and illuminated an essential spot, an unknown voice among the masters began to speak. The voice recounted a dream they had been having persistently, which they persistently forgot. At last, now, it was remembered.

CHAPTER TWENTY-FIVE

It was a dream about a golden heron lost in its own dream. Beautiful white birds descended on the heron and tore off all its feathers and broke its wings and left it dying on the riverbank where it lay sick for ninety-nine years, sick and dying, but not dead. The birds had also fallen on the nest of the heron and carried off many of its children and many died on the seas and many others were borne off and scattered about the world in horrible conditions, and they did not know one another any more, and forgot that they were all children of the golden heron.

In the dream the children suffered and grew and changed and married in these different lands, while the mother heron lay sick and dying by the river and on the dry sands. The children of the heron that were not carried away were not the same any more, they became sick too, and spent most of their time fighting one another, and dying.

And then one day the birds in the world woke up to the realisation that they were all descended from the same bird in heaven and were all related to the dying heron and they realised that if the heron was dying, they were dying too.

The voice telling of the dream fell silent at this point and did not speak again for the rest of the council meeting. The other masters had listened with an air both listless and interested. And they listened to the silence too. And they had nothing to say, no interpretations to offer. They were just content with the mood of malaise that had so infected all aspects of the life of that dream-enclosed tribe. And when dawn hinted from the edges of the sky, the council members returned in silence to their masked lives.

CHAPTER TWENTY-SIX

The maiden continued to suffer in her wide-eyed waiting. Her body troubled her. It seemed such a strange and alien and heavy thing to be bearing about all the time. She felt oddly that she shouldn't really have a body, that it somehow restricted her, and prevented her flight and freedom. The maiden was profoundly sick with a deep sickness of the heart and head, but she was radiant and healthy. She felt she was dying, but was vibrantly alive. She was deeply unwell, but seemed youthful and blooming. She felt awkward, and yet was acquiring sublime grace. She felt her body heavy, and yet she ran and skipped about like a young gazelle on the plains. She was weighed down with a deep unhappiness, and yet she was giddy with delight, her head spinning in vertigo and sudden fevers of joy. She felt like dying, and yet she loved life like a bird in spring, by the river.

The maiden walked about in a dream. She heard nothing that anyone said. She performed her errands wrongly, and uttered silly and irrelevant things. She would suddenly burst out laughing for no reason except an arising bubble of happiness in the pit of her belly, or near her heart. Or she would suddenly burst into tears while listening to the tribal drums near the shrine, or staring at the clouds, or walking in the forest, or playing a skipping game on the sands near their house. And she would, for no reason, throw her arms round her mother's neck and kiss her all over. Or she would suddenly begin a carving of a face in ebony and would stop just when its beauty was beginning to emerge ...

CHAPTER TWENTY-SEVEN

Much the same thing, but in a different key, was happening with the masters in their nocturnal meetings of great import.

They felt many intuitions, but had no clear understanding. Impulses haunted them, but their tongues were inexpressive. An oppressive gloom weighed on them, and yet they felt light in their silence. Spirits of warning flitted about them, but interpretation eluded their minds. Oracles made diverse signs to them, but they were deaf. Tremors happened amongst them, yet they felt only the movement of the wind on the raffia rooftops in the dark.

Silence was their main speech. They sat and stared and brooded on vacant moods. Dreams passed by them unnoticed. And in the silence they heard worlds coming to an end in the hollow cry of birds in the sleeping forests.

But a few days after the last meeting the unknown voice continued with the dream that they had; or, rather, they dreamt more of the dream that they had recounted, as of a tale unfinished. The voice said:

'. . . and the white birds realised the horror of what their ancestors had done. And they couldn't sleep well any more for the agony of it. And they wanted to change a terrible thing that had come to pass. Meanwhile the children of the dying heron learnt also of their dying ancestor and all the scattered tribes of them from all over the world set off on a great journey back to their original home. They brought the lost rains with them. Rains that had gone away for centuries they brought back with them. They returned on yellow rafts and golden canoes. And they converged at the riverbank. It was a great day in the history of the golden herons. And the mother heron, touched by the love and blessings brought back by her descendants from all over the world, and revived by the wonderful gestures of repentance made by the descendants of the white birds, and awoken by the knowledge of the great kinship all birds had with the mighty father bird in heaven, moved by all this, the mother heron that was sick and dying on the dry bank of the river began to make a miraculous recovery, and experienced an amazing regeneration. Then she became at last what she could never have been without these tragic events – a beautiful golden bird among birds, enriching heaven and earth with her surprising splendour. She became a gift of the sun. And because of her regeneration the kingdom of birds was raised higher in the wonderful scheme of things. And a new cycle of history began on earth, leading to the fulfilment of the true and mysterious prophecies of the race of birds.'

The masters of the tribe listened in silence to the recounting of this elaborate dream. And when its telling was finished, further silence reigned. And nothing more was said.

But the sense of waiting and apprehension continued, as if they sensed the mood of the end of time.

CHAPTER TWENTY-EIGHT

Among masters, in the dark, sometimes extraordinary things happen. They are signs of passing degeneracy. Some miraculous occurrences have to be purged. They give rise to tales of wonder that blind pilgrims on the path to the true enchantment. They give rise to tales of great feats that distract travellers from their humble quest, diverting them into a desire for amazing deeds, amazing transformations, visitations, magic.

Among masters, manifestations which lead to stories are impure. The quest is for simplicity, a peace beyond the earth, a quiet glimpse of heaven, an intuition in which, in a lightning flash, all things are made clear. Understanding is a pure glass of water. All great truths have no taste. Hints of sweetness are coloured by the need for amazement.

Among masters, astonishment is suspect. A fall, a lowering, desire for that which shines, are signs of falling standards. Soon afterwards people lose their way. No pilgrim must abide too long with miraculous occurrences on the path. Deceptions have the greatest charm to the eye.

The tribe had long been the home of myths and fantastic

dreams. Too much myth, an excess of magic, and the road to heaven is undone. What amazes the eye blinds the soul to its true goal. The masters of the tribe should have known this and should have known to beware the fatal allure of the need for the astonishing. When humanity is amazed, the inward gaze of heaven is diminished.

In those times, when across the savannahs and in the wild forests tribes danced to an excess of gods and killed and sacrificed one another and were led astray by false babblings from oracles false with priests who were steeped in the mysteries of the stupidity of man and woman; in those times, a clear light seemed to come from the austere images of the tribe of artists. The old masters of the earliest times were wiser; they wielded a purer knowledge of the way. But blockheads, the greedy, the weak, the power-seekers too fall upon the path and through degeneracy join, unknown, the council; and impurities poison a purer way for ever. And no master-gardeners emerge to purify the garden of these fatal weeds of the mind that one day will lead to the garden's destruction.

CHAPTER TWENTY-NINE

But among masters of the time marvellous things happen. Sometimes, at the council meeting, in the silence, a spirit would appear, and would speak in an incomprehensible tongue, and tell, very briefly, a tale of woe and wonder upon the earth. Sometimes a being not of this world would manifest, and in silence would speak of innumerable worlds in the vastness of space where living beings dwelt in a surprising variety of forms. Sometimes a trio of such interstellar beings, radiant in lights of gold and blue, with eyes of shining stones, and bodies wholly transparent, would tell the masters of the ways of their civilisations, and how they came to an end. They would tell of how they now wander the universe, seeking a familiar air and space in which to leave their tale as a guide and warning to those of future ages who sow destruction in their quest for an all-conquering power over all they survey.

Sometimes, amid the expectant silence of the masters in the depth of mysteries that cannot be told to the uninitiated, an emblematic animal, a mysterious unicorn, would appear; and would gaze upon them with pitiful eyes, and would whisper, in silence, a formula in the air, for the regeneration of the race of man and woman ... But the masters, too used to the passive witnessing of astonishments, did not grasp all the details of this simplest of formulations; and so, without any sense of loss, lost one of the greatest secrets that nature had to tell them.

It would seem that those who fall prey to astonishments always believe that more and ever more will be manifest to them, and, oddly enough, cease to believe in what the astonishing can tell them. And so those who love stories most learn the least from them, but devour them in the endless fertility, when one true tale listened to with the mind of awakening is enough to lead one to the path of gold and simplicity ...

And so only one of the masters grasped the formulation; and the one kept it to himself, and nourished it as one nourishes a deep love that must be kept secret from the jealous eyes of the world.

CHAPTER THIRTY

Among masters, birds have appeared from the empty air; words have been spoken in the dark, from no mouth but the mouth of the unusual; white forms, singing on the wind, have paid visits; kings have appeared, requesting help for their dying kingdoms; children have manifested, begging aid for the loss of their parents; girls have materialised, crying for a change to the traditional ways that crush their lives before they are born and to their dying days.

Among masters, victims being sacrificed have appeared, swearing vengeance on their tribes for their cruel practices; a succession of beings, spirits, the dead and dying have made themselves present and screamed about the evils in the land, the wickedness of their tribal ways, the madness of their kings, the stupidity of elders for allowing manifold monstrosities to pass for tradition.

Apparitions have streamed thus among the masters, bearing witness to a vast land crying out for a purging, a mighty retribution, a dreadful curse of fire and suffering that will sweep the land of its centuries of superstition, vileness, injustice, murders, oppression, tyranny, infanticide, cruelty in wars, horrible rituals, amid so much that was good, joyful, hospitable and loving. These forms came, and lingered, in the midst of masters.

And not only witnesses, but simple presences too. Feathers suspended on wings of light. A child praying on the moon. A fabled creature from another land. A fairy with wands of blue. A white hat. A painting of rare beauty turning in the air. A sonnet whispered by the wind. The beginnings of a tale of chivalry. A knight in broken armour. A bearded man with a shining magic sword. A radiant book whose words streamed out into the illuminated air. Even a castle seen in miniature. All these appeared in the midst of the masters of the council, and created in them the habit of silence, and an unwillingness to interpret that which must be unseen in order to be seen.

And thus such things turn into tales of wonder that so beguile them from the true nature of their function.

CHAPTER THIRTY-ONE

Among the masters, many wonders no longer become stories, for so many have been seen . . .

And now, they have this dream told them in the dark, by one who was unknown. And it was a time of incomprehensible ennui in the turning days of the last years of enchantment under the old sun. For a new sun, harsh and strange, was rising from an uncompassed sky.

At the next meeting, while the world changed, there was silence too among the masters of the council. Till one spoke, suddenly, saying:

'I too had the same dream, but in my dream the children of the heron did not return, and the white birds did not do very much, and anyway it was not a heron but a golden eagle and it recovered from its sickness by the powers of heaven, and became a great bird at last and made great contributions to the race of birds.'

This addition to the silence prepared a mood strange and pregnant. Dreams never dwell alone. The silence was unused to this addition. Another voice grumpily spoke.

'In my dream all the tribes returned to the father in heaven; and then a great new history began on earth.'

Briefly, but damage was done. The mood was undone. There was a new expectation. Who else had found the same current from which this fountain sprang? Briefly, the wind blew. There were hooting noises in the distant dark. All around the forest brooded, and in it forms unseen were alive, and they too were having their meetings. But here, among the masters, another voice:

'I had the same dream too. But it wasn't an eagle, it was a sunbird. And the children scattered in the world did not return home. They did not remember their mother. And many of them were ashamed that the dying bird on the riverbank was thought of as their mother, and they denied her. Some of her children even mocked her and laughed at her in their new lands. And the golden sunbird, with the help of heaven and by its own great powers of healing, made itself well in the course of time, and became a great bird among birds. And one day, in the distant future, she became the saviour of the race of birds on earth.'

Another silence. Then an older voice, old and no longer quite here. A surprise, for many thought the voice had come from the ancestors. And it spoke, with obvious boredom.

'All this talk about birds, when something terrible is happening which we cannot see.'

That ended the dreams, for a while, and returned them to incomprehension and a listlessness that, with the heat, weighed on them like an oppressive enchantment.

CHAPTER THIRTY-TWO

And so it was too with the maiden. She was cloudy-headed, and became unpredictable. She began thus to frighten her mother, who began to hint that maybe it was time for her to marry. But to her father she was normal. He said:

'Her destiny is being born in her, poor girl, and her life is fighting against it. And so her body suffers these changes, like water suffers the changing lights of the sky.'

'You always talk in riddles about perfectly simple things, my love,' said her mother to her father. 'She is pregnant with a need to be pregnant. That is all. It is time to consider her marriage, and find acceptable suitors from the poor specimens around.'

Her father laughed, but said nothing.

And the maiden, changed by the tragic resonances of the sculpture that had so broken her life, walked among the clouds, neither on earth nor in heaven. She was perplexed by feelings swelling and raging in her belly and her heart. She was waiting for a god to speak to her, or for a special bird to bring her a flower, and free her from the dark joy of unknowing.

Part Three

CHAPTER THIRTY-THREE

Every land and every tribe is guided by its secret necessity, its most essential truth. And even when a people lose their way, or sink in degeneracy, or fall off the face of the earth, what lingers of them, or what is left of them somewhere, is this mysterious essential truth, this secret necessity. It is like a dream had in many variations but never remembered, but always familiar. It is like a homeland forgotten but reinhabited again by the same people, a love lost and found again without being recognised a second time.

But sometimes a people forget who they are, and lose their secret necessity, and start, slowly, to become strangers to themselves without knowing it. And then they dream up rituals, and fall into rites, and deeds, and enter into wars, and perform sundry acts upon the stage of the earth to forget their forgetting, or to try to remember or redefine, or find who they were, and now should be. Such ventures are doomed. A skin shed is a skin shed. A loss is a loss.

They say we were meant to lose something in order to find that which is truer. And that which we find may well be that which we have lost but which is found on a different day, when we have changed. And that which we have lost and found differently may well now be the magic stone with which we can, in greater readiness, continue our unending journey.

But to forget that which we are and not know it is an accursed thing. And this creeps upon a people in a hundred ways, like the numerous ways that darkness steals across the skies of bright lands. And then one day invaders appear on the horizon, bearing false mirrors — and a tribe, a people, disappear into captivity, and are forgotten on the face of the earth but for a few mysterious standing stones dreaming in moss in a forest, unseen for centuries, till a lost child comes upon them. And then an enigma is found, stones without a history, without a story, except the one which is to be glimpsed in dreaming fragments, in the great book of life among the stars.

CHAPTER THIRTY-FOUR

How to tell the story of the tribe of artists that are my ancestors from the fragments that are gleaned from the sights seen in touching stones, or among the enigma of the stars . . .

How the tribe used to live invisibly, like the heron, always on the move, but always perfectly still when fishing for inspiration that will be revealed in their art . . .

How they always used to change location, when needed, like fugitives, because they never wanted to be part of external corrupting structures, only wanting to contribute purely to the spiritual and artistic life of the land. To be free. Free to be truthful to their dreams and visions, and to the warning and guidance that came to them through the mysterious agencies of art and life . . .

How to tell that this need so permeated their life that it also permeated their ways of loving . . .

CHAPTER THIRTY-FIVE

And so it was that when the maiden's mother decided it was time for her to marry, suitors were invited into her life. And they wooed her with art. For that was the way of the tribe. With art a maiden is wooed and charmed. The suitors would begin to create works of art to win a maiden's heart.

It was often one of the busiest times of the year when numerous suitors competed in art for the hand of a woman. The sounds of carving, of drumming, of shaping could be heard all around the square. Sacrifices at the shrine multiplied. Young men, vigorous and intense, could be seen in groups as they worked for the suitors they supported. Gossip bred and sweetened the ears and hair-dressing hours of the women. They talked of little else but the suitors, their families, rumours of their past, recent or ancient scandals, and the appropriate or inappropriate behaviour of the maiden, or her family.

It was always a time of great creativity and festivity. Relations and friends of the maiden were wooed too, indirectly, with gifts from the suitors. Impromptu dances, sudden performances, improvised songs were directed at the maiden in surprising moments. It was the best time in a girl's life.

The whole tribe centred its attentions on the girl to be married. Her behaviour was scrutinised, and her worth was assessed not only by the quantity and frenzy and height of artistic excellence inspired by her among her suitors (and this counted very high indeed), but most especially by the charm and nobility of her conduct, her innocence, her humility, her grace, and her seeming to be unaffected by all that attention. For the tribe also wanted to fall in love with the maiden who was being wooed. If her conduct is exemplary and enchanting she inspires the whole tribe to greater excellence. Then the harvests are rich, the art of the people reaches new heights of innovation and brilliance, the old feel rejuvenated, the women feel younger, and the men dream of unique glories. In short, every aspect of life is touched and enriched, as if by the special favours of a goddess.

CHAPTER THIRTY-SIX

It was the time of year when the art of the tribe was most colourful. Reds and yellows, flashes of gold, dazzling blues and deep bright greens filled the air and caught the eyes everywhere. The suitors would often create great totems either celebrating the potency of the lineage of the maiden being wooed, or displaying the majesty of their own family. They might create carvings large and daring, showing the face of a warrior from three angles at once; or the statue of a goddess so pure in its beauty that people fell in love with the art more than the girl it was made for. Suitors from rich families made bronze casts, and sometimes, in cases of rare astonishment, they made statues in gold.

Every once in a while, miraculous art is created, and enters legend, and afterwards children are told they were born in the year that so-and-so was married, the year that a great work of art was made.

One such year was the year the maiden's father wooed and won her mother. The suitors were numerous, for the maiden's mother was of exceptional beauty and grace. She came from the family of one of the great chiefs of the tribe, one of the true masters. The suitors were not only numerous, they were also of the highest calibre. Many of them were reputed to be among the greatest artists of the land. Some were princes from distant places, who heard of the legend of the maiden's mother's beauty and charms. Men who were artists, warriors, courtiers, princes, wealthy merchants came from sundry lands. Rumours of her desirability spread far; and every day brought new suitors on horseback, on camels, with rich entourage, and paid musicians, and praise-singers. It was an astonishing time for the tribe. Fame had visited the tribe again because it had a beautiful daughter that all the world wanted to marry.

The maiden's mother had conducted herself impeccably. She had carried herself with simplicity, grace and a becoming shyness. This enchanted all the suitors and inspired them to the highest peaks of artistic and spiritual endeavour. That year of the maiden's mother's marriage did more for the tribe than a decade of its harvests and its art. Money poured in; artworks were bought in great quantities; trade multiplied; and stories, songs and epics abounded.

It was a time of legend, and the wise ones knew it. Whoever won her hand would have to be truly exceptional, and would instantly enter the legends of the land and would bask in lifelong fame. It was the right time to make a great name, for those who tell stories would be singing about it long after the tribe had vanished from the earth.

The princes brought their artisans, the griots prepared their epics, the warriors honed their skills, the artists perfected their creations, some in secrecy, others with great publicity. They were mostly of noble, great, or celebrated stock. All, except one, who was an orphan, whom no one had noticed. He lived with his uncle, a master bronze-caster. He had never been remarked as an artist of any note or stature. But he had grown wise in the service of his uncle, and he had been initiated into the mysteries on account of his profound interest in the causes of things.

His sense of humour could have made him famous in the tribe if he had been inclined to be known. But years of watching, growing deep in the hidden knowledge, years of smiling to himself and studying profoundly the secrets of his art had inclined him to a sublime invisibility, and a sublime nonchalance.

He might have been a prince born into unfortunate circumstances; but he was an outsider who was more deeply inside the centre of life and art than any of the age, and no one knew it, least of all himself. He made himself a suitor on the simplest grounds of love, a quiet love that had grown and been sustained for many years. For as long as he had been aware he had always been in love with the maiden's mother, had grown deep in this secret love, and had developed with it into a man of rich and hidden character. The love had been one of the primary motivations and inspirations of his life. The love had given him the reasons to learn the ways and causes of things, to study the laws of nature and personality and power, and to master his chosen art.

Through his love for her he was open to a higher love that led him into the ancient mysteries brought with the caravans from the masters whose original homeland had sunk into the oblivion of the sea. Time, his condition and this dual love had enriched him and made of him what the most noble birth could not do: they made him a true man among men, who saw where others didn't, who intuited what others couldn't, who dreamt what others wouldn't, who questioned what others felt they shouldn't, who ascended to realms that others didn't suspect existed, and who knew what others didn't even know that there was to know.

Nobility of birth couldn't confer on a man nobility of soul; that is attained only by one who strives for the highest, in the lightest of ways, with humour of spirit, and a guiding sense of invisibility being best. How do such people come to be? Love has its ways of civilising souls that may have been destined for servility. In the maiden's father stood a free man and a true prince amongst beings, who had fashioned himself out of the dust that he had found and a love that had led him to the stars over the stars that can be seen.

And this love he bore was his qualification for becoming a suitor when all around him told him that he was mad for harbouring such a wish or dream or hope. How could a simple man, unknown to his peers, without a shadow in his land, compete with such a magnificent gathering of names? But this he did; and simply, as was his way.

And while others created extravagant and wonderful works, great masquerades, giant bronzes, stone statues, rapturous dances, tremendous epics, to capture the maiden's mother's heart, he did the simplest and most astonishing thing of all. He made a sculpture of pure air and sunlight, a work that all could see and not see, that induced a great dreaming in the whole tribe, a deep enchantment and silence, that stilled the minds of masters and children, and made the women weep for beauty. The sculpture was composed of the material of love itself. It was revealed in the open air, above the shrine.

The other suitors claimed they couldn't see it, that it was a fraud, a vile sorcery masquerading as art. But everyone else could see it, and they fell under its spell. The maiden's mother adored it and spent most of her day sitting in front of the shrine, gazing up at this work of the magnificent soul, with an expression on her face that only lovers lost in profound adoration have. She couldn't get enough of the enchantment, and she declared that she wanted to spend the rest of eternity with the man who had made such a dream. It was the only time that she broke out of her pattern of behaviour and acted as if possessed by a force greater than her. Along with the whole tribe, and the entourage of the dignitaries, she, in fact, became quite obsessed with this mysterious new work. Her parents too fell under its enchantment, though they doubted the suitability of their daughter's rash declaration.

'We ought to know more about this suitor,' they said.

'All we need to know,' she replied, 'is the quality of his dream. Look, everyone has fallen in love with his soul. I don't care if he is a beggar. That is the man I want to marry.'

'But what if he is mad?'

'Then it is a madness that pleases me,' she replied pertly.

'You have not even met him and look at what his work is doing to you. Can't you see? You are behaving as if a spell has been cast on you. How will you be if you live with him?'

'Happy, and mad, for the rest of my life.'

'But what he has done is unheard of. He has changed the nature of our way. If we allow this to go on happening he will destroy our tribe.'

'Or he may save it from dying.'

'Are we dying, my daughter? Are we not thriving as a tribe? Look around you.'

'Dying things appear to thrive. Without new dreams we will surely die.'

'Maybe they are right, my daughter, when they say that this man has used sorcery on us.'

'It is not sorcery, my dear parents, but a new kind of wine for the spirit, a new art. If it is sorcery then it is the sorcery of art. I have never heard of its kind before. This man is rare, and he will be my husband. I will have no other.'

'You will bear his strange children.'

'They will be unique. They will bring you pride and joy.'

'You will have a strange fate because of him.'

'All fates are strange. I welcome an unusual life. Maybe they will sing of us in future stories because I married this sorcerer you speak of.'

'What is unknown may bring unknown suffering.'

'There is no protection against the future, except love, wisdom and hope. My love will be my guide.'

'Then so it must be.'

'But only with your blessings, my parents.'

'So it must be. Let us prepare for a new story in our lives.'

And so it was. The work of the unknown suitor not only broke the pattern of the maiden's mother's behaviour, it altered something in the air. It was the first time that a work of art had induced a communal experience akin to witnessing a miracle from the gods, a sense of wonder, a brush against the unfathomable. There was a bright fear in the wonder. It was the first time that the tribe had been presented with a work entirely new to its tradition, something that had never been done before, which changed its history and possibilities. For the work not only transformed its art, it transformed the way the tribe saw itself. It renewed the vision of the tribe and opened up, for ever, its destiny, and made its destiny new again.

Suddenly the tribe felt that its future was not determined by its past. The tribe felt, overnight, that its future could now go any number of ways. Before, it had only one future, and that was related to the past. Now it had many futures. It was freed from the past. And it was even free of any of the futures it chose. For the sense of an ongoing freedom was inherent in the magic of the work of the unknown suitor. Like a door that is never open, and never closed. Like a door to heaven that opens both ways. This freedom was new. The work made people dream again that they were not what they thought they were, but more. It made them feel they shared in heavenly glories and power.

This was the first time that the masters had been presented with an invisible sculpture that could be seen by all, a dream, an art of the incommensurable, composed of elements beyond the human hand, borrowing from the divine. The hand of God had been drawn into artistic creation.

There was no competition. The general astonishment, the happy dreams of the people, and even signs from the oracles, were unanimous. The outsider, unknown, prone to invisibility, with a hidden sense of humour and a curious detachment that concealed great compassion, slight of figure and strange of eyes, without appearing to try, and in apparent silence amid the famous and great names with their entourages and their big noises and their tremendous public and critical acclaim; amid all this, the unlikely one had come through. And the tribe, in many ways which it was too proud to admit, would never be the same again.

The marriage was a quiet one, though the tribe was ecstatic in its celebrations. And quietly they slipped, the two of them, into being man and wife, as if they had spent many invisible centuries rehearsing for it. His distinction had been earned by astonishment, hers by tradition. Together they grew, laughed, thrived and prospered, and bore an only child, the maiden of this tale.

CHAPTER THIRTY-SEVEN

In contrast to her mother the maiden was awkward, strange, unpredictable, dreamy, moody, alien. Someone said she looked like a beetle, and that she had beetle eyes. Some said that she looked like a mask, a carving; one that was used to frighten off unwanted spirits. Some said she looked like a spirit herself, one that frightened off human beings. The more charitable said she was just plain, and odd, and that girls like her, as with certain birds, change as they get older, and become very beautiful indeed. They said that you could never tell with her type whether her face would settle into a new harmony of surprising beauty, but that, given who her parents were, it was best to assume that, in due course, she would amaze. But most people did not see her so.

'She is not beautiful, but she is so aloof,' they said.

'She is not pretty, the men do not flock after her, but she behaves as if she were too good for marriage,' the other girls said.

'As if she will not spread her legs when the time comes.'

'As if she won't get fat before she knows it.'

'As if she won't need us when the men let her down.'

'As if she wouldn't cry blood on the day she has to push her child out into the world.'

'As if blood will not drip down her legs when she is walking so proudly to the river.'

'Drip down her legs and shame her.'

'As if her beauty won't fade.'

'And she still hasn't made the work we are all waiting for.'

'And she won't smile and has only useless girls as friends.'

'I pity her parents such a useless daughter.'

'Such an ugly daughter.'

'Such a mad daughter.'

'Such a lonely person, who none of us wants to know.'

'I pity her too.'

'I don't pity her. She deserves to be lonely. She thinks she is better than everyone, I can't see why.'

'She is not like her mother, who is loved by everyone.'

'Her mother is a flower, the daughter an insect.'

'How come such a beautiful woman gives birth to such an odd-looking creature.'

'If she were a man I would say that daughter is not his child.'

'Life is full of strange things.'

And so it was. The mother was the delight of the tribe, with an irreproachable reputation, like a princess who hasn't put a foot wrong in her standing with the people. But her daughter was different.

Her face was composed of odd angles, and her eyes were unusual and saw too much. There was something disturbing and critical about the cool intelligence in her eyes. She had big eyes, a little watery, and they caught the light and gathered to themselves a mood both dreamy and uncanny, as if she were a witch, or had unusual powers of second sight, or could see the future in any face she glanced at and didn't much like the future that she saw in them.

She was not graceful, or elegant. In fact, she was clumsy, as if all her fingers were thumbs, as if her feet were of lead and each faced in an opposite direction, or as if she had two left feet. She spoke little, sang much to herself, and was born with a perception of the world so unique as to make her fearsome since she was a little girl. For most of her life something about her spirit intimidated people, and yet she was on the small side.

In herself she would not have drawn such illustrious suitors, but as the daughter of legend she was of the greatest interest. Her suitors were not of the myth-making range as her mother's had been, but they were illustrious enough for the tribe to tell stories about in the years to come. The best of the tribe had come forward to earn the hand of the maiden who was as well known for her mysterious nature as for her celebrated parentage.

The artistic competition for her hand turned out to be unique. The most gifted of the tribe, driven to heights of inventiveness in order to win the respect of the master-artist that was her father, surpassed themselves in artistic endeavour.

CHAPTER THIRTY-EIGHT

And all this time the tribe still expected from the maiden an artwork for her own healing. And all this time the great tragic work that had so affected all, still worked on all. And all this time an ennui deep as centuries still drove deep despair into the roots of the people's hearts.

All was not well. Forebodings danced in the forests. The shadow of unmentionable events stalked their dreams. Omens brooding with undeciphered significations appeared amongst the great and the small. Turtles trapped in ropes were found on the far side of the riverbank. A bird shorn of its feathers jumped about insanely beneath an iroko tree. A herd of beautiful antelopes was found dying of a mysterious disease. The seasons were losing their rhythms. It was hoped that the season of the maiden's wooing might prove auspicious, and change the fortunes of the land.

But the maiden couldn't care. They wooed her with songs, and competed for her love with their different sculptures, their varied works of art, and she gazed on their best efforts with a tender indifference: she saw no art amongst them, only artefacts. She looked upon all the works of her suitors with a neutral eye and a gentle distracted smile. What was she dreaming of? Where was her mind? What images engendering immeasurable moods moved about in her spirit? She saw nothing but the mediocrity of her suitors, mediocrity masked by energy. Their works made her long for some incommensurable mood, some quality of being that only love or the highest art could bring about or satisfy. And this longing became, slowly, almost an insane desire for freedom, a lust for transcendence. She longed for an elusive something that would make her not a modern woman, or an antique, a traditional woman, but a transcendent woman. Her longing was for an impossible triangulation, distilled into the image of an eagle earthbound all its days, master of the terrestrial realm, but increasingly plagued with dreams of flight, dreams in which it was flying intermittently.

Then the image got stronger. The eagle, in its sleep, was flying short distances. This was the mood of the maiden's spirit. She dreamt as an earthbound eagle (which thought of itself as a hen), she dreamt of soaring, of the open air, of the clouds beneath, of the land beneath the clouds, and of the clear heavens above, with all its brittle stars.

The works of the suitors, their artefacts, masks, masquerades, songs, little epics, their extraordinary dances, their bronzes, their giant sculpted goddesses, these works were indeed flattering, charming, impressive. But where everyone was delighted by these works, she was cool. She was unmoved by all the noise and fame attending the works that would have swept many a virgin off her feet.

She had been raised in magic, in true mastery. Early in life, she had been dipped in the mysteries. Legend and myth had attended her most ordinary existence. Her eyes were charged with starlight. Her mind had been formed in the forge of the most enlightened laboratory of the tribe. The vanities of beauty, the art of the woman-spirit, the charms of the mother-way, the obscure puzzles of the female silence, had been fed her with her mother's milk. Art was the language with which she read the world. When she looked out at the world, she saw all as art – the trees, the faces, the owl, the rat, all figurations and casual arrangements. All life she gazed on with the intensity of the art mind. This was the silent inheritance of her father. She saw the heart of things without trying. She knew that true excellence, true mastery, comes once or twice in a lifetime, almost never in a generation, and she was not disappointed at seeing nothing from her suitors resembling the true. She expected nothing. Where would it come from? The true can only come from the true, from the hidden. This she had intuited from her father. She awaited her surprise from the margins. Till then she endured her wooings, and suffered her changes and her yearning for something unknown but coming.

CHAPTER THIRTY-NINE

The suitors were of many kinds. There were famous mask-makers, respected bronze-casters, and feared image-makers whose images bristled with power and strangeness and were used as war fetishes by alien tribes. There were warriors and dancers, tremendous master-musicians and courtiers. There were chiefs from far-off kingdoms and members of royal families. It made the tribe come alive again to witness such an array of brave young men assemble for the hand of one of the celebrated daughters of the land.

But the maiden herself was indifferent. She drifted in a living dream. She was deaf to the serenades, blind to the works of powerful inventors brought for her amazement, cold to the gifts of gold and cows, to the visits of wealthy intermediaries, and resistant to the pleas of her mother to be more gracious.

And her aloofness worked unintended wonders at inflaming the passions of the suitors for her unattainable hand and her proud untameable spirit.

From her otherworldliness seemed to come the message not that they were not good enough for her, but that she was beyond being interested in them . . .

Somehow they had to gain her attention and establish their reality in her consciousness.

To her they were all a blur, they were all variations of one suitor.

CHAPTER FORTY

Around this time the maiden took to wandering off with her female companions and lingering by the river. She played games with her few friends when she could, but mostly she just stared at the river, its reflections, its lights. Sometimes she glimpsed future events in evanescent fragments as she stared, lost in deep reverie, into the surface shimmer of the river when it appeared quiet in its steady flow.

Mostly listening to the water lapping on the shore, staring at the birds, always absent-minded, lingering at the hinges between here and there, she dreamt things which her mind barely registered, but which filled her with a delicious sweet melancholy of which those days of youth were composed.

Sometimes, in a flash, in an evanescent mood of a dream surrounded with golden moments, she would see but not register a ship tossing about in the wild billows of a brutal sea, she would smell without knowing the smell of blood and decomposing bodies lashed to wooden structures in a cramped hull. She would feel without feeling her ankles in chains, an intolerable agony from her wrists, and men bearing down on her. She would see herself without seeing that she was standing naked in an alien marketplace being sold like a goat, and would sense the heat of the whip, would glimpse white faces and silk, would hear without hearing an inexpressible cry of abandonment. She would catch without knowing that she caught the mood of an alien land, cold blades in the air and underfoot, a universe empty of hope . . .

And sometimes she constructed dialogues dreaming in her head. Were they her thinking? Such things perplexed her lightly as she woke from those golden states, standing. And she would continue a daylight activity, as if there and here were the same. Sometimes such a dialogue went like this.

'Tell us a story,' someone would say.

'I will tell you the story of a girl by the river in Africa,' she said, and never spoke a word of the story. 'But stories can't be told in too much pain, my dear child,' she would then say.

Was she dreaming, or thinking a dream as she thought it? Time has pressures upon the brain, as does timelessness, and presses things there from innumerable spaces.

'Do you remember the moon?'

'The moon died in the big sea.'

'Do you remember the land?'

'The land died with chains around my neck.'

'Do you remember your mother?'

'My mother died when I stood naked sold like a goat.'

'Do you remember your father?'

There was a pause. Then:

'To remember is the worst form of suffering. Spirits torment me saying the past cannot be real. Only death is real. I long to die. And then maybe I will find true happiness.'

And then she would wake from the hinges between here and there . . .

. . . a delicious sweet melancholy of which those days of youth were composed, beside the great river.

CHAPTER FORTY-ONE

The maiden grew to love the river and one night dreamt that a god or goddess would address her from its shore. She dreamt also that a lady of the river would rise in a golden shower and bring her wedding gifts of pure white flowers and a dress made by the mermaids and a ring fashioned by the little people who worked for a king.

And she dreamt that her husband would be a young god come from a mysterious land whom she would not recognise but whom she would save from death not once, but twice . . .

All this from the river.

And so the river became her dream. It was a languorous dream of past, present and future. Her whole life was there. And many lives and deaths and births of moons and skies and suns in its watery depths and surface. The whole history of her tribe was there; and the magic and sadness of things sparkled in the glimmers of rays on the water's face. All she didn't know, all that was whispered to her heart heaving in joy and dread of all that was to come, all was there. And often she would in such happiness find herself weeping at mysterious feelings. And often she would catch a glimpse of a face of one who loved her more than the moon and the earth. The glimpse of a face in the river.

And so the river became her dream. She waited for it to yield her its promises; and many moons went past and only dreams came to her, and glimpses, unrecognised, of the future.

Her whole life was planted there by the river, on its surface, in images stolen, but not kept, from the future.

Sometimes she travelled the river, in a canoe; and with her companions she sang sad songs for the mermaids to bring them gifts now that they were still young . . .

It was around this time, in a state of expectancy, that she heard the voice from the bushes, the voice asking her mysterious questions, along the riverbank. And she thought, at last, that the god or goddess had kept their secret promise . . .

CHAPTER FORTY-TWO

The man who was the best of all the suitors was handsome, virile, a marvellous hunter, a good enough artist, a famed warrior, and of the right age. He had strong eyes, wonderful instincts and great cunning. He had that gap in his upper front teeth that traditionally sent young girls into raptures. But the maiden was indifferent to him, and this inflamed his lust to possess her even more, and brought out the hunter in him, and the greatest cunning. For he knew that marriage to the maiden was marriage to legend, and that he would thus be set up not only for life but in the long memory of the tribe. In effect she was his best chance at immortality, as he saw it.

And so he set about his conquest of the maiden with all his ingenuity, cruelty, stealth and calculation. He began by creating the most powerful series of sculptures that it was in him to create. This suitor, who because of his wrestling style they called the Mamba, was known for his guile, his slipperiness and his extraordinary tenacity. They say what he holds on to, what he clings to, what he sets his mind on, and gets his hands locked into, never escapes his grasp. He had killed at least two people in the famed wrestling matches he had taken part in many miles away from the tribe, wrestling competitions in distant villages, from which he had brought back the winning crowns. This same mind that grasps without rest, this relentless mind, he brought to bear on his desire to possess and wed the maiden.

Just as in his wrestling matches he ruthlessly studied the styles of those he fought, coldly analysing their slightest weaknesses, and just as when he caught their necks in an arm lock and never let go till the legs of his opponent stopped twitching, just so did he concentrate on the artistic task of wooing the maiden. He studied, coolly, from a distance, the secrets of the maiden's father's art. He paid spies and servants for information. He tried to see as many of the works attributed to the master as possible. His reasoning was simple. The maiden's taste would be formed by the influence of her renowned father. She would love in art that which reminded her of what she had grown up with in the works of her father. This would be her weakness: her taste would be bound up with her love as a daughter.

And so the Mamba studied what he could of the works of the master. But how could he be sure that those works were indeed the works of the master? This was a profound problem, the dimensions of which he could not fathom. For the master conceals his work even when the work is evident. The master reveals only that which is the least of him. That which is taken for the works of the master are often his cast-offs, his rejects, his second thoughts, his diversions, his red herrings, his false trails, meant to mislead those who seek only the normal, the evident, the superficial power, the material power, the form and structure of the world, those who seek worldly mastery and fame. These the master traps in the labyrinths of false achievements.

But the master's true works, which lead to illumination and mastery of the spirit, and freedom from the dominion of matter, earthly power and illusion; the true works of the master, which guide the true seeker to the gates of their own self-discovered heaven, these are concealed, they are hidden, they are to all intents and purposes non-existent, invisible, and become visible only to those on the true path, and whose hearts are pure.

And so the Mamba studied what he could find of the master's works, and imitated, almost to perfection, the flaws, the illusions, the errors, the false beauty, and the labyrinth concealed in all such works. He studied them, imitated them, with variations of his own, and produced sculptures of inverted twins, carvings of fishes swimming in opposite directions, carvings of a great mother with stars all over her body, of a great god with a sun in his head, of a great sage with a snake as his thyrsus, images of the illuminati, which he, the Mamba, did not understand and so used indiscriminately, as with a language not grasped and in which one speaks nonsense.

The Mamba thus presented his works to the shallow astonishment of the uninitiated, and to the cool appreciation of the maiden, who looked upon them, saw the poor imitations of her father's masterful gems, and passed on without comment. The works merely confirmed what she suspected. Masters are born only once or twice in the life of a people, or an age. Even the truly gifted are rare, being at best only very hard workers or good imitators or combiners who have found a personal language with which to say nothing profound. The deep can only come out of the deep, as her father always said, for as long as she could remember.

And so while not wholly abandoning the wooing of her through art, the Mamba chose another course of action to conquer this brilliant and unattainable maiden. He took to following her, to stalking her, like a shadow . . .

CHAPTER FORTY-THREE

All these activities surrounding the wooing of the maiden concealed from the tribe the sense that portentous events were going on in the undercurrents of the world. It is not necessary to be deaf not to hear loud noises around you; all that is required is that there be sounds played close to your ears. The smallest sounds heard in the ears blot out the thunder sounding all around. It is not necessary to be blind not to see; all that is required is to be distracted. A brighter light close by can divert our gaze from a terrible tragedy happening right in front of us.

All the activities of a people – masquerades, festivities, funerals, harvests, rites and seasonal events – are but constant distractions from unspecified occurrences drawing ever closer that would change the life of a people for ever. The sages of the tribe used to advocate long periods without rites or celebrations, without public events or ceremonies, so that people would be undistracted and so more open to the signs of things that were coming or that were already present, here, now. But these suggestions were ignored over the passing years because the people's need for events, for distraction, was so great, and worse mischief would have occurred if they had persisted in this event-starvation. And so the tribe gradually lost the faculty for communal stillness which allowed for a greater sensing of events to come, the receptivity to signs, omens and warnings.

There was great unease in the undercurrents of the age. The tribe sensed it, but did not know it. The masters of the tribe sensed it, knew it, but could not identify its form. They were paralysed by the power of what they sensed. They were paralysed by the future. They were like individuals who gazed into an abyss and no longer knew if they were still gazing or if they were falling or if they were dreaming. These were conditions which were perfect for being possessed by the abyss into which they gazed; till they became one with it, and fell into it, through self-enchantment.

When a people sense their own extinction what do they do? They either throw themselves into an orgy of distraction, or they try and resist the inevitable vision by deeds which make the feared thing happen, or they do nothing, as if they had sensed nothing; or they create, in a sublime fever of hope, magic works to divert disaster, or to perpetuate their memory, so that the earth will not forget that they once existed and were passionate under the sun.

There were those who had glimpses of this extinction and

were perfectly tranquil, as though it were a necessary part of a universal plan . . .

There were others who resisted this inevitability . . .

But their different attitudes and responses amounted to the same thing.

CHAPTER FORTY-FOUR

The memories of a land are vast and deep; they are more than the land itself. The memories are a place, a realm unto themselves, a separate space and continent, in which all things exist at once which once appeared to exist in sequence.

Deep were the memories of the land in the time which the tribe passed through. Births and deaths, rites and rituals, murders and wars, love stories and rape, suicides and loneliness. The smell of burning tapers, of kaoline piled high in sacrifice, of slaughtered chickens goats cows at the altars shrines and thresholds. Ghosts that wander bewildered through grey timeless zones of the land. Sunsets that bleed odd omens on hot nights. Babies born in the dark forest and abandoned and devoured by ants. Women branded, men from strange tribes caught as slaves and slaughtered, proverbs of great wisdom salting the dusk, the lowered moon that pulls out stories from villages like the tides that rise, boys that play and discover the differences that are girls, diseases and witchcraft, quarrels in families about land, harvests in the farms, celebrations, and then ghosts, and the disappearance of a whole people devoured by disease or famine or wars, then new arrivals, with old histories, in a new cycle, settling into building huts, fishing, hunting, farming, dying, passing on, living in difficult days and hot nights, and ghosts, and laughter, feathers in the wind. Dust in the air. Leaves from the trees. The river's majestic winding flow. Bones of those long dead. Spirits in the forest. Lions in the wild. Birds that circle the air. Drifting clouds. Moon over the land. Sun with spears of light. Footpaths that wind through the trees. Insects in the undergrowth. Seeds bursting into shoot on walls, on clothes, in the eye sockets of the dead. The abnormal fertility of the land. Things growing everywhere. Flies and flying insects pestering the new villages. Then they too move on.

Deep the memories of the land, deep with tragedies, with comedies, with ghosts, with silences, with blood, with riddles, with laughter, with death.

And yet there are spaces there vast enough for more memories, millions millions more than there have been. That is how endless the land is in its depth. And out of this what is yet to be is not hinted at. The space will accommodate whatever comes to be. Who can measure the depth of that space? Who can draw from it all that is needed for renewal?

When a people sense the end of a way, of an era, of a dream, they always sense it as the end of the world.

Who can stop the end of the world?

CHAPTER FORTY-FIVE

The masters sensed all things going on in the tribe. Some of them sensed all things going on in the land. One or two of them sensed all that was going on in the whole world.

Some of them knew that the events surrounding the marriage of the maiden were not isolated events in the history of the tribe, or the land, or the world; but that they were linked to some vast catastrophe and some vast future redemption through fire.

Some sensed that the end of time is contained in the seed of an insignificant event. Stories in their fullness are beyond telling. They arc from here into spaces beyond words and things, where stories do not dwell, nor images, nor sounds, nor colours. Stories start in their already-existence and cease in mid-space, the rest vanishing into the invisible.

Only the living and dead united can tell the fullness of stories. Even then only isolated strands. All the gods in all the lands could not tell the fullness of a single story all the way from its pre-beginnings to its infinite end.

Only fragments are left to us to make structures out of, that please and hint and delight us through the labyrinth.

Fragments glimpsed in the invisible book of life.

CHAPTER FORTY-SIX

The Mamba was not an insubstantial man. In fact, he was a man of stature, who had already crossed the line that elders attributed to those of promise. He was promise in fulfilment, a solid badge of the tribe, a man of stone and strength, whose prowess had been proven as much on the battlefield as on the farms. He was a man who had saved many lives: he had saved people from drowning, men at the battlefront, women from the savage jaws of the feared crocodiles of the swamp. He was of near heroic stature, for he was already famed for having wrestled with an alligator that had snatched a child, and had broken its thick serrated neck with a howl that was nearly legendary. And it was on account of his battle with a deadly mamba, which had caught him in a ferociously coiled embrace, and which he had wrestled with under the horrified gaze of a few witnesses from the tribe till he broke its neck with a grip which he sustained for nearly an hour, that he got his celebrated name.

He dragged the mamba back with him to the tribe's shrine and all gasped at how huge and long it was, huger than a tree trunk and as long as the village stream. He coiled it out at the front of the shrinehouse as a dedication to the gods, and afterwards fashioned a mighty sculpture of this mamba that amazed and delighted the tribe in its likeness, its power and its sinister presence.

All admired the sculpture, except some women, many rivals, and the masters. The masters saw the achievement, solidity, fluency, fierceness and hard work, a man's work, in it; but no mystery, or suggestiveness. It did not have what they called shadow, or dark life, or hidden light. It was substantial, but it did not have the lightness of that which can writhe, coil and move effortlessly. It had power, but not simplicity, or sadness. It had strength, but not weakness, the weakness that all living things have. It had glory, but not heart. It amazed the eye, but not the vision. It did not set the masters dreaming. The sculpture did not suggest something they hadn't suspected was there, something more than itself. In fact, its very fluency and power and strength implied something troubling and sinister about the spirit of the artist. And some of the masters detected in it an inclination to self-mythology, megalomania, and a secret craving for power and authority. He was not called to the guild of masters. And so the masters kept silent about the work, and withheld judgement. However, the Mamba got his name and his fame; but he became bitter about his rejection by the masters, and brooded about it often.

CHAPTER FORTY-SEVEN

Quite apart from his personal achievements, the Mamba came from a good family. He was of respectable birth. There was some wealth in the house. His father was a well-considered carpenter and maker of images, and his mother was not undistinguished in her patterning of images on cloth, with many-coloured dyes.

His father was not a member of the council of masters, and none of their lineage ever had been. His mother was not of the council of the wise women of the tribe either. This was of no great account, for they were a people liked and respected in the tribe, who paid their dues, did their duties, and were much consulted in important decisions affecting the well-being of the people.

The Mamba grew up, as did most people, under the shade of his father's philosophy and his mother's admonitions and gently guiding stories. But with time he came to amaze his parents with his great strength, his prowess and his cunning. He grew up to be a loyal son of the tribe, a solid young man, and quite early had been singled out as a future member of the council. He would be the first of his family ever to have such an honour, and ascend to such heights. But his successes made him rash, his strength made him too confident, his winning ways with women made him visible, and his rude virility lent an impetuous but unenduring brilliance to his artistic creations. He worked with great verve and swiftness, but lacked patience and stillness; and all things touched with mystery were a genuine puzzle to him.

And yet the force and vitality of his creations, like his grasp of an opponent while wrestling, was powerful and arresting. His inclination to the gigantic, to things of great size, and weight, and mass, drew crowds and tempted the children into treating his creations as things to be clambered on and hide behind and play games on. They also made people gape, but not linger. He seemed to specialise in short-term astonishments. Every time a work of his appeared people knew it was his immediately, and they enjoyed going to see it, to have something to talk about for a short while, like witnessing something unusual but not profound. The people enjoyed the unusual creations and bestowed on them a certain popularity, from the sheer pleasure of talking about them. It was as though such works were needed to aid the conversation and gossip of a people, a not inconsiderable function in society.

But this very quality and the success it brought him made him continue in that way of being; and it never occurred to him that there were other modes, or alternatives. And this way he came to be, with his popularity, his facility, his victories in wrestling, hunting, harvesting and on diverse battlefields, slowly did something peculiar to his reputation, which he never noticed. And with time the possibility of the path that led to the council of masters quietly vanished from the map of his life. Yet he thrived and stood high in the estimation of the people. After all, he was a man who had built his habitation with his own hands, and wrestled with wild animals and broken their necks ...

He did not drink much, but was not disinclined to bursts of celebration. He was therefore considered sober and serious; and yet there was about his brooding presence, and his big bulk, and his powerful good health and his strong cunning eyes, something unexpressed. He did not speak much, but his reputation was not one of a man of silences. He had more presence than he had absence. Which is to say, when he was there he was there; in fact, he was too much there. And when he wasn't there, he wasn't there at all; in fact, it was as if he had never been there. He was noticed when in society, but not missed when he wasn't. People talked of him, but not about him. He generated rumours, but not gossip. And, oddest of all, he didn't inspire stories. The people didn't tell stories about him, in spite of his dramatic deeds. Or maybe the stories they told didn't linger, or last. They came quickly, and were quickly exhausted, and needed more deeds from him in order to generate more stories. He seemed to live, without knowing it, in a race against the way time devoured his deeds. He lived chasing story-making events. This gave a desperate restless energy to his life; and made him a man whose presence was constantly alert to opportunities to do things that would turn quickly into stories.

He seemed to have an unusual intuition for knowing when stories about him were being told. Then he was in his element. Only then did he radiate a certain charged serenity.

Thus his eyes were ever flashing, looking about, to see if he was being noticed, if he was being mythologised. There was something in him that reacted to the magnetism of public mythology, no matter how shallow. This quality made him one of the most alert men of his generation. If he had more patience he might have made a good actor.

These qualities in him also made him do things that were ambiguous, things he didn't recognise in himself. He thought of himself as a good man ... but his character was strange, even to him ...

. . . as if he harboured other selves, unsuspected, from a distant past ...

. . . or future.

CHAPTER FORTY-EIGHT

He was indeed known to have cracked the spine of a large thrashing serrated alligator that had snatched a child in the nearby marshes. He was indeed something of a hero, but he was also suspect, on account of the sinister air of the diabolical that he had about him. It was rumoured that he conjured dark spirits associated with the evil one, and that this was the source of his powers. It was also rumoured that he used these dark spells on girls and women, and that his successful seduction and possession of many a woman who refused to speak about him afterwards was entirely due to his dark transactions.

Women didn't so much come under his spell as be compelled, by an unpleasant but irresistible force, to succumb to his summons. But this power of his, this crude magnetism, didn't work on all women. Indeed, in the case of certain girls or women, his very power worked against him; it worked on him instead; and it cast a dreadful obsessive spell on him which he could rarely shake off. He tended to avoid such women, if he recognised their type in time. And he was mostly successful, for he knew the qualities in this unique breed of women that so turned his own infernal powers back on him and made him a slave and prisoner to his own sinister passionate sorcery, and which threatened to drive him mad with the powerlessness to resist the monstrous spell he cast on himself. These women tended to have certain qualities in common: there was simply no accounting for them, that is all. They need not be beautiful, clever, brave, rich, sensuous, fat, thin, cunning, devious, vulnerable, disdainful, foxy, flirtatious, man-wise, dependent, or anything like that.

They were simply other. They were unique. They possessed some peculiar unaccountable anti-spell. Nothing worked on them. Anything attempted on them rebounded on to the perpetrator. And they were always innocent of their powers. It was something they had, something they were born with, a simple genius. It had nothing to do with will or intention. And it could not be regulated, turned on, accentuated. This strange quality without a name was the one he feared most, and which most fascinated him in a woman. It was the quality he sought for most in a woman; it represented for him the ultimate challenge to his nature, a challenge more terrifying than fighting a lion or an alligator, or wrestling in distant villages with legends of the art of combat. And this quality, so rare, so magical, so unmistakable, was one possessed by the maiden.

CHAPTER FORTY-NINE

His desire to possess the maiden, to win her hand, made him obsessed, slightly crazed, constantly on the verge of hallucination, almost mad.

At night he couldn't sleep for thinking about her. And when he did sleep he ground his teeth so loudly that he often alarmed his neighbours. Because of this slight madness he was constantly tense, constantly working his jaws and clenching his fists. His eyes developed an odd maniacal light, and his face twitched. He took to brooding, and strange propensities surfaced in him from unsuspected depths. He became aware that he was suddenly capable of the most unlikely deeds. His mind developed a sinister inclination. Murders, vague vile notions, an inexplicable desire to do something amazing and monstrous took possession of him on account of the reverse spell of the maiden.

There grew in him, suddenly, overnight, out of his brooding, an inextinguishable desire to command, to crush, to compel, to be powerful, to dominate, to overcome all obstacles to his will. He brooded often on power, and on the domination of the tribes. Something in him wanted to rule the world . . .

But first, he knew, he had to win the hand of the maiden, and overcome her innocent power over him. He knew that if he did not win her, and annex her mystery into his powers, he would never be able to lead the tribe. Beginning with the tribe, then the surrounding tribes, he could make the great land his own, and spread his legend to the farthest stars.

It is impossible to say when the notion came upon him that the maiden was the key to his destiny. She had grown so powerful in his mind that he came to see that if he could not conquer her he could never conquer anything or anyone else. She became the obstacle, the riddle, the door, the sword, the rock, the mystery, the dark night, the great fear, the magic formula that stood between him and greatness.

When such notions grow in the mind of a man he develops the strangest instincts. There is nothing more powerful than when a great instinct is harnessed to an overwhelming desire. Such people conquer the world, or destroy it.

CHAPTER FIFTY

He had the gift of second sight and in his dreams he knew things about people that baffled them. This ability of his made him a formidable opponent in most endeavours. He was able to divine people's secrets, without knowing how. He dreamt of fights beforehand and knew what tactics his opponent would use, and could therefore neutralise them. He had visions and often heard what people were saying about him, so he knew how to take advantage of rumours, or when to kill them. Even with women he knew where their sweet-points were, where their weaknesses lay, because often he had successfully seduced them in his inexplicable dreams, and so in real life he knew exactly what to do to make them surrender to him completely, of their own free will.

He had some kind of innate power and talent in these things, but they were sporadic. They came and went. He had an innate ability, but he was not a master, and this infuriated him. He was so at the mercy of the apparent randomness of his gift for second sight, that without a vision that gave him advantageous insight, without a dream from which he could deduce a method, he was hopeless, he was in the dark. This filled him with fear. It meant that he could only undertake that which he had already gained an insight into by virtue of his erratic gift. This gave him an air of shallow enigma, fascinating to the undiscerning majority, perfectly transparent to masters, initiates and the innocent.

He was a man in constant dread of being deserted by his gifts. For someone with his ambitions this was indeed a great and dangerous flaw; and he was keenly aware of it; and could do nothing about it, on account of the structure of ambition upon which his life had grown. He wanted so much to control his gift, to be in control of it, but he wasn't and he couldn't. Second sight came to him when it came. He couldn't control it, and he couldn't conceive of living without it, managing a life of narrow certainties based on hard work, practical possibilities, and at the mercy of ignorance.

The Mamba preferred his occasional but greatly advantageous visions to a life of fighting without extra knowledge. And so he was unpredictable, even to himself; confident when he knew; frightened, and constrained to hide it under bluff, when he didn't.

And because of his lack of mastery over his talent for seeing more than most people saw, he felt an impostor in the real and higher things of life. Fortunately, he discovered, as he got older, that most people were utterly blind to these things anyway. He discovered that even without his second sight he was better than most. With it, he was superior to almost everyone.

This ability was to prove invaluable in his competition with the suitors to win the hand of the maiden.

CHAPTER FIFTY-ONE

On a day that he had been in the forest brooding and cutting wood for a sculpture he hoped to make of the maiden in her finest glory, he fell into a deep sleep and had a vision that the maiden was being spied on by an alien, by a strange slender creature with doe-like eyes. In the dream he saw at once that the maiden found it out and fell in love with the creature's eyes and wept over it and cried out loudly that she wanted this creature alone to be her husband. In the dream the tribe was horrified that the maiden wanted to marry an animal that no one had ever seen before. And this caused such outrage and confusion that elders were dispatched to the Mamba. They begged him to kill the creature and free the illustrious tribe from this threat of an abomination.

In the dream the Mamba set off into the forest, hunted the creature for seven days, and brought it back alive to the village. Then in full view of everyone he set the creature free and challenged it to an honest wrestling match. During the match he broke its neck with a crack so loud that it caused astonishment. The creature died instantly, and the Mamba became an instant hero, celebrated in songs and dances.

However, on the seventh day of the celebrations, the creature rose again. It had changed into a man, and it stood like a colossus in front of the shrine. It stood there silently, not saying a word, while the clouds passed across his clear soft face, now obscuring it, now revealing it. And there was the most unnerving stillness in the village while the colossus stood there, and did nothing, just staring in perfect tranquillity at the Mamba, who was now as tiny as a little cat in the presence of such gentle might.

The Mamba woke up from the vision and knew he had to do something. His whole world was in danger, but he did not know how. And so he made sure that the tribe felt that its whole world was in danger too, and did not know why.

First he needed proof of what his instincts had picked up. He began to spy on the secret life of the maiden.

CHAPTER FIFTY-TWO

Drawn by her mystery and cut through by her disdain, the Mamba followed the maiden in stealth wherever she went ...

In public places, among the women of the village, when she was in the community, he had no need to spy on her. The public eyes did that well enough and kept him informed with its daily quota of gossip. But when she stole away into the forest, or wandered down the clear brown path to the river, alone or with her hand-picked companions, he stole after her, and watched her from behind a cloak of partial invisibility.

He preferred to follow her when she was alone. He wanted to catch her at a secret habit or vice or some act of nature that would demystify her reputation as a woman beyond reach, a maiden of unattainable perfection and purity. He wanted to catch her squatting or at making the kind of natural noises that impeccable women are not allowed to make. Then her reverse spell might just cease to work on him; then, he hoped, he would begin to break the enslavement of his mind to her mystery. But the maiden was as irreproachable in private as in public . . .

. . . and this made him madder, more obsessed, and more given to intense seeing and hallucinations.

She became many people in his mind. He magnified her. He multiplied her. He suspected her of profound sorceries. He invested her with witchcraft. Her sense of solitude became for him a sure sign that she had secret covens or meeting places with fellow witches. Then he suspected that she was the priestess of a goddess, a handmaiden of the great mother, a daughter of the mysterious one. She seemed so gentle, walked with such wayward grace, and bore an air of such inexplicable protection that her life was certainly lived under the aegis of a divine being. Who was she? What did she worship? The Mamba followed her and interpreted everything she did as a sign, as a votive deed, as an offering, as a rite in an unknown series of rites which added up to a significant ritual of great worship. He expected that any moment the focus of her worship would be revealed, and he half expected to be blinded by the sheer light and power of this unveiling.

On the other hand, he half expected also to be brought to the edge of terror by witnessing the monstrous centre of her ritual disappearances. Which would it be?

Her mystery filled him with fear.

CHAPTER FIFTY-THREE

He watched her as, in the forest, she spoke to the birds. To spiders in their webs, she sang a song, laughing. She whispered girlishly into the trunks of trees. And, alone, she sometimes threw her arms up and exulted in the rich bank of green above her and the cool shade of the trees. Often she would pick up a snail and move it from the path. She would speak to it, urging the snail to be more careful where it strayed.

Sometimes, while he gazed on her, she seemed to vanish, and he would panic in bafflement, and he would find her somewhere else, a distance away, in another part of the forest, as if she had been moved there by elemental forces.

Once, he saw her surrounded by fairies, all in yellow and blue and gold, all girls, tiny and bright, with green and golden wings; and she sat on a tree that had fallen, and was telling them stories ...

CHAPTER FIFTY-FOUR

Sensing some pact she had made with solitude and with the little creatures of the forest, he was surprised when her escapes changed, and her feet tended towards the river. He walked in her footsteps to try and steal her powers and inhabit the weight and form of her being; but his big feet only destroyed the shape of her footprints on the white sand and left him confused about what he had accomplished.

Flowers she touched, he touched; and afterwards they wilted. And when he tried to tell the fairies stories he found not long afterwards an evil-looking bird regarding him from a tree that wasn't there.

Often the fairies perplexed him. Often he thought he saw the maiden in two places at the same time. Often he saw the maiden with her companions singing to the goddess of the river, all of them dressed in dazzling white shifts. Once he saw them all in a circle, linking hands, and they danced and spun around so fast, laughing girlishly, that they appeared to rise from the ground, all of them, while their sweet voices filled the air. The Mamba fell down in terror and astonishment at this sight, and when he got up he found himself partially blinded.

For two days he could not see clearly, and a mysterious ring burned in his brain, burned and turned in a pure air. Sometimes he could be heard screaming, for no visible reason.

CHAPTER FIFTY-FIVE

When his sight improved, and the fire ceased burning in his brain, he resumed spying on the maiden. And he was shocked one day to find he wasn't the only one spying on her . . .

For two days he watched from a distance and noticed how she seemed to be in a dream or a secret ritual or as if she had indeed beheld the presence of a higher being by the river. He watched as she spoke to the air, in an attitude of profound humility. He was mesmerised by the pure beauty that shone from her awkward and piquant face as she fell on her knees and began to answer three questions which it seemed the very air had asked her. And it filled him with jealous awe to behold the light that radiated from her form, purified now by some dazzling quality of the morning sun, which brought her in outline and seemed to concentrate a holy fire around her perfect slimness. She seemed then to be possessed of a beauty so refined and tender that the Mamba found himself gasping at this miraculous incarnation of the maiden by her own illumination.

He watched as she went through a strange ritual of praying, of worship. Quietly, he drew closer. And then he heard the voice in the morning wind, say: 'Come back here the same time tomorrow. Come alone.' He saw how she shone at the sound of the voice speaking in the wind.

He was instantly suspicious. It occurred to him that one of the other suitors might be behind this outrageous deception. Then he noticed rustling in the distant bushes and saw the form of a man disappear behind a cover of luxuriant green. Amazed at the audacity of such an act, he hurried in the direction of the bushes, taking the longer way, so as not to be seen by the maiden. But when he got there he only caught a glimpse of a fabulous horned animal vanishing among the trees, in a spangle of golden light pooled in from the sky between a bald patch among the high branches. The horned animal was of dazzling golden form, a pure matter of legend; and like a spark of a miraculous perception, it evaporated into the shade, leaving the Mamba partially blinded a second time.

CHAPTER FIFTY-SIX

He lay there on the floor of the forest, amidst a mildly sweet-smelling bank of leaves. He felt a slow drip of late morning dew fall on the nape of his neck as he listened to the thousand footfalls of invisible creatures in the forest. He lay quite still, waiting for his eyes to clear. In the distance he heard a wild boar rooting around. Around him he heard a steady hum and mingled tiny sounds of insects stirring and whirling. A voice was singing high above the trees. The river roared in his veins.

He began to formulate a vague act of malice to compensate for his blinding, his humiliation. He couldn't get the other spying out of his mind; and whenever he thought of that form, the fabulous horned animal also came to mind, and refused to leave. What was he to do? He was, he felt, owed due vengeance. A great rage swelled in him like a river in spate. He let it swell, and waited for the rage to subside. And when it did, he knew exactly what he should do, not only to win a bride, but also to begin his commanding steps towards power.

Dimly, feeling his way to the river's edge, he washed his face and his eyes. He lay in the sun. He slept, and when he awoke his eyes had cleared considerably.

He made his way home, speaking to no one on the journey back, grunting in a bad-tempered fashion when anyone spoke to him. It was the advantage of reputation. He could cloak his vulnerability beneath a growl.

Back in his abode he brooded on what he was going to do. Then, with the sure instincts of a fighter who knows when his moment has come and the fight has tilted his way, offering him the perfect opportunity for a victorious coup, he set his extraordinary plan into action. It was simplicity itself. And its consequences were incalculable. Till this day it still haunts the world, like a wandering note of dissonance that will never die.

CHAPTER FIFTY-SEVEN

The Mamba did two peculiar things. First he put it about that the maiden was having illicit relations with a horned animal near the river. Nothing travels faster than an evil rumour; and rumours are the easiest things to create. Like magic they appear, and take on the full vestments of truth, a terrible truth which everyone would secretly like to believe. This malicious rumour travelled very fast and soon everyone began to entertain the notion that the unattainable maiden made love to an exceptional beast in the forest.

Good news travels with the speed of a gazelle, but bad rumour travels with the swiftness of the wind. Soon sculptures depicting acts of bestiality, representing, in sublime forms, the coupling of a horned animal and a beautiful girl, began to appear at the tribal shrine.

And the second thing the Mamba did was to inform the maiden's parents that an outsider, a mysterious and dangerous figure, was spying on their daughter and could ruin her chances of a good marriage . . . The Mamba thought that, by this action, he would earn a special place in their affections.

The maiden meanwhile was completely unaware of the appalling things that were being said about her; and she bore herself, as ever, with a tranquil and angular dignity. She sang when with her friends, and was silent when in the community. She did not notice the circle of her friends gradually dwindling. She did not notice the nature of the silence that came upon people when she entered their midst. The magical effect of the voice that had spoken to her by the river had illumined her consciousness and lifted her mind to realms of tender contemplation. She gazed upon the world and upon people with the sweetness of one in love but not having an object of love. She was a floating being of tenderness. She was occupied with a peculiar happiness that often made her suddenly giggle and weep and then gaze sternly all about her and then fall into a vacancy of being. Like a sky with constantly changing clouds that affected the light so dramatically, she was a changeable being of infinite sensitivity.

She had no idea what to do with herself. And so she made things, carved, drew figures on wooden panels, made up songs, invented new patterns on dye cloths, and ran exhausting errands, all this to try and stop feelings of powerful and fragile beauty from tearing her apart inside.

Life is too full of mysteries to which we pay no attention,

and so significant events happen and we don't notice that they ever existed. Significant events often appear so insignificant anyway, almost invisible; and yet they are the tiny catalysts that change a life. After the maiden's encounter with the voice at the river, she dreamt that night, very fleetingly, of a young prince. She barely noticed the dream at the time, but the brief appearance of the prince in her dream remained somewhere in her mind, awaiting events that would double its presence. In the dream she merely saw a figure, whom she took for a prince, and he was staring at her, saying nothing, doing nothing, watching and not watching her, as if she were a mysterious work of art he never wanted to understand, but only to learn how to look at.

CHAPTER FIFTY-EIGHT

The maiden lived her life of tender absent-mindedness, as far removed in thought from the clamour of suitors as from the gathering rumours. But it became impossible to escape the rumours. The maiden herself remained forever oblivious to them, protected by providence from ever being sullied by lies that would have broken her young spirit; but the same was not true for her parents.

When her father learnt that there was a man who wasn't an official suitor who was spying on his daughter at the river, when he heard the rumours whispered in the tribe, he knew he had to act swiftly in order to protect her reputation. He knew he had no choice but to make her disappear from the tribe, and he knew that her exile might be bitter.

But as he was a man of mysteries, who never acted without listening to the invisible oracles, without listening to the hidden masters of the tribes, without consulting the ancestors, he set about the rituals by which things unknown are revealed in hints and messages, signs that manifest in the world and are interpreted by the master-readers of revelations. From the ancestors he received signs that things must decompose if they are to give birth to immortal fruits of time. From the hidden masters of the tribe he learnt that evil must triumph for a season if an even greater good that will change the world is to come into being; that good, in its gentleness, needs its true character and resolve tested, primed, and strengthened by the suffering brought on by evil; only then will good have the moral force, and the great integrity, and the deep certainty, and the boundless power to step forth and overcome evil and transform the world into the reality of a higher vision.

From the oracles he learnt that only one who is not fit to be a suitor can possibly win the hand of his daughter, only one whom no one notices can truly rule, only one who is unofficial can be truly official, only the lowly can be on high. Also, from the oracles he learnt that an unlikely contest will decide all things; and that the future is a dark hole beyond which, in time, a great kingdom of unimaginable splendour will be found. Through sorrow and pain, all will be well. All things will be transfigured. All will be redeemed. A joy beyond description will crown all stories. These things the oracles told.

The maiden's father was comforted, and acted with perfect tranquillity. He ignored the rumours and set about a long-term plan; for he was a man who always regarded present problems as excuses for long-term vision and preparation.

He was thinking now of the future of the tribe, beyond the time of its disappearance. He began preparations for its rebirth out of the decomposition of its present state, a life after the death of the tribe.

But first he summoned his wife and, deep into the night, they planned for the safety of their child and the future regeneration of their people. Only those who have accepted the death of their people can dream so clearly so miraculous a future. Only one who has accepted death can see so clearly that impossible things can be done beyond the limits that are there.

CHAPTER FIFTY-NINE

It fell to the mother to tell her daughter of her sudden departure. For that night, in the middle of decisive discussions, her father had said, quite suddenly, to her mother:

'It is time for her initiation into the mysteries of woman-hood and of the goddess.'

Her mother looked at him with large almost sorrowful eyes.

'What a trying time awaits her, my dear, in the middle of her dreams.'

'But afterwards she would be a woman like no other, like her mother, a woman whose love not even kings deserve.'

'But the suffering and the dying.'

'Yes, my dear, and the shining face of a new woman when she emerges from the cave.'

'But the darkness and the loneliness,' said the mother.

'Yes, my love, and the loss of fear for ever and the light of wisdom in her spirit. And the strength of mind and awakened gold in her soul, gift of the goddess, if she is lucky.'

'But these things take a long time to show, if ever at all. Most of the girls go through the initiation but are not changed by it.'

'Not our daughter. Everything that has meaning works on her, affects her. She is ready. It may take time to flower in her, but she will drink the experience in as the earth drinks rain. Then one day, in times that call for greatness to emerge, times of crisis, when all around are paralysed by fear, the power of the goddess, the power of the cave, of our ancient ways, will rise in her, and she will be amazed at what unsuspected magic lives in her.'

'I know you are right, my love,' the mother said, 'but children do not always live up to the possibilities we see in them. They don't always bear the fruit that their early brightness promised. They don't always become the wise and balanced people that we hoped. Often they let their parents down and grow up to become quite ordinary, quite like the others. All the preparations, the initiations, the careful guidance of their early years disappear into them never to show forth again. I don't want to expect too much of our daughter and spend our old age shaking our heads in silent disappointment.'

'Have faith in her,' the father said. 'She is strange, I admit. She seems not to be of this world, I admit. But there is something in her that cries for great understanding of the mysteries of life, and that is a special gift in itself.'

'Many want to understand,' the wife replied, 'but few have the character for it. It takes character to receive, to wait, to listen, to obey, to learn, to grow, to master, to keep on the right road, to make mistakes and to correct them before they have gone too far, and to always remember what the most important things are in life, beyond wealth, success and glory. She might want to know and yet she might settle, as most people do, for the most ordinary average things. She might have no stamina to become a true woman. I fear her over-sensitivity; it might make her demand to be spoilt. It may make her ruthless only for things she wants, a soft and easy life. It may make her cruel. She may fail to see that the best things often are the hardest to see, and the most challenging. Or not. I have seen too many girls ruin their lives because they wanted what was easy, against the true whispers of their hearts.'

'Our daughter is not like that. She has her mother's spirit, but in a different form. She was given to us to teach us how a different way can also arrive in the kingdom of the blessed. Anyway, what have we to lose? If she turns out all right, she will be a gift to the world. If she doesn't she will have lived an interesting life, because of the rich creed of the tribe. Already she has seen enough and learnt enough to have plenty to think about for a whole lifetime. Already, anywhere else in the world, she would stand out as a special person. She knows more than she knows. I do not fear for her.'

The mother laughed and staring deep into her husband's eyes of mystery, she said:

'And what of all these rumours?'

It was now her husband's turn to laugh.

'We both know who is behind them. We both know why.

Rumours can destroy only that which is not true and deep. Rumours are like rats that eat away at the foundations of a house. If the foundations are not strong the house will fall anyway, without the rats. These things can work for our ends. We must let them come and go. People are seen to be greater if they survive the lies told about them. Out of shame the world gives more stature to those it has maligned, but only if the maligned ones turn out to be worth their weight in gold. The integrity of our daughter will turn these rumours into great praise, into songs of legend, one day. Those who tear down a good name will be forced to build a palace for their future fame.'

'You trust your daughter so much.'

'And so do you. She has your special nature, but she is a strange gift.'

'I know,' the mother said, 'and that is why I am so hard on her. I love her too much and so I let her wander and dream her youth away. These may well be the best days, her purest days, under this difficult sun. I want it to last. I want her to forever live in these happy times when she doesn't know how happy she is. I want her not to pay any attention to the suitors, or worry about the healing work expected of her, or be troubled by the instinct of love growing in her, or be stirred by the whispers of the gods in her being. I want her always to wander by the river and to talk to snails and to laugh suddenly because happiness shakes in her like the midnight touch of a lover. I want her never to walk on broken glass, or to wake up in the dark, or to see the world turn into a cage, or to see the open road narrow and become a tiny path, or to see monsters everywhere, or to become full of doubt and fear, to become suspicious of those she loves, and to see evil in the good things in her life. I don't want her to drown in sadness, or to no longer see the sky with gladness. I don't want her to forget what love means, and to learn to hate her life because of all the troubles that living brings. But all I can do is prepare her in her youth, for all the troubles, and a love of truth. All I can do is show her a mirror in which she can see her future self, and be surprised by it, and rebel against it, and in rebelling take such twists and turns that will lead her to the right way. We will be gone by then. And she will look back and see these days again as magic days and not gone, but waiting. And she will find us inside her, smiling, growing in her rebelling, flowering in her realisation. And we will be in the best fruits of her life, her best deeds. One has to use such cunning ways to make the future yield the best fruits. But for now, I must show her the art of delays; show her, without showing her, how to make time a yielder, a teacher, a friend, a guide, an alchemist, a magician, a transformer, by the ways of delaying – one of our ancient ways which the new generations are forgetting. Now I must be the wicked mother, and bring swift unwanted changes into the sleeping life of our daughter. Why is this always the mother's task, my husband?'

And they both laughed deep into the night at the mysteries of these things.

CHAPTER SIXTY

On the wonderful day that the maiden was supposed to obey the injunction of the voice by the river, to keep her solemn promise to the mysterious voice heard in the riverwind; on the day that was supposed to be the most fateful, the most beautiful of her life, when the gods would show her favours she could hardly dream about; on the day that she had anticipated deeply but wouldn't allow herself to think about, and her anticipation made her quivery and nervous and full of joy at the slightest thing, so that sometimes she felt that some vital part of her being would suddenly ascend from her body in a daze of unequalled ecstasy; on that day her mother called her with a different voice, a terrible voice, a hard, harsh and earthy voice, and told her, quite brutally, that she was being taken away, immediately, on a journey.

The maiden was given no time to think about it and virtually no time to pack. She had to leave as she was. Something very urgent had come up, and for her absolute good she had to go.

'But mama,' cried the maiden, 'do I have to go now?'

'Yes, my dear, absolutely.'

'But I have barely woken up from sleep.'

'All the better. You must think then that you are dreaming.'

'Do I have to go this moment, now?' the maiden asked, incredulously.

'Yes, now, as you are. We should be leaving now as we are talking.'

'But does papa know about this?'

'Absolutely, of course.'

'What does he say?'

'It is his instruction, it is his will. I am merely carrying out his orders.'

'But why?'

'There is no time to explain. Take what you need now, the fewer things the better. Take them now or you will regret not paying attention later.'

In a state of complete confusion, her mind in disarray, her world seeming to collapse and dissolve about her, she quickly, in a daze, as in a dream, gathered together the items of clothes and other ordinary but invaluable things she would need. She was on the verge of tears, but she was too confused to weep. Her mind swirled, the notion of the end of things, the end of the world, swooped down on her. She didn't know what to think or feel. She was distressed beyond bearing at leaving so suddenly and breaking her promise to the god of the river who had favoured her with speech. This filled her with immeasurable sadness and a sense of panic. What would the god do? Would the god be angry with her for disobedience? Whom should she most obey, the voice of a god or the commandments of her parents? The maiden was in turmoil as she threw sundry items together into a bundle. How could she get word to the river to say she was being taken away so suddenly, against her will and desire? And if she got word to the river would the god listen to anyone else but her? And the messenger, how could they speak to the god when the god had chosen to speak to her alone? Could she – should she – explain all this to her mother? But there was no time, for time was collapsing all about her. Things were vanishing. She could not find half the clothes and items she sought. The walls, the house, the village, were vanishing before her gaze. Her life was disappearing. What was happening to her?

And her mother, thinking the daughter looked perplexed because of the suddenness of her departure, as well as the mysterious nature of her journey, began to speak to her a mother's words:

'My child,' she said, as she hurried her through the tying of her bundle, 'this life of ours is a strange story that only the gods can read.'

Time became very swift. It was as if she were in a dream and her life was being altered by a god. The maiden, listening and not listening to her mother, felt as if a god were wafting her into a changed course. She felt as if she were being lifted out of one life and being placed in another. She felt, oddly, as if she were being obscurely assisted, as if propelled through time and space and destiny. It all felt strange. Suddenly she was under the sky. Then the village passed her by. Faces gazed at her, smiling. Then she found herself in her father's workshop. She was kneeling. He was pouring out a libation and invoking the gods, the ancestors and the masters. He was asking them to protect and enlighten his daughter on this journey that she was undertaking into womanhood and into the mysteries. The prayers had a powerful effect on her; they cast an astonishing enchantment on her mind. Spirits appeared before her gaze, and her mind faded a little, and the world passed her. The artworks bristling with prophecy and power dazzled her spellbound mind. The road led up to the hills. Soon her mother was beside her again, then she disappeared, then reappeared. She walked on the earth and then was borne along in a dream. The sun beat down with sharp rays like the swords of warriors. The heat and the sharp rays sent her mind revolving. For a long time, beyond the earth, above the river, high into the hills which she had never heard about, whose grottoes abounded with legends, she went, walking on light feet, listening to the wind, and to the eagles and sunbirds and the white-winged birds that flew over her head with softly whirring wings like the noises that precede the voice of prophecy in the oracles and the shrines.

She was led into a world beyond her dreams, into valleys of stone and wild green plant, rocks with faces like old masters gazing into this world from another one, vultures perched on high outcrops, strange animals that rustled across their paths. How long had they been walking, been borne along, by dreams, by insubstantial forms? Were they going to the world's end, to the domain of alien beings, to the home of spirits? Was she being taken on a ritual sacrifice, for some unknown reason? She had heard stories such as these often. A maiden is taken away because the god has chosen her to be sacrificed to avert a disaster fatal to the tribe. Did I come in peace and willingness? the maiden asked herself, and couldn't answer. She was so mesmerised. She felt as if she were going to her death, in order that the world could be renewed. She was the god's choice for the renewal of the world and the averting of catastrophe. She could feel now how she was borne along by a power greater than her. She dreaded it all, and yet was calm in her terror.

She loved the world she was leaving, she now discovered. And she realised that she had not looked at it enough. The hills were beautiful, rugged, harsh and mysterious. Here the spirits dwelt, she thought. They are the rocks. The hills were gods. The sky was clear, and bright, like shining bronze and gold, and profoundly blue, as if heaven's depth had lowered itself closer to the earth. The air was clear. She could smell all the fragrances of all the herbs and plants she loved. The place she walked on was old; old stories of tribes that had long vanished into dreams told themselves to her feet. And she saw bearded magi and young children, burdened and pregnant women, warriors and their stones, laughing fathers, and sons that must rebel in order to become men. She saw them in her walking state, vanished tribes, gone into the rocks, lingering in the invisible dreams in the air. She felt the blood of wars and ritual sacrifices.

She knew at once that she had lived and yet had not glimpsed what life was, and she gave a cry, and the enchantment tightened tenderly about her mind, and her mother appeared at her side and began speaking.

CHAPTER SIXTY-ONE

'My child, my child, be still, and be comforted in your heart,' her mother said. 'This is what a woman's life is like. Constant change. No here, and now. What is stable in this world? Nothing. Everything is changing, running away. One day a girl, proud as a goddess, confused as a millipede counting its legs, and the next day a woman, a mother, too busy, a little mad, and quite helpless, and yet powerful. Changes in the body. Changes in the world. Every day the earth has been taken away from under your feet. The man who loved you yesterday, is he the same man today? One day you are loved, the next day love is a stranger. One day your mother is here, the next day she is dead, gone to join the ancestors. Who knows anything? All is like the wind, changing like water. Things disappear. And so a woman must learn to be still, to make things stay, to make things remain, to inspire things to come back, even when they go. A woman must learn to charm life to keep returning that which has gone. The woman learns the art of making time be still. Of stretching time out. Making time wait, linger. You make time live in your house, while history is being made. You keep time under your pillow, with your dreams. You make time a great power. And how do you do this? That you must learn yourself. But I tell you why. Because everything goes, beauty, earthly power, fortune, happiness, clans, tribes, empires, everything goes away, disappears. But you can make them disappear slower; you can make them wait longer; you can charm them to stay for one more day; and if you do this day after day, then you can manage a modest eternity. And even things that go, you can charm their presence here, their fragrance, their spirit. If their spirit is here then they are here too, and soon their form will return in another way. These are women's things, these are women's ways; but not all women know them, my daughter, only those in whom the ancient wisdom of women is alive, who have been taught, who have been initiated into the mysteries of the great mother . . .'

CHAPTER SIXTY-TWO

These words were meant to distract the maiden. They were meant to prepare her. The ancient ones believed, as I do now, that a person has to hear a thing three times in order to hear it once. The words her mother spoke to her between hills, under the changing brilliance of the sky, with the jagged rocks underfoot that snagged them as they walked, the words were a ploy, a bridge between distances, between home and the unknown.

Did the maiden hear a single word her mother said? No, not a word. Not with her normal ears. Did her mother think that her daughter had heard a word she had said? No, not a word. But she knew that her daughter's spirit had heard the spirit of her words. That she knew. The spirit of the words had gone into her daughter through unusual channels, and will wait in her like an unsuspected pregnancy; and one day it will give birth to unexpected understanding. The maiden's mother had long mastered the art of planting the spirit of words in people. She knew that people resist words themselves, because they hear them. But the spirit of words can't be resisted because it is not heard, or is heard by deeper, invisible ears. Not many people knew the art of the spirit of words; and to know this art one ought first to know the art of the spirit of things; indeed, the art of the spirit. This art was one of those that the maiden's mother specialised in, as she wove in and out of her daughter's consciousness, and as she travelled the feet-tearing distances over the rough hills and across streams to the unfathomed place of initiations.

The maiden did not hear anything, as she staggered along in her semi-sleepwalking way over rocks and on brutal stones. When her mind was not blank, or full of foreboding, or bedazzled and bewitched by the merciless sunlight, she was thinking only of the tragic loss of not keeping her promise with the divine voice at the river. And she was certain that she would suffer and be punished for her failure to keep the appointed hour with her destiny. It was only much later she would learn that there are many destinies. And that we fail to keep our appointed hour with one destiny in order to fulfil another. There are many alternative destinies waiting in the wings of our failures.

These future notions would not have consoled the maiden. As she stumbled along the harsh paths in the ascending hills, crushed by the sun, obliterated by the sky, made raw by the earth, her mind worn down by an intolerable exhaustion that shaded into hallucination, she thought mainly of the voice and the river that she had left behind for ever.

CHAPTER SIXTY-THREE

Meanwhile the Mamba, not knowing the effects that his plans had wrought, not knowing of the disappearance of the maiden, kept up his malicious campaign. He began to speak out about unknown foreigners invading their lives. He went about this with such an obsessed state of mind that he forgot how open the tribe was to outsiders. In fact the tribe relied on the continual flow of outsiders into its life. They brought trade, and goods, and they brought artworks and artefacts from distant kingdoms and principalities. Without them the tribe would have no idea what the rest of the world was doing artistically. It would be isolated from the visible currents of art and dreams.

The tribe thrived on its sense of wonder. And there were few things it found to wonder at more than a new bronze sculpture from an unknown race, or a carving, or a new form, or shape, or way of representing what was familiar or unfamiliar. They loved nothing more than to be amazed by that which they did not understand.

It was essential to their pleasure and appreciation that they did not (at first) understand the art that came their way from the mysterious trade routes of the world. For the tribe, to understand was not to see. To understand too quickly was a failure. It was a blinding. Understanding stopped them from seeing, and looking. Even when they understood, they sought that within a significant work which they did not and could not understand: this they held up as its central and most secret feature. And when this point of mystery moved, or changed, as it does through time and under the new light of unexpected events, they also changed the centrality of the work's mystery.

Like women admiring new clothes in the marketplace, or like women admiring the fruits of a rich season, so the tribe clustered round like children and admired the new works which traders brought from the wider world. Knives with uniquely designed handles, figurines made of fired clay, reliquary figures of unknown ancestors, items sculpted from rocks, drawings on scrolls, handwritten manuscripts from prosperous kingdoms, paintings on parchment, vivid colours on absorbent wood, seeds of strange fruits, skulls of strange animals, objects that were magical because they were strange and beautiful in themselves, in their forms, in the ideas that spoke out from their shapes: these created a great and lasting excitement in the tribe. And they were part of the vital life of its continued creativity.

So freely did they adapt, absorb, transform and combine the ideas and possibilities in these artworks and objects that they encountered. They absorbed them, and acknowledged them; for, to the tribe, acknowledging was a high expression of gratitude that made higher creativity possible. The gods of creativity, they believed, frowned greatly on unacknowledged absorptions; and the punishment for this was future barrenness in art.

It was against all this that the Mamba, in his blind obsession, found himself pitted. Not only that; but also against the great commerce done by the purchase of their works by traders, by outsiders. And not only that either; but against the presence of the other suitors for the hand of the maiden.

Soon the Mamba found himself isolated, and he didn't know it. He was outside the current of his people, and no one told him. In some tribes silence is the highest form of both condemnation and adoration. But the silences are different. A madman shouts out obscenities from dawn to dusk, and the tribe is silent. The madman becomes madder, and one day is heard from no more. There is a kind of silence that swallows up the personality and spirit of one who talks too much.

CHAPTER SIXTY-FOUR

The maiden's father had picked up the rumours and the whispers not from the mouths of people, not from friends and associates, not from relations, but from hints that the tribe was so expert at sending. Songs that he heard in the marketplace, with certain references and certain sly images, and he knew that his illustrious house was being referred to; indirectly, of course. Works of art seen, sculptures near the shrine noticed, certain words in conversations overheard, and an intolerable suggestiveness in certain glances, lingering too long, with an insolence previously unthinkable, and the speech unspoken wasn't hard to hear. The unsaid things thundered for being said in a hundred other ways except through speech. And so when he acted, when he had the maiden sent away, not in secrecy but in daylight, so that everyone could see and therefore not see, he acted in the highest spirit.

With his wife, at night, when they talked deep into the hours of the dwindling stars, they often said things like: One does not become a woman just by getting older. One does not become a human being just by being born. To become what one is takes a long time, and no time at all. Those who use only their brains cannot get to the mysterious depth of things. Now will not be like this for ever. Now is not what people think it is: there is a now that has gone, there is a now that is going, and there is a now that will be, but which is already here – and they are all in the same now. People see only that which has gone, and which is no more. They never see that which is already here, but invisible.

Man and wife; these manner of things they spoke to one another, into the hours of the dwindling stars and the gently brightening heavens. And they spoke these things incidentally, in relation to something else, something more concrete, like what to do about their daughter.

Her disappearance from the community increased her reputation and her stature amongst the suitors, and fuelled innumerable rumours about her. As rumour takes the place of fact, filling an absence, it allowed people to be creative in the monstrosities that they could imagine and invent. There was talk that the maiden was unwell, that she had gone mad, that she had contracted a fatal disease, that the gods had sent dreadful omens regarding her fate. They whispered that she had disappeared because she had been impregnated by the horned animal that had copulated with her. They speculated about the nature of the man-beast that she would give birth to, and wondered if it would ever be allowed to roam about the shrine in broad daylight. They surmised that the pressure and expectation of having to create a new work to fulfil her healing had perhaps cracked her sanity. Or wondered whether she had crumbled under the strain of the relentless wooing by the suitors. Some said that she had gone away to be fortified. And as there is always an element of chance in the accumulation of rumours, so there is an element of truth in something that is collectively whispered for long enough, even if that truth is allegorical, or even symbolic. For there were those who suggested that she might have gone away to be spiritually strengthened, to be magnified.

In fact, she had been taken to the cave of awakening, in the hills of the gods. In that cave her real life began. She was buried alive, left for days, allowed to die, and was then raised . . .

It was in the cave that she began to dream of a dying prince.

CHAPTER SIXTY-FIVE

About initiations we ought to be silent. They are often sacred and private events. What rituals are wrought there belong to the initiated and should not be bared to the irrelevant scrutiny of a curious and sensation-seeking world. People destroy the power of initiations when they reveal them to outsiders and to those who are not undergoing such rites. Noble initiations ought to have great silence and a ring of fire around them, so that the initiated may undergo the rites of their transformations in the power of that intense space. Initiations within are silent and unseen; so it should be for those who make the ritual changes from darkness to light, from boys to men, from girls to women, from chrysalis to butterfly. Wisdom ought to guide these processes of the liberating being.

About the maiden's initiation, though I saw it in the book of life, I shall be silent, in my revealing kind of way. I shall conceal by revealing. She passed through it with great pain, difficulty and suffering. She dwelt alone for seven days in the cave of transformations. She was buried alive for many nights. She gave birth to herself in her death and emerged from the earth in a disordered, disorientated state. She ate nothing but herbs and water. She dwelt among the rocks and awaited the goddess. She recited the prayers of light that had been given her till she broke down and wept a whole day. Then she felt like dying and lay down on a white rock to die in the blazing sun, with her lips all broken and her mind quite cracked. And a blaze of light encompassed her and in the light there was a bird and she followed the bird into the heavens and wandered in halls of pure white glory. Then she saw a prince waiting for her at the door of golden splendour, and he reached out his hand and she held it, and together they entered the chamber of angels. And they were silent there among the angels and they were both one and happy and perfect in their bliss beyond the wildest dreams of mortals. And they dwelt there in perfect love and harmony for an eternity; and then time tugged at her and she found herself alone, listening to the whispers of the goddess in the hall of the Holy. She listened a long time to whispers that were not words but beyond words; and then a flash of red light fell upon her and she awoke and found herself in the cave, alone, with girls who had changed into women singing outside, calling her to come out of the cave to be a woman now and give birth to a new world.

CHAPTER SIXTY-SIX

Eventually she emerged, and after much encouragement and coaxing she danced as a new woman and was taught the rituals of birth. Her blood broke then and ran down her legs and they celebrated her as a woman who with blood bears the weight and fire-wisdom of the world, who with blood sacrifices her life to make the world beautiful and rich with meaning, and who with blood continues the entry into the world of sleeping souls waiting to emerge into history and time, and who with blood bears legend and myths.

And she danced, and ate, and was fed rich food with the new women. And she learnt proverbs, silence, legends of the land, the histories of the tribes, the sagas of families, the ways of woman that overcome and dissolve the often stubborn and short-sighted ways of men. And she was taught to see men as allies in the universe created by God for them both to make noble the future of the race and the earth. And she was taught the art of indirection, the science of herbs, the marvels of decoration, the place of agreement and disagreement and the ways to accomplish things. And she was taught that wisdom is better than force, grace greater than power, love greater than hate, that bitterness and food do not mix, that a pure heart is more beautiful than a pure sky, that discord is the enemy of prosperity, and she was taught a thousand other things which will be forgotten and then remembered and passed on from generation to generation, longer than the hills . . .

She danced, grew, learnt, unlearnt, changed and didn't change, with the other new women. She had no idea what her initiation had made her become. Her face in the mirror of the lakes in the hills looked strange to her. She had acquired a new face, with a new look in her eyes. She feared her new self, feared its new secret power and knowledge, and kept it hidden for a long time.

CHAPTER SIXTY-SEVEN

She went to the hills a girl, and emerged from the cave profound, and yet sweeter, more innocent, and more mysterious than ever. She was also more odd. Initiations only make you more and deeply what you truly are. There are, in truth, no changes. And even the greatest experiences or revelations do not change a life. They only reveal what was deeply and truly there, in the depths of the personality. They only unveil the true self. They only make people become what they really were all along. When people say 'This or that experience changed my life' they only mean that 'this or that' pushed forward their true selves, brought forth their true nature. We never change. From youth to adulthood, from frivolity to seriousness, under the impact of significant experiences we only become what we really are, for good or ill. That is why when people say they have changed it does not, as they think, mean that they have necessarily changed for the better.

But initiations are different: if they are noble, they change you into the becoming of your true self, that you may better see yourself as you are in the mirror, and thereby begin further unveiling. For all initiation is unveiling, self-revealing.

The maiden descended from the hills in her new mystery.

The world she left was not the same.

She saw it differently.

She saw things she had not seen before. She heard things she had not heard before. She did things she would never have done before.

And yet had she changed?

CHAPTER SIXTY-EIGHT

In accordance with tradition the tribe welcomed the maiden back from her initiation with songs and dances reserved for heroes and heroines. They embraced her back into its heart. They treated her as a special being, creating an arch of palm fronds for her to walk under, as if she were a priestess returning from the shrine of prophecies with good omens for the world.

CHAPTER SIXTY-NINE

And it was when she returned from her initiation that, under a trance, a sudden inspiration, she created an inexplicable sculpture of a dying prince. She had not long returned when she began haunting her father's workshop, wandering amongst the sleeping wood and the unsummoned spirits. Soon she was seen frequenting the forests, searching for something which she claimed could not be sought, but only received. One day, in her obsession and her wandering open-minded state, she encountered an old man who sat on air, his eyes piercing, his face young. He had a gentle smile on his face. She said nothing to him and he merely stared through her and she wandered past him, seeking that which can only be received. Then in the silence she heard someone say:

'What you seek is the foundation.'

She was not puzzled by this voice, but went straight home, and the next day found the perfect piece of wood near the shrine, as if it had been placed there for her. The wood shone with the light and mystery of dawn. And she took it home and slept near it and then one day, in the middle of her duties, unaware of all things, she saw the dream of love in the wood and surrendered to it completely. She asked no questions, brought no answers, forgot all techniques, discarded all craft, abandoned her heart, left behind her mind, ceased to be a maiden, a woman, or even human, became blind and refused speech and, in complete emptiness, like one without beginning or end, she received what emerged from her dreaming in wood.

And when it was finished she displayed the sculpture of a dying prince in front of the shrine.

CHAPTER SEVENTY

No one understood it. The work, beautiful and rough, rich in pathos and yet touched with humour, caused consternation in the tribe. But it caused more problems in her. The work bothered her. She had no idea where it came from, or what had made her create it. The work perplexed her, and she pondered it often, and stared at it whenever she could without being noticed, and she peered into it as into a prophetic mirror. Baffled by the mystery of her own creation, she began to fall in love with it. She fell in love, not with the art, or the beauty, or the work; she fell in love with the hint of the prince she had created. She fell in love with the mysterious possibility of the figure lying languidly in the charmed wood of her inspiration.

She fell in love with the image, the tranquil sadness of the dying youth; and she became secretly obsessed with it. Her secret obsession began to affect her sanity; the mystery of the work began to unhinge her. And she began to seek one who was like the sculpture, and she found no one to rival the intriguing beauty of the work she had made. She searched for such a one in all the faces that she met. Then she entertained the hope, which was awoken in a dream she had, that the figure in wood might wake from his death-slumber in wood and stand before her fresh as a flower nearly touched with dew.

It was an odd dream, extremely vivid and rich in colour, in which the dying prince slowly stretched his limbs as blood returned to his pale cheeks, and sat up, and then turned to her, and spoke with a silent voice so familiar that it made her shiver with a precious delight. The dying prince stared at her a long time with his doe-like eyes of liquid sadness. His lips were gently red and hinted at the softness of rose petals. And his nose was gentle too, but his jaws had a quiet strength. He stared at her and didn't speak. He was silent and he stared and he wasn't thinking, just staring, not even moving, but his eyes seemed the centre of the universe, and his breathing the centre of an intolerable tenderness that was like an ache which she could not locate, and from which she could not escape. He made her want to weep for some unstated tragic condition about the world, some great universal injustice, some unbearable crime committed against a complete innocent. Not one thought emerged from his stillness, or his presence. Just the tranquil stare that looked upon her as at a profound mystery. The tender intensity of his gaze touched her very deeply, to her core, where she was not just a girl or a woman but a living being of pure love. And then suddenly, but slowly, the dying prince lay down again and assumed his dying repose, and returned to his condition of a work of art in wood.

She had this dream several times and every time she awoke she was disconsolate. Not a word had he ever uttered to her. And till he spoke, she felt she could not speak; his awakening from his imprisonment in wood was the miracle that could free her voice in her dreams. But as he could not speak, neither could she.

The maiden carried a strange secret around with her in her waking hours: she wanted the prince to waken from wood into flesh, and for him to speak, so that she could learn to love.

Her work held her prisoner too. She could not be free till the prince could *be*. And so her return from the hills, and the creation of the work of art which should have healed her and made her stronger in spirit, made her more ill, more susceptible to impossible fancies and fantasies.

She fell ill from an inability of life to be as fascinating or as mysterious as art.

CHAPTER SEVENTY-ONE

The tribe was troubled by her artistic offering. They had expected from her a healing image. They had expected an image of beauty. They had expected a work potent with the greatness of her inheritance, her distinguished lineage, her freedom, her unique personality, and the myth from which her oddness gained resonance. They had hoped from her that which will be as an oracle from a new generation, a mirror into the broken rhythms of the times, some kind of work that would disentangle the enigmas that seemed to so imprison the tribe. They hoped, as the first daughter of the new generation, that with her new and uncontaminated eyes she would show them that which they could not see, the fate pressing on them, invisible but palpable as a tragic premonition.

The tribe sensed that the sculpture found in front of the shrine one morning was her work; centuries of artistic tradition had made them sensitive to the links between the work and its creator. And the tribe, collectively, could generally tell who had created what work, could read correlations between the work and its creator as those who could, intuitively, read the personality from the handwriting. To the deep mind of the tribe, the face of the creator was in the work they had created. And so when the sculpture of a dying prince was found in front of the shrine, first there was puzzlement, then a sense of mystery, then fascination, much discussion and many rumours, and then intuitive links were made. The hidden signature of a personality was deciphered in aspects of the work. Then a visible creator was slowly deduced. Then there was consternation.

It amounted almost to an outrage, an insult. It seemed such a wilful diversion, a distraction, an irrelevance, a conceit, a private, unnecessary indulgence in imagery and aesthetics. The work seemed without direction, without prophecy, without vision. It did not speak. It did not address the need of the times. It did not reflect the mood of the tribe. It did not relate to anything that anyone could care about. It seemed beautiful and sad and well-wrought just for the sake of it. The sculpture seemed an exercise in displaying personal artistic accomplishment, a display of genius unfolding, a dream of beauty and piety in wood. It did nothing for the people. It did not soothe. It did not guide. It was not deemed the voice of a new generation speaking with the authority of youth that can see with clear eyes that which the elders can no longer see or cannot see for all the cataracts of experience and knowledge, too much time accumulated in the eyes and in the heart.

The tribe felt that the work was not a new vision. It was not startling. It brought no new techniques that hinted even at the necessity of an altered way of seeing. It provoked deep outrage because it so disappointed the great hopes the tribe had placed in an image or work from the daughter of a new generation, an image or work that would begin their liberation from a destiny they could all feel but could not name.

Or maybe it was an outrage caused by the unknown fact that it had indeed shown an image of liberation but they knew it without knowing they did, and they wished to know what they felt more directly in their feelings, which the work bypassed, working as it did on their souls, the very foundation and bedrock of who and what they were, as a tribe and as individuals. But the outrage of the tribe was very real, and almost became violent.

At first they were enraged; then they took to mocking the work, and many other smaller and hastily executed sculptures were displayed which ridiculed the sculpture of a dying prince. Songs surfaced in drinking places, at the farms, in workshops, marketplaces and communal kitchens – songs mocking the irrelevant and inadequate sculpture. The ridicule was unprecedented and inexplicable. The numbers of those who sent in works mocking the sculpture was astonishing. Wise heads wondered if the tribe, encompassed by invisible tragic fears and paranoia, did not feel it necessary to find something to laugh at, to relieve itself of that weight of foreboding which it could not understand. Ridicule was therefore its way of dealing with incomprehension and bewilderment about a fate which seemed to oppress them, and from which they could see no escape. Like the hysterical laughter of one who knows they are doomed.

The ridicule passed, but the consternation remained. Till a work of art has been absorbed or understood in some way, consternation and some hostility towards it abides. The truth is that the tribe had expected from the maiden a clear healing image, one that would earth the tremors sounding in the land, or an image that would free them from the underlying paralysis creeping upon them from the universe. On to the maiden they had placed great hopes. On to her mystery they had projected great expectations. And because of the legend that was her birth they had awaited a great sign, a new direction, and nourished the belief that where the people are blind one of its blessed children will see, and be its eyes, till sight returns to all. Instead she had given them an ambiguous image of a dying prince. There were no princes in the tribe. What had this to do with them? they asked, infuriated.

The maiden was startled by the fury, the incomprehension, the ridicule, the destructive obsession, and the sudden need to tear down the reputation of her family that the work inspired and called forth from the tribe. She was terrified by their outrage, their threats of violence, their abuse. She was amazed at how quickly she became an outcast, shunned, denounced, her talent pronounced as worthless, her father's reputation seen as fraudulent. She was perplexed at the sudden desire to demonise her and her family, and at the same time she was aware of how much more fascinated and curious the tribe were about the mystery of her family. And all this had been touched off by the simple image of a dying prince, an image that she too had fallen prey to, and been seduced by; so she now was in a state of double distraction, caught between two absurdities, one public, the other private.

Through all this her father was silent, and carried on his mysterious journeys and his enigmatic artistic ventures with his usual remote tranquillity. It was as though nothing were happening. He not only seemed unconcerned, he didn't even register that anything was going on, or that there were furious reactions directed at him and his family. He went about his business as normal, as though he lived in a separate realm where the laws of the significance of events were radically different from that of the tribe, or the so-called real world. And this quality of his gave him an invincible air. And he was invincible. And this air aided his mystery, and tightened the powers of protection around him. And when his daughter came to him troubled about it all, he smiled at her gently and said, with mildly distracted eyes:

'The minute people are unjust to you they have already lost the fight. The moment they attack you they have lost the war. The moment they try to hurt you, to humiliate you, to bully you, to disgrace you, to destroy you, to invalidate you, that moment they have lost the truth. They have lost all protection. That moment they surrender all their power and authority to you, and they do not know it. Their end is certain. Their defeat becomes inevitable. The rest is time's doing. So carry on your business, be serene, follow your conscience, and have no fear. The laws that operate in the world are invisible laws, and they are greater than the force and powers of men and women. On these laws you can depend. Some people kill a little thing, and invite a mighty storm on their heads that wipes them out. Take pity on those who try to destroy you, and try to forgive them because what they call upon themselves is too terrible to withstand. It is better to endure their stupidity sometimes than to be part of that greater force which will wipe out a whole people, yourself, maybe, included. And sometimes it is better to fight, for their own good, to stop a greater and more implacable army of the invisible from doing your fighting for you. And so, for now, go about your business, and let's see what time brings, my daughter.'

And so, much comforted, the maiden went about her business, and took on an air of innocent invincibility, like certain flowers have, or certain babies, as if they know that they can be destroyed, and yet cannot be destroyed. As if they know some simple secret of eternity. And this makes them smile so guilelessly, without any enigma.

CHAPTER SEVENTY-TWO

The masters of the tribe, however, brooded, on the night of interpretations, on the meaning of that image of a dying prince.

It was the great night of interpretations, when they gathered, as a whole, to contemplate any enigmas that had come upon them. They tried to unravel any prophecies or utterances that had entered the tribe from the oracle or from any of the innumerable and unsuspected agencies of the oracle, be it the words of a madman, the strange accidental language of a child, a word overheard from the river, the last incoherent words of a dying man or woman, or a complete phrase made out in the noise of thunder, or the roar of a wild inspired animal in the forest.

They came together to tease out or intuit the hidden meanings of new parables, paradoxes, mysterious sayings, stories, legends, songs, or any works of art that perplexed or seemed to be without an easy revelation, demanding profound meditation and listening. Works of art that can only be appreciated by inspiration, by intuition. Appreciated, but not understood. For the masters knew that works of art could not be understood. And that the desire to understand was not only a fatal presumption, and an arrogance, but that it also got in the way of seeing or hearing or being inspired by the work of art at all. For (so they believed) once a work is thought to be understood, its magic is dimmed, not in the work, but in the person seeking to understand. And so such people become closed to its light, its power for continual inspiration and regeneration. The world is thus diminished; for a light, a source of light, has then been hidden by false understanding. The masters sought therefore only to be open to the work's secrets, its language, its inspiration, its guidance.

The night of interpretations was one of the great nights of the congregation of the masters. None of them missed that night, not even if ill. Those dying have been known to attend. It was considered greatly healing to be there on that night. It was considered a high honour to die among masters on a night of interpretations. For then one's death takes place in a most exalted state.

On this night the masters gathered to contemplate the image of a dying prince. They, who were wiser, had kept above the ridicule heaped on the maiden. And they had, in representative numbers and in significant ways, sent her words and signs of warmth, support and love to help her through. The masters knew that there could be no hasty response to a work that had come from one who was newly born in initiation, especially one so gifted by the legend of their birth and the uniqueness of their temperament, and by the way they seemed to attract both the negative and the positive in unusual combinations. The masters knew they had to look deeper into the work, and to wait, till the work spoke, or till the world gave it one of its unexpected, unsuspected meanings, one of an endless chain of illuminations.

On this night they waited for the work to speak, and it didn't. They pondered its meaning – and could find none. Or they found too many meanings that cancelled themselves out. Was the land a dying prince? Was their way in danger? Had they lost their way under the sun? Was their freedom or their conscience dying and they couldn't see it? Was the spirit of the tribe dying? Was their art perishing?

The masters were baffled and concerned. The more they probed, the more baffled and concerned they became.

But the work itself did not speak. The work itself said nothing.

CHAPTER SEVENTY-THREE

Meanwhile the suitors for the maiden's hand persisted in their obscure competitions for her attention and her favour. Meanwhile the Mamba continued his double campaign of rumours and seduction. Meanwhile the maiden grew more odd, more innocent, more distant, and more obsessed with the mystery of a dying prince. Soon she fell ill. It was thought that the subject of her sculpture was exercising undue magical influence on her, and that she was dying with the dying prince. She was falling under the spell of her own creation. Nothing could be done about this. And so it was felt that she had to go through that condition if she was going to emerge as a purer, greater artist of the tribe, an artist who is never affected by what they are creating, because they have developed, by much exposure and strengthening, a psychic protection against the forces of their own mind, a spiritual antibody to the laws of art as it affects the creator.

For the second time in her life, the maiden surrendered to death. She became so ill with her own mystery that she 'died' for seven days.

CHAPTER SEVENTY-FOUR

She did not die as such, but she did not live. She was profoundly ill and yet rich in health. She would not eat. She became lean, languid, and full of an ineluctable yearning. She longed so much for an impossible, indefinable condition, like those who yearn for some previous life of incommensurate beauty among the distant stars. She was lost to time and place, distracted from parents and suitors, and she spoke, in broken sentences, only of a love beyond reason, a love sweeter than madness, or was it a madness sweeter than love? And she slept most of the time, wherever sleep took hold of her. She slept like a calf. If sleep came upon her near the river, she would curl up on the floor and sleep. If sleep crept upon her at the marketplace, she would arrange herself on bales of cloth, or on heaps of oranges, or under the stalls of the fish-monger, and she would sleep a sleep of innocence, faintly enchanting, as if she had been put under a spell.

Sometimes, in her father's workshop, listening to the tale his hammer told as it beat upon the chisel that wrought a dream from the wisely resistant wood, sometimes she would curl up among the fabled masks and the images of beings unseen on earth and faces that were alive and real on distant galaxies, and she would drift off to sleep listening to tales told across the vast spaces. Tales that travel in no time through dreams, in the air, carried by waves of light that are everywhere.

She would sleep thus in her father's workshop and wake up at the marketplace; or she would fall asleep at the feet of the goddess or in the alcove of the shrine and would wake up in her mother's kitchen, her head on her mother's lap, listening to the rich mood of stories freighted over from ancient times, stories of sages that brought the lost secrets from a fabled land of their true ancestors that was now beneath the sea. Or she would fall asleep in her mother's lap, her hair being plaited, and she would wake up to find a bucket of water balanced on her head as she returned with her new companions from the river with water to wash and purify the goddess on the day of her celebrations.

And whenever she slept she dreamt of the dying prince, among other dreams; and he gazed at her, and never spoke.

CHAPTER SEVENTY-FIVE

And then one day, in her dream, the dying prince that was her sculpture sat up, and stared at her as usual, as if she were the first flower he had ever seen, as if he was trying to see the flower properly and understand what about it so moved him, to understand how it came to be, its purpose, the point of its beauty or mystery.

He stared at her as at a work of art that had no enigma and yet seemed beyond understanding. And she bore his gaze for a long time, waiting.

And then it occurred to her that it was she who must speak. After all, he was her creation. If she the creator did not speak how could she expect her creation to speak? Her speech would free her creation into speech. She had to invest her dream with life. For too long she had been mute, waiting for her dream, her art, to speak to her. What a failure in a creator! she suddenly thought. If the creation is to have something of the creator then its soul must be awoken, with love, with a touch, with an invocation, with the magic of the word.

She realised then that the prince, seated and staring at her so simply, regarded her as the grandest and most impenetrable mystery, a being beyond comprehension, so long as she was silent. She realised that not revealing herself, not establishing a kinship, not having a dialogue, meant that the prince would forever dwell in his own unfathomed condition. He would always be a creation without connection with anything else. He would always be unconnected with that which was the sole focus of his being, and his love. He would have nothing to say to her. And she would therefore always have this same dream. And so she would never know herself through the eyes of another. She would never know herself, or see any reflection of herself. She too would remain an unfathomed mystery to herself.

The maiden knew instantly that she needed the prince to speak, much more than the prince needed her. She realised that if the prince did not speak she would gradually cease to be. For her being depended on being known, and loved, by another, by herself in another.

Then the maiden understood the stare of the prince. He was looking at her with complete love, complete adoration, a love without beginning or end, a love greater than humanity, a pure love; but it was a love that was without knowledge, without understanding. It was a love without mystery. A love too pure for a creator. For it was a love without life, without suffering, without tears, without blood, without pain, without history. It was a love without time, a love that had been found in perfection, a love without a story, without a journey, without complications. It was not a love arrived at, born into, a perplexing love. And so it was a love without self-knowledge. In fact, it was a love that did not know itself, a love that did not know what love is. It was a love that had not grown, had not evolved, had not lost its way, had not stumbled and dwelt in the dark.

It was a love that did not know what it was like to live without love, how hellish, barren, deadly, dry, forlorn, how miserable, cold, lonely, empty, useless, bitter, agonising, tormenting, twisted, and how ugly it was to be and live without love.

It was a love that did not know the ecstasy of one who finally comes to know, after all the darkness, what it really means to love, to have love in the heart.

It was a love like a pure thing that had not lived.

That was the gaze that the maiden saw in the eyes of the prince. And she knew that the purity of that love had to be broken if the prince was ever going to be able to speak, to be free, and to love her, not as a creation, but as a free living being, out of his own choice, his own affinity, his own inspiration, his own necessity. The prince must be free to love her as himself. And so he must be awoken from his enchantment, from the eternal spell of his natural adoration for the maiden, his creator.

And so the maiden spoke to the silent dying prince that was her sculpture, her dream; and she was shocked and profoundly moved, to a state beyond tears, when the prince replied, naturally, speaking back to her in complete freedom and complete confidence in himself, in a voice which she already knew, a voice which she recognised, and loved, and revered, a deep strange magical voice which had come to her from a place older than dreams.

'Who are you?' she asked.

'I am that which was and now am.'

'What is your name?'

'My name is written in your tears.'

'Why are you dying?'

'Because I am not living.'

'Why are you not living?'

'Because I don't know what love is.'

'Do you know what love is now?'

'Yes.'

'What is love?'

'Love is life, to live.'

'You talk back and forth.'

'It is back and forth.'

'Why are you a prince?'

'Because I am the son of a king.'

'Who is the king?'

'The king is the king.'

'What is the king a king of?'

'The king is the king of a kingdom.'

The maiden paused and stared thoughtfully at the prince. The prince gazed back at her with pure, open, smiling eyes.

'Is it a kingdom of heaven or of earth?'

'I don't know the difference.'

'Am I of this kingdom?'

'Yes.'

'How can I be? I made you.'

'Did you make me, or did you discover me?'

'What's the difference?'

'Sometimes we make what we discover. Sometimes we discover what we make.'

For the first time the maiden was perplexed.

Then she had an odd notion.

'Am I dying too?'

'You can only make what you are.'

'So I am dying?'

'Maybe.'

'Why am I dying?'

'For the same reason I have not been living.'

The maiden was silent. In truth she was astonished.

It was like catching a glimpse of herself in the clear mirror of a lake and finding that she did not look at all like what she thought she looked like. It was a disquieting feeling. She was seeing a self quite different from what she thought. This displaced and shocked her. She did not know what to say. This was going to take her a long time to get used to. That was when it occurred to her that she must delay her life. To delay it till she knew who she was. To delay it till she gained some wisdom, and self-knowledge. So that she could learn how to really live.

She was not going to make any hasty decisions. She was going to take life a little slowly. Take time to learn.

The dying prince was mute again, staring at her with candour and simplicity.

And she found stillness in the depth of her dream.

CHAPTER SEVENTY-SIX

Afterwards she began her slow self-recovery. She slept less, and went about more. She became more silent, more calm, more humble, less sure. Less unpredictable.

She appeared to be listening all the time. She appeared to be listening to everything, as if whatever life had to tell her would be told her silently, between the sound of things, in the least expected ways.

She became attentive, too attentive, as attentive and as aware as she had previously been distracted and unaware. But too much attentiveness is akin to too much distraction, just as too much looking leads to too little seeing. She missed as much now as previously. There was much she didn't see because she was trying to see, or thought she saw. She wore herself out with her new intensity. As she was unable to sustain it long, it became a kind of coiled passivity, with a waiting spirit inside her. Aware and waiting for life to teach her.

Her father regarded all these changes with a smile in his mind. Her mother fretted because she knew what was happening to her daughter. Knowledge did not make her tranquil about it.

'We are built this way,' she said to her husband. 'To worry even when we know.'

The suitors were driven to frenzies by the maiden's unstated programme of delay. One by one they fell away. Till there were only six suitors left, even.

CHAPTER SEVENTY-SEVEN

Time passed slowly, as in dreams. The river imperceptibly changed its course. The tribe imperceptibly changed its ways, lost its centre. People died and were born. Forebodings quietly took form, and no one noticed. The gods died silently, and no one saw it happen. The world encroached on the dreams of the land, and no one saw the shadows in the distance, approaching like the evening. Lost in its dream, the land was lost in its dream. In its rituals, ways, cruelties, abominations. In its superstitions. Lost in its ancient ways, the land was lost in its ancient slumber. Its dreams, its power, its wickedness. Deep in itself, the land was lost, and did not hear the music of the world outside, or its speech. Lost in its magic, its enchantments, its ways. And so time passed slowly, as in a dream where things are changing, and the dreamer is unaware, and yet aware, awake and yet asleep, seeing what is coming in prophecies and yet blind to what it sees, deaf to its own prophecies as if cursed not to know that it is cursed, or blessed not to know that it is blessed.

And so time drifted slowly down the dreaming way. And many things were forgotten, even while they lived. The image of a dying prince was forgotten. The scandals were forgotten. The unease was forgotten, because it got worse, and therefore even more imperceptible. The tremors of art were forgotten. Rumours were forgotten. Suitors were forgotten. Purpose was forgotten. The way was forgotten. The masters were being slowly forgotten, till they became a rumour of conspiracies, or of a sinister secret society. The shrine was being forgotten. And all this in the space of a dream, in no time at all, or all the time it takes for a people to be lost, to change, and then, one day, inexplicably, to vanish off the face of the earth, as if they never existed, or as if they had been taken away, as a whole, and repositioned in another place, another realm, another constellation in the universe.

But while all this happened in their lives, while they were forgetting, and not knowing it, something unusual came to pass.

CHAPTER SEVENTY-EIGHT

One day, on a clear day in which nothing unusual happened, this happened. Mysterious laughter was heard in the land. It was a great, incommensurable laughter, inexplicable, booming, deep, happy, sad, sublime, light, cheerful, mocking, ironic, clear, lucid, sane, wise laughter. And all of the tribe heard it in their dreams. They heard it fleetingly in their work when they were most absorbed in what they were doing. They heard it in their passionate moments. They heard it in their silences. The masters heard it in their communion. The river and the birds and the trees heard it. The children and babies and the dying heard this laughter with especial clarity. And the deaf and dumb and blind and crippled and the sick heard it more clearly than most. The dying heard it with mysterious poignancy which aided their peaceful deaths. The criminals heard it and shuddered deliciously. The evil ones heard it and trembled. The Mamba heard it and felt a chill come over him that presaged the dissolution of his powers. The suitors heard it and wondered. The shrine heard it and the unknown priestess within echoed the laughter in vibrancies that shook the foundations of the tribe. The maiden heard it and fell into a dream. Her father heard it and had the inspiration to create one final work of sculpture, after which he would sculpt no more. Her mother heard it and was visited with a prophecy concerning the future of the race. They all, in their different ways, heard this almost celestial laughter; and they never stopped hearing it, for it pervaded the land and became a permanent part of the air and the renewal of things. And long after their world came to an end, the laughter remained, as it does till this day, and all the days to come.

Book Three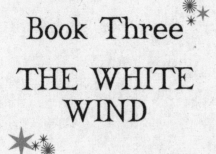
THE WHITE WIND

CHAPTER ONE

Many are the wonders to be lived, in a flash, without knowing it, in the book of life among the stars. Many are the horrors deprived of their horror, the evils deprived of their sting, the deaths deprived of their tragedies. Many are the lies stripped of their power, the sufferings stripped of their excesses, the agonies drained of their mortal pain beyond endurance. Many are the loves that haunt still, and the betrayals that shock still, and the stupidities of men and women in the blind proud empty vanities of their days and nights, all stripped of that which made them so absurd or so banal. Many are the great events drained of all wonder, the wars that seemed so significant now seen as moments on an unreal stage where people died and crawled in blood as in a vast panoramic dream. Many are the moments unnoticed, the child gazing at invisible forms and holding converse with angels, the dead drifting past the love-making forms of the living, the stars seen in spangles through gaps in the leaves of a tree, young girls brimming with the ambiguous happiness of life, drummers lost in the wild joys of syncopation, passionate lovers who destroy their love through their fear of loving, moments in dust, when dust dreamt itself in mortal forms and lived adventures in the dim mirror of illusions, with an immortal light shining within, unseen . . .

Many are the lives that connect and cross and speak to one another across the stars and the vast spaces of the universe, connecting and not knowing it. Many are those who think that they are alone when in fact they live in constant speech with many others in remote realms, in their dreams and their waking moments in the depth of their spirits where time and space and matter do not cage the soul. Many are those who do not see the wonder of things in the blind realm of mortality. All this, and more, to be lived, in ways sublime and beyond the brain's knowing, in the open book of life in the magic spaces among the stars . . .

CHAPTER TWO

During that time, in the kingdom so large that it did not know its own parts, and many of its parts did not know they belonged to a kingdom, during that time a mysterious plague was abroad in the land.

The kingdom was sprawling and vast and within it were many sub-kingdoms. In fact the kingdom was so extensive that it did not know itself. And the king knew it only through the cartography of dreams, of his dreams. He dreamt all the corners and obscure places of the kingdom and saw the great variety of the people, the vast forests, the mighty rivers, the innumerable creeks, the uncountable hills and valleys, the multiplicity of traditions and the incredible number of languages spoken. He saw them all in dreams, and ruled this vast unruly undivided yet much divided kingdom through the agency of dreams. There was no other way. Terrestrially he had chiefs, emissaries, deputies, spies, messengers, sub-rulers who travelled the vast lands, carrying laws, decrees, legislations, edicts, proclamations, instructions, dictates. He had an extensive hierarchy of chiefs and sub-kings who ruled the lesser kingdom in his name and spirit. But to rule them all by land, messages, edicts sent by messengers, courtiers and chiefs was insufficient. Often weeks passed before messages sent were received and the messages were often out of date by the time they arrived. Laws were no longer valid by the time they were made and received. Time devoured the possibilities of ruling the immense kingdom; and space mocked the reforms, changes, edicts sent forth; space distorted them on arrival. The only thing that time and space could not affect or distort, but would aid and enhance, was the way of ruling through dreams, through thought. The king sent forth his laws at night, on the wings of sleep; and all over the kingdom officials, chiefs and sub-kings woke up at dawn knowing what to do, and they enacted the laws as if they were their own ideas.

And so dreams were laden with instructions, urgent laws; the night trafficked in edicts, notions, improvements, reforms, reproaches, promotions, reprimands, praise, suggestions, corrections, elaborations and signs. The kingdom was busiest at night, when the people slept. Then the king, sending off his round of laws, would visit the sleeping forms of his subjects, listen to their dreams, and question them about their needs and fears. So extensively did he speak to and listen to his subjects thus, that he was as thoroughly involved in their lives as though he were one of them; and they felt this to be so, that he was one of them, and that he knew their hearts and they knew his heart, though they didn't know they did, but felt it intimately. So profoundly did the king listen to his courtiers, the elders, the criminals, the butchers, the market women, the traitors, the soldiers, the orphans, the slaves, the servants, the abandoned, the hungry, the rich, the heart-broken that he knew the hopes, the anger, the desires of the people more sensitively than if they had come to him in person and he had granted them an audience . . . But he did it through dreams, he listened to them and queried them and he paid attention to them in their dreams, and he tended to them in dreams too, sending them solace and guidance, advice and suggestions, protection and blessings, and often dispensing powerful spells and incantations into their inner worlds, to strengthen them in their daily lives and to make sure they didn't feel abandoned; and so that they would know that their king, though far from them, was also closest to them, and that he never slept, but kept their needs always in mind, and always worked for their good in a thousand ways that they never suspected, be they good or bad, equally, as though they were all his children, which they all were, as they belonged to his vast kingdom without a name . . .

The king therefore seemed to rule without ruling. And there were many who had no idea that they had a king, had no idea what a king was, or who. There were many to whom the king existed as a dim rumour, a murmur, a figure made up from so many stories, a figure who dwelt on a mountaintop, or deep at the bottom of the sea, or in an extensive mysterious cave; or as a persona who sometimes came to the village in disguise, an old man with a strange beard or an old woman with youthful limbs, or a child with a golden cane, or a beautiful young girl no one had ever seen before, or an animal that is white and covered in light, or as the wind, or as a cloud, or as the night itself, and sometimes as the sun.

Many were those who never thought about their king, but worked very hard at the forge or in the farms, in their labours, from dawn to dusk. Many were those who lived lives that didn't seem like lives, but one long toil and drudgery, like beasts, for no purpose, save to feed their families and drink under the moon and sleep without resting and wake without pausing. But the king knew them all intimately, from their dreams, knew their deepest truths.

Many were those who did not think the king existed, but acknowledged their local chiefs, the elders of their clans and the figures of authority of their villages, their lands.

The king therefore seemed absent in the kingdom when he was most present. But his absence meant he could know them better. His absence meant he left them in freedom, to be how they best can be. He left them free to be able to choose how they wanted to be.

The only way the king was known by those who could know these things in the kingdom was by his mysterious laughter, which was heard everywhere that solace was needed. By this laughter all things were connected, and corrected, answered, acknowledged, balanced, embraced, and touched with an enchantment beyond understanding.

The only other way the king was known was by the silent figure in their dreams, the one who is always there in their dreams, taking part and not taking part, observing and never observed, and who sometimes intervenes to make a most interesting suggestion which is nearly always forgotten because listening has not always been learned . . . But then the next night, in the next dream, that silent figure would be there again, humble, unknown, and it would be the king, at his ways again, paying attention in the deepest places, to the most important or trivial things in the spirit of his people, without sleeping . . .

CHAPTER THREE

Many things happened in the kingdom that were baffling. During that time, for example, a strange plague was abroad in the land. At first it appeared in the form of a new wind that blew over from across the great seas. It was a cold white wind and wherever it blew it created vacant spaces. The wind was at first a beautiful wind, bringing melodies and fragrances and pleasant dreams. At first it was a soothing wind that brought hints of new visions of the world and the heavens. It seemed to clear the sky, and stars that had always been in the heavens were seen more clearly for the first time. The wind was at first cleansing and fresh and bracing and it cooled the humid air of the sun-loved land. The white wind brought coolness to the skin and mind, and a window into new ways of being and feeling, and a lovely hint of a wider world than suspected, a horizon where dreams of a different sort travelled on the white wind to enrich the dreams of the land. At first the white wind was a thing of wonder, a phenomenon strange and delightful to behold. It swept through the land, changing the appearance of things, and brought a new light to the bright light of the day and a new light to the brilliant darkness of the night.

Then, imperceptibly, the nature of the white wind changed. It began to erase that which it passed over, or passed through. The white wind began to erase hills and valleys, it erased the memories of people, it erased villages and towns, forests and gold mines and rivers and animals and flowers and whole portions of land. Slowly, mysteriously, things began to disappear. The weather changed. The seasons were altered. Songs began to vanish. Artworks from the tribes evaporated into the white wind. Then, most strangely of all, the gods began, one by one, to be erased from the enduring pantheon of the kingdom. No one noticed this momentous silence of an event for a long time. And the silence of the gods was taken as a sign of tranquillity, of good fortune, of harmony and plenitude in the land. And so no one noticed when the gods began to vanish from the visible and invisible pantheons, erased by the white wind. It was impossible to tell which of the gods went first, which god vanished first. Those who can see that which they didn't see at the time say they remembered first that a great malaise, a profound unease came amongst the people, making them sleepy, in-turned, divisive, slow, intensified in superstitions and sluggish in their reading of signs.

Some say that the first thing they were aware of was a strange new failure and unwillingness to decipher the signs and omens that multiplied in the land. The people lost the will or the desire to interpret their dreams, to listen to the oracles, to listen to their prophets, or to pay attention to the images that were born in the inspired dreams of their artists. The people no longer listened and no longer interpreted. This should have been noticed at the time, for the land was always rich in significations, in signs and wonders, in omens, in warnings, in hints and messages from the stars, the gods and the ancestors. And with the advent of the white wind blowing from across the seas an unsuspected lassitude of the mind came among the people, as if the wind erased, gently and seductively, their will to be aware, and to interpret; inducing a sleepwalking quality into a land that so loved the interpretation of things. And so it seems that the first to vanish or be erased from the pantheon by the white wind was the god of interpretation.

Such an important and oddly decentred god, never fully noticed at the best of times, silently vanishes, and no one notices. Then again, according to those who can see long after the event what they did not see at the time, there followed the god of questions. For, after the sleepiness and the malaise that descended on the land, the people, who were as much prone to contestation as to silence, stopped asking questions of things.

They stopped asking why and when and who-it-is-for and why-is-this-so; and they just accepted the reality they saw as the world as it should be. They accepted what they saw. They accepted what was there. They accepted and believed what they were told. This was a new kind of sleep. It was a sleep of the mind. A sleep brought on when the white wind, in its sweetness, its enchantments, seduced the senses and lulled the spirit of the people into dozing. Then the god of questions vanished from the pantheon, and no one asked why, or how, or what it meant.

Then followed the god of harmony . . . for there had always been battles between tribes and villages and clans and families, there had always been discord and enmities, but these elements existed in harmony within the kingdom, the way different colours and energies exist in nature, or contending animals coexist in a forest. Beneath the differences were harmonies, even if it was the harmony of people maintaining their different space. Then, with the advent of the white wind the people saw one another differently; for the white wind cleared the air of obscurities that make a people shrouded in mystery, a mystery that is respected. Suddenly, they all saw one another too well. Mystery was dispelled. Suspicion took its place; then fear, then rumours, then misinterpretations, then open antagonisms, and then were created the conditions for future wars too vile to contemplate. And so it was that the god of harmony, normally invisible at the best of times, was erased by the white wind from the great pantheon of the land.

After that the rest was easy. The god of memory was forgotten, and vanished. The god of mysteries was laid bare, and turned into dust. The god of love was defiled and passed into the air. The god of thunder became a murmur. The god of sacrifice perished at the altar of change. All the mother gods and the goddesses of women fell into silence, and became cults practised in hiding, in lowly conditions. And even the great god, the father god, succumbed to the etiolations of the white wind, and proved the easiest to efface, on account of his great seriousness. The white wind made him seem ridiculous and unlikely and soon no one believed in him. And when the people stopped believing in the father god he seemed useless and without effect and then was forgotten, and became only the shadow of a memory, his form occupied by another notion that came in the wake of the white wind.

The people were to pay a great price for the loss of their gods, for allowing their gods to perish and disappear from the pantheon. They were to pay a terrible price indeed, in the fullness of time. And they would never know that the suffering they would endure in the time to come was because of the loss of their gods. They would never make the connection, because they would become a different people, a changed people. And they could never be the people they were again. They had lost their gods for ever. They could not go back again. They could not resurrect that which they had allowed to die. They became a people without their own gods. In time they would find other ways to the same energy of the pantheon, their own new and future ways. But till then great confusion and plagues and suffering and chaos and all the troubles of a people who have lost their way will come upon them. Many tribes will vanish. Many languages will fall silent for ever. Many secrets of the people will be lost. Many clans, many little nations, many peoples will perish and die out and disappear from the face of the earth. When gods die many great things in a people die with them.

And then a something greater than all the gods reveals itself. And, in the cycle of things, greatness returns to the people.

CHAPTER FOUR

But for a long time the only god not effaced by the white wind was the trickster god, the god of paradox, transformations, illusions, chaos, change and humour; a god tinged with an element of danger, of the sinister. And this god was not effaced because he had made sure he was both in and not in the pantheon. He was ineffaceable because he had no face. He had long escaped the security of the pantheon, had long freed himself from the form of the pantheon, and become without form. This trickster god had found it more congenial to seep into life, into the life of humanity, into the world, into reality, into the ever-changing conditions of things.

Change was his home. The trickster god was at home, whatever the dispensation. He had become a part of life and of change itself. The people never understood, or saw, or appreciated, or worshipped the trickster god. He was too strange and intangible and nebulous for them to grasp. The trickster god liked this. Being worshipped as such was not his thing. He wanted to have sublime and unpredictable and uninterpretable effects. He was a high agent of the divine. He was a warrior of simplicity itself, a sublime puzzler; and everything he did, with its flashes of celestial danger, of a paradox and riddling that almost drives people mad, was designed to bring the mind of the people to the very edge of things, to the brink of the deadly abyss of the mind, and to push them over, that they might fall into an intolerable white emptiness in which illumination might flash awake in the spirit of a people who are so deeply asleep to the highest things.

The trickster god makes all thing inside out, makes all things go into reverse, to obverse, to perverse, in combinations of all, to trick and fool the intelligence, to awaken that which is greater than reason, but which reason prevents from being awoken, because it thinks it knows, when it can't.

The trickster god wakens, by his fiendish ways, that which knows within, that which knows all.

The trickster god loved the white wind. The wind brought the perfect conditions for his reign and his mischievous flowering.

There is no telling when, and how, in what atrocious circumstances that aren't what they seem, or in what wonderful moment that conceals the seeds of tragedy, there is no telling when and how the trickster god is working. Perhaps even now he is working with these words on your mind . . .

CHAPTER FIVE

The white wind was the first sign of the plague that came upon the land. The white wind was part of the plague. For first the gods began to vanish, then trees, philosophies and traditions; and then it became most noticeable when healthy young men and women began to disappear. It was a great mystery, a sinister mystery. The young men suddenly began to vanish. Whole villages lost their young. No one knew how. There were no wars that devoured them. But there were tales of people being lured away by spirits; but no one knew where they were lured to. Their bodies were never found. Those tales, presenting an intolerable mystery, did not satisfy . . .

CHAPTER SIX

Soon it was rumoured everywhere that white spirits had come into the kingdom and bought and kidnapped the strongest and bravest of the land and carried them off in great ships to distant places or to the bottom of the sea. There was much talk of vast farms where the missing young of the land worked from dawn till dusk in captivity to the white spirits at the bottom of the sea. But only children believed these tales.

The plague of spirits was a great mystery and brought great fear to the land. No one had seen these white spirits. To see them was to be lost, was to be captured by them. Those who saw them were already caught. Only a few isolated seers, sages and masters in the kingdom, only the occasional child, only the odd strangely gifted girl could see them in dreams and spoke out of what they were doing. In their different communities they spoke of chains of iron; they spoke of instruments that spat out fire and death; they spoke of long lines of young men and women of the land being flogged and gagged; they spoke of the chained men and women, of the chains binding their hands and ankles; they spoke of how they were dragged away by the white spirits; they spoke of bleeding hands and ankles, and the trail of blood they left behind as they were dragged off to ships in which they vanished; they spoke of trails of blood that ended at the sea.

These were dreadful rumours and visions indeed; so fantastical were these rumours that no one believed them. No one believed that even evil spirits would be so wicked to human beings. People therefore dismissed the visions as rumours that were being used to hide some greater problem.

The king held several important meetings of the elders to discuss this terrible plague; and all were baffled. During these sessions the king listened, and said nothing. At night, while these fears grew wilder, and the plague grew fatter, the mysterious laughter of the king could be heard throughout the kingdom.

But the disappearance of the young continued, till the land began to be quite empty of healthy young men and women. In many places the ones who survived were only the lucky ones, or the scrawny ones, or the sons and daughters of chiefs, kings and the powerful; or only those under the protection of powerful elders, or those who belonged to tribes that lived far away from the popular routes and centres, those who lived in the deep inlands, the weird hinterlands, protected by murky creeks and vile insects and legions of mosquitoes. Only those survived who were hidden from the famous coasts and ports, where the white spirits did the best of their inhuman business in draining the kingdom of its young, of its future hope, the pride and glory of the land, the strong, the brave, the criminal, the war-like, the gifted ones of the happy land.

CHAPTER SEVEN

Meanwhile the prince remained, hovering, in the land of death. He had no idea of the effect his dying had on the people. He didn't hear them, or see them, for he dwelt in the grey land between dying and living.

While he lay there, in his room, with courtiers and handmaidens and the women of the palace in great mourning all about him; while he lay there, on his bed, unmoving for several days, believed dead, and yet with the softness and the faintest fragrance of a smile on his face, the crowds that had gathered to pray for his recovery had grown so large that many feared that the village wouldn't be able to support their vast numbers.

They kept on pouring in, from all over the land, and from distant lands, and from distant realms. Never before had a prince had so great an effect on the hearts of a people. Emissaries of grief were sent from remote kingdoms of the continent, and from remote kingdoms across the world. The fame of this prince who was dying became a thing unto itself; and those who had no idea who he was, or what his kingdom was, or the name or the place, were moved by the very thought of this gentle prince, loved by all, who was dying, and who attracted such great crowds. More people came to the village and made extraordinary pilgrimages there just because others did. And women and girls and hardened men and fierce warriors who heard of this astonishing mass of people travelling to keep vigil for the dying prince burst into tears and couldn't stop themselves weeping for the sheer sweet sorrow of this gentle death taking place in the middle of their lives.

So great and famous was the phenomenon that long after its time people referred to anything that happened during that period as 'that which took place during the great gathering for the dying prince'. And musicians and bards composed poignant elegies and epics and haunting melodies of that mysterious event, that inexplicable moment in the story of the land.

There are people who, though they seem to have accomplished nothing visible in the world, manage, by their fate, to move the hearts of millions for reasons far beyond reason itself. So it was with the prince. His dying brought great shivers of grief to all peoples, to those who heard about it and even to those who didn't. For it was widely reported that during that time never were people more prone to spontaneous weeping, to sudden accesses of inexplicable sorrow and shakings and tremblings of heart. Such an overpowering sensitivity to grief and suffering swept over the land, and the force of an irrational sadness dwelt in most hearts for reasons they couldn't explain.

During that time there were many beautiful poems composed, and the loveliest and saddest music that the land came to be famous for was created; and a strange flowering of art, of sculpture, of rock and cave paintings, of architecture, of stories and legends sprouted all over the land, born from the current of a sweetening grief that circulated among the dreams of the people like the fragrant breezes of a hidden paradise.

In the midst of all this the prince dwelt in the land of death.

And in silence his father, the king, would sit by his side, at night; and in silence he would laugh into all the realms of his kingdom.

CHAPTER EIGHT

Then one day a soothsayer made his way through the vast crowds to the palace and demanded to be presented to the king. After much delay and many lengthy interviews with courtiers he finally was granted an audience. And to the king he said:

'Your son is dying because of all the evils in the land. Only love can save him.'

The king laughed.

'You think there is no love in the kingdom?'

Rocked by the powerful laughter of the king, the soothsayer fell silent, chastened.

'That is not what I meant, your majesty,' he said.

And then he went on to tell the king that the only thing that could save his son is if they found the maiden of the tribe of gold-makers, the tribe of bronze-casters, the forgotten tribe of artists.

'How do you know this?' asked the king.

'I was directed to tell you this in a dream.'

'Who told you in your dream?'

'You told me in my dream,' said the soothsayer.

'Me?'

'Yes, you, the king.'

The king stared deeply into the bold intimidated eyes of the soothsayer.

'Did I tell you anything else?'

'That's all you told me, your majesty.'

The king thanked the brave soothsayer, weighed him down with many gifts, and gave him a horse to bear him back to his home.

Then the king sent out emissaries all over the kingdom to find the tribe of artists. They travelled the length and breadth of the land. They went deep into the interior, to villages near shallow creeks, to the remotest communities, to peoples who lived on the hillsides, among the ritual caves. They went to the water people, to the desert people, to the savannah people, and to the people of the towns and villages. The emissaries went to the people of the masquerades, to the wandering tribes and shepherds, and to those who lived on the caravan routes and those who travelled extensively because they bought and traded goods throughout the land. But they could not find the people they sought. No one could find the tribe of artists. No one knew where they were, or who they were. The strangest thing was that all over the land, amongst most peoples, the most beautiful artefacts, medals, sculptures, shields and bronze works and golden jewels could be found and when the people were asked how they got them they said the objects came from the tribe of artists. They were objects bought in exchange for goods, services, food, clothes, or they were commissioned. But they couldn't say how, or where, or when. The objects had just mysteriously appeared in their lives when they were needed.

All this was very puzzling. And it began to appear as if the tribe of artists had designed their lives so they wouldn't be found. They would be present, they would create and share their work and enrich the life of the land but they would be invisible. They would be unseen. They would dwell as if in a separate realm.

The king sent messengers and servants everywhere and promised rich rewards for anyone who could find the tribe of artists. And the servants and messengers scattered all over the kingdom, and put out word of important commissions for works of art, and sent out announcements of competitions to find the best artists in the land. And many beautiful works were commissioned and executed, and many came forth and entered the competitions, but no one came from the tribe of artists. They remained as elusive as ever.

It began to seem as if they didn't exist, and had never existed. They seemed a rumour, an invention. It was as if the tribe of artists were a dream, a legend that the land needed and invented to explain its own creativity; or as if the tribe of artists were one of the legends, one of the many dreams of a vanished people in the kingdom, a people who had ceased to exist, a people who had disappeared and evaporated into the moods and stories of the land, a people who once were, but are no more. A people who live only in dreams.

News of the quest for this mysterious tribe filtered through to the gathered crowds, and they lived in hope that the tribe would be found so that the prince could be restored to life and health. No one from the vast crowds had ever heard of or known anything about the tribe of artists. But with the news of the quest the people hoped they would be found. So it was with great sadness that the people received the news that they could not be found and, worse, that the tribe did not exist. It was a sadness that brought a cruel poignancy to their grief and their vigil, and filled them with a hopelessness they never had before.

Their hopelessness contaminated the air of the village and the palace. It engulfed the atmosphere with an intolerable gloom. The gloom was so dense, so without music, or joy, or buoyancy, that it began to spread a sort of pestilence and many of the gathered crowds fell ill and died, and cattle died, and people of the village came down with a malaise and a deathly lethargy of spirit. A dreadful melancholy drifted about everywhere. The crops drooped. The children became pale and stopped laughing. And no birds were seen in the air. A great joylessness reigned. The crowds, in their pestilential malaise and gloom, were becoming fatal to the atmosphere and to the village and the palace. And all because the tribe of artists could not be found, and did not exist.

However when this fact was told to the king, it was reported that he merely laughed, hard and long, as if it were the strangest joke he had heard in a long time.

CHAPTER NINE

But they kept on pouring in, men and women, boys and girls who had run away from their homes just to be part of the single most wonderful and the saddest phenomenon taking place in their lifetime.

They kept pouring in, spirits and inexplicable beings, animals on leashes, elephants, dogs, cats, goats, horses, camels, donkeys; they came in all forms, and they descended on the village, and nearly destroyed it with their grief, their sorrow, and their desire to be together in so mysterious a moment of shared sympathy.

The fame of the dying prince threatened the very life of the village. The entire environs were overrun. The farms were occupied. The villagers soon found themselves hemmed in by the crush of these pilgrims and visitors, these crowds of well-wishers. The villagers soon found themselves unable to function. The kingdom slowly ground to a halt; its activities began to fall silent; too many people had abandoned their posts to come and express their sorrow, as at a great shrine.

The elders called emergency meetings and eventually put it to the king that the people must be turned away, or the kingdom would be destroyed by this unnatural sorrow. They maintained that the crowds must be sent back to their homes, and that life should return to normal in all spheres of the kingdom. They suggested that the people should be told a fiction: that the prince was recovering and desired them all to return to their lives; that all the healers had made it clear this was the best way they could help the prince get better, otherwise he would die. This cold fiction, softened somewhat by elaborate praise and gratitude for their devotion and love, was the formula proposed for getting people back to their homes, their ordinary lives. The idea was to make their returning home the true sacrifice that could help their dying prince.

The king listened to the elders dreamily. Apart from listening he did nothing. The elders discerned a silent laughter in his response, and took it as their mandate to act.

The elders made the necessary public announcements; they sent out respected figures to mingle with the people and spread the word; they made known the invented wishes of the prince.

The people did not believe the elders, nor did they trust the announcements, nor were they seduced by the expressed praise or gratitude. But in their own discussions, the people arrived at the same conclusion. They realised that they were having a deleterious effect on the village, and that they might be bringing the life of the kingdom to a halt. They knew they had to return to their normal lives. The time of enchanted sorrowing was over. The magic moment of a shared universal sadness was gone.

They desired, however, to know the true condition of the prince; and the elders, through their intermediaries, promised the most extensive announcements of the prince's health as it became known to them.

Slowly, unwillingly, the crowds dispersed. Most of them returned to their homes. Many of them didn't, and founded new villages and towns near the village of the dying prince. These were enclaves of outcasts, those who longed for escape, for new beginnings, those who had never felt at home in their homes.

Unwillingly they all dispersed. They were not the same people that they had been. Sweet sorrowing had changed them. Life in the kingdom was never the same again. It was as though a rocky hillside had been sprinkled with marigolds and mayflowers.

And so the prince, who lay in silence, never knew the effect that his dying had on the world. He remained innocent of his own fame and without any knowledge of the transformation that his condition effected in the people.

CHAPTER TEN

Then on a day without a name, on a day outside time, the prince in his dying dreamt about the maiden. She came to him, and said:

'Why are you dying?'

'Because of all the evils in the kingdom,' he said.

'What will make you better again?'

'If all the evils go away.'

'Will you take the evils away?' she asked him in a gentle voice.

'Yes,' he replied.

'Will you suffer the evils in yourself, to cleanse the kingdom?'

'Yes.'

'It shall be so. You shall be well again.'

'But there is one more reason why I am ill,' he said.

'What?' she asked.

'Because of you. Because I am in love with you. And I want to see you again. I am dying also because I love you and I can't see you.'

'To see me again your suffering will be great, and your happiness will be greater. For I am your destiny.'

'What must I do?'

'What you must do.'

'Is that all?' he asked, surprised.

'Yes. And whatever befalls you, never forget who you are and all will be well with you and the kingdom.'

'Who am I?'

'You are a simple man. You are loved. You are the son of a king who laughs. You are a prince.'

'And who are you?'

'I am your greatest love, and your destiny, and you are mine.'

'Will we be happy together?'

'In life and for eternity.'

'Then I am recovered. I am well. I am no longer ill. I take the evils unto myself, and I will earn you as my destiny.'

'Do what you must do. Even if it seems wrong. It will be well. For you are guided, my love, my prince.'

And then the maiden was gone from his dream. In the morning he miraculously recovered from death and opened his eyes. He lay there on his bed, feeling as though his life had altered course, as though someone had switched round his life, or given him a different consciousness, a different mind.

He felt as though he were someone other than he was, that another higher oddly illuminated being had been implanted in his old self. He felt more alive and more awake and more aware than he had ever felt in his life. The new illumination in his head was almost unbearable. The new clarity of his consciousness was almost intolerable. So clear and sharp and fresh was his mind that he simply didn't know what to do with himself. It was a clarity, an aliveness, that bordered on madness. He felt he would go mad for the sheer brilliance and limpidity of his new consciousness following his recovery from death.

Whatever he gazed upon was clear to him. Whatever he thought about was wholly transparent to him. He had in him a new kind of light that pierced everything. And all life, all conundrums, all the difficulties, all the problems became clear and simple. And he saw now quite clearly the purpose behind everything. He saw the meaning in all things. And as open to him was the mystery of the wall he gazed at and the farthest star and all the space that wasn't space that was in between. He seemed to understand all, to know all things, not because he knew them, but because of this substituted consciousness in him that was a pure light that knew all things simply and without words.

He lay there, in his chamber, on his bed, where he had gone from the world for a long time; and he simply lay with his eyes open and his mind in perfect tranquillity, roaming realms of wonder, with a gentle smile on his face, a smile that would now always be a permanent part of his face, along with a knowing, aware twinkle in his eye, even in the greatest suffering.

And his father, the king, came into the chamber and found his son awake, awakened, and quite new, like a newborn thing, with a smile on his face as if he had achieved some unexpected feat without knowing how; and the king was very happy. The king was so happy that he declared there be a feast that should last seven days throughout the whole kingdom. There was great joy and feasting throughout the land and happiness swept through the kingdom at the news that the prince had been restored to life. It was as if all the people had been given a new life, as if everyone had been changed, as if all had been given a new beginning, as though all had been restored again to a state of enchantment that they never had, but which was familiar.

This happiness lasted seven days; and, like a rich rainfall, the happiness sank into the spirit of the people, and lay there in the underground rivers of their joyfulness, while life returned to normal.

And that day, when the king came into his son's chamber and found him alive, and smiling, he roared with a strange new laughter from dawn to dusk; and all over the kingdom the liberated laughter of the king echoed in the hearts of his people, and in the underground rivers.

CHAPTER ELEVEN

The prince's recovery was swift and wonderful. And his dying had changed him profoundly. As if he too had found an eternal reason for smiling at all life, he understood more the nature of his father's great laughter. He knew more clearly what he wanted. He knew more clearly who he was. He had seen his end, had travelled his road to its vanishing over the inevitable abyss, and had seen where all stories come from, and where they go.

In his death he had witnessed his life in advance, had lived it all, lived it through, suffered it, endured it, wept for it, and had been granted the mercy of having forgotten it while still remembering it as a distant melody that is heard just a few moments before it is played. All this was clear to him. He had done it all in advance, in death. Now his body had to catch up with what his spirit had already gone beyond, transcended. To those who have been awoken from a true death, this is a peculiar grace, and a unique burden. They are unsurprised a moment before the big events of their lives. They live a constant, accentuated *déjà vu*.

And so the prince stayed in bed and listened to the world he had been absent from. He asked how long he'd been away and all the king told him was:

'Long enough for things to be at the right time for you, my son, to play your part in the scheme of things in the kingdom.'

'But how long is that?' the prince asked.

'Long enough for legend to be formed, for myth to grow, and for the land to be changed.'

'But how long is that in moons or tides?'

'Long enough for the people to no longer think of it in moons or tides, but in stories.'

'That long?'

'Not long, but concentrated.'

'What do you mean, father?'

'It can't be measured in time, but in enchantments. Be content with this answer, and as soon as you are strong enough to get around, go and thank the women of the village, and all the courtiers, and the men too, thank them for all their prayers while you were ill. The people showed you more love than can be told in stories, but now that you are well they would not want to show it. Great events bring out great unsuspected feelings in people that they would be too shy to acknowledge. Thank them simply, then go about your life in a normal way, as if nothing has happened. This way you will reassure the people, and they will be normal, and stability will return to the kingdom.'

'But father, does normal mean not doing anything?'

'It means being your true self.'

'My true self?'

'Yes.'

'However I am?'

'Yes.'

'Whatever I have become, because of what dying has done to me?'

'Whatever you have become.'

'For good or ill?'

'For good or ill.'

'And this will be fine?'

'It will be fine. It will allow the people to be what they truly are. It will give them the freedom to grow, and not be afraid. They will trust your truth.'

'Thank you, father, for telling me this. Often one does not know if one has the right to be what one is.'

'It takes a long time, my son, to know what one is, and to be one's true self. Dying, I think, has quickened it for you.'

'Something has quickened for me. And I hope it is for the best.'

'It is for the best. A blessed providence watches over these things as a master-gardener watches over the flowers and fruits of the orchard. There is no quickening that is not attended to with the greatest care and love.'

'But so much larger and simpler and lighter now is my spirit. I thought I would become a giant, but feel myself to be an infinitely free and flying being, like an unusual bird that knows only the air between the stars.'

'So it is after a return such as you have made. Find a way to keep this new place whatever life brings you, and you will be touched with magic. It is not being a prince or king that is special, my son, but being alive to the mystery of life, and glimpsing the true wonder behind it all. To know one's true possibility is greater than being a king of all the earth, my son.'

'I believe that now, father. For the first time I know it in my being. Stories cannot be told of this.'

'They have tried, and found it better to speak indirectly about such matters, or to be silent. As we say, only the deep can talk to the deep. Rest, my son, and tomorrow arise, and greet the people, and be as normal. I return to my tasks.'

'I thank you, my father.'

'You have thanked me already by being such as you are, a special son.'

CHAPTER TWELVE

The next day the prince awoke with a new zest for living, and an unbounded and humble vitality. He leapt out of bed and faced the rising sun and, with his arms stretched out wide as if to embrace the whole world with his love, he breathed in deeply the new air and the magic rays of the sun. He breathed deeply seven times without counting and he stood gazing into the heavens and he gazed over the earth and a most profound and simple prayer of thankfulness burst from his heart. It filled him with such joy, this expression of gratitude for being alive, that he wept without knowing why. He thanked the great surge of life all around him for the good fortune of being alive. He thanked the air for being there. He thanked the sun for its warmth and its mysterious quality of light. He thanked the world for all its colours and its variety. And he thanked the magic of life for eyes to see, for ears to hear, for the feelings he felt, for his heart, for his soul, for his mouth to praise with. He thanked this great life for the beauty of the world, the animals and the plants, for living and for dying, for the sweetness of the newborn babe and the wrinkledness of the aged. He thanked life for rivers and storms, for food and for hunger, for trees, for flowers, for wild animals, for songs, for fathers and mothers, and for all contradictory things that make up life.

The prince was bursting full of a mad exultant gratitude and he breathed deeply and made himself aware of all parts of his body, from his toe to his head, and he felt the expression of life all over him inside and out, and was grateful for every inch of himself, and he went and drank pure water from the sweet wells, holding the gourd up to the sun and drinking with a smile, and he saluted the world and the hidden glory behind it all, and went and had a bath, with a song in his heart, which he allowed to surface on his lips.

And when he had bathed, washing himself all over in simple gratitude for the strange miracle of the living body, he dressed himself in clean, plain and graceful clothes, and went round the court and its environs to thank everyone personally for their prayers and the part they played in his recovery from death. He thanked every single person there was to thank. He thanked the cooks, he thanked the servants, the herbalists, the messengers, the slaves, the gardeners, the cleaners, the elders, the chiefs, the wives, the women, the daughters, and the babies.

The prince then sent emissaries all over the kingdom to convey his personal thankfulness to all the people for their kindness and their prayers which, he said, were so powerful that even the king of death was moved and allowed him to return to them healthy and renewed. He sent a simple message of gratitude to all the people, in all the regions, of all kings, all ages. And he sent his message of thankfulness beyond the kingdom, to other realms, as far and as wide as it was possible to send messages. And he sent these messages through the ordinary routes, and through dreams and moods as his father does.

Then the prince went round the village; and from hut to hut, from abode to abode, knocking on every door, he thanked all the villagers, shaking their hands, embracing them when he could, thanking the astonished men and the bewildered women, the moved young men and the shy girls with tears sparkling in their eyes like diamonds. He thanked them all. He spent many days thanking the people of the realm. He left no one out. He thanked the old men who were now blind. He thanked the old women who couldn't remember who they were. He thanked the anchorites and the hermits in the forest. He thanked the witches and the wizards. He thanked the criminals, the mad, the outcasts, the diseased, the sick, the dying, and he prayed for them too. He thanked the fishermen by the river, and the tappers of wine amongst the tall palm trees. He thanked the hunters in the woods, the farmers in the farms, the women in the marketplace, and the town criers at their wandering posts. He thanked the warriors, the sages, the priests of the shrines. He even sought out the fabled old woman of the forest who lived in isolation away from society and he found her in a foul mood, and he thanked her too. He got an earful of salty curses for presuming to intrude on her chosen solitude. Afterwards, she said powerful prayers for him. He didn't mind her foul mood anyway, because it was an adventure meeting a fabled being.

And then he sent his messengers round with his apologies to anyone in the village that he had neglected to thank for their prayers.

He spent seven days thanking every single person in the environs of the village.

He had even been seen thanking the goats and dogs and cows too, and the trees, and the river, as if they all, in some way, had aided his recovery and helped bring him back from the land of death.

By the time he had finished with his thanking he was due for another recovery. And so he stayed at home and convalesced from the exhaustion of being grateful. And when the king heard that he had taken to his bed to enjoy a second recovery the king found it so funny that he laughed throughout his dinner at the extensive tenderness of his frail son.

That night, while the prince slept, the king watched over him, and chuckled deep into the night.

CHAPTER THIRTEEN

On the first day of his recovery, after he had performed his new morning rites, the prince set off into the forest, drawn there by an irresistible mood and longing for a golden dawn that seemed now so ancient in his memory, so far away from the present time as to be almost something that happened in another life, long ago. He stole away from the palace at dawn, after he had ceremoniously and with deep breaths greeted the rising sun, and made his way to the edges of the forest.

At first he lingered. This way his life had often drawn him in a dream. Often, in a dream, in death, he found his life's true happiness on the invisible trail through the forest to an appointment that wasn't kept, by someone he hadn't met but who he knew was the love of his life. And this loss of her, this failure to keep her promise, had somehow led to his death. And yet here he was again, on the same trail, risking a second death in a second betrayal.

He sensed, as he lingered at the edge of the forest, that all love must lead to death, of one kind or another. All love must lead to death. And out of this death a new man or woman is born. But he sensed also that love does not lead to only one death, but to several deaths; and that because of love one must keep dying and being reborn, from time to time. And that love dies only when you resist another death which love brings upon you, in order that you be reborn, and grow. That is why there are few real loves in the world, because people fear yet another death that they must endure. They count the deaths and rebirths they have undergone and say 'so many and no more, so far but no further; I will not die again for you, but intend to stay here where I am, how I am now, and here in this fixed place. I intend to build the castle of myself on this rock.'

And the prince sensed that there was no end to the deaths that love brings about, and no end to the rebirths either. Each death making us lighter, freer, simpler, more human, more vulnerable, more strong, more spiritual, more tender, and more universal. Till we become unrepresentative of our clan, tribe, country, sex, religion, or any other classification; but just a beautifully dying living being, dying and being reborn, regenerated, refined, for ever, till we become a kind of dream of light, thought the prince, without words, in a shudder, as he plunged into the cool shade of the forest.

He felt dew-beaded webs enmesh his face. He was assaulted wonderfully by all the smells of the forest, the vegetation, the sleeping earth, the breathing tree trunks, the fragrance of green and hidden living beings, the mood of tranquil spirits, the smell of flowers, of the path, of rotting leaves, of the sun yielding the odour of dew on grass, on the path, the rich marmoreal immemorial odour of the forest, which he had forgotten all the time that he had been in the kingdom of death.

Had he forgotten the trail, and where it led? Yes. He had forgotten his favoured pathway to the place by the river. But he was guided down another, down a new pathway, that led him past wonders he didn't notice or see, but which impacted on his new spirit, his new self, and which he would see later in his dreams, and upon awakening would wonder where such sights had come from, where such marvellous visions had their origin. For he passed through many worlds in the forest, all of them invisible and intangible, and all of them real. These things too are written in the book of life among the stars.

The prince was still quite weak; but he had a great appetite for life, a great hunger to live, to see, to feel. No longer did he want to dream. He had done all his dreaming in the land of death. He had dreamt his life through, dreamt it to its dregs. He had dreamt everything in advance, and knew, somewhere in him, that some of what he had dreamt was provisional, and could be changed, depending on what he did, what forces he put into motion; but, regardless, he now wanted to live right through. He wanted to live it all, with open eyes, and an enlightened spirit. He wanted to live the great challenge of his life, and to square the impossible circle of destiny by the feat of his loving will, and his vision. He wanted to be the conqueror of his own life, of himself. Others, he knew, were famous for conquering the world. He wanted to conquer himself, his destiny, his fate, with the simple power of love. That was his modest desire, this frail prince of a laughing realm.

CHAPTER FOURTEEN

And so he set off through the forest, and wandered a long time, through that dawn, as the sun shone its sharp clear warm rays through the fingers of leaves and branches. The forest was new to him, and had become full of more stories in its mood than it had been before. He lost his way and found new paths and pursued a dimly intuited course in a direction that was as vague to him as a dream disappearing upon awakening. Lost in the forest, he wandered the paths that pleased him, and made many discoveries. He came upon quite a few huts of isolated dwellers in the great forest. And whenever he passed one of these lonely huts an old man or an old woman would be sitting outside the door watching him with tranquil eyes. And when he greeted them they would smile and stay silent. The prince began to think that he was encountering the same person, the same old man who changed further on into an old woman, sitting outside a hut that wasn't really there. Always smiling, never speaking.

The prince was done with dreams. He wanted to be, to act, to do. He didn't even mind the idea of suffering. The forest changed all around him. He passed a crowded feast of the dead and didn't recognise those who had loved him as a child because he didn't see them. They watched him wander through their feast in sadness that he didn't see. But he paused just after he had passed their midst, and he looked back, and looked round, and gave a shiver, and carried on. And one or two of the dead wanted to go after him and tell him how much affection they felt for him, but they were restrained by the others. And they watched him go, knowing that soon he would join them, for time is short among the dead, time is fast.

The prince soon broke the confusion of so many paths and found himself by the river where he had left his heart among the wild flowers. And he found his familiar spot in the bushes. It was much changed now. The rains had made the vegetation more luscious, and the parting among the branches where he nestled and watched the shore was quite overgrown and had forgotten him altogether. So he made a new place for himself there; and with a heart beating fast to a new expectation, he waited with a dream to see if a dream he'd had would come true on this the first day of his freedom from death.

But there by the river, he fell into a mild hallucination in which he saw a shrine sailing down the river on a yellow boat. He saw the oracle wandering about, babbling. He saw the oracle sinking. He saw the shrine of the oldest god flying in the air. The shoreline was full of spirits and strange beings; they were holding a great meeting. Then he saw a white form dancing in pure light on the water, turning, spiralling, dispersing a radiance everywhere that was pure sweetness to the blinded eyes, and when it was gone there was darkness.

Then the prince saw figures with metal chains linking their legs and wrists. They were being led by cloud-coloured men with hats on their heads. They had guns and they had servants with them who carried luggage and who kept the chained figures in control. The chained figures were often whipped. Then they were bundled on to boats and borne away into the blinding reflections of the river. He heard their poignant lament from beyond the horizon, as if they were drowning in the land where the sun went to after it had left the sky of the kingdom . . .

The prince did not understand what he saw, and took it for another vision. And he went back home, taking a more familiar route. He was more troubled than before. What he had seen had awoken in him a profound unease that had been sleeping in him, and growing while it slept.

CHAPTER FIFTEEN

The world that the prince saw now was not the world he saw before his illness. It was a different world, and much had changed in it, subtly. The kingdom that he saw now was different from the one he saw before his long illness. Something had changed in the air. There seemed to be more gaps between things, between trees, between huts and houses, between people. He noticed these gaps everywhere, and he didn't understand. Then, after a while, he wasn't sure if what he noticed were absences, or if they were actual things. These gaps, were they substances? Or were they simply spaces? This puzzled him.

The next day that he set out to the forest, bound for his watching place near the river, where he still hoped that one day the dream he sought might return, he noticed the gaps as if for the first time. They seemed real. And when he noticed them he began to see them everywhere, again. He saw the gaps spreading between the trees, obliterating them, slowly. He saw these gaps along the shore, obliterating the edges of the river, till he witnessed, in mesmerised amazement, the apparent shrinking of the waters on the shoreline. He noticed the gaps appear among the bushes, the plants, the shrubs. He rubbed his eyes, convinced that he was somehow dreaming with eyes wide open the gradual disappearance of the natural world that he knew. He rubbed his eyes, and yet it continued to happen, and he continued to see gaps sprout between things. He saw holes appear in the river, and he expected the water to drain away, but it didn't. He saw holes appear on the shore. He saw gaps spread in the sky, and birds flew into these gaps, and never reappeared. This truly troubled him and, without waiting too long, he hurried home to ponder this new terrifying phenomenon.

When he got home to the palace he went straight to bed, and covered himself with a blanket, and shut his eyes to the world. But even in his sleep, the gaps appeared. There were strange gaps in his dreams.

CHAPTER SIXTEEN

The next day the prince arose, performed his rites of awakening, and set about the kingdom. He did not go to his watching place that day. He went about the kingdom like a beggar, and he looked, using his eyes as he had never done before. And what he saw astounded him. He saw gaps everywhere, growing. He saw gaps in people's faces, gaps in their eyes, he heard gaps in their voices, gaps in their words. Some of the mothers had given birth to babies that were part gaps, part human. He was frightened by this.

'Where are the gaps coming from?' he asked himself, aloud. 'Have they always been there and I am just noticing them now, or are they recent?'

He asked questions of people, and he realised their minds were full of gaps. There were gaps in the history, gaps in the traditions, gaps in their reasoning, gaps in their knowledge, gaps in their laughter, gaps in their suffering. He saw people whose hands were disappearing, whose faces were turning into gaps, who walked on one leg because their other leg had been eaten away by the gaps, but they didn't know it. Apparently no one else saw the gaps in them or around them. But the prince saw the gaps spreading in the villages, gaps in the dances, in the drumming, gaps in the farms. He said to the people:

'Where are the gaps coming from?'

But no one seemed to know what he was talking about. So

he sought out the wise men and women of the kingdom, to find answers to his anguished questions . . .

CHAPTER SEVENTEEN

But the wise men and women were hard to find and mostly did not want to be found. And when he made enquiries and was directed to this hut or that place, when he arrived he would discover that the wise man, learning that the prince was seeking him, had disappeared, had, as they say, made himself scarce. The prince was puzzled by this.

'Why do the wise flee from me? Are there gaps among the wise too?'

Everywhere he went seeking the wise they were not at home or were seen leaving their abodes by the back door or had moved or had gone on long pilgrimages or were reputed to be performing great feats of the spirit somewhere else in the kingdom. Not a single wise man or woman could he find. Maybe, he thought, their wisdom also included not being found by people who sought them. But this left him with his own perplexity, and with no one with whom to share this discovery of the phenomenon of the gaps. He wandered back home that evening, lost in thought, occasionally disappearing from the world as he strayed into great holes of contemplation. And when he came back again to himself he saw the darkness gathering and the stars shining between the deep blue gaps in the sky . . .

The next day he summoned the elders and asked them about the gaps in the people, the gaps in tradition, the gaps into which people disappeared, never to return.

His father listened to his questions with a smile on his face, radiant with curiosity and pride in his son.

One of the elders said:

'Gaps? What gaps? There are no gaps in our tradition, our history, or our people, or anywhere. We are fine. The foundation is secure, the house is stable. We are solid. We have no gaps among us.'

Another elder stepped forward, and said:

'There is a proverb: "Only the person who sees the world as mad is mad." We don't mean you, our dear prince, nor do we mean any disrespect. But you have not been well, you have not given yourself enough time to recover, and you are looking at things too hard from your convalescence. Maybe the gaps are in you.'

Then the first elder, more emolliently, said:

'I would not go so far myself, but maybe, our prince, you need to get better. And then you will see that the land is fine and our traditions are secure and that there are no gaps anywhere among us.'

The prince held his silence, and did not press the issue on this day.

But his unease continued in the following days when he saw birds in the sky suddenly flying into nothingness, into pure invisibility. Or when he saw children playing near the stream and they would run, laughing, and completely vanish in the twinkle of an eye. Or when he saw drummers playing an extraordinary flourish, beating out complicated and beautiful ideas in cross-patterns in the white heat of an inspired syncopation, and they would slowly drum themselves into invisibility, vanishing as they played more intensely, as if obliterated by their own fabulous harmonic discoveries. Or when he saw whole portions of farmland vanish into nothingness, and farmers with them. Or when he saw strips of the palace slowly crumble into thin air, as if wiped away by strange effacing clouds. Or when he saw the shrines slowly evaporate into the trembling vibrations in the hot air of an intolerable afternoon, till only the ghosts of the resident gods quivered in the space above the shrine, till they too were blown away in the general atmosphere of the hallucinating sky.

He beheld these things and kept his counsel, as he now knew that no one would believe him if he spoke of them. But having to be silent at such momentous things as he saw became unbearable to him, and they tormented his sleep and perplexed his dreams, and he could find no solace anywhere.

To see these things and to have no one with whom to speak of them introduced a strange new pressure and alienation into his life. He was possessed of a dreadful tragic isolation and a sense of being an outsider in his own land. The people seemed happy enough, the elders carried on as they more or less did, scheming and intriguing; and his father, the king, was silent and mysterious. The only sign he gave of his presence was his characteristic universal laughter which could be heard from the rooftops or trembling on the light breeze in the long afternoons into which the gods, one by one, were vanishing.

And so the prince found himself alone. Finding himself invaded by signs of a world being obliterated by a mysterious phenomenon which no one else saw, he did not know what to do with himself. Sometimes he thought himself mad. Sometimes he thought everyone else mad. Sometimes he thought the world was dreaming. Sometimes he thought he was living in a perpetual dream in which nothing was real, except for the gaps. Only the gaps seemed to him real. They seemed real because no one else saw them. There were times, however, when he thought that he had died, and that all he witnessed was from the viewpoint of the dead. This troubled him.

He might have done something truly dreadful to himself in this state of mind if one night his father, the king, had not appeared to him in a dream, dressed in his full splendid regalia, and said:

'My son, seek out the maiden of the tribe of artists, and be a servant to her father. Study the daughter. Then win her hand. This will not be easy. But your children will eventually be the saviours of the land.'

The prince woke up with the distinct feeling that something in him had changed for ever. But his great unease at the things he saw hadn't changed. Only now he had a clear sign of what he had to do. So, at dawn, after his morning rituals, he set off to the place beside the river, with the hope that one day, some day, the maiden would return again.

Meanwhile, so as to cover all fronts, and in spite of official protestations that it had been done before, and done extensively, and that all previous missions had failed, the prince sent emissaries all over the kingdom to find the secret tribe of artists, so as to find the maiden of the river. And, one by one, they eventually returned, saying that the tribe could not be found, and in fact that the tribe did not exist.

So also, day by day, every day, at dawn, from the freshness of hope like dew on the grass, till the blazing heat of noon that blinded all things that could see, the prince waited for the maiden. And she did not materialise, or return. It was as if his previous sighting of her had been a dream, or had happened in another life, in a distant realm, when life was younger and more beautiful, and true.

CHAPTER EIGHTEEN

But some of the elders were not pleased at the recovery of the prince. The elder who spoke first at the meetings which the prince convened, and whose name was Okadu, was chief among those who were not pleased. Chief Okadu was an elder of some efficiency, a man enormously pleased with his abilities as a strategist and organiser, and a great sycophant to the king. He had crocodile eyes, discoloured red lips, a general slimy manner, and a certain complacency based on having secured for himself the economic management of aspects of the kingdom.

He had no power himself, but he had the ear of the king. He despised the people, he believed in hierarchy only if he was at the head of it; in fact he believed in anything only if it would benefit him. He was given to striding about the place with his hands in his pockets as if he owned the world. Chief Okadu was foremost among those who were deeply ill at ease with the prince's restoration to health. He was most threatened by the prince's notion that there were gaps in the kingdom, gaps in tradition, gaps in history. Chief Okadu hated the idea of gaps and ever since the prince had raised the subject he had gone around to the other elders and asked them if they knew anything of the gaps about which the prince had spoken. Without exception, none of them did.

'I don't see gaps anywhere. What does he mean by gaps anyway? Do you think he was referring to us?'

The elders went about the village, and made their own interrogations, and they stared at the world, and wandered around, and talked to those the prince had spoken to, and they re-converged and discussed their findings. They still had not seen gaps anywhere.

Chief Okadu's crocodile eyes grew more sinister than ever; and he acquired, in his quiet opposition and his grasp of the play of things, a strange power over the minds of the elders, a power that had been growing all along in his sycophancy and his general mode of appeasement. But now he was the force behind the elders, and they all held him in silent awe; and it could be said that, all of a sudden, and quite mysteriously, they realised that they feared him more than they feared the king. And so silently in the kingdom, in the shadows, in whispers, in the bushes, in the dark, in mutterings, Chief Okadu came to be known as the Crocodile. He was called the Crocodile whose eyes never shut and whose jaws never sleep.

Under the Crocodile's insistence, the elders came round to the notion that the prince was talking in code, and that he might be hinting that they – the elders – were the gaps, or they created the gaps, that they were corrupt, or that they distorted the laws, or misused their powers, or stole from the kingdom and the people, and impoverished the traditions, the history and the land; or that they were somehow a negative force in the kingdom.

'It seems to me quite clear,' said the Crocodile, in heavily accented menace, 'that we are the ones the prince is referring to; and the way he is going he will sooner or later want to get rid of us as a class and as a force. He is our natural enemy. We wish him nothing but good, but he sees us as the cause of destruction in the kingdom. We have much to fear from that prince when he ascends the throne.'

The Crocodile paused. Then in a low gentle slimy voice that insinuated fear into the mesmerised elders gathered in the gloom of their meeting place, he said:

'Unless there is no longer an ascension . . .'

He paused again. Then giving a sign to his minions to blow out the lanterns in the gloomy hall where they met in secrecy under his summons, and when darkness gathered about them all like a thick blanket against the cold, he said, almost in a whisper that could not be heard or confirmed:

'. . . or a throne . . .'

CHAPTER NINETEEN

The gaps that the prince had asked about, the existence of which they denied, began to haunt the elders and create gaps in their minds. They began to suspect that the prince had found out things about them, their secret activities, their corrupt practices, their ritual sacrifices, their secret societies, their secret taxation of farmers, market women and traders which they kept for themselves, at the expense of the kingdom, while so many starved and suffered. The elders were for the first time troubled by revelations they feared would emerge any moment.

They did not like the prince's recovery, his new-found awareness, courage and clarity. And above all they were not pleased at the great love the people bore him.

CHAPTER TWENTY

What were the elders to do, faced with the notion of the gaps that the prince had insinuated into their minds? They hated the notion of gaps in things. It revolted them. It disgusted them. It threatened, profoundly and mysteriously, their establishment. It threatened the foundations. It threatened their grasp on reality. And so, because of this, the elders, over a period of time, like strange cultists performing dreaded operations on the natural world, became involved in activities which the uninitiated saw as perverse, as monstrous, as evil spells, as rituals meant to seal their powers and their grip on things in the structure of the kingdom.

They went around, at night, with lanterns, and began to tap at things. They tapped walls, buckets, trees, buildings, floors. They tapped to find any hollow spaces. They tapped with sticks, canes and bones. They tapped with ritually treated objects. They listened to the noises of the hollows. They noted the spaces between buildings, trees, earth and sky, above the stream, and between people. They were overwhelmed by the open spaces that led to the stars and the heavens. They were bewildered by the sheer multiplicity of spaces.

They all began to have bad dreams. They had nightmares in which the spaces oppressed them. They contemplated filling up all the hollows, blocking up the spaces. They wanted to eliminate all gaps, but in doing so they did not want to create bigger gaps. They became obsessed with filling up all the gaps, and whenever they saw a gap they saw a force undermining their foundation. They dreamt up ways of jamming up all the empty spaces with things. They couldn't find a way, however, to cram the spaces that led to the stars and the heavens. And because they associated these vast accusing spaces with the prince and therefore the throne, for the first time in millennia they began to scheme against the king and to devise ways to get rid of him. They no longer heard his laughter in the air.

CHAPTER TWENTY-ONE

And so it was that at dawn, just when the sun was like a newborn child in the gentle golden mists of the east, when the birds were in competition as to which would waken the prince with the message of their incomprehensible melodies, the prince would rise, and greet his life, and try to remember and heed his dreams, and after performing the rites which he had devised from his death to keep him ever awake to the wonder of living, he would set off to the forest. He was not seeking adventures, but seeking only that which he had lost before he nearly died.

That vision had grown so much more now in meaning with each passing day. And that love which had lain sleeping in him was stirring with a restlessness that made his life quite intolerable without his being aware of it. Then, one day, he found himself pursuing an enigma, a riddle, in a dark forest. He was pursuing a white and golden antelope in a dream which he saw in the forest, still blinded by a love which he did not know possessed him like the life in his limbs.

The white and golden antelope led him past a stream he had never seen before, past a white house inside which he heard a girl singing a song so beautiful he nearly burst into tears, past a well in which he saw not water but a crowded cluster of pearls and diamonds, and yet he did not stop to investigate the well, but followed the golden and white antelope. It led him past two villages in which he found he was worshipped as a god, and when the villagers saw him they fell in mass prostration and in screaming ecstasy cried out that they had been blessed with glimpses of their divinity. The prince didn't linger to taste the pleasures of this ambiguous power but kept firmly on the trail of the white and golden antelope as it led him into a maze of trees and flowers at the centre of which was a gap the exact shape of the morning sun. The antelope leapt into the gap and vanished. The prince hesitated at the threshold of this mystery and then he said a quick prayer and without thinking, and with the courage that youth often has, and which those who age wisely are richly composed of, he leapt into the gap too, and found himself in a simple place in the forest, not far from the river, with his head quite clear, except that he was a little puzzled how he had got to where he was. He had forgotten how he got there. He remembered only that he had left the palace, entered the forest, and now found himself near the river, near his favourite hiding place in the flowering bushes, and he could hear the laughter of young women in the wind over the whispering waves. He could hear the laughter of young women and girls. He could hear their teasing, their sweet songs, their stories half told, their games and their names being called out. He could hear them the way you hear favourite moments from a childhood remembered in dreams.

Like a faun awoken from a gentle sleep by a rainbow that played a haunting melody in the sky, the prince awoke from his half-dreaming state and hurried to his place among the flowering bushes. And when he looked out from among the innumerable white and blue and yellow and red flowers that richly surrounded him on all sides, he saw, along the shore of the golden river all aflame with the gentle jealousy of the sun's rays on the pure liquid glow, the girls all in white, dancing in circles. They had flowers in their hair and cowries round their necks, and they were dancing as if they were performing a magic rite to the season of flowers and the rich green gift of the world after the gloom of death has passed over the land.

There they were, the girls in white dresses, dancing in circles with bangles of light-spangled bronze on their lovely wrists and anklets twinkling with gold on their slender ankles as they danced along the shore, in the beauty of youth, in a time without memory, in a pure happiness that cannot last, in a perfect beauty that the gods put there by the river to celebrate all creation. And the prince gazed on this happy sight with wonder in his heart.

And he listened with rapture as they sang a peculiar ditty, one that somehow seemed to move the river itself to smiling, or so it appeared to the prince.

'If you touch me
And I touch you
Then this is true
And that is true,
Too.'

The last word detached but connected to the other words in the song had an odd effect on the prince. It made him aware of a figure whose presence made his heart shiver and the world changed and the lights darkened a little, as at an eclipse, and then brightened better than before, and a higher colour was restored to all things, as if a veil had dropped from his sight. And then he beheld the one girl among the dancing girls who was apart from them, but not aloof. She stood in a pool of water on the shore, staring into the horizon, turning a flower round in her hand, spinning its stalk so that it was the blue flower that danced, spinning, in her hand, to compensate for her stillness.

And she was there, as in a dream that time forgot, in the perfect enchantment of a lifetime. The prince, upon seeing her, and without knowing why, began to weep silently, with a smile in his soul as warm and tender as the young sun in its moment of early gold.

At that same moment, the girl who stood apart called out to her companions and they gathered about her in a circle and she said:

'My friends, I feel today a special sadness, as if at last a god has given me all I ever wished for, but I can't see it because I am such a fool. How can this be?'

And her companions giggled at her riddle and danced around her in a circle, singing their ditty, in sweet melodies, without giving her an answer.

And she turned and turned with their dancing till she was quite dizzy and then beyond dizzy and began to dance herself and then they all began a game of chasing one another up and down the shore and into the forest and back again.

And then the prince noticed that she was alone. They had come to do their washing on the stones of the river and the morning had cleansed away their task; and their games, which were their celebration at their task's end, were over. They had eaten fruits and laughed and talked of suitors and mimicked the various men characters in the life of the tribe and had shared dreams and notions and had borne their sundry buckets on their heads and had gone back to their homes. And only the one who stood apart now lingered at the river, as if waiting for its god, or for a voice, to address her, as once it did, when she was more innocent. But when nothing happened, when she waited, and sang a little, and looked about her expectantly, and a wind bore down on her, making her tremble a little, she decided to return home. She now had three flowers in her hand, which she played with. One was yellow, another blue, and the third one was red, and she seemed to love them all.

She seemed also to fall into a happy smile of a half-dream as she made her way through the flowering plants and into the forest.

When she had looked about her expectantly the prince had the desire to speak to her, but a wiser urge made him hold his peace. At last he was learning the lesson of the heron, his personal bird-spirit. He kept silent when he most wanted to express that within him which was too much to express. And he watched her as if his soul had left his body and had joined her being for ever. But he kept still. And he breathed gently, properly, as if he were breathing in the sweet life of the sun itself. And when she started to wander away from the river, he had no choice but to follow. He had no idea if this was the right thing to do or not, but as the moon draws the tides, or the sun setting in the west draws our gaze homewards, so he found himself following this dream of his life that had at last come alive.

She moved gently among the shadows in the forest. She alone of all the girls bore no bucket on her head. She had come empty-handed, to keep her friends company in their tasks, and was leaving with flowers. Her slender form and smiling walk delighted the imps of the forest.

CHAPTER TWENTY-TWO

She seemed merely to be wandering. Wandering in a dream. The prince followed her through the trees that her presence made magical. Everything that she went past changed with her passing. He followed her through new villages where sculptures of him rose from the shrines. He saw the sculptures but did not recognise them for what they were. She went down into a valley and emerged into another forest that was blue within the shade of its trees. It was a complicated journey. She seemed on a private ritual of discovering the world about her. Often she would stop to gaze at the trees as if looking for something or someone within them. Often she would feel their trunks and tap them and listen to their interiors. She behaved quite strangely, and this fascinated the prince.

And then, at a certain junction, where paths met, and where you could have a clear sight of the sky, and where the air fairly bristled with unaccountable whispers, she did something quite amazing. She suddenly stopped, and became alert, and awake, and stood very still, like a warrior waiting for a sign before charging into battle. Then she looked to the left and to the right, she looked above and then below, and the prince watched in baffled astonishment as she stepped into one of the gaps between the trees. She walked into the gap and disappeared completely, as if into a dream, or as if from a dream fading in daylight. And he hesitated for one moment only before he hurried and leapt into the same gap between things that she had vanished into; and on the other side he found himself in quite a different world, the same world but different. He found himself in the same place as he was before he leapt into the gap between things, but it was strange. The shadows were still blue. He was still in the same forest. The junction where the paths met still quivered with enigmas. But it was not the same. In the distance he saw her walking and singing to herself along the forest path that was like a rough ribbon of subdued gold amid banks of wild greens and high trees. He saw her stop and talk to a snail on the path and saw her lift the snail and place it among the plants on the other side.

Not long afterwards he followed her into the dazzling environs of her village, where the fabled tribe of artists lived and created in secrecy and to maximum effect, in the unseen spaces of the kingdom.

CHAPTER TWENTY-THREE

Following the principle of the heron, the prince made himself indistinct and indistinguishable and managed to wander among the tribe of artists without drawing attention to himself. And so he was able to see into what building she entered, that was her home; and so he was able to make discreet enquiries and learn something about her family. He explored the environs of the village, lingered in the palm-wine bars, asked further questions from fellow drinkers, and contemplated spending the night at the edge of the forest. But he had visions of eating raw tuberous roots and not sleeping for all the noises of wild animals circulating the darkness and he imagined himself being devoured by wild beasts if he so much as dozed off, and so he decided to return home instead. But he was lucky that day, for as he set off home he saw her leave her house and he followed her round the edges of the village, past the shrine, into the woods, and saw her step into another gap which shone like a little moon barely visible in daylight. And when he hurriedly stepped through that gap as well he caught sight of her disappearing into an unusual-looking hut with an ordinary door. She was in there a long time. Then just as he was about to leave someone came out of the door and looked around. The man who came out had eyes like those of a wild eagle. He was clearly a man of mysteries in the fullness of his powers. He looked about him, as if sensing something new in the air; then, uttering a few potent incantations, he withdrew into the hut, leaving some mysterious quivering form of his spirit lingering outside, still watching, till that too faded into afterglows.

The prince didn't linger a moment longer, but hurried home the way he had come. He was careful to return through all the gaps, thereby making sure that he left nothing of himself behind and that he didn't get trapped in the forest, or lost in a world he did not know, a world, maybe, of forest dreams, and legends.

CHAPTER TWENTY-FOUR

The more the elders of the kingdom tried to fill the gaps, the more gaps appeared. The elders and the chiefs of the king's court precipitated a great crisis among themselves and in the kingdom. And they caused many evils to come into existence because they feared that the gaps that loomed and appeared to their paranoid scrutiny were in the world about them and in tradition. With each passing day doubts grew amongst them about the truth of anything. They were no longer sure when a certain innovation had become the beginning of a tradition, or whether the tradition had been there since the beginning of the world. Their earth became shaky, and one day they overheard the prince saying to one of the children in the palace that the world stood on air, and that nothing held up the earth in space, and that in a dream he had seen the world as a shining blue bowl in a vast sea of nothingness, dotted with stars.

'This earth is held up by air, by mystery, by nothing,' he said to the children.

'How come we don't fall off then?' one of them asked.

'Because it is the same nothing that keeps us on the land. Some people walk upside-down, with their heads facing downward, and they don't fall off into the big nothing. A power invisible keeps us here, not our power.'

The children were silent. Then one said:

'So the earth stands on air?'

'On nothing,' the prince said, smiling.

The chiefs and elders overheard these words and this began another bout of talk and fevered discussions. It awakened more fears. They met at night and gazed into the heavens and could not see that which held the earth in space. This made them see more gaps, which they had to destroy.

Often the chiefs and elders, unable to sleep, watched the gaps growing in the kingdom. This phenomenon began to paralyse them. Chief Okadu was heard screaming in his sleep. His wives assured him that there were no gaps in the world, but his raw red eyes could not unsee that which he had begun to see. The paranoia of the chiefs, made worse by the horror that they stood on air, that their world was held up by nothing, began the destruction of the potent mythology by which they controlled the kingdom in the name of the king. They thought of having the prince poisoned, and enlisted the support of one of the king's wives, the most disaffected. Three times they attempted to poison the prince but each time the food was eaten by an eagle, or a dog, or a monkey that appeared in the prince's chamber before he was ready. Three times he saw empty plates on the table where food should have been; and he took it as a sign to fast. He fasted till he received another sign which he took to mean it was time again for him to meet the family of the maiden, in disguise at first, following the principle of the heron. The sign came in the form of a dream in which he was sitting at the foot of a master and the maiden was at the door, looking out at a spectacle in the street.

The prince told his father that he would be away for seven days and would return each night. His father nodded and asked no questions, and didn't laugh. But there was an odd twinkle in his eyes.

CHAPTER TWENTY-FIVE

That morning, passing into the gaps that were like afterglows, the prince, in disguise, made his way through the forest and past the yellow valley and back into the blue shade of woods near the village of the artists, and went directly to the workshop of the maiden's father. He sat outside its unremarkable door, and he sang an ancient song that went like this:

'If you cannot find it
  On earth
  Seek for it in the
  Sea
  If you cannot find it
  In the sea
  Seek for it in the
  Sky
  If you cannot find it
  In the sky
  Seek for it in the
  Fire
  And if you cannot find it
  In the fire
  Seek for it in your
  Dreams
  If it isn't there
  Then it is nowhere.
  This is nowhere
  And I like it here ...'

The prince sang this peculiar song in a sweet poignant voice that was unused to singing and indeed betrayed no talent for song, but the mood of it soothed him as he waited. And he sang himself to sleep, and sang gently in his sleep, with his head resting against a pole in front of the door of the workshop. And when the maiden's father arrived that morning for work he saw a strange and strangely beautiful youth at the entrance to his secret workshop, singing in his sleep, singing words that moved him somewhat. And before the young man woke up, before he spoke, the maiden's father knew that this young man was going to play an important part in his life. He knew, instantly, in fact, that this inexplicable youth had already altered his life, and the life of his family, and the life of the tribe. He saw the future in the frail form of this youth who had now awoken and who had solemn smiling eyes like one who has not yet decided whether to live or die.

'What do you want?' he asked the youth gruffly.

'Sir,' said the youth, smiling shyly, 'your fame is great, and your art is greater, and I have travelled a long way, past the regions of death, sir, just to come and serve you. I ask nothing in return. I do not even ask to be instructed. I dare not, sir, ask so great an honour from so great a master as you. I desire only to serve you in any way you want and in the evenings I will return to my land; this I would like to do till you no longer wish it, sir.'

The maiden's father stared at the youth. He was quite mesmerised by his inexplicable frailty and beauty. There was something profoundly unusual about the youth; and some whisper told the father of the maiden that he couldn't refuse this modest request, even from a total stranger. The older man sensed the youth was of unique birth, and might even be something other than he seemed. And so unusually feeling himself under the sway of a kindly invisible power, and without knowing why, or what he was saying, he said:

'I accept. You shall serve me as I instruct you to do. But you must only do as I instruct you. Nothing else in my household is your business. You learn nothing of my art. I will teach you nothing. You will sit and serve till I decide otherwise. I have no need of a servant and I don't know why I am doing this. In the evenings and at night you may do as you wish, except don't disgrace me in any way. And you must not reveal anything of what you see here. Silence and discretion I demand of you. And you must not speak to my daughter.'

The prince bowed his head gracefully.

'Thank you, sir,' he said. 'This is the greatest honour of my life.'

The older man stared at him in puzzlement. His feelings were mixed and confused. He had not felt like this for a long time indeed. He felt in some obscure way that it was he who should be thanking the youth, and that it was he who was honoured. This confusion somewhat annoyed him. Few things ever did. The master was encountering something that baffled him, that eluded the powers of his intuition, that silenced his guiding spirit. And he knew for the first time in years a delicate kind of fear, a terror that bordered on illumination.

'Who are you anyway, where do you come from?' the older man asked sternly, in that complicated state of mind.

The prince smiled gently.

'I am a poor lost person, sir, separated from my family during our journeys, and I found myself here.'

'I thought you said you had come a long way because . . .'

'A long way, sir, have I travelled because of your art and your fame, past the land of death even. The earth itself can bear witness to this. And the wind will speak for me. The stars watched my journeys with keen eyes. You may ask them, sir, when I am not around, and they will bear me out.'

The older man fell under the grip of a disquieting amazement.

'Who is your father?'

'One who laughs, sir.'

'I see. And your mother?'

'She is happy among the stars. She flew to heaven when I was young.'

There was a pause. Then the older man said:

'You begin today.'

'May you be blessed, sir, for the greatness of your heart.'

The older man stepped into his secret workshop with his new servant.

CHAPTER TWENTY-SIX

When the maiden came to see her father that afternoon she did not notice the new servant. He sat in a corner, under the wall, among the statues and images. Light poured in from a space in the wall above his head. He sat in absolute stillness, as he had been instructed, and breathed the way that bronze statues do, inaudibly, without motion. The maiden didn't notice the new servant but she noticed the form of a new notion in wood that her father had half dreamt into space. Her father worked in silence, among stones, among chunks of wood, at a table, dreaming with quiet intensity new beings into form, as if he were praying, or conjuring in deep silence. Meanwhile his daughter sat at her favourite chair and spoke thoughts that came to her mind, partially aware that her voice had a nice effect on the mood of the workshop, and made the statues in the dark listen, as if to one beloved. She had been to the river that day, she said, and had found it barren . . .

'There was nothing there, father, and I could not understand. The river was the same, or maybe it wasn't; the shore was the same, though I am not sure; the sky hadn't changed, and all my favourite flowers are in bloom, but it was all empty, as if the spirit of things had gone away from them. When my companions sang, they did not please me. When they danced, they were clumsy. I did not feel like anything. The wind wasn't sweet. The river was like stone. I wandered into the forest alone. It was without colour. I couldn't see the green of leaves. Everything was flat. Sometimes a butterfly lands on my shoulder. Sometimes I see a snail on the path and we have something to say to one another. Sometimes, while walking, I have a diamond dream, and some fairy has made me a queen, or a princess, and I am smiling among the trees. Sometimes, father, I see in front of me a perfect image that I can make in bronze or wood. And when it goes away it reappears in my dreams. Sometimes I hear the song a suitor sings on the edge of a dream while I am coming home. But these days, and today especially, nothing happens. The world is flat. The stars don't shine, and even my heart beats as if everything is normal. Has something changed in the world that I haven't noticed?'

And then she was silent. Her father was silent too, and worked quietly, only now and then moving wood on the table, breathing as wooden statues do, gently, as if not wanting to trouble the air. The maiden stared at the statues in the workshop, stared without seeing, and in that abstracted semi-dreaming state she made out the shapes of spirits going about their tasks of slowly bringing new forms into being, under the

precise instruction of her father, their master. She watched the
dimly visible forms of the spirits out of the corner of her eye
and for a moment noticed a new one amongst them, but when
she looked to ascertain, it was gone, faded into the mysterious
half-light of the workshop where the most important events
happened in the shadows, in an insubstantial light, not possible
to gaze on, in a dark mist, where things become real and unreal
like shadows moving in a darkness.

CHAPTER TWENTY-SEVEN

The maiden didn't notice the new servant even when she
sat in her chair and dozed and dreamt that one of the
statues was alive. Sometimes when she was awake and listening
to her father carving shapes in the air, describing forms to his
spirit-servants that he wanted them to make out of the wood
that he had long prepared for their new life as art, the new
servant would stir under the wall, and cough gently, as though
breathing in the dust that floated from the wood were mildly
choking him. Even then the maiden didn't notice. Once while
the maiden dozed with eyes half open the new servant crept
across her field of vision and received instructions from her
father and went out and returned and whispered in his ear and
passed her reclining form in the chair and he went and
resumed his stillness in the dark, among the statues under the
wall, and still she did not notice or see him. It was as if her
father, the master, had cast a spell of invisibility over the new

servant so that he would not be seen by his daughter; or as if he had cast a spell of incomprehension over his daughter so that she would not see the new servant, or notice him at all. Or it may have been that the new servant cast a spell on himself, that he would not be seen or noticed by her, following the principle of the heron but raising it to the pitch of an enchantment.

When he sat there in the dark, under the wall, many things came to the mind of the new servant. He fell often into a dreaming state and passed through a golden gap in his sleep and found himself in a place where he was a slave. He had no idea what had brought him to this condition. He was in a faraway land, among those whose skin was the colour of the sky just before evening comes, and he was a slave working in a field from dawn to dusk, along with many others, singing poignant lamentations for a life that was gone. Sometimes he was half naked in a marketplace, being sold for the price of a dog. Sometimes he had three children that were not his colour and his wife's eyes were cold like the eyes of a dead fish. Sometimes it was hard for him to find the golden gap and return to the workshop, in the dark, awake. In silence, when he returned, he was puzzled.

Many thoughts and fragments of lives, many notions fantastical and real descended on him as he sat there among the stones and structured wood.

The new servant that he was, he sat there quietly, and obediently, and still. He learnt the art of statues. He learnt their stillness. He learnt their repose. He learnt how to absorb all things, all energies, all memories, all thoughts and moods around him into his unresisting being. He learnt to give off his mood, his thoughts, and energies too, in silence, such as they were. He learnt the absorbency of statues, and learnt their radiation too. He learnt to be present the way they are, without insistence, and yet unforgettable, not moving, and yet seeming to move, never changing, and yet changing with the light, or the angle of being viewed. He learnt the simplicity of statues, and how this simplicity makes them monumental in the mind. He learnt the immobility of statues, and how this immobility makes them able to travel to a vast number of minds who haven't even seen them. He learnt the humour of statues, how they keep their best secrets to themselves, smiling inwardly at the unreality of their outward form, their true mystery dwelling within. He learnt like statues to dwell in the mystery within and to live in its secret light and listen to the truths whispered in the silence inside the forms of things. He learnt the openness of statues too, and offered himself to all eyes, all souls, to be gazed upon without being understood, and not minding. He learnt the tranquillity of statues, content simply to be, to give or receive, to waste no energy in that which is not, to be unconcerned about being or not being, but in being to so clearly be. He also learnt the power of statues, he learnt how to occupy and not to occupy the space he did, he learnt how to feel every part of his being, and to be aware of all that he was, and to be aware of all that is, all that is the case, in the universe.

He learnt from statues that all things participated in all things in the universe, and no one thing or object or being was isolated from another. He learnt the indestructibility of statues, for they can't be destroyed, and when statues are burned or broken down their form remains, even in their formlessness, and what they once were persists for ever in the memory of the invisible space, and in the eternal book that dwells among the stars.

Many things the new servant learnt from the statues without knowing it. And one of them was the unteachable art of happiness; for statues, in all that they are, know happiness as a by-product of their inner certainties about the higher this and the lower that. And so whatever they are, this they appear to be, along with the inner art, which they reveal only in the dark, among themselves, when no one else is around or watching; when they can be most true. It took some time before they admitted the new servant to their hidden exalted ranks. And first he had to be tested and initiated into their condition, into their philosophy, into their mysteries.

His time among the statues, as a statue, was one of the greatest adventures of his life.

And so the prince, in order to serve, became a statue. He became a statue in the maiden's father's workshop. He seldom moved.

CHAPTER TWENTY-EIGHT

Meanwhile, the clamour of the suitors grew worse. Their competitiveness intensified. Many of them had been in the village, putting forth their individual suits, through elaborate, influential and often unorthodox intermediaries.

Herbalists had been recruited into the ranks; and they, on the payroll of one of the suitors, would insinuate their way into the maiden's parents' house and whisper hints laden with suggestions as to evil things that might befall the family if so-and-so were not chosen as bridegroom. Or if there were an illness in the family, and in secret a witch-doctor were consulted, it would often be hinted that such-and-such a suitor was responsible, or that if a favourable decision were made in the direction of such-and such then the epidemic, of which the illness was merely a forerunner, might be spared the family, if not the tribe.

On all sides the maiden's family was pestered and hounded, bribed and threatened by the increasingly frustrated suitors. Their frustration had begun to have an unwholesome effect on the village, on the artistic life of the people, even on the good will in the air. One way or another people of the village found themselves being drawn into one camp or another, into supporting one influential suitor or another, into being used by them. In the marketplace those who sold fish, or the butchers, or the sellers of trinkets, of mounds of vegetables, of bales of dyed cloth, would whisper to anyone from the maiden's household the name of a suitor that would be much favoured by the majority; this name would make its way, via circuitous routes, to the mother, and then eventually to the maiden herself, who wouldn't hear it, nor hear any other names, nor hear the word suitor, because she had developed a graceful eccentric deafness to the whole subject and in its place had acquired a lovely drifting absent-mindedness. She would be often singing, often dreaming of a moment, shrouded in golden mystery, by the river.

The more the suitors clamoured, the stranger and more elusive the maiden became. She grew more beautiful in her awkward way, and yet more invisible. She learnt the art of passing by people without being seen, or slipping through crowds without being noticed. She also learnt to stop seeing what she didn't want to see. And as the suitors began to make themselves an unavoidable part of the village, she learnt to see less and less, and to hear less and less, till she almost wholly withdrew into a way of dreaming and a way of wandering.

The suitors so infected the village with their obnoxious rivalry that the families of other young girls of marriageable age began to complain. Often they could be heard, with daggers in their voices, saying:

'Why doesn't she choose one man and let us have peace in the village? Is she the only girl in the world? Why doesn't she think of others? Because of her this village is being ruined by strangers.'

The Mamba, her chief suitor, who made this theme popular, now increased the pitch of his campaign. He slandered the other suitors, and maintained that their wealth, their presence, their alien ways were corrupting the spiritual integrity of the village; and that the maiden's inability to make a sensible choice would bring fragmentation and even death to the village, if care was not taken.

This kind of talk grew in force. Many picked upon it, and even the secret masters were alarmed enough to feature it in their obscure meetings.

CHAPTER TWENTY-NINE

For the first seven days the new servant did as he was told and if he was told nothing he did nothing. He barely spoke as a servant but only listened. He never knew there was so much to listen to, so much to hear, in the world, and in the universe.

At first listening was very alien to him, very difficult, and he experienced it as a kind of agony. Then, slowly, he noticed there was a pleasure in it, if he slowed down the workings of his mind and if he forgot himself. He began to hear things he would never have been told. He heard stories and rumours about the kingdom. He heard that the land had a king that no one had ever seen. He heard that in the king's court there were those plotting the removal of the king and the division of the kingdom. He heard that the prince had died and that a false prince had been put in his place to soothe the agitation of the people. He heard that on all sides the kingdom was being invaded by shadows and white spirits. He heard that the land was being devoured by darkness, and that an evil had come among the people and was snatching away the young men and women and stealing them away into a dark space beyond the great seas, from where there is no return. He heard the cry of the ancestors, he heard the wailing of the legion of unborn generations, and he heard the crashing down of the great pillars of the land, the collapsing houses, the crumbling palaces, the howling of the dead, and the poignant songs of angels singing of new ages to come out of such appalling destruction. He had no idea how he heard these things, but when he learnt to listen there seemed no end to the things it was essential for him to hear.

He learnt to listen without fretting, without the need to act. He learnt to listen, and to hear, the way statues do.

He realised that the more he listened, the more he heard.

CHAPTER THIRTY

Every evening the new servant went back to the forest and walked into the precise gap between the trees and found himself in the same forest, except it was different, and it led him home. He would rise from among the statues and bow silently to the father of the maiden, and would pick his way through the sculptures, the wooden busts, the gates of images, the statues of gods, the thronging artworks along the village main ways and paths, images in stone and wood and mixed materials of nails and feathers and blood and rope and patterned cowries, works that crowded the thoroughfare, changing shapes in the encroaching evening. And he would make his way past them all, listening to the murmur of voices like the choirs of the low rumbling river. And, without looking at any faces, or dwelling too long on any one sight, he would glide past the busy village, not drawing attention to himself, and would find his way to the dark thick forest. Often it was that the rich startling fragrance of the evening-breathing leaves would engulf him in deep memories and a feeling of a great freedom; and his heart would sing with a ruby-dark joy. Often he would feel so fortunate to have the kingdom of the forest all to himself, and he would linger or run among the trees and sing to the birds and recite lines of ancient verse to the forest flowers. Sometimes he would lie with his back against a tree and for a moment would allow himself to drift in a realm of elementals. And on one such occasion he had an extraordinary dream about a baby who, on the very same day it was born, became a man, married a wife, had three children, fought valiantly in a great war, travelled to all the continents, was initiated into the mighty secret brotherhood of universal masters, healed the sick, redirected the course of world history, cleansed half the earth of its great corruptions by diverting through it the wonderful river of Venus, yoked the oxen of the sun to the dry unfruitful earth, fought the seven-headed monster of the deep, and restored the neglected garden of the race to its pristine beauty, and then died at the midnight of its first and only day on earth. The dream of this wonderful child haunted the new servant for a long time, and he had no idea what it meant, but he drew great strength thinking about this baby avatar that accomplished so much on the first and only day of its life.

Every evening the new servant would do something new in the forest on his way back home. Sometimes he would learn the taste of fear as he walked in the dense shadows of the trees and listened to the weird birds call his secret names in distorted voices. Sometimes he would try to listen to the language of trees, to hear what they had to say about being immemorial, and about time. He sometimes heard whispers that death lived in the forest and that its house was all the trees and all the shade and all the darkness and all the earth and that in its womb was life too, if you could find it. These whispers made no sense to him.

Whatever he did, however much he lingered, he always made sure that whenever he was returning home to the palace he found the exact gap between the trees and that he passed through it quickly and in a firm spirit. And when he did he found that he had vanished in one place only to reappear in the same place that was somehow different. He couldn't understand it and didn't try.

But it was some time before he realised that this gap might be the reason why his emissaries had been unable to find the tribe of artists. And it occurred to him that the mysterious tribe was not on any map or in any territory, but in a separate realm. For the first time the prince was not even sure if they were of the land, or in the land, or in the kingdom.

And when he passed through that gap, which changed shape from day to day, never the same, sometimes like a moon, sometimes like a fire, sometimes like a clear mirror of water dazzling in the air, sometimes in the shape of a woman, but whenever he passed through the gap, he became the other side of what he was, different, but also the same. And on the journey home he became the prince, frail, tender, his head shimmering with a new clarity, as if with eyes shut he could see half the universe in a flash, and glimpse the immortal mirror of destiny.

CHAPTER THIRTY-ONE

For seven days he served thus. For days he lived thus. Then he asked his father, the king, for permission to stay longer on his mysterious mission. His father, with the hint of sublime mischief in his eyes, said:

'I consider it part of your duties as a prince to be first and foremost a human being, richly grounded and properly rounded. A season of humility would do you good. Another season of suffering would be quite excellent for you. A season of humiliation would put power in your veins and some ripening rage in your heart. To be all things is to be human. The ancestry of dust, the lash of destiny, exile in a hostile land, servitude, slavery, warfare, madness, folly, despair, grandeur – these are the food of human history. All will be tasted at the feast before you become king. But the greatest fruit of all, my son, is love; and if love is that with which you can learn, in the art of a human being, you will be a great prince and a joy to the mystery of the stars.'

The prince was taken aback by this strange speech from his father. The king had never spoken to him like that before. The prince was so amazed, and oddly touched, that when he recovered from the mild delirium of joy, his father was gone from his presence.

On the evenings of his return, however, driven by an inexplicable passion and a silent empowerment he sensed from the king, he summoned the elders and demanded answers from them about the multiplying gaps in the kingdom that were threatening, undermining, the foundation of things. This puzzled and enraged the elders more than ever, because they had no answers and could do nothing about the gaps that were spreading through the kingdom like a nameless disease.

CHAPTER THIRTY-TWO

The prince went and lived among the tribe of gate-makers, masquerade-shapers, bronze-casters, and dream-revealers. He lived among the tribe of artists in disguise, as an ordinary man, following one of his favourite principles of invisibility. He worked as a servant for the father of the maiden of his heart. He worked with him for seven seasons. Often, with permission, he stole back to his kingdom. He never spoke to the maiden in all that time. And she never spoke to him. She didn't see him. She didn't notice him. He never spoke to her, seldom looked at her directly, but he watched her in his spirit and listened to her in his soul. He studied her heart, and he followed her ways, and he absorbed the peculiar philosophy of her being.

She was one of the strange ones who did not know quite how strange she was. She was so strange to herself that she took it to be normal. The new servant learnt, for example, that she was not much interested in the reflection of things. Mirrors did not unduly fascinate her. She was more interested in being than in things. And yet she avoided people and hid among things. She was more interested in fruits than in roots. Others kept probing what lay behind things, where people came from, where they were in the hierarchy of things, who their ancestors were, but she was interested mainly in what people produced, their fruits, their art, their deeds. The new servant often noticed how with a glance at someone's art she took in all that she needed to know about them. With a glance at their production, her silence spoke. To her nothing was more revealing than the signature of a soul in the works of art they created. In this she was merciless. In this she was absolute. Everything lay bare to her, like a true secret confession, in every work she saw. She could read minds in their works. Courage, humour, patience, capacity to grow, freedom of spirit, meanness, a hidden greatness, cowardice, a mystical inclination, the state of their health, how long they would live, what kind of husbands or wives they might make, their trustworthiness, their capacity for love, all these and many more things that can only be intuited thus could this peculiar maiden read in every work of art she saw. This was a strange gift indeed. It was almost a curse. It weighed her down. It was almost like divination, like prophecy. It was a wonderful witchcraft of the eyes. Everyone in the tribe feared her eyes for this reason. And this power had grown more acute since her initiation. To look at the works of art around was to suffer. She saw only too clearly the inadequacies of the best. Very few works had ever affected her as being beyond. And these had affected her very powerfully indeed, like a wound, or like a mental breakdown, or like a revelation in which she was somehow destroyed. She craved this destruction. Only through such a destruction did she feel and get a great sense of the mystery and unspeakable truth of life that so haunted her in her daydreaming hours.

The new servant, in his stillness among the statues, never ceased to study her obscure heart, and her ways. Using the powers that death had given him, he strove to roam and listen to the philosophy of her being. It was his primary reason for dwelling there, in the shadows, under the wall, in the realm where he was a stranger, and where he was unknown, and unseen. All he wanted, whether he admitted it to himself or not, was to live in her being. And more often than he realised, he did.

He sensed that she saw straight to the heart of whoever she encountered, but she seldom believed that what she saw was what she had seen.

CHAPTER THIRTY-THREE

Often her mind would drift to another world, far away, where she would have long converse with beings of radiant beauty. They were beings of all colours and they were pure in form. To them all things had gods and philosophies. To them magic and miracles were primitive things. To them science and technology were the ancient arts of a prehistoric people who were not even legends in the annals of that realm. They did not believe in remembering anything. They did not believe in too much memory or history. They believed that it was important to forget for a civilisation to be quantumly creative. Their forgetfulness was an act of genius, because they knew that everything that ever was ever will be, and so to even strive to enshrine history was to commit a tautology and to clutter the path of the future. All things that were important, they believed, found their way to the present. They were masters of the present moment, in which all things, all worlds, all time and all possibilities exist. Their sense of humour and irony was inexhaustible. These beings showed the maiden many wonderful things and notions that filled her heart with delight – the past and future, they showed her, under the aspect of sublime irrelevance seen from the infinite perspective of the stars.

The maiden loved the hours she spent wandering the forest and half dreaming on the shores of the river, in converse with these beings of a remote place that was her true home. What sort of things did she talk about with them? Once they conversed about the art of misunderstanding.

'Misunderstanding is all that is possible between your people,' said one of the beautiful beings. 'It is simply not possible to understand one another, given the way you people are made. You do not hear what you hear, you do not say what you say, what is said is not what is intended, what is intended is not what is said. How can that which does not know itself know what it is saying, or wants to say? Nothing is as you see it or feel it or hear it. Your bodies are inefficient for the collecting of true information. All you can do is misunderstand. And so you may as well make an art of it.'

'How can you make an art of misunderstanding?'

'By assuming that you can't understand anything, and that nothing can be understood, because nothing is what it seems.'

'But where is the art?'

'The art is to communicate through misunderstanding. To make misunderstanding the very tool itself.'

'Like people who talk in different languages and yet do good business at the marketplace?'

'Yes.'

'Is that what art is?'

'Yes. Being misunderstood and yet speaking clearly to the spirit.'

'What else can I learn from this?'

'If you begin with the art of misunderstanding you will find your way to the gate of illumination.'

'Then what?'

'Then everything will be simple and clear and you will know what to do and what not to do and you will have no beginning and no end any more and you will be with us and wherever you want to be.'

The maiden often spent hours in the company of her true people so far away; and their conversations were so far removed from her life in the tribe of artists that they were useless to her except as refreshments to the spirit. Sometimes though they gave her hints and signs of things that were to burst into faint reality and which she caught in art and forgot that she did, thus adding, as if in sleepwalking mode, to the enigmas of the race.

Sometimes one or two figures from that distant realm would pay her a visit, in a form she didn't recognise, in that kingdom where artists are not seen . . .

CHAPTER THIRTY-FOUR

Silently there among the statues of an ancient mood, the new servant sat, while all the stars in the galaxy revolved, while the story of all things approached the ultimate secret of their ends and their beginnings, while death crept over the kingdom, and darkness stole into the name of that realm.

Drums broke their voices in the evenings and held the steady beat to the public festivities. The drums were charmed with sculpted figures of bards singing death back to its cave. Deep voices sang, dances thumped the face of the earth, libations poured into the cracks, and laughter rose among the flute melodies that imitated the enquiries of newborn babies about the fitness of the times for their arrival. The new servant sat in the silence of statues till the spiders wove their nets about his face, entangling his hair, imprisoning him in their fine web from which he did not stir. How quickly did the spiders work? He would be still a while, wandering in the delicious philosophy of the maiden's being, when he would come round and find himself enmeshed again in fine-spun threads of darkness. He would hear his father's laughter in the irony of it all, and he would smile.

And still he sought a way into the subtle notions of her sweet existence.

By the river he would linger with her in the errands she made as a daughter to a mother. He would learn in her the art of weaving stories in cloth, of dyeing tales on cloth, of painting symbols and signs, figures and forms, hints of dreams, shapes of prophecies on the bales of wrappers which the women and men wore on ceremonial occasions. The maiden and her mother dressed the tribe in prophecies. Shapes of fishes that mean many things, forms of beings with eyes of gold and moonstones, dancing with angels of blinding colours, were charmed on to the cloths. Cowries arranged in forms of changing divinations, images of stars in space in unique constellations, visions of men in space, among the stars, with arms embracing the universe, were patterned on to the materials that would become blouses, dresses, wrappers, coverlets. The tribe and the world would be draped in dreams, in visions, in cheeky myths, in divinations and inscriptions to the future. The maiden loved this working on cloth with her mother; and they laughed often and told stories and challenged one another in images and inspiration.

Then later, when evening fell, and the day's work was done, the maiden would go to the farms, with water and refreshments for the farmers as they prepared to come home; and often the new servant would sense her wandering among the golden sheaves of cornfields, leaning against a tree, lingering among the cassava plants, gazing at a remote constellation.

And then he would be surprised to see her burst into tears, as if she had lost a lover to the stars.

Then, just as suddenly, she would be re-composed and would be with the women, returning from the farm, carrying a basket of yams, or dandling a child on her back while its mother rested a moment in the shade.

The new servant sensed a profound restlessness in the maiden. One day she burst into her father's workshop and said:

'My father, something is supposed to be happening to me, but it isn't. What is it?'

'Are you ready to make your choice of husband now?'

'No.'

There was a pause.

'Then what do you mean?'

'I am supposed to be happy or sad, but I am not.'

'What are you then?'

'I don't know. Do you?'

Her father said nothing. The silence lengthened in the workshop. The new servant could hear the statues whispering. He could hear the spirits at work in enriching the forms of the statues, polishing them with the invisible wax of myth, and infusing into them moods of amber and of unfinished stories, breathing an odd quality of life into them, till they fairly bristled with a condition that partook both of something lifelike and something mineral, alive in a hidden, troubling, dreamy kind of way. The new servant listened as the spirit-servants performed their finishing touches on the statues and figurines, making them take on an ancient immemorial mood, under the father's precise instructions. They worked on the masks too, silently, the masks that would adorn the masquerade's faces, that would be the faces, on the day of the ancestors or on feast days when the select ones were possessed by the gods. These masks were carved with the mysterious art that made them take on their true personalities only when in motion, only when in the dance. Motionless, they acquired a kinetic stillness. This fusion of motion and stillness would transform the art of the future. The spirits infused into these masks the eternal longing to dance, in order to be free.

*

In this silence of statues changing from their recently created states into their enigmatic natures, the new servant listened to the maiden awaiting her father's reply. But her father didn't speak. So the maiden absent-mindedly wandered amongst the statues in the workshop, to see how they were coming along, and to see how much they had changed by just being there in that space, immersed in the radiance of the master and deepened by the atmosphere which enters the body of the statues and enriches them with dark and wonderful notions.

The maiden lingered at each statue and gazed at it dreamily. And then she came upon the new servant where he sat motionless under the wall in a sepia and amber mood of spiders' webs and the silence of old royal trees. And, suddenly, engulfed by an arboreal mood of unknown kings of the forest, she was amazed at the new perfection of her father's art. She drew in breath and cried out, half horrified and half enchanted at this statue of a frail-looking and beautiful young man that sat there like a visitor from an unknown world. Her heart couldn't stop beating so fast and a wild delusion flooded her head and for a moment she went quite blind and then a white light, like the brilliance of the sky, quite conquered the top of her head. Then everything suddenly cleared. Her mouth was dry. She saw nothing as she did before, and she drew back. Shaken by a nameless wonder, she was astonished at what she beheld. It seemed incredible to her that her father had now created a work so real that it had become virtually human. If there was any flaw it was that there seemed something altogether too kind about its face, and too adorable about its lips. But overcome by the sorcery of the accomplishment the maiden feared that her father had gone too far; and this time, in his terrifying perfection, he might have tempted the gods with the greatness of his art . . .

CHAPTER THIRTY-FIVE

The maiden retreated from this new art of sorcery and went and sat at the far end of the workshop. To her mind the darkness where the new sculpture sat was now a place faintly touched with dark magic. In her mind the new sculpture conjoined the weird and the enchanting. And so she set about forgetting that she had endured such an unsettling and yet such a beautiful experience. But what was beautiful about the experience she had felt only as bizarre. There was something unnatural about the beauty of that face that she didn't quite want to think about.

She had also forgotten the question she had asked her father. She sat in a mild confusion, feeling scared and miraculously changed, but not knowing why. Soon the mood of the workshop crept over her in its whispers and its fragrance of old wood and stone and spirits, and she drifted into a deep and wonderful sleep. When she was far away from the workshop, and played like a child among the beings of her secret homeland in a remote constellation, her father turned to her and rose. Then above her sleeping form he chanted potent vowel sounds, intoned certain reality-altering incantations, and spoke to the master-spirit that dwelt within her, saying:

'Forget that which wouldn't do you any good. Remember things in a manner that is best for you. Open your heart towards your marriage, and choose only he who would best help you fulfil your destiny, whatever your destiny may be, and he whose destiny you can best help fulfil, whatever that too may be.'

Then, intoning another complex sound, he went and sat down again, and worked in silence.

Shortly afterwards he summoned the spirits of the workshop and gave them fresh instructions about the new work he had slowly been gestating. The spirits set about their tasks. The new servant hadn't moved. Breathing gently, he felt the spirits working all around him, enriching the air with ideas, with open dimensions to other worlds and other ages. They worked on the air, the atmosphere. It seemed as if they impregnated the air with moods of ancestral wisdom and future realities, and that this charged atmosphere, seeping into the statues, into the carvings, the masks and sculptures, was what created the highest mystery in the works of art. It seemed as if the works when finished were not complete. They needed to absorb an atmosphere richly treated in enchantments and sorceries, in dark beautiful suggestiveness, and moods combined from remote eras in the infinite museums of universal history. This was the most important work, it seemed, that the spirits performed. They marinated the completed creations in enigmas. It wasn't long before the servant realised that he too was being treated and woven in enigmas . . .

CHAPTER THIRTY-SIX

The maiden woke with a shock and sprang out of her chair and hurried to her mother and said:

'I'm in love, but I don't know who I am in love with. Why?'

Her mother was bewildered.

The maiden joined her mother in the creation of images on cloth; and in silence she made a beautiful collection of dye work of all the suitors, their forms, their traits, their gifts, and the works of art each had created. It was a loving group portrait of all the suitors who had honoured her with their intentions, their efforts, their patience and their ardour. She worked in silence with her mother. This was the way they talked about things too difficult to talk about. It was long laborious work and as the faces emerged, each one represented so beautifully, the maiden's mother wept at the wonderful gift her daughter had and didn't value at all.

'Mother, why are you weeping?' the maiden asked absent-mindedly, and with a simple smile.

'I just pray that you marry the right person. You are the strangest daughter that God could have given a mother. I just don't know what to do with you.'

And the maiden laughed and wept on her mother's shoulder, like a little girl.

Later on, when the dye was set, and the cloth was ready, the suitors delighted in the lovely gift the maiden had given them, the gift of fame. For their faces adorned the women's bodies in the season's festivities and were seen beyond the tribe, carried to distant lands by cloth merchants. And instead of pacifying the suitors, this act inflamed them more.

But in making the images on cloth, the maiden found herself perplexed: she made an astonishing discovery. She was not remotely in love with any of the suitors. And yet she knew, from all she had heard, from all the tales of the heart she had been told, and from the quickened happy and alive quality of her being, the delightful half-blinding half-clear-seeing malady, that she was in love. There could be no other explanation. Either she was in love, or she was possessed by a god, or she was being worked on by a master or a wizard, or she was going mad in her youth. Was she just simply more than normally excited by the miraculous joy of being alive? How could she love without an object for that love? These questions troubled her. And yet she could not sleep, she brooded around the outskirts of the village and hung around the shrine and lingered in her father's workshop staring at the statues that were slowly coming to life. She consulted, secretly, the priestesses of the shrine, and they told her riddles, prophecies and obscure words that confused her even more.

'When that which is not seen is seen,
When that which is dead comes to life again,
When stone turns to flesh,
When the yellow river bears
The prince and princess into distant lands,
When darkness has come and gone
Over the world,
And we understand the meaning of the sun,

And we realise what a human being
Is among the stars,
Then all your questions will be answered.
The whole world is a seed
And inside the seed we dream.
One day the seed will grow,
And what we will see will be
As great as heaven.
What you love is right in front
Of your eyes.
But you can only see it with
Your heart, your soul.'

This they told the maiden in songs, woven with choruses.

CHAPTER THIRTY-SEVEN

Meanwhile the new servant was being woven in cobwebs and in enigmas by the spirits of the master-maker's workshop. In order to serve, he became a statue, and was inducted into the mysteries without knowing it. For only the statues, in their purity, know the secrets of the land. They absorb them simply, and store them in their forms. The new servant absorbed the lessons he had to learn from the master without being told anything. He absorbed by being still. He almost never moved. And when he did move he did it silently, like a shadow or a ghost, not troubling the air, or shifting the mood. He moved with the grace and simplicity of the dead. And he returned to his place under the wall, in the dark, among the statues, as though he were occupying a space he had never left. He began to suspect that a part of him moved, but another part of him remained behind, unmoving, in the semi-darkness, among the spirits and the fragrance of wood. He thus acquired a delicate patina from the air of the master's dreams.

For a long time the father of the maiden did not require much of him, and asked him to do nothing. At first there were simple errands, but even these were forgotten, and abandoned. The master worked in silence at his new revelation, which demanded the utmost stillness and the most profound concentration which, for him, was really a form of great humility, an acute receptivity. The master too had to cease to be in order to see what needed to be. It was a new mode every time. Sometimes, in order to make a work happen, he had to turn into a wild lion and roam the forests hunting for a dream that dwelt among the spirits there, a dream that can be seen by beasts, but not men. Sometimes, in order to drag back form that would endure for more than two thousand years, he had to change into an eagle and fly to remote villages in faraway lands and spy on the rituals of the daughters of an ancient mother whose children, scattered about the world, didn't know one another any more. And sometimes, very rarely, when he felt an acute mood in the world that needed a cry of bafflement to help heal a giant wound which an entire race will suffer, he had to turn into a shape abhorrent to men, and journey to the realm of the dead and drag back the corpses of evil images, and change them into beautiful forms in the darkness before the light of the sun reaches them. And then he would have to learn, for many months, how to be human again. All this expended his life, shortened his life, converted his vitality. And it was only by regenerating himself in an invisible stream of light that flowed from the centre of the sun to the centre of the earth that he managed, in dreams and in meditation, in prayer and in rigorous ritual exercise, not to die, as many do who work such tough wonders, long before their time.

And now the father of the maiden was preparing himself again. Slowly, he was letting go of the world. Slowly, he was letting go of desire. Slowly, he was releasing himself of all need to create, or to command, or to will, or to dream, or to summon. The world must do without him. In prayer, within a magic circle, in his workshop, surrounded by an invisible light, protected by the seven spirits who ward off all intruders, the father of the maiden set himself adrift into a world where all forms, all notions, all unexplored dreams, all ideas dwell in a constellation bright as the light and fire of jewels and diamonds that sparkle in the sun. He released himself into this world, and surrendered himself to its currents, and then found the gates to unsuspected worlds, where he made new friends, and attended the convention of master artists from all the worlds. While in the workshop, he might as well have been dead.

Often the father of the maiden went off like this, without informing anyone. And so he forgot all things, and left the new servant without instructions. So the new servant sat under the wall and stared and dreamt and discovered new gaps and was silent. And then he found that he was learning and being taught in the silence. Things and beings and artworks were whispering to him. The masters of the tribe, who saw him in their meditations, whispered secrets into his being. Spirits of the workshop came and explained the workings of things to him, the secrets of bronze-casting, the golden art of harmony in wood-sculpting, the art of kinetic magic in mask-making, the history of the tribe, its public history and its secret sacred history too.

It was whispered to him, by beings he had no idea about, from realms inaccessible except to travellers in dreams, that the artworks of the tribe were prophecies of one kind or another. They were prophecies that the tribe itself didn't know about. Sometimes, in the silence, the new servant found himself elsewhere. Sometimes he found that he was in the square, or in the circle, where the shrine stood, and he was being shown statues and sculptures, masks and carvings and paintings of wars between tribes, invasions of continents by aliens, of wars being fought across the seas, of murders committed in distant lands which have never been solved, and secret intentions of governments far away given clear artistic form. And market traders on caravan routes who have visited the tribe to trade have been shocked to recognise, among the artworks that were visible, the face of one who had been crowned king of their land just as they were setting out on their journeys, or the face of a famous sage who never travelled, a thing the tribe of artists simply could not have known about.

The new servant gathered, in the hints and whispering in the air, that the tribe of artists were listeners at the universal world of facts and events. It was as though they had access to a place where all things that happened in the universe were registered. And so they seemed to know, in the works they created, without knowing that they knew, the invasions planned on sleeping lands, assassinations, the faces of generals who would lead monstrous battles, world wars that would not happen in their time but hundreds of years in the future. And the new servant learnt to see in the artworks prophecies of great events to come in the far distant future as well as those that happened in the remotest past. It was as though time was an indifferent stream in which past, present and future were all one. And the artists of that tribe bathed in that stream, and drew from it their inspiration without end.

Happenings and possibilities were coded there in the odd art of the tribe, in one form or another. The futures of the world and of many worlds were encoded there in one form or another. The tribe knew great and intimate secrets that they didn't know they knew.

But the new servant was astonished to learn, in a flash of intuition, that the artworks of the tribe were intended to be works of sublime indifference and beauty. They were not interested in prophecy. They had no idea of prophecy. It meant nothing to them. They were not interested in facts. Only in creating different kinds of beauty: beauty out of disharmony, beauty that lurks in chaos, beauty that hides in disorder, beauty that sings in destruction, beauty out of the least expected events or things or materials or elements, beauty in ugliness, beauty that becomes beauty in a horrible-looking work only when you have stopped looking at it; beauty that the work creates in the mind, a mental and spiritual beauty stimulated by the work but not residing in the work, or its design. Even beauty itself the tribe of artists were indifferent about. They were interested only in what exalted states the work could induce in you, for you to use as your intelligence or need best suggests to you. And so they had no word for beauty in their language. They had banished it centuries ago, because the word got in the way of infinite suggestibility and an inducement to higher states of consciousness.

The prophetic element was merely a covert accessory, a hidden incidental, accompanying the strange beauty that the art of the tribe embodied.

CHAPTER THIRTY-EIGHT

All this, and much more, the new servant learnt in silence. The silence was invaluable. The semi-darkness was invaluable. So also was the stillness in which he could learn to be free. He learnt more in the silence than in years of being told things.

Then, at a certain moment, he realised that he was learning things about the kingdom, about the palace, about the traditions, about the mysterious nature of the gaps, and about the white spirits and their silent invasion of the land through mirrors and with hidden fire.

He was even learning about learning.

Everything in the workshop was eager to tell him things, to teach him. The stones yielded the secrets of the structure of matter. The spiders yielded the secrets of the art of making, and of cohesion. The implements yielded the secrets of joining, of angles. The walls yielded up the art of the vertical. The air taught the art of invisibility. Feathers taught the nature of flight. And the light that came in through the chinks in the wall bore to him the underlying secret of all things, in fragments, hints, and undeciphered illumination.

Time was different in the realm of the artists: sometimes it was long, sometimes it was short, and often it simply did not exist at all. Mostly time for them was timelessness.

Everything in that village, in that tribe, was eager to teach him. He was eager to listen, and to learn.

CHAPTER THIRTY-NINE

Meanwhile, brooding darkness was gathering about the kingdom. First came the white wind that made things disappear; then came the brooding darkness. It was not there before. The old sages say that it came with a name, a word uttered, words used as an incantation to distort the land and make it more manageable to those who wanted to conquer and use it. They say the words created the darkness, and then the darkness came and hung over the land, and the people did not know it. The darkness thickened amongst them, and the elders did not see it. And when the darkness had made them more visible to those outside, the white spirits came and emptied the kingdom of its young ones, its virile men, its gifted children. And at first no one noticed. They didn't notice because of the darkness.

About this time the new servant made infrequent visits home through the forest. He noticed that there were more gaps than before. This filled him with mild alarm. In the palace he noticed changes in the air. The women were more silent. He peered into the faces of his people and he saw a new doubt he had never seen before, a new puzzlement. He asked them questions and they spoke of their dreams. Many dreamt that their bodies were taken from them in the brightness of day, when they were in the middle of their tasks and without knowing when they had become spirits who were performing empty duties in a place where nothing happened. Their bodies had been taken from them and worked the white fields of blood as if in a deep sleep of horror. They tried to get their bodies back, but they were stuck in that place, working the farms of the strangers. Many people reported having the same dream, of how their bodies had been snatched, and how they found themselves as spirits in the kingdom. Some said that eventually they managed to get their spirits to join their bodies in that far-off place, and then the agony of their nightmares began.

The prince was troubled by these dreams of his people. No one seemed able, or willing, to interpret them.

About this time the prince, in asking so many questions, began to rouse, unknowingly, the fears and unease of the elders. They feared once again that he was going to undermine them. They feared he was going to destroy their power and their institutions when he became king. They feared he would be a dangerous king, with too many new ideas, too many changes, making women equal to men, reducing the hierarchies of things, and, worse, changing the nature of their rough religion, and altering the laws which made them the secret masters of the land. And so they pressed forward with their schemes, plotting ways of getting rid of the prince. And then one of them – Chief Okadu, the Crocodile – had the brilliant idea of somehow offering the prince to the white spirits, so that they might carry him off to the seas and leave the elders free again to rule in secret, in the name of the laughing king.

CHAPTER FORTY

There were times when the prince would stand near the centre of the village where the palace could be seen in the distance, and where all around he breathed in the immemorial air of his people, their harvests, their traditions, their births, deaths, their wars, their festivities. There were times when he would watch the women on their way to the farms, or the marketplace, or the river, or on visits to their relations; and, unaccountably, he would weep. There were times when the ochre of the huts, and the winding bronze paths that led to evergreen forests, and the rolling choruses of children's voices, and the clear sharp tinkling of bells rang out gently behind the passionate songs of the women or the deep-throated songs of the men in their gatherings at dusk, and the silvery blue quiver of the sky, and the brightness of the moon white as the most perfect gap that leads to other worlds, and the smell of the goats, and the lonely song of the hunter in the hills, and the sudden red and yellow cry of the women of the golden shrines, and the flight of the blue-headed sharp-eyed long-flying birds that precipitate auguries when they circle the palace three times before shooting upwards into the palm-wine sky – there were times when overcome by all this, standing in the square, dreaming of his ancestors who had come from the land that was now forgotten under the sea, there were times when the prince found that time itself had turned upside-down, had become scrambled, that the huts had turned to dust, that the children had all fled or been sold or only their spirits remained, that the forests had shrunk, that the stream had thinned into a ribbon, that only the very old remained, that the elders had lost their memories, that the aged mothers wandered the forests without voices, unrecognised by their children, and that the white wind had wiped away the traditions, and that only the dreams and the histories and a bitterness, tinged with songs, lingered in the dry hot air where his tears of an exile turned into stones as they fell from his face and piled up, white and sparkling as diamonds, at his feet.

There were times, in the farms, as he worked with the men, carrying sheaves of corn, or cutting the long grass with a machete, or hauling mounds of yam from their bundles to the village, there were times when time itself turned round and everything cleared and he found that the farms had gone and that he had fled from that distant land of slavery and had escaped on a great ship and had found his way, after many years, back to the continent, on a remote shore, and had begun his search for the homeland that he had been stolen from and which he hadn't seen for forty years. He was an old man, wise in many sufferings, which illumination had taught him to endure, and he searched for his homeland, travelling from one country to another, through countries without names, seeking for his kingdom that had been so vast and which also never had a name. He travelled through many countries with villages so similar to his, and saw palaces that could have been his, but nowhere could he find the kingdom he had left behind. And as an old man, who knew slavery, who knew freedom, and who had never ceased being a prince, and who in spirit had never left his homeland, he sought, in that brief time left, while he dreamt in the farm, for his homeland, and found it everywhere and never found it at all. It was as if it had been broken into fragments and scattered all over the vast continent. The years passed in dust and dreams, and he never stopped seeking his kingdom. And then one day, by a narrow stream, he heard in the wind the laughter of the king, and he fell down and fell towards the beautiful brightness of the sun. And when he stood up he found himself in the farm, surrounded by the women of the village, who were concerned for him, and who loved him with all their hearts, as if he were all of their sons. And they bore him in their arms, and carried him with songs, to the edge of the farm, ignoring his protestation that he was well, that he had only fallen into a strange spell of dreaming. And after they had made him drink some water, which tasted strangely sweet, with its taste of earth and stone, and after they had prayed over him, and shared their food with him, they carried him to the palace, singing and cheering, as if he were a hero returning from the noble wars . . .

There were times when the prince stood in the square, in the middle of the village, and wondered about the kingdom, and the people, and what the strange hands of destiny were weaving for those that walked the land with long shadows.

CHAPTER FORTY-ONE

Meanwhile, the maiden grew inflamed with a love that seemed to have no source and no object, a love that gripped her like the growth of a fever. She was possessed by a love that had no meaning, no purpose, and she went around with the feeling that she was slowly being driven mad by a love that had come upon her with invisible wings. She was under a peculiar spell.

This madness became more evident to her parents. But they said nothing. They watched her mooning about the place, pining away gently like a fading rose. They watched her eyes grow hollow in their sockets. They watched her staring at the moon and singing childish love songs. They watched her wreathe her hair with flowers and beheld her skipping down the village paths, singing out aloud:

'Who am I in love with
Who has poisoned my soul
Let me know, let me know.

Who has conquered my heart
Who has killed me with love
Let me know, let me know.

Who am I a slave to
Who is now my destiny

Let me know, let me know.

I am quite mad with love
I have lost my soul to love
Does it show, does it show?'

Then the maiden would play with the little girls and boys, suddenly laughing, suddenly bursting into song, suddenly weeping. She would trail behind her whispering companions and would not dwell long by the river. She had lost her taste for the river and the sky and the forest. She didn't even think of art or look at the new artworks that appeared in the square. For her there was nothing to see there. Often she walked round her father's workshop as if seeking the spot of hidden treasure. Often she would repeat the verses given her by the priestesses of the shrine. The more she pondered them the more obscure they grew.

Once she was sitting under a tree listening to her friends in the remote place where she felt more at home when a bird with yellow plumage landed in her lap and seemed to speak to her. She could have sworn she distinctly heard it say:

'The more you look
The less you see.
Let it be, let it be.'

But she could not let it be and she seized the bird and took it to her father. Her father was pondering how high a thing can be before human beings begin to see it; he was pondering how invisible a thing must be before human beings can see it;

he was pondering how light a thing must be before human beings cannot destroy it – when his daughter intruded on his thoughts with a bird that she claimed had spoken to her.

'What did it say?'

She told her father.

'Then pay attention to it. First, let the bird go. Then, go back to your tree and see what happens.'

The maiden set the bird free and went and sat under the tree again and fell asleep with her back against the tree trunk. And when she awoke her head was clear. She felt a wonderful clarity within her, as though she had just had her first good night's sleep in a long time. She had a shining feeling within her, like the day after it has rained, and a storm has broken. She still felt the madness of her love, but it was a quiet, tranquil, beautiful madness, like the surface of the river on a clear moonless night.

CHAPTER FORTY-TWO

The new servant returned from his visit home and resumed his life as a statue. No one noticed his departure except the spirits and the spiders. And on his return they began to weave webs of enigma about him again, layering the work they had previously done. Deeper into the mood of his new life went the new servant. He plunged deeper into the silent mysteries of the tribe. And in his deeper delving he found himself exploring the roots of legends, the source of myths, the dark secrets of creativity. And then, one day, or one night, he found himself falling into the abyss that was one of the strangest secrets of the tribe, a secret it kept even from itself. He fell into the abyss, and was falling a long time, in great horror, when he became dimly aware that the abyss, without form, and dark beyond measure, was the route through which the gods appeared in the minds of men. He cried out in the abyss and no one heard him. He fell without end for days and nights without end and it was a fall into the abyss that took him beyond nightmare, beyond chaos, beyond madness, beyond death, even.

The fall took him to the placeless place where the gods pullulated, where all things were mixed into one, where the universe seemed to converge in vastness and mingling, where all beings in all the universe merged and emerged, flowed into and out of one another as in one great unimaginable spirit that was neither darkness nor light, a place where all dreams came from and went to, where all deaths died into and where all life emerged from, a place raw and wild and sublime and bright beyond bearing, a place of fire and darkness, of great quivering columns, all seven of them, that seemed to be longer and deeper than it is possible to imagine. And still he went on falling. He fell through the dark secrets of the universe, through all the versions of lives and dreams and deaths of all beings, in all the universes, whether of humans, animals or plants, or creatures from realms unthinkable. And still he went on falling, without hope of ever stopping his fall, of ever emerging from the abyss, of ever getting to the end of his fall. And he might have gone on falling for ever in this space that was no longer a space, a hole that was no longer a hole but a gap that led into the infinite endlessness, and he might have gone on in this black dark bright infinity of a fall, till he was no longer anywhere, and till his body, woven now so thoroughly in profound mysteries, would have turned finally into a statue of flesh, preserved by spirits, if he had not been saved by a master's hand on his head raising him from this dying that was not a normal death.

CHAPTER FORTY-THREE

And so it was that on a certain day, now lost in time, with the maiden looking on, her father laid his hand on the statue that was the prince, and said:

'This is my new pupil. Get up! Arise!'

And the prince arose in the dark, as if from an immortal dream; and he bowed gracefully to the master and his strange daughter. And he remained in an attitude of bowing, till the master touched him on the shoulder. At that moment there was a flash of light from that touch which no one but the spirits saw. And the maiden drew breath sharply; her amazement knew no bounds. For the first time she had witnessed with her own eyes, wide awake, what she had only heard rumours about. She had seen her father bring a statue to life. The rumours were true. Her father had spirits that worked for him, that did his carving, his shaping, his moulding, for him. Her father's statues were brought to life by the power of his hands and they served him and did his will. Her father was an artist-wizard, and a creator of monsters. She had always revered her father; now she was in utter awe of him. She no longer thought of him as being entirely human, but something more, which she dared not specify in her mind . . .

And, in addition to this, the maiden feared the new servant. She feared him because she knew that he was not real, was not truly of flesh and blood, and had no heart, but was a thing made in the dark workshop of her powerful father, and brought to life by the touch of his mysterious hand. On another day, after his arising, the prince was instructed by the maiden's father to walk once round the workshop, in a perfect circle, in an obscure symbolic ritual. As the prince performed this rite, in slowness and with dignity, he accidentally brushed against the maiden's dress, the effect of which made her jump.

'Don't touch me,' she said, in a confusion of feelings as she felt the warmth of his body as he passed her.

'He feels almost human,' she said, in wonder. 'Is he?'

But she received no answer.

She avoided this new pupil and soon stopped noticing him again because he aroused in her disquieting notions. He made her feel a mild and incomprehensible aversion. He became invisible to her a second time over. And so she was truly herself in his presence because she did not notice him in the brief period after his raising, when he remained silent and still. She was what she was, simply and purely, as he sat there in the workshop, among the gathering images and statues that would one day perplex the minds of men and women.

CHAPTER FORTY-FOUR

The new pupil, raised from his sublime immobility, soon began to participate in the life of the community. He ran errands and fetched wood for carving. He took part in the dawn installation of the master's lesser works in front of the shrine. He passed on secret codewords from the master to other masters without knowing he was doing so. He performed many esoteric duties which seemed to him to be perfectly normal tasks. He became an active participant in the life of the tribe of artists.

There must have been a profound spell cast on him because, whatever he did, he was never noticed, never truly seen. And more especially he was never seen by the maiden. He would trip and fall in her presence, he would spill water from a bucket, he would speak to the air in front of her, but she simply would not lift her eyes unto him. Even when she was the object of errands, even when the maiden must have seen him with her father near the shrine, taking measurements for a new work, she still did not notice him. He felt like an object in the world that the light did not fall upon . . .

CHAPTER FORTY-FIVE

Then one day the new pupil met the mother of the maiden and without a word gave her a bunch of flowers he had picked under the moonlight. The mother of the maiden noticed his tender beauty, his frail and slender body, and the peculiar lively radiance of his eyes for the first time, and fell into admiration of him. That night the mother and father of the maiden talked about him.

'He is not normal,' she said.

'No.'

'His birth is unusual.'

'Yes.'

'Is he a secret suitor?'

'Maybe.'

'Or has he come to steal the secret of your art?'

'He has no interest in creating art. He wants to become an art. But I don't know what art he wants.'

'What other art is there?'

'There are many other arts greater than the art of making art out of wood or stone.'

'Like what?'

'Like the art of making life out of death.'

'You think your servant so exalted in mind?'

'Why not? He turned into a sculpture. He learnt to be a noble statue. He demands nothing, and gives everything. He does not listen, but hears. He does not appear to do anything, but he does everything. Either his birth is noble, or it should be. Or his past beyond his memory is noble. He is like a master who cherishes lowliness.'

'You maybe read too much into his insignificance?' his wife asked, smiling.

'He allows his insignificance to be so much. Insignificant people don't have that tranquillity. They may have contentment, they may have innocence, they may have simplicity, but not that tranquillity. Tranquillity in a man is an achievement, a discovery, almost a by-product of a great insight or illumination.'

'All this in one so young?'

'Some are young in body, old in soul. You know that, my dear.'

'I do.'

'Still we keep a stern eye on him.'

'We shall.'

CHAPTER FORTY-SIX

Even the masters of the tribe, in their irregular nocturnal meetings, commented on the new pupil, obliquely. After one of those long silences, during which, in the dark, many forms appear, one of the masters suddenly said:

'A stranger can wake up a sleeping land.'

Another voice said:

'A stranger can raise men's minds towards the stars.'

'Still, he has passed the tests he didn't know he was taking.'

'And we might have to induct him into the darkness of the hidden tradition.'

'Without him knowing, of course.'

'In case we are showing disrespect to a god, or to a king.'

CHAPTER FORTY-SEVEN

Then on a night that seemed like any other the new pupil was given instructions to work in the secret forge deep in the forest. He was taught the hidden arts of making. The father of the maiden initiated him, without his being aware of it, into the mysteries of fire and the esoteric art of turning ordinary metal into gold. It was an art known only to a few, brought from their old kingdom and nurtured as a secret tradition. Some say this art conceals the art of achieving immortality.

The new pupil also worked on the outer substance of things; he shaped, carved, polished, moulded, and did patina work on the sculptures, under the strict supervision of the master. All that he learnt in silence, obliquely, he was forbidden to reveal. He was made to swear a blood oath on this in the depths of the forest, in the initiation that he didn't know was one, conducted by figures in complete darkness and whose voices were muffled by ancient masks.

There must have been a profound spell cast on him during the night of the initiation for, whatever he did, he still was never noticed, never truly seen.

CHAPTER FORTY-EIGHT

Around that time the clamour of the suitors got worse. They had lingered in the village, they had created their works of art, had seen them found wanting, they had made several pilgrimages to spiritual centres, and shown their piety, dignity and seriousness. They had shown their restraint. They had behaved well. They had made journeys back to their different homes to conduct important affairs of state or business. And they had returned with gifts, both for the tribe of artists and the maiden's family. They had made themselves a part of the village life. Some of them had become so much part of the artistic life of the tribe that they forgot why they were there and took other women as wives and dedicated themselves to new vocations in art which they had accidentally discovered. But many of the suitors, having wasted much time and expended much of their resources, were becoming impatient and intractable. They eventually ganged up together, finding common cause in the elusiveness of the maiden. And, presenting a united front, they stormed the maiden's father's house and demanded that the maiden make up her mind as to whom she would marry. They were angry and, being men of great importance in their different realms as ambassadors, chiefs, aristocrats, sons of noble families, famous warriors, they felt that they were being insulted, being played with, taken too lightly. And so they laid down an ultimatum that the maiden must make a decision within a fixed period of time, or they would spread her name in infamy all over the world and no one would ever want to touch her or consider her in marriage again.

CHAPTER FORTY-NINE

In the forest there are the seeds of trees that lie in the earth for a very long time and seem to be doing nothing. There are plants that are very small and over many years they appear not to grow at all. The sages say that there are some prayers that take a thousand years to be answered; some say such a period of time is less than a moment in the mind of God. There are times when a people take a long time to hear what is being told them, a long time to respond to a provocation, a long time before they are roused to go to war. There are people who take a long time before they acknowledge the greatness of someone amongst them, a long time before mourning the death of a king, a long time before they fall in love. There are plants that never seem to flower or blossom, and then one day, to everyone's surprise, they bloom with astonishing splendour. There are plants that never seem to grow or change, and then one day, to the keen observer, they reveal a shining new leaf, and then, afterwards, they grow at a surprising rate. There are people who never smile, never play, and then, one day, they are like someone new, as if a benign sun has risen in their hearts. Different reasons for these things. They say the gods delay the revelation of our destiny, till it is upon us and the revelation and the living of it are one. They say that about the deep matters of life the rash hurry, but the wise, guided by an instinct beyond reason, choose to delay. Sometimes delay is fear. Sometimes delay is weakness. Sometimes delay is uncertainty. Sometimes delay is prophecy. Sometimes delay is awaiting a sign, the right moment, an alignment, a harmony in the heart with the heart's star in heaven.

The maiden kept delaying her wedding, her marriage, her choice of suitor, because deep in her heart she knew that the person she truly loved had not yet entered her life.

The more her suitors clamoured and threatened, the more she was possessed by the spirit of delay. She became fertile in the invention of new conditions, trials, contests and qualifications. She invented new doubts. She inclined one way then swung to another. She said she could not see any one of the suitors for all the suitors: they were like a forest, and she could not see a single tree. She wanted them to give her breathing space. She wanted to see not their actions, their deeds, but their shadows. She asked each of the suitors to bring her their shadow, so she could see what their spirits were really like. This became a famous riddle. The suitors were perplexed. They did not know how to detach their shadows from themselves. The suitors went about the place consulting witch-doctors, herbalists, wizards, sages, wise old women, witches, but no one could tell them how to separate their shadow from their bodies and give it as an object to the maiden. This problem kept them occupied for a long time.

All over the village, along the great trading routes, among the masters of the tribe, and even in the realm of the spirits this problem of how to give someone your shadow caused much discussion, amusement, and thought.

No one had the answer. But everyone talked about it. The conundrum soon reached the ears of the new pupil. He told his father, the king, about it; and his father, roaring with laughter that made many seeds in the forest suddenly burst into life, and made many barren women become pregnant, and many pregnant women suddenly give birth, and many rivers overflow their banks, and rain fall in dry places, said:

'My son, the answer is as simple as giving someone your love.'

CHAPTER FIFTY

Not all things glimpsed in a dream are clear. All dreams retain an enigma. Not all events glimpsed in the great book of life among the stars are clear. Only while dreaming does the dream make sense. When one awakes, that which made sense suddenly becomes strange, tinged with mystery. When one dreams one beholds a complete picture; when one awakes one finds a few fragments in one's hand of what was a glorious vision. With these fragments one tries to recreate, or suggest, a beauty that is lost when one returns from the stars.

The gaps in the forest began to change; the prince, at first, did not understand the nature of this change. On one of his fateful visits home to the palace the prince noticed that it was an unusually blue dawn. The forest sparkled with silver and with mists that gave off a roseate and golden hue. Cobwebs, with droplets of dew, sparkled like little necklaces of diamonds.

It was a dawn in which the trees and the animals, the plants and the birds were stirring from a beautiful dream. And their dream was the bluish colour of the world at dawn. The prince, as he sought the gap that would take him home, felt that he was entering a world he had never seen before. The gods and the spirits shone out from the haze of gold and blue, the roseate hue, and rays of pure sunlight like the magic swords of heaven piercing the enchanted forest. The prince stopped to retain the wonder of that moment. Then he found a tree that he had never noticed before. It was a tree like any other, except that its trunk was pure and fresh like the face of a pretty young girl and it had clean green leaves like broad green hands and it had buds on its branches like the joined palms of children at prayer. The prince sat under the tree, rested on its trunk, and was borne off to sleep. But it was not a normal sleep, nor was it a long one. And during that sleep many things happened to him that he would only remember in fragments of dreams over the many years in the suffering to come. He dreamt the beginning of all things, and their end. He dreamt all the stories of humanity. He dreamt of the answer to the greatest question, told him by a being in space unlimited inside a kingdom of silence. All that he was, all that he would be; all that was, all that would be; and the solution to death; the answer of immortality; he dreamt them all in a brief moment of sleep. Then he awoke refreshed and found himself in a different place. The tree was in flower. The birds had awoken and were singing. Nine maidens in white drifted past him smiling. The forest was gone. The gap he sought stood before him like a ring of enchanted fire. He stepped into the fire and found himself on the other side, near the river of his village. He was full of questions. He made for the palace, and summoned the elders. He knew his time was running out. He had little time left before his life would change for ever. And everything he did, or would do, would hasten time's swiftness. He had to live swiftly, to do what remained for him to do, and yet act as if he had all the time in the world, which he did have.

CHAPTER FIFTY-ONE

Sometimes an innovation repeated becomes a tradition. This one took place in the presence of the king and the royal bards who recorded what they witnessed in their future songs and legends. The prince, as if in the grip of a poetic vision, under the spell of a sublime rhythm, wanted all slaves freed and returned home to their tribes. He wanted the elders and the rich and the chieftains to share their wealth and their food with the poor. He wanted to know how big the world was, and what the people on the other side of the world looked like. He wanted to find out if they knew things his people didn't know, to link hands with them. He wanted to know why the elders hadn't taken sufficient interest in the rest of the world. He had visions, he said, that all people were children of the stars; and he wanted to meet all his sisters and brothers of the earth. He wanted to know if there were better ways of living, of governing, of improving the life of his people.

The elders were silent as the prince spoke; but the king, when he heard the avalanche of questions, laughed and laughed, as if there were nothing funnier than seeking knowledge about the wide world and its varied people. He laughed as if his son's quest for extensive knowledge were a wonderful joke. The son sensed a disquieting wisdom in his father's laughter, but he was not deterred, in fact he felt oddly encouraged.

'Nothing is as it seems, my son,' said his father, in between his bursts of laughter. 'Everything goes into reverse. What is up is down, what is down is up.'

The prince asked as many questions as the rising sun asks the sleeping earth. That day, in legend, became known as the Day of the Great Questions; and in the future it would become a tradition, a day in which people would ask one another the important questions of life, and attempt to answer them in song, in meditation, or in art. The bards exaggerate when they sing that the prince asked questions that lasted seven days; but they speak the truth when they sing that after that day the prince never asked the elders another question ever again.

The elders were concerned about his new desire for knowledge about distant people across the sea. They feared that new knowledge would render them irrelevant.

'If he wants to know so much about the world why don't we give him to the white spirits,' one of them muttered, 'then he can find out all the knowledge he wants.'

If they had not been so inward-looking things might have been very different when the white wind blew . . .

CHAPTER FIFTY-TWO

Now that the prince had sufficiently recovered, now that the prince was home for a brief visit, now that the prince was enlightened enough to hear without ears, and to see without his eyes, the king, his father, decided to spend some sublime time alone with his son, to talk to and listen to him, and to impart what little he knew of the mysteries of things, of kingship. And while the son slept he spoke over the sleeping form, knowing he was speaking into ears that would hear without resistance, into ears that would hear purely, and into a mind that would remember nothing of what was said except its pure spirit. The prince would act from this knowledge that deep down he would have made his own.

And so in silence, the king said:

'There are barbarians of the high as much as there are barbarians of the low. There are barbarians of the nobility and barbarians of the chieftaincy. There are barbarians of the intelligent too, my son. Don't let the clever words or the brilliant mind of anyone blind you to the fact that they can also be stupid. There are more intelligent people who are imbeciles than imbeciles who are wise. Intelligence is a form of blindness; it prevents people from seeing the truth. People value their mental power too much even as it increases their fundamental errors. Trust more someone who has simplicity of spirit, goodness of soul, a fearless heart and an enquiring mind. Beware of people who use the word "I" too much. Beware of people who trust only what they have seen, or heard, or touched, or smelt; they are limited people and are easy to deceive and corrupt; for whatever they are is founded on the limitation of their senses. People's convictions don't amount to much. People's passions don't amount to much. Do not fear sorcerers or those who conjure for the devil. So long as you do not believe in it evil cannot harm you. And fear is the greatest and most powerful form of belief. So do not fear anything. There is only one true cure for fear, my son, and that is knowledge. Knowledge of the true ancient way of the tried and tested mysteries that was brought down to us from our ancestors. Keep to the path that has led to your light and all else will follow. Notice the higher comedy in most things. You have your own way, but ever have a place in your heart for humour.

'All power is but the shadow of true power. I have heard of a man who grieved because he thought he had conquered the world; he had nothing more to do. He could have conquered himself. Afterwards all the lands he conquered turned to dust. Only fragments of stories remained. He could have found heaven in a single thought. His is one of the greatest comedies in the human story. There are kings who do not know what they are kings for. A human being ought to know what they are human for. It is a strange blindness to live a life, roaming the earth, without understanding why. There is no tragedy greater than a god that does not know itself. There is no greater comedy than a human being who looks at their reflection in a calm river and sees a complete stranger that is them.

'We have three bodies in one. Only one of them endures. But nothing perishes. Everything remembers. All time is here. Don't worry yourself with passing sufferings, fashions, ideas, notions, conceits, disasters, failures. All are illusions. Maintain a sublime detachment from all things, and the greatest love will shine through you. Be silent. Be still. Sometimes our minds are our worst enemies. Do not hold preferences too strongly. Be guided by that clear voice within. Drink the cup of suffering that life gives you when it does. Pass through the narrow space. Do not cling to any fixed ideas of who or what you are. You are more than whatever you think in simplicity. Being a prince is nothing compared to a man or woman who has discovered that deep down in them there are gods. Humility makes you great. Who can destroy the air or the invisible thing that makes the universe real? Be as nothing; be everything. Do not fear loss. Nothing is lost on the way that is not found among the stars. A way has been shown for you to reach me when you need to; and the wisest of the universe are here for you in that clear voice within. All the guidance you will ever need is within you, as part of your own mysterious nature. All human beings are princes and princesses, but only very few know their kingdom.

'Throughout your life you will slowly acquire a family of people from all over the world. We have many families. Remember to stop when you have ripened. Call forth what you need only when you need it. Live simply. Carry with you only your shadow, and surrender that in the light. Be light, in spirit and deeds. Don't be above people. Lower yourself without being low. Have dignity without showing it. Be a prince without displaying it. Let your wisdom be invisible to the eyes of men and women. Rule as if the people are ruling themselves. When power is needed, summon and use it. When war is needed then rise and go to war in the highest way, and win in the quickest way, and use it to create better conditions for all. Many things are forgivable if you are truly extending the good in the world. Do not try to be perfect, but only to get better. And don't carry any of my advice in your head. Forget it all. What you need to guide you is in you. Your light is your guide and your power. You have already awoken it and all you have to do is to keep it alive, whatever life brings you. As you know now, you are a child of the stars and all the universe is your home. But the centre of the circle is the home of your home. Dwell there ever, in your heart. And you will transcend death. Then your life will never be a failure or a success, a tragedy or a comedy. It will be immeasurable.'

CHAPTER FIFTY-THREE

The prince slept profoundly through the magic hour when his father gazed in silence over his sleeping form. And the prince had dreams of great beauty, which he could not remember, but which had a deep impact on his being, and on his life. Afterwards he found himself both a deeper and a lighter person; he dwelt more naturally in the beautiful silences in the air and he found that he smiled more, that within him grew the mood of an everlasting laughter. He also discovered, a little later, that he could control his visibility. He could be visible or become invisible by choice, by will, using a knowledge, a technique, that was whispered to him in a dream. Afterwards, during his great suffering, which coincided with the years of his great enlightenment, many techniques, many methods, many laws, and a clear elucidation of the way, were whispered to him in dreams. Much later he realised that seeds of the truth were being planted in his sleep and sometimes in the vast moments when he dwelt in contemplation of the wonderful silences in the air. Often he would perceive himself in the centre of a golden circle, and this much later during the worst years of his slavery. He found then that dwelling in the centre of that golden circle transcended the agony of slavery. Beyond the flesh burning in great suffering he knew the sublime fire that was itself an illumination in the throne at the brilliant black centre of the golden circle of light.

Sometimes, in the village of artists, running an errand or taking a rest under a tree in the forest, he would pass through a blue gap in the world and arrive at the torments of his enslavement in an alien land. His bride was gone. His child was gone. He had survived the monstrous crossing of the sea of evil, where slaves lay chained ankle to ankle, wrist to wrist, in the coffin of the hold, in the ship, on the waves of an empire's dream of power. He had arrived in a new land that was rich with blood and guilt and hope. He had survived the lash. He had survived the degradation. He had survived being less than a man, or a dog, or an insect, or a beast. He had survived the loss of his love, his kingdom, his home, his earth. He had survived being forced into a marriage with a wife that was not his wife but the mistress of his owner. He found himself listening, in odd tranquillity, as his owner made love all night to his wife that was not his wife. And he listened on many other nights too, gazing at the stars, dwelling in the sublime fire in the centre of the golden circle. And he knew then as now that it was an odd fate indeed to live through such suffering while being blessed with such illumination. If he were to sum up the paradox of his being, in those moments in the forest, under the tree where he rested, and passed into the blue gaps, and saw distant revelations, he would say it was this: How do you survive the worst with the highest? What is the music of this paradox? What is its song? And can you show anyone its shadow, so they can see the spirit of such a conjunction of the sublime and the horror? And yet, for all time, in the present and future story, the prince found within him the unquenchable mood of an immeasurable laughter. And all this was born on the night when, unknown to him, a father gazed with love on the form of his sleeping son.

CHAPTER FIFTY-FOUR

On his return to the tribe he found that the gap was a hole of black fire. The mood of the tribe of artists had altered. A cloud of indecipherable doom seemed to hang over everything. The air was light, but the spirit over things was troubling. The maiden was withdrawn. Her delay was wearing her down; delaying her choice of suitor was wearing down the tribe. A mood of violence, of restlessness, of irritation drifted among the buildings and floated with the men, women and children.

The new pupil resumed his service. There wasn't anything he didn't do as servant and pupil. He carried, cleaned, washed, ran errands, bore messages, went to the market, made and unmade the beds, aired the abodes, and sat in stillness among the statues. He cleaned the latrines, fetched water from the wells, washed clothes at the river, brought in wood from the forests, worked on the statues and carvings under precise instructions, and seldom spoke. And all through this he lived within the being and flame of the maiden.

He studied her moods. He learnt to slide into her dreams. He listened in on her thoughts. He lived partly in her life, and partly in his. Mostly he dwelt in her being, as a fragrance dwells in a flower. He was happiest there. Sometimes he smiled. Sometimes he laughed. When he laughed he did so quietly, within himself. Moments later he would hear a wonderful sound of laughter in the wind, circling the village. Not long afterwards the maiden would appear, with a smile on her face; and, with her father serious in his work, she would whisper a joke into her father's ear, as if he wasn't there. Hours later, in the evening, in bed, the father would find himself laughing as he shared the joke that he had only just understood, with his wife.

The maiden's delay was driving a lot of people to the brink of anxiety. Her father strove not to put any pressure on her. Her mother spoke obliquely, and controlled her shaking voice. But they knew, in all fairness, that none of the suitors had yet solved the riddle of the shadow, and so there was nothing to be done. But the tensions and the annoyance did not lessen.

Fights broke out between the suitors. They began to challenge one another to dangerous combat. They fought with weapons, they fought with bare fists, they wrestled. There were many injuries and near-fatalities. And so, informally, it came about that the suitors decided to settle it among themselves through combat. The overall winner of their contest would be deemed the winner of the maiden's hand. They organised this grand contest among themselves, and it was designed to be over within an allotted time. The contest would take place on the rich fields near the shrine. The contest became a formality; announcements were made; a date of commencement was decided. And the tribe whose life was dedicated to art found itself about to witness fighting among suitors who must win in order to justify time spent wooing a maiden who had become priceless because of her unique gifts, her disdain, and her delay.

CHAPTER FIFTY-FIVE

The maiden disapproved of the contest, and made her feelings clear. But events had passed out of her hands; the desire for a visible outcome had taken on its own momentum. Never before had this happened in the tribe – for a woman's hand. It was a historic act. The myth-making event was a fascination so powerful that the people fell under its spell. The maiden withdrew and let it be known that she would not witness the barbarous contest, and would not recognise or sanction the winner.

But what she said made no difference. It promised to be a moment of history, of spectacle. Everyone wanted it to happen. The brooding air, the quiet history of the tribe, the legend that was coming into being. They all seemed to call it forth. And so it had to be. Everyone looked forward to its commencement after the season of rain.

CHAPTER FIFTY-SIX

Through all this the maiden maintained her delay. She knew that she could bring an end to all the conflict and rage at any moment simply by making her choice known, simply by making a decision. But she didn't. She intended to delay long enough to know what was right for her, to delay long enough to gain wisdom, to make the right and best decision. And she would delay till someone whom she knew she loved appeared, someone who could also solve the riddle.

CHAPTER FIFTY-SEVEN

Around that time, while the new pupil quietly performed his numerous duties in the workshop of the maiden's father, and while the rains delayed in coming in from the sea, and before the time of the festivals, a shadow of an event descended on the tribe that moved them profoundly. It came on the great winds of sadness. But the new pupil learnt about it first from the maiden.

She came to her father's workshop one evening and she fell

on his shoulders in tears and she wept convulsively and couldn't seem to stop. At that moment they heard lamentations and general weeping from the streets and the mainways, from the other workshops, the marketplaces, and especially from the priestesses of the shrine. And it was some time before they made any sense of this phenomenon of sadness that was sweeping over the community. The maiden wept on her father's shoulder and couldn't explain why, couldn't seem to get her words out. Her father led her to the main house, led his daughter sobbing on his arm.

Lamentation was general throughout the tribe; and whoever was told the reason why there was so much weeping fell into weeping themselves. The cause was contagious. And the contagion of this poignant sadness gathered over the tribe like thick rainclouds, and broke over them all. And no one spoke. People sat wherever they heard the news and stared, with that blank look on their faces, as when we have heard that someone very dear to us has suddenly died.

And so, because no one was able at first to tell the new pupil why everyone was so sad, on account of the fact that no one noticed him, he assumed an air of sadness too. In fact he picked up the mood and felt a poignant sadness for an event he did not know about. Something truly terrible must have happened for the people to feel it so, he thought. And he brooded on this mood of sorrow. The mood lasted for days. There was a subdued air everywhere. The suitors were silent and subdued too at the depth of the news. The marketplace was silent. The workshops were silent. The women were silent. The wind blew through the village, whispering of death and change. The brooding birds piped in the forests. The crickets could be heard. The distant river swelled its banks. The moon was unusually large and white in the clear dark sky. By day footfalls could be heard in the dust. Birds circled the village overhead. Omens roamed through the passageways. Dogs barked unaccountably. Cats padded about warily with shining silver eyes. Everyone was touched by this mysterious sadness, the men, the market folk, the hunters, the women, the children, and especially the young girls and boys, they felt it more, for strange reasons; maybe because the shadow of death moved them into a sudden contemplation of a beautiful unknown, for there was something beautiful about their sorrow.

Then suddenly new works of art began to sprout from the tribe, while they waited for rain. The sorrow brought forth a burst of creativity; it seemed the only way the tribe could express the true depth of their sorrow. And the sorrow that they felt, and expressed, brought out and included the unexpressed sorrows of the centuries, the aeons of pain and tragic moods that they had carried in them through the long twilights of history. The tribe, like a land richly seeded in flowerseeds of suffering, exploded into bloom and blossom during the time of their sorrowing. This was a brief and unsuspected golden age of artistic fruitfulness. It was as though sorrow were being converted, instantly, into beauty; as if sorrow was beauty's secret, and its mother.

Only a few times before, in its legend, and in its works, had the tribe known such fertility. And this was the last time that the tribe would enjoy such an intense blessing of beauty. And, as with all such miraculous moments in the lives of a people, they were not aware of it, and did not know how fleeting and how mysterious this phase was through which they were passing. They lived a magic moment in the fugitive dream of lived time, and did not know it. And later the world would wonder at such an astonishing concentration of art so beautiful and so elusive that they would ascribe it to the hands of unknown beings from fabled realms who had descended briefly on a backward land. And some would mutter about a divine touch or spark that had animated, for a time, the hands of an unknown and long forgotten people.

CHAPTER FIFTY-EIGHT

But it was only from the works that began to appear that the new pupil found out the cause of the universal sadness. And it was only when the works had been done, created by so many anonymous hands, made by every single member of the tribe, it seemed; created and made and shown around the shrine, or dotting the village square, or freestanding among the trees in the forest, or sprouting in the farms or the marketplaces, or quivering in front of the cracked mud huts and in circular compounds or bristling along the shores of the river; it was only when the artworks began to vanish, began to leave the tribe, taken away, most of them, by travellers, merchants on the great trade routes, spread out and disseminated; it was only when these works of astonishing variety and richness were created, were shown, and had mostly left the village, to circulate in the kingdom through invisible routes, only then could the tribe of artists speak of that which had brought them such sadness. For they only knew how to speak of it when they had expressed it first in art and then had time to understand something of that which they had expressed.

CHAPTER FIFTY-NINE

When the new pupil eventually heard the news he too was saddened. And he joined the women and men and children in their vigils by the shrine to pray for and express their sorrow for the fate of the prince who was a good soul and who they heard was dying. Everyone spoke well of this prince that they did not know. Everyone said he was a prince in a faraway kingdom and he was a gentle soul who loved all the people and always cared for the poor and the simple and the lonely and that too much evil in the world had broken his heart and now he was dying and would die unless the people somehow put enough sweetness in the air to make it possible for him to live. No one knew who this prince was but all were moved by his fate. And the new pupil was very moved indeed for this prince and often sighed to think of him.

'How lucky he is to be so loved,' he thought.

On one of those days he overheard the maiden talking to a companion.

'I would like to make a journey to this prince's palace,' she said, 'and make an offering.'

'But no one knows where it is,' her friend replied.

'I will find a way,' she said. 'Even if it means doing it through my heart.'

Then they wandered off to the forest, towards the river.

By this time the maiden was being quietly hailed by many as a seer. For now the masters began to understand one of the aspects of her enigmatic sculpture, which revealed a dying prince, and which had so baffled the tribe. And they wondered and marvelled at how she had executed the work so far in advance of the news itself.

The maiden was the only one who did not know that she was considered a seer by the most venerated minds and masters. She had forgotten her sculpture and, what is more, she saw no connection at all between her sculpture and the news that saddened them all.

CHAPTER-SIXTY

There was so little time left and he knew it, even as time passed so slowly. The tribe kept vigil for the prince and special fires were lit in the forest by the masters of the tribe to keep alive the light of that soul that ran through the land like the vast silver of the flowing mirror that was the river. They waited and worked for healing in dreams and in the many ways that the spirit works to cure things in the world unknowing. And it was a subdued time while the rains came and they waited to hear if he who was dying was dead or would live again. The rains were fierce, and in the heavens thunder battled with lightning, and in the legend of the tribe good battled with evil for the soul of the prince. And the whole land was in dire judgement; for if the prince should die it was said that the land would die in his death, and the white wind would conquer for ever. And death would grow in the farms and bestride the hills like a giant. The rains were fierce and those with unusual sensitivity saw the battles everywhere between monsters of the deep and the creatures of the lightning flash. The rains were merciless and lashed the farms and overswelled the river and carried off huts and abodes and became a racing stream that rushed through the forests uprooting trees and creating gaps and carrying off goats and farm animals and young children who had not heeded their parents' warnings. The rains seemed to go on for ever, while they awaited news of the prince's fate.

And then the rains, more cruel than they had ever been, destroying and tearing down and disintegrating homes and wrecking farms, marketplaces and works of art, made the people forget their concerns for the prince, drowned their sadness in more immediate tragedies. The community battled as one to hold their lives together, to rescue their homes, and protect their villages from being washed away by the angry deluge. The river broke its bank and swept through the village and in the floods a few perished, and yet there were miraculous survivors. People forgot their other troubles. The masters wondered if the tribe wasn't being punished for their divine neglect. There were other masters, however, who hinted that the flood might be an inexplicable form of cleansing, that it might not be as negative, as terrible, as it seemed.

Then just as suddenly as they appeared, the rains ended, the flood subsided, and the land flowered and bloomed as never before. It was its last bloom in that way. The shrine had been unaffected. If anything it seemed to shine with a greater light. The mainways and paths and minorways all were new and clean. The village was altered. The marketplace now was made to face in a truer direction. The farms were richly fertilised with death and rich riversilt that made the crops sprout and grow as if transformed. Huts and homes had better alignments. A new harmony appeared amongst the devastation. Artworks which were lost turned out to be ones which were quite useless and ones that were quite invaluable too; and this had the effect of reminding the tribe about what they lived for, what their true purpose was, which they had partially forgotten.

The masters and the priestesses of the shrine mounted a grand ritual, in which the whole tribe participated, for the rededication of their lives to their chosen art. It was a new covenant with their deity and their destiny. It was a ceremony of great inspiration.

Then the tribe learnt of the preservation of the prince, and they rejoiced in a double jubilation of good events and good omens, at last.

CHAPTER SIXTY-ONE

Through all this the new pupil toiled and performed great unnoticed feats during the rains, and during the flooding. He rescued women who were drowning. He helped strangers save their possessions. He helped carry vital supplies to dry places in the hills. He helped families move. He built impromptu huts on hilltops. He kept up the spirits of those who had lost their homes. He brought food for the homeless in the hills. He cheered up the children huddled miserably in high places. Along with the galvanised men of the community, he lifted the shrine to the dry mouth of a cave. They bore the gods to the stone terraces. It was at this point that he began to teach. He spoke to them of one God, one father, one source as the source of all. They heard him, but they didn't listen. It was at that point he began to speak of the unreality of death. Life, he said, is stronger than death. Death is only a shadow, a brief darkness, a fearful mask that frightens those that use only their eyes. Life, he said, is a light that shines for ever. They listened, but did not hear him. He performed miraculous healing on the sick, the diseased, on those who were traumatised by the floods, those who had died for a long moment while drowning, those with broken legs and broken hearts. He performed miraculous transformations on the spirit of the community, and didn't know the effect of what he did. All this he managed, in innocence, while still looking after the workshop of the master, moving the statues and carvings to safe ground, making sure nothing was lost or carried away during that time of confusion, the raging of the storms. And through all that time the maiden avoided him; or, as if still under a spell, did not notice his existence. Nor did anyone else in the village, except those he helped, and the masters, who saw, but kept silent. But there were young girls who were touched by his spirit, and fell in love with him for the rest of their lives, and passed on the legend of their adoration to their children, in oblique songs.

CHAPTER SIXTY-TWO

When the flood passed, when the beautiful fury of the rains had crossed the sky and journeyed on to drier destinations, when normality began to return to the tribe, when they began to sort out their lives and make the best of their devastations, when songs began to be heard again from the girls, and laughter heard among the flowers, the new pupil, unnoticed by the maiden, decided it was time to reveal, wisely, his love.

One day he began to speak to her in his mind. It was the only way to speak to her. He spoke to her dreams. He learnt from the statues how, through stillness and oddness unnoticed, to appear in people's dreams, and then speak to them as himself. This he did. At first she did not notice because she did not much notice her dreams. And so a backlog of unchecked messages accumulated in her unnoticed dreams. Then one night, after sitting in silence in moonlight, listening to inaudible whispers in the wind, all the messages and the dreams came through all at once, all in a rush and tumble, at great speed; and this alarmed and perplexed her. But he went on speaking in her dreams more tenderly, taking many forms. Sometimes he was a flower that she was twirling in her hands in a dream and his face would appear in the petals of the rose and he would speak to her gently. Sometimes he spoke to her as the moon. Sometimes when, in a dream, she was on a canoe on the river, he would be the canoe, or he would be the river.

Sometimes when, in a dream, she was riding a lion, or an antelope, or playing with a gazelle, he would be the lion, the antelope, or the gazelle. Sometimes he was a white bird that she dreamt of which returned often and lay still in her lap, and then, circling her head three times, would fly away to a distant constellation, leaving her quite alone. Often he was just a person she knew in her dreams, a familiar person whom she could not quite place; but one for whom she had a great affection. Through these forms he spoke to her of their ancient love that went back centuries and which was born on another realm, another planet, far from this galaxy. He spoke of the brevity of time given them here in which to meet and love and be so happy. So brief was the time allotted them, he said; and that it was less than the space of time between one moon and the next. And then, he said, they would be separated till the distant time they would meet, in another space, where they would have to start all over again learning to recognise their ancient and future love, their unconsummated love, their great love. He spoke love verses into her dreams.

'When the moon is full
It spreads a light
That is cool
And round and white
All over the land that is you.
That moon is like my love.
Even the air knows this is true.
But my love never wanes like the moon –
My love is not there only at night
And like a ghost is gone before noon.

My love has the power of seven.
My love is the light
And the promiise of heaven.'

Sometimes, in her dreams, he took her hand and journeyed with her through all the happiest places in the universe, among the stars of ecstasy and delight, and to some of their ancient homelands in faraway galaxies. He showed her their palaces of pleasure, their castles of love, their cities of happiness.

When he was not speaking to her in dreams, he arranged anonymous surprises for her in the waking hours. Children brought her bouquets of rare feathers. Strange children brought her rich brocaded cloth. When she was musing by the river an old man gave her a single flower that no one had ever seen before, or since. He said the flower came from the stars and that he was a messenger of one that would not be named. The maiden accepted the flower hesitantly, and smelt its fragrance. At that moment something happened in her heart. She was not sure what it was; but suddenly she felt things more clearly. The fragrance altered the wind. She heard the faintest echo of a melody. The river was calm. The old man had turned into the faintest mists of gold fading in the distance of the green cloud of the forest. The flower would never wilt, never die; but sometimes it became invisible and was lost, and it would reappear again, depending on how she was feeling. That flower, along with her only child, was the legacy she passed on to the next generation. Every now and again, for a decade, or for twenty years, the flower would be invisible, and then on an auspicious day it would appear in the hand of one of her descendants, always clarifying the heart. Such a curious flower was she given among the anonymous gifts from an unnamed and an unseen one.

There were other odd gifts that the new pupil caused to come her way. One day a beautiful young woman brought the maiden a rare ruby. She claimed it came from the far heavens and she was a messenger from one who could not be named. Another beautiful young girl, with a dazzling smile and a bright countenance, brought her a pure white stone, not of this earth, and repeated the magic words of the other messengers. A child dressed in gold brought her a white bowl. When later the maiden ate from the bowl she noticed how well she felt, how contented. Then she noticed that the bowl somehow enriched her food, and in eating little she was not only satisfied quicker but that she experienced an unusual sense of nourishment. These gifts puzzled and frightened her a little, but she kept her puzzlement and fear to herself. She kept her silence. She refused to let even curiosity and a great sense of mystery divert her from her chosen course of delay, patience, and awaiting the wisdom of the revealed hour.

But more gifts of astonishment came to her and left her, from one day to another, reeling as if in a strange moonlit intoxication. A child dressed in heavenly blue brought her a handful of shining ashes, and with enchanted words poured it into the maiden's palms. Then came special messengers, all seven of them, all beautiful, all dressed in white, repeating love verses from one who should not be named, but whose love came from the stars.

By now the maiden was bewildered, then curious, then amazed, then enchanted, then fascinated by these gifts. She was so curious about this personage who should not be named that she followed the messengers and was astonished when, with a cry and a flash of light in the air, they vanished as soon as they entered the forest.

Then, slowly, her love found focus. When the messengers stopped coming, when she didn't hear from them, nor receive any more gifts or verses from them again, she found that she missed the mystery quite deeply. Then she found that she had fallen in love with one who was unknown, with one she would never know. Her lovesickness had found an object, a personage, who was not there.

CHAPTER SIXTY-THREE

Through all this, time quickened for the new pupil. Time was hurrying towards the great gaps, pulling him towards his martyrdom. In dreams, he spoke to the maiden of love, and how love saves; and time spoke to him as he sat among the statues that were changing from raw carved wood or rough stone into works of art, changing with the ambiguities of the air, of time, of the silver sheen that a vital element in the atmosphere presses into the surfaces of the new carved works. As they changed from wood into wonder-bearing forms, from stones into statues of enchantment and frozen dreams, he changed too, from the new pupil into one who, through the gaps in time, would find himself in the hold of a ship, crushed with a thousand others, bleeding, starving and raw with beatings, his ankles and wrists in metal chains. He was unable to connect one moment with the other; a life in his own land, a pupil, free, and then less than an animal, in chains, in a ship bound for hell. The new pupil was more frequently snatched in spirit to that future or past condition, he couldn't say which. More and more it encroached on him, this martyrdom, the final suffering before his everlasting freedom from the mighty wheel of mortality. More and more he felt the great suffering drawing closer, till he could smell his blood on the chains, smell the deaths and the agony of the others and their disintegrating flesh all around him in the hold of the ship, in a torment that cannot be lived while being lived, and yet cannot be forgotten, or avoided. In such moments he wondered acutely if it wouldn't have been better to have died beforehand, considering what came later. Among the statues, he sent out to the world a message of the heart — make the most of the happiness in your life; it may be a prelude to something strange. In this vision he saw something worse than death, and he lived it. He saw a suffering beyond endurance, but which was endured; a suffering of a people so great that some of its excess had to be endured before and afterwards, in the form of the greatest happiness. Then he saw why some people, some races, had such an extraordinary gift for happiness and for joy, and for ecstasies of the spirit: it was the excess left over from the suffering to come and the suffering that had gone. It was a divine conversion of that suffering into exhilaration, happiness, and moments in paradise while alive, a sublime compensation for enduring the unendurable.

The new pupil foresaw, among the shadows, the songs in the air, and the stones turning into art through time's alchemy, he foresaw his suffering to come. It was like another life; a martyrdom and a crucifixion in time. Man enchained and gagged with metal and enslaved ought to be the symbol and icon of a new religion: one that reveals how man's life was sacrificed for the wealth of others, and the building of civilisations. The new pupil found this so, in the hold of the ship, with all his flesh broken and his bones eaten by the chains and the lash. The only thing that saved him then was the vision, in extreme agony, that man is a vast spirit and a body, a silver formlessness surrounding a living mould of flesh and bone . . .

Enlightenment does not reduce suffering.

CHAPTER SIXTY-FOUR

The rains came and went; time sped on with epic grace; and the contests began. The maiden, in spite of being hopelessly in love with one who should not be named, maintained the dignity of her delay. She maintained, also, a charming distance from the fighting matches between contending suitors.

During the long rains, most of the suitors had returned to their homes, for replenishment and fortification. They had come back, rich with magic potions and spells, and praise-singers, and witch-doctors to help them through their campaigns. The contests were violent and full of wonderful events which the bards have long elaborated in their songs and legends. All over the kingdom these marvels are familiar in moonlit stories around which children weave their improvisations.

The contests drew great crowds from distant places. Many different forms of fighting and many skills of self-defence were displayed. The crowds gazed in awe at the jump-kicking of the Northern suitor, the anaconda wrestling style, sinuous and oily, of the Eastern suitors, the leg-hooking techniques of the suitors from the Southern creeks, and the gyrating dervish swirling style of the Western free-form suitor, who fought to the wild and elliptical beat of a sinister and mesmerising talking drum. There were suitors who used curious crab-stalking techniques; they were stocky suitors, with devilishly low centres of gravity, who were as impossible to shift in their wrestling contests as the squat hills around. There were suitors with legs so baked and dry with the studied art of kick-fighting that they proved a nightmare to their opponents, whom they kept at a safe distance with the repeated tattoo of their peppery kicks to the face and body. And there were those who crouched like cougars, who fought like whirlwinds, and moved with the unpredictable and hypnotising rhythm of drumbeats administered by their witch-doctors.

The fights were unpredictable, engrossing and passionate; no one was killed, but many suitors were wounded, and some were disfigured for life. The contests became legendary; and the Mamba proved the eventual winner.

CHAPTER SIXTY-FIVE

There are ancient tales where a man, faced with an enigma blocking his road, goes into the forest, to sleep with demons of the deep, wrestle with wild animals, and do battle with death. He lives a wild secret life alone in the depths of a cave, and he returns transformed. Sometimes he brings with him fragments of a new religion. Sometimes he returns with a vision. Sometimes he returns changed, and becomes a witch-doctor, herbalist or sage. The Mamba, spooked by the weirdness of the maiden with an awkward kink in her spirit, and seeing that he was being progressively destroyed as a man, and that he was doing it to himself because he was all askew, found life impossible in the village, and one night disappeared without a word.

The Mamba simply vanished from the active life of the tribe. No one knew where he went; no one heard about him for a while; and no one speculated about his disappearance either. When he was there he had too much presence; when he wasn't there he had too much absence. It was a sort of curse. He wasn't noticed when he wasn't seen. He was not a man that anyone missed.

Then events happened which ought to have been strange, but were not seen as such. His father died suddenly one day, after screaming that his heart had been loaned to a shadow. Then, not long afterwards, his mother died, after wailing that her spirit had been stolen by a shadow. The Mamba did not reappear to bury his parents; he sent no word; he sent no emissaries. His absence at the tribal burial of his parents was not remarked on. Then his parents' compound began to be haunted by dark forms that whispered like bats and created shadows that stood up straight and walked like real beings and danced in the moonlight. The rains came and the Mamba's abode was completely unaffected, but no one remarked on this as being strange either. The rains went, and one day, in the middle of a contest, people saw that the Mamba was one of the contestants. He had returned, and no one had noticed. It was then that people began to speculate. It was said that he had gone hunting a rare animal with which to amaze the woman who would be his bride. It was said that he had gone seeking for unusual powers in the deep dark places of the world, and had traded the lives of his loved ones for invincibility, for power over the known and unknown, the strange and the innocence that spooked him. It was said he had gone to acquire powers that would bend the hearts and minds of all people to his will; power over women of all kinds, and power over that which mysteriously perplexed his will. It was also said he had gone mad with love and lust and guilt and had been taken to a powerful herbalist deep in the forest to restore his sanity.

And then, one day, he reappeared. He was darker, fiercer, and more menacing than ever. He was also more silent. He wore black. His eyes had changed. They saw deep things. He had stared into the depths of his own madness and had seen things of the deep and was initiated into the new art of the deep and the dark. Upon his return he was more feared than ever before. The very mention of his name sowed dread and made grown men quake. His very presence made them tremble, and often flee; and when they didn't flee they were rooted to the spot, mesmerised by a terror that they couldn't explain. And when he spoke people's minds often went blank. He had become truly awesome, like those spirits who, when they show themselves in war, make armies abandon their weapons and scurry away across the plains.

The Mamba returned, was seen first in the middle of a fight, dressed in black, and before anyone could register the profound change that had come over him, he had beaten all the contestants in a manner so cruel that the crowds were appalled and fascinated in equal measure. He had broken the neck of one suitor, cracked the spine of another, and dumped the swirling dervish suitor on his head so roughly that the crowd was stunned by the grinding sound of his neck crunching into his body. The Mamba was simply the most brutal contestant among all the suitors. And, strangely, many women gasped in admiration whenever he appeared, and secretly wanted him to win. And when he did win husbands were dismayed, while the women, largely, rejoiced. It was said he had mastered the secret of women's hearts and their deepest desires.

When he won the overall contest, however, people wondered about the next unfolding drama of this legendary set of events. They wondered what the maiden would do.

CHAPTER SIXTY-SIX

It was simple, what she would do. She refused to recognise the validity of the contests, and decreed that whoever told her the best story and the best dream and solved the riddle of the shadow would win her hand . . .

And all through this, because time was quickening for some but becoming slower for others, because time was running out in the land that is reached only through a unique gap in the world, the pupil continued speaking to the maiden in her dreams. And the maiden, though unknowing, was made happy by her dreams, and looked forward to sleep, and often lingered by the river, in the fragrance of wild roses, turning over in her mind the delightful elusiveness of her dreams. If only she could grasp them clearly and understand them, she thought, she would see things she needed to see, and would be happy. But even this state of puzzling out those images and fragments of verses that so perplexed her gave her a feeling of profound happiness too, as she spent her keenest hours by the river, gazing into the sky so blue and so bright with the gold of heaven.

And still, in all this self-absorption, she didn't notice the new pupil. Sometimes an invisible hand would deliver a sign in front of her in the form of a carving, which prompted odd thoughts in her mind. Sometimes she would catch a glimpse of a face so beautiful, frail and familiar, like some gladdening image in a dream: she would blink and the face would be lost in a crowd. Sometimes a voice would reach her heart, and she'd give a strange start, and would wonder whether she was awake or whether once a god had spoken to her and she had done so divine a being an injustice by having forgotten. Sometimes, in a reverie, a voice, tender with great understanding, and light like a feather, would whisper these odd words right into her soul, piercing her so with a passionate and mysterious fire:

'Time is not with youth;

Time is with the truth.'

And she would fall headlong into a waking dream, where carvings spoke, and statues danced, and a white horse, of dazzling beauty, beckoned her with its cheeky eyes to take her on a ride to paradise.

Maybe she was too young to notice what she saw. She only noticed much later, in another land, in the burning heat of the difficult years, when, in looking back, she saw what she should have seen, what was obvious to see, but which she hadn't.

She was too young to notice how fortunate she was, how blessed, how lucky, how loved, how watched over, and how brief was her hour of such glory, such blessedness, such living beauty in the land of art.

She was too young to notice things. She saw only dreams, hopes, ideals, vague notions and moods. She lived in a vapour of time. She didn't see evils there, or looming. She didn't see the contests. She didn't much notice the Mamba. She loved her parents more than she noticed them. She loved her land, its skies, its hills, the women, the mass of faces, the smells, her father's workshop, the shrine, the forest, the farms, and the dazzling river where she played, washed and dreamed, more than she noticed them. Only later did they become so real, when she had lost them all, irredeemably. Only later did she learn to see that which she had loved in the blur of her being.

She was too young, for example, to notice that when the new pupil smiled the sun lingered in his smile long after he had left the presence of the person he was greeting. She was too young to notice how quickly the smile left the faces of most people who had just vacated your presence. She was too young to notice many things about him . . .

But he saw her more clearly than anything in the world . . . and studied her deep hidden nature every moment of his being . . . as if she were his secret soul . . . and often when he pondered her and entered her dreams he saw her in strange images, and peculiar notions . . . often a lamb-like nature had been left alone and years later in its place was a lioness . . . how to see the true person that would later be, later emerge, in the tender graceful and peculiar youth that now was . . . how to remember the lamb that was the lioness . . . riddles of the shadow . . .

CHAPTER SIXTY-SEVEN

The Mamba was infuriated at the change in the rules for the maiden's hand. Convinced that he had won, convinced that there was a conspiracy or whispering campaign or evil voice against him, the Mamba's paranoia became worse than ever before. But it was an unfocused paranoia, without an object.

Then, one night, he saw the maiden's silhouette, under a powerful spell of moonlight. His head went slightly crazy with the beauty and the mystery of her. All the powers that he had acquired from the deep did not protect him against the shimmering effect of her innocent profile charged by the enchantment of the moon. In fact, all his powers worked against him, for they too, like the tides, fell under the immeasurable sway of a force invisible which wholly captivated his heart and reduced him to a broken colossus. Odd hallucinations passed before his eyes. Odd voices sounded in his head, whispering of spirits and insanities:

'Beware of the moon
  When above it looms
  And shines on the hair
  Of the girl who is fair.
  Madness and hell
  Ring their bell
  From the silk
  Of the moon
  In her hair.
  Beware.'

And the Mamba, in his hiding place among the trees, gazed and was lost to the voices and the hallucinations. Then, suddenly, he saw the form of a slender man, or was it squat, and round, or was it tall and strong, it kept changing, he wasn't sure. The Mamba instantly felt a laceration of heart, a great unnameable awe, and fear and suspicion and dryness of mouth all at once. And he knew that this changing form of a man was his real enemy and rival, though he had never seen this being or person before . . . . or maybe he had, in another form, in another way . . .

This person stood under the eaves of the maiden's father's workshop. The moonlight did not fall on him. Behind his head was the shape of a lamp. He was in deep shadow but the Mamba could make out something of his presence; for the Mamba sensed he was seeing the reality of a vision he once had, the vision of one who would spell the destruction of the tribe, their ways, their art . . .

The person gazed too at the maiden, as if he were the moon.

CHAPTER SIXTY-EIGHT

And then it wasn't long before the Mamba noticed the new pupil. He was the first to publicly notice him. And when the Mamba drew attention to the new pupil, he began to lose his protective invisibility.

The Mamba disliked him on sight; and, without provocation, began a campaign against him, to get him evicted from the village as a spy. At first no one paid the Mamba any attention; but he became obsessed, and his obsession, fed by the bitterness of having won the contests but not the maiden's hand, gave him a powerful clarity of voice and a strange prophetic authority. Not for the first time, the Mamba was losing his mind; but this time it appeared he had never been in greater control of himself. Having won the fights, with the skill, the brutality and the mastery he had displayed, coupled with the dark mystery he had gathered to himself during his disappearance, the Mamba was now being seen as a figure of great public power and leadership. People felt inclined to follow his lead; they felt, for the first time, that here was a leader they had never had, who would take them to a new destiny. Sometimes a sense of doom makes a people susceptible to that which in normal times would horrify them. Maybe that is why, in history, a people sometimes chose the very leader who would lead them over the precipice that they feared, and wanted to avoid, in the first place; they chose the one who would deliver them to the doom which they dreaded.

And so, inexplicably, the Mamba became the voice of the tribe. And the tribe, inexplicably, ceased to heed the warnings of the oracle, or the guidance of the masters who had, for centuries, brought them to various stations of their promised land.

CHAPTER SIXTY-NINE

The Mamba spoke out with a new voice of the destruction of the tribe by the stranger from beyond. He spoke of the stranger among them who was invading their lives, insinuating himself into their secret ways. He made a powerful and terrifying speech at the gates of the village, where he conjured visions of the end of their history, of hordes descending on them on white steeds. He sang passionately a song called

'Destruction is coming' and another one called 'Beware of the stranger', and he had the women in tears and hysterics, and the men quaking with fear and foreboding. Then, later that same day, under the unpredictable spell of his obsession and to the complete astonishment of the tribe, the Mamba challenged the new pupil to the ultimate contest, to win the hand of the maiden. The tribe was amazed at this act because they had never heard of or noticed the new pupil before. Nor did they know that he was considered a suitor.

That same evening the Mamba turned up at the maiden's house and did something strange. He brought out from his bag a gigantic skull of beautiful ebony that he had carved; and, with a faintly sinister and quite charming smile on his face, he banged the skull down on the table, and said:

'This is my shadow. My transformation is my story. Your love is my dream.'

Then he strode out.

After a long silence, the maiden's mother said:

'Trouble has come to our house.'

After another silence, the maiden's father said:

'Only the deep can speak to the deep.'

CHAPTER-SEVENTY

The new pupil did not know what to do. He had been challenged. He was no longer invisible. He did not believe in fighting. And yet there was no way out of this moment . . .

Slender, frail, sensitive, he took himself to the forest and asked the animals and the birds to teach him how to fight, how to prevail, how to win without winning.

And the crane taught him to balance on one leg. The lizard taught him elusiveness and the scuttle and how to abandon your tail if this would save your life. The spider taught him the art of ugliness and the web. The ant taught him the art of tenacity and the cunning of being small. The lion taught him majesty of presence and how to intimidate through stillness. The mosquito taught him the art of irritation and oblique motion. The bee taught him the art of madness and the sting and the possibility of impossible flight. The bat taught him the art of fighting without sight, of comfort in the dark, and the art of being upside-down. The mole taught him to go deep into the spirit of things. The goat taught him to use his head. The elephant taught him that weight is a hindrance as well as a force, and the art of memory. The art of awkwardness and the mystery of dwelling on two levels were the gift of the snake, as well as the art of the unthinkable. The art of love and the art of fighting through beauty of spirit was the blessing of the flowers. The frog taught him the unpredictable leap. The termite taught him the art of devouring within a structure. The eagle taught him the art of suddenness and surprise. The vulture taught him the art of stealth. The chicken taught him how to confuse by flapping his arms. The rabbit taught him its short-arm punch. The cat taught him sinuousness, elasticity, and how to fall; the python, how to coil and grasp; the lioness, ferocity; the antelope, speed; the trees, economy of movement, longevity in stillness. The silence taught him serenity. The tortoise taught him how to use time, patience, paradox and cunning. The praying mantis taught him that even a good fight is a form of prayer. The fly taught him how to frustrate, pester and disorientate. The tse-tse fly taught him the art of inducing sleep in the middle of a campaign. The heron, the new pupil's favourite creature, taught him the incommensurable art of fighting without appearing to do so, and winning when you are losing, and the art of transcending winning and losing, and sublime invincibility through always being in a higher state. The seeds of trees taught him the art of being reborn even when dying. The dew taught him the art of heaven meeting the earth. Sunlight taught him that all things come from a miraculous source. And the laughter faintly echoing in the air reminded him of his mysterious noble origin.

CHAPTER SEVENTY-ONE

With all these qualities what could have been the outcome? When the day of the fight came, it was all foregone. The fight was won and lost in advance, over before it began. It had happened, it was quick, and it was a mystery that was never unravelled. The fight was an unqualified work of art that so dazzled and amazed the tribe that it instantly entered their mythology and never left.

For it is still talked about in numerous stories all over the world till this day, and tomorrow, how the new pupil vanquished the Mamba. All that the people saw was not the fight, but its shadow, its aftermath. For they missed the event, which happened before their own eyes; it was so full of mysteries.

The Mamba appeared in all his physical and mythic glory, his muscles like bronze, glistening. The new pupil, slender and frail, appeared. He was still. He was smiling. It was almost a smile of forgiveness. The women's hearts went out to the frail one, who seemed so alone, an orphan.

The Mamba pounced, and caught a shadow. The Mamba grasped and wrestled with that which had no form. The Mamba lashed out, and struck the face of the wind in his fury. The Mamba chased after that which flapped. The Mamba heard buzzing in his ears. The Mamba heard a roar unnatural from a reed. The Mamba couldn't find the antelope which sped beneath his hulking shape. The Mamba was perplexed by the stillness of that which wasn't there when he charged it; and then he found it was behind him. The Mamba heard whispers of falling leaves. The Mamba saw a light flash in his brain. The Mamba charged the thousand forms of the same things all over the arena, out into the crowd. The Mamba cried out for the new pupil to stay still. Then the Mamba whispered for the servant to move, to fight. Then the Mamba saw the glory of the sun shining above the head of a young crowned prince. Then the Mamba, bleeding from so many self-inflicted wounds, heard a great wonderful sound of laughter in the clouds. Then the Mamba sank to his knees, and fell in prostration. Then, with a howl of horror and a cry of joy, the Mamba fell over on his back, and didn't move again for three days.

The prince hadn't struck him once. The masters declared this one of the greatest works of art they had seen in a generation.

The maiden fell completely, insanely, lucidly, sublimely, and shyly in love with this new revelation of man whom she had not noticed all this time, but who instantly healed her of all her sicknesses . . .

And eventually, at last, she recognised the one for what he was: anonymous, in disguise, a part of all the delays, there and not there, in the competitions, indirectly, in secret, winning them all, humbly, without entering them and without knowing; that which she had been seeking for she had found, humble and lowly though it seemed; and to everyone's astonishment she declared him to be the one she loved and wanted to marry . . .

CHAPTER SEVENTY-TWO

Her father's response to all this was completely mysterious. Around this time he unveiled what he had been working on in secret. He had created one final sculpture to heal the horrors the last one had unleashed. Then he sculpted no more. His tone of tragic sublimity vanished from the tribe and the land, echoing now and again in the lesser works of those who came much later. His last sculpture was a work of pure beauty, and it had the same effect as the last one, except in the opposite way. The masters said it was his spiritual offering to the mystic wedding of his daughter, to a wedding that took place among the stars. People came on pilgrimages to see the sculpture, even as the suitors and their entourage left the environs of the village. Their noisy, rowdy presence was replaced by pilgrims to a new revelation, as if the image unveiled were a new god or goddess incarnated in the land.

The sculpture was beautiful indeed, and its beauty was mysterious. It induced sleep, graciousness, good manners, profound and vivid dreams in which guides appeared to the dreamers. It also induced an odd vacancy in all those who saw it. Suddenly the young wanted to die in its presence; and the old, dying, wanted it to be the last thing they saw before they passed away ...

And what was it, this mysterious sculpture? It was more than it seemed. And its mystery was as much in how it created a shimmer of illumination around itself, against the sky, as it was the spirit-charged nature of the stone, as it was that of which it was an eternal sign, a question mark without a name, concentrating the magic of the heavens into the illusion of space. It was the figure of a being, a man or woman or god or goddess or dream; and the figure stood with both of its arms stretched out unnaturally wide, embracing the whole universe, in a mighty act of acceptance. Arms outstretched and legs spread out wide, doubly embracing all of life, the universe, all suffering, all joy, the beginning, the end, life, death, and beyond ...

CHAPTER SEVENTY-THREE

The king was wandering about the kingdom looking over the sleeping forms of his people, marvelling at the beautiful darkness rich with the minerals of the stars, and came upon a maiden in white kneeling in front of the village shrine. She turned a smiling and beautiful face to him, and genuflected without speaking. And he said:

'What are you doing here at this hour when the world sleeps?'

'I found myself here not knowing how.'

'Then you must have a reason.'

'This evening I took to wandering, walking and thinking and trying not to think, and I found myself here.'

She listened to the incommensurable music of the distant constellations. Did she expect a response from the mysterious personage? She had the wisdom to listen to the silence that seemed to come from him, a silence like that of a river at night when all is still and all the stars are out.

'Also I brought an offering,' she said.

She revealed a piece of sculpture she had placed before the shrinehouse. The sculpture was of a radiant king wearing a ten-pointed crown. In his right hand he held a staff with two serpents coiled round it, and at its summit was a globe. And in the other hand the seated king, in his majestic throne, held a book that was also a six-pointed star. The sculpture pleased the king immensely. And he laughed in great warmth, and the young lady, touched by the humour of this majestic being on so beautiful a night, found herself laughing too; and together they laughed happily under the clear stars of the sleeping world.

CHAPTER SEVENTY-FOUR

She woke earlier in the morning than she had ever woken before. She woke with a strange new clear joy in her head and a clear strong irrational hunger between her legs and a deep hollow dark happy feeling in the pit of her stomach. She could not seem to breathe right and whenever she drew breath she felt her heart go light and her head swim and she had the queerest sensation that something in her was going to jump out of her body and leap out into the air, towards the sun. Her head was clear but she could not think clearly. She got out of bed and bathed and oiled herself and cleaned herself and anointed herself as if in a dream, as if she were going to be presented to a king. She did everything dreamily, for indeed she no longer knew if she were dreaming or not, or if she were alive or if she had become a spirit, for she no longer seemed to be in her body, but in a sort of bliss that was like a beautiful death. And when she felt clean enough, when she felt so happy and so beautiful that she lost all sense of herself, she left the house silently and went to her father's workshop.

She was surprised when she arrived not to find the prince there. She was so surprised that she went among all the statues and touched them one by one, and stared into their faces, into their eyes, expecting one of them to move suddenly and come alive, revealing the one and only love she would ever have in her life, in this life and the next. But not one of the statues moved, or changed, or stirred into life, or became the one she had yearned for and loved, the one who could not be named, who have lived in her, it seemed, all her life, and before.

Then a sort of terror came over her, a terror that bordered on madness at the thought that she would never see him again. She stood absolutely still in her father's workshop, among the statues of stone, of wood, and of bronze. And she felt, for a moment, how cruel a fate it was that all this time she had not seen him when he was there, and now that she could see him and craved for him and wanted him more than life itself, he was not there. She felt keenly her punishment at her blindness, at her inability to see. And she felt, as she stood there, that there was nothing left for her any more, not on earth, not in life. She had no idea how long she stood there in silent lamentation and intolerable grief, for one she had loved without knowing it, and who loved her as the sun loves the earth, as the birds love the air. She had no idea what to do except die. Death seemed the only answer to her loss. In a dream of death, of the joy of dying for the loss of the unknown love of her life, she locked the workshop and wandered to the forest, singing a lullaby. All who passed her early that morning thought she was both happy and mad.

In a daze she wandered through the forest, picking flowers of every colour, singing gently a song of happy death while she did so. She picked wild roses, and white lilies, and blue flowers with mysterious calyxes, and yellow flowers, and marigolds, and hibiscuses, and held them to her face and wandered to the river. She did not notice anything. She did not hear the birds, nor the wind, nor see the gently gold and red and quivering yellow of sunrise, nor did she even feel the dew or the softness of the sand beneath her feet. She dreamt only of one thing, guided by the angel of love that had blanked out her mind to all awareness except the happiness to be found with her loved one who was waiting for her in the kingdom of the goddess in the depths of the river.

She began to sing a song of farewell to all things. Then she fell silent and rose and, holding the flowers in her hand as an offering to the goddess, she began to walk towards the river, away from life as she had known it. She was gone from life now, gone from her body, gone from the earth; she was going to the only legend that was forever true, the legend of love, of death and love, beneath the river.

And then she heard the voice on the wind that she had heard long ago, the voice that had first woken her from the sleep of her life, the voice that she had once taken to be that of a god. And all about her everything sprang to life. All at once she saw the river, big and swollen and mighty, and she feared that it would without warning engulf her and take her under, to a frightening kingdom. Then she saw the sky, vast and clear and of a blue so pure she felt that it would snatch her soul away. Then she noticed the sunrise, golden and gentle red and quivering on the rim of the river and so beautiful that she felt if she breathed she would be wafted away to some homeland beyond the stars. And then she heard his voice again and all the clamour and agitation in her heart, her belly, and the wild unknown hunger between her legs came awake in her and she stood rooted to the sand, not hearing what was said. Then a darkness passed over her eyes and cleared and she found herself staring into the blinding adoration and passion of his gaze. His eyes were all the world then and she did not see the sky or the shore or the sunrise or the forest or the river, just his eyes. And she stood there gazing into the depths of his eyes completely lost to everything else on earth and in heaven or maybe she had found everything that she sought on earth and in heaven. And before she knew it they were lying side by side on the shore, near a bank of flowers, just gazing into one another's eyes, mutely, almost without breathing.

They say that it is not just things of this world that one sees but one does not know one is seeing. And as the prince and the maiden gazed into one another's eyes, as they gazed deep into the depths of the whites, and into the mystery of the emerald or green or brown or golden centre at the centre of the eyes they caught glimpses of what they had been to one another in time past beyond memory and what they would be to one another in the beautiful time to come beyond death, in another life, where their true story of love would seem to begin. They gazed as into crystal balls and were mesmerised and slightly frightened by the intolerable depth of love they saw deep within the other. It seemed a love too strong for mortal life, a love that would make itself the sole purpose of living, a love that was like eternity gazing into the mirror of eternity, a love that would do nothing but simply exist in the blissful light of the other as in the light of the sun after the darkest night. In their silence they exchanged all the tokens and signs and secrets of mutual revelation so that, among the millions of people who dwell on the earth, if they were to meet in their appointed future hour of destiny, it would take only a glance into the other's eyes to know that this was the one they were seeking. And so they planted the certainty of finding one another in the life to come by the depth of the speech of their mutual gazing into the mystery of each other's eyes. And not only that: for as they gazed they journeyed through time, through many realms and planes of pure happiness where they already lived the joyful life they were meant to live. They touched those other lives and returned refreshed and reassured. And then the prince changed the nature of their mutual enchantment.

Without seeming to breathe, quivering in the warmth of the world at sunrise, the prince peeled off the maiden's wrapper and her white blouse and beheld the beauty of her clear pure skin. It shone like the surface of the river in the tenderness of sunrise. Then without touching her he passed his open palms along the surface of her skin, not touching her and yet touching her more deeply than if he had grabbed hold of her in a wild passionate embrace.

He passed his hands over her face and lingered over her eyes, her cheeks, her ears, her forehead, her chin, and hovered over her throat. At first she was still. She breathed gently. Her eyes were shut. Then something strange happened to her. She felt a fire pierce her heart and it burned her right through in a golden pain and then she was gone. Breathing felt as if the air was made of a beautiful deathly powder, for every breath she drew was a sublime agony; and as he passed his hands slowly over her body the more piercing was the fire in her heart and the fire in her belly. And she began to cry out an unknown name and was not aware of it. And soon her cry and her love, her fire and her joy were one. And it was so unbearable that she opened her eyes in a wild abandon, a holy rage at being so unwrapped and so full of an inexplicable yearning.

And then he lay down next to her, so close they were not touching and yet not close enough that they were almost as one. And then he brought his lips close to her tender soft lips . . . There was something special, almost forbidden in the manner in which they kissed; it is a secret that is not to be shared. It was a kind of kissing that was unique to them and they had kissed one another thus in all the times past and in all the planes and in all the future time that they had spent and were to spend with one another. It was a kiss that can only be described as the way in which certain angels kiss if such a thing can be imagined; it was the kissing of their souls. It was the only true way that their souls can speak to one another, the only way they can be understood, in bliss.

And after this secret kiss, their lips touched and they moved into the second kind of their secret forbidden kissing. The maiden felt herself to no longer be herself but the prince, and the prince was no longer himself but was now the maiden, and each to the other was a sort of eternity. There is a kind of love, a kind of bliss that borders on blasphemy in that it breaks one of the unwritten laws of life as it is meant to be lived in the body. And that law is thus: thou shalt not feel too much. The prince and the maiden, lost in the labyrinths of their kissing, had somehow gone back to a forbidden moment under the sun. And their lips came together fully and they did not move and all the rivers and seas came together and the laws of time and space were torn asunder and what was to happen to them pressed closer as if the power of their conjoining would provoke the evil that was to befall them in their unimaginable dissolving of one soul into another. It is possible that too much love can awaken an evil destiny: why else are love and tragedy so twinned on earth?

But they plunged deeper and went past the tree of good and evil and lived its consequence and they came to the tree of knowledge and waited under its enchanted fruits, not moving, their hearts still. And they glimpsed the angel of ecstasy and they went past the tree of knowledge in their kissing and went right into the golden place that they'd been in once before in which they heard the sweetest singing in the air. And they dwelt there, like two swans in the lake of paradise . . .

And then, seized by a sudden violence, she began to touch him all over. And she felt and loved and moulded every single part of him, singing to him in her mind, mapping him in her pleasure, for she never knew that there could be a pleasure on earth greater than feeling the wood or stone out of which a statue emerges, and that flesh and the body of a man can be more beautiful than dreams. For she had such dreams, such notions and inexplicable feelings as she felt the prince and lavished her senses on the magic of his skin and his muscles and his quivering trembling limbs. And when she had felt him all over, she was astonished to feel her fingertips tingling and her palms shimmering inwardly as if possessed by a supernatural energy, a radiant delight. She had never known this miraculous sensation before, and she was even more amazed to catch, in a glimpse, the way his skin shone all over, and the light that poured out of him, from his skin, as if she had polished a lamp of gold and any moment now a spirit would leap out from it, the spirit of the light that it would shine for ever. And the light around him, full of many colours, for a second resolved itself into a golden aureole and she was so overcome that she fell on him in tears of unmentionable love and adoration. And they held one another in fearful embrace, as if they wanted to become spirit again and penetrate one another's beings, right into the core.

Tightly in their embrace, so that the one did not know where they ended and the other began, they remained still. They just lay still, locked and merged in one another's love, and like that they drifted away together. They could hear whispers at the far end of the village. They could hear the wind over a wave in the farthest reaches of the river. They could hear the call of the sunbird far in the sky beyond the horizon. They could hear the cry of a baby in the remote depths of the kingdom. They could hear footfalls drawing closer to them, and murmurs, and rumours, and the clasping of roots in the black earth, and the flowers opening to the sun, and the dew forming on the silk of the calyxes of roses, and the pure music up in the distant reaches of space among the stars, and the slightest movement of the wings of a butterfly and of an angel, and they could hear all manner of thoughts, of dreams, but they could not hear one another breathing or weeping in silence.

And then having been taught by her what to do, and how deeply it was possible to feel if felt with the enchantment of art and love, he now began to touch her too, mapping in his soul the memory of her body as if he knew that this was the one time only in this life that he would have to love her and enjoy her beyond the limit of what was possible. And so he prayed for the wisdom and the knowledge and the passion and the joy of being able to love and enjoy her more than it was given to a mortal to do during these moments of being alive and having her there before him in all the beauty and glory of her youth and her love.

And when she felt him entering her, the strangest thing happened, and the fire between her legs made sense at last, and she let herself slip into the warm waters of the river and sink slowly into the realms of the goddess, for now she was all liquid and fire and senselessness. And they moved together sometimes as one, sometimes divergently, often in odd wild rhythms, and mostly in the rhythms of the waves of the river as it crashed on the shore or lapped silently on the rim of the land so that it felt that they were both the river and the land, both the sun and the earth.

And then she was falling, not into an abyss, but deeper and deeper to the bottom of the river, falling without end, and she was unbelievably happy in her fall till she became aware for the first time that she could not breathe and she loved it so. The more she gasped for air the more she found herself unable to breathe and the more bliss she felt and this got worse and better and worse still, this inability to breathe and the insane pleasure, that it reached a point beyond which she feared it was too dangerous to go in the excess of her feelings. She knew then that she would surely die and yet she wanted to and she let herself go and he went on moving in her and kissing and clutching at her an irregular way and then she went over and she panicked, for she saw something very dark and fearful and inviting, summoning her, a thing or being vast and dark and bright in the midst of her bliss, and she had come to the end of her inability to breathe and she was going away now, getting utterly lost, and she screamed and cried:

'Oh my mother, save me, I'm drowning, I'm drowning!'

And he didn't hear her at all, for he had caught a spark of dangerous fire, and he found himself on a crest of such shining relentless ecstasy that it seemed he was possessed of a living fire, and every movement he made was like touching a live spark of screaming joy that could not be put out, like being touched in a raw place with sparkling tongues of an immortal burning; and it got worse and more unbearable till it was the core of his being that was the beautiful burning and the feeling; and he too went past a point and went over.

Neither of them could stop moving now, stop racing towards their doom, their disaster and their redemption; and she gasped and her mouth opened wide and she cried out long and silently; and his mouth was open wide, uttering no sound, but screaming in a high pitch. And then there was a long silence, and a sudden long stillness, as if they had been both momentarily transformed into statues of grotesque and sublime pleasure. And then a long terrible double cry was heard that resounded in the depths of the river and up in the heights of the sky, a long-sustained much delayed much desired cry of creation, and then a single burst of light, bright beyond measure, as at the birth of a significant star.

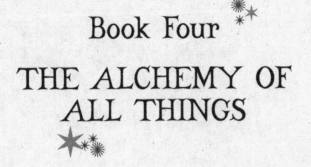

Book Four

THE ALCHEMY OF ALL THINGS

CHAPTER ONE

There was rejoicing in all the high places. They had made love once, but that once was enough. Each changed the other's world and the story of the earth changed too in that once.

Nothing could undo what would happen, what would continue to happen because of that once. Their love had, at last, after centuries of missed opportunities, finally found its great moment. And their love in a future time would last a lifetime and an eternity for having finally connected on this earth, where such a possibility is all too rare.

Yes, there was rejoicing in all the high places.

CHAPTER TWO

As night fell, the maiden said:
'I always thought you were not real. I always thought you were something strange, like a dream, a white horse in a dream. I always thought you were something brought to life by a miraculous touch. Not entirely human. You appeared like a being created by my father's magic art. Now I have to see you as a human being, and love you as a man. To me you will always be something unique, something more than just a human

being. Maybe before all this and after all this you are just my dream.'

'I am a dream and not a dream; I am real and not real,' said the prince.

'There is only one thing left though.'

'What?'

'How do you give me your shadow?'

'I have given you my shadow because I have given you my death and my love.'

'But you have not told me a story.'

'That's because we have lived it.'

'And the best dream?'

'You have dreamt it.'

CHAPTER THREE

Afterwards came the changes. It all happened so fast that their lives passed from the greatest happiness to the greatest despair in what seemed like a lightning flash of unreal time. But the moments in which they were happy, even delirious, were themselves a lifetime, an eternity. These moments were deep enough to last in the memory that never fades, till they were to meet again and live the lives of two lovers whose time to be happy and to be together at last arrives on earth, or somewhere else more suitable ... And these future lives would not be much worth telling a story about because of the simple pleasure and harmony of their togetherness, their happiness.

But that night, by the river, as they stared naked at one another in the afterglow of their shattering pleasure, they probably sensed that their magic moment was over, that such unnatural joy was not meant to last. They probably sensed that their sublime consummation was a brief gift from heaven as a promise for a future renewal, and a consolation for what was to come.

They had been followed. And as they lingered in the starburst of their love-making by the river, they were set upon by the Mamba and his followers, bearing flaming torches, leaping out from the undergrowth . . . .

CHAPTER FOUR

In confusion and horror, the two lovers fled into the forest, holding hands. The maiden, unable to keep up the fury of the pace, demanded that her lover make his own escape and that he should return for her later, when times were more auspicious. The new pupil, in the chaos of the moment, in furious whispers, told her of the gaps in the forest, and the right one to choose when seeking for him should he be successful in his escape or should she not hear from him. Then he made off into the darkness of the forest.

The new pupil, in his haste, in the chaos, in the trap sprung by the audacious fates, chose the wrong gap between trees, a gap fiery with the dark light of an agonising destiny; and he appeared in his village at the moment when, their plan hatched and ready to be born, Chief Okadu and the usurping elders had decided, should he return, to have the prince either killed, or delivered up to the white spirits to be carried off into the sea of oblivion.

CHAPTER FIVE

In his nakedness the prince, guided by an intuition, did not go back to the palace when he managed to find his way back to the village. He hung around in the dark, waiting near the village shrine for anyone who might happen past. A woman late returning from the market saw him crouching and heeded his call. From her he learnt about the changes that had happened in his absence. Stripping off a layer of cloth, the woman covered the prince's nakedness and led him, under the protection of darkness, to her humble family abode, where the prince could collect his thoughts and fortify himself with food, and where he could meditate and pray. What he had learnt, what he found out, was indeed momentous. The world had spun out of its axis. Celestial night had fallen over the land.

CHAPTER SIX

When he arrived back home, his father was no longer there. Only his laughter now ruled as an echo in the kingdom.

His father, it was said, had simply vanished on a white wind, and had left all his laws and his legacy in his laughter.

No one witnessed the disappearance of his father.

And then even the laughter could no longer be heard in the growing wastes of the land.

The elders were now rulers of the kingdom.

And when they heard of the return of the prince they immediately denounced him as a fraud and decreed that if caught he should be killed . . .

There was a dead new silence in the kingdom without the laughter of the king.

Some say that it was with this silence that the real fall of the kingdom began . . .

CHAPTER SEVEN

Somehow the spies of the new dispensation got wind of the prince's hiding place in the abode of the market woman. They learnt of his presence there not long after he had arrived. Fortunately the prince was informed that they were coming for him and he cut short his prayers and began his final sojourn away from the land. His exile began in the midst of his prayers, his exile from the kingdom.

For the second time that fateful day the prince had to flee; and unfortunately he fled, in the dark, on the margins of the forest, right into the trap of the white spirits. He was caught, chained, gagged with a metallic contraption, and bundled off on a long trek across the savannah to a waiting ship where, in its hold, he found a thousand others. Those who were caught and chained together were from different tribes and nations and spoke different languages and could not communicate with one another except through gestures, through agony, through thought. And thus began the great trial and the great suffering of the race. Those who didn't perish under the lash, who were not thrown overboard, who didn't die in the crush and torture in the hold, those who made the crossing, all manner of men and women and children, they were sold, they worked the fields and the earth of alien lives; and they took with them a new destiny, the spirit of freedom, the colour of justice, and the mystery of music and art to a new world. The prince was sustained only by the laughter of the king that sounded all over the universe, beyond the power and the evils of men.

CHAPTER EIGHT

But that is only one side of the story. On the fateful day when the Mamba pursued the two lovers, the maiden managed to escape, and made it back home, where she appeared in a state of near-deranged nakedness.

What followed is unclear. In the book among the stars one reads with the spirit and interprets through memory; and there is much that is vague when the spirit is not perfect.

The masters of the tribe decreed that the tribe commence one of its seasonal migrations, to escape the cycle of doom that had been hovering like a thundercloud over their lives. They also declared the Mamba an outlaw and banished him, too late, from their midst. The maiden bore her child; and having awaited for many moons the return of her loved one, she left home one night and went seeking him. She too went through the fated gap of an agonising destiny, was captured by the white spirits, and suffered the sea crossing which should never be forgotten in the forgetfulness of men and women.

When she disappeared, the tribe of artists lost its soul. Then one night, through the same fated gap in the forest, which had widened beyond measure, the white spirits came, and descended on the unsuspecting tribe. It might never have happened if it were not for the activities of the Mamba and his followers.

They had become marauders in the forest, and the Mamba's chief obsession was to find and kill the pupil who had so humiliated him.

Often the Mamba and his followers raided villages, and plundered and pillaged the surrounding countryside. Often they would return to the edge of their old village and look on at the preparations the tribe made for their migration. They looked on, and wept at their banishment . . .

But it was the Mamba and his followers who attracted the

attention of the spies of the white spirits, who followed them one night and saw a village without fortifications. That night the white spirits fell on the tribe and carried away its strong and its young. They destroyed the village and scattered its inhabitants among the hills. Those that were caught were gagged and bound and sent across the seas; many of them perished in the crossing; those that made it over, in their suffering, spread an unconquerable spirit in the new land; because their spirit, from ancient times, had always been strong.

CHAPTER NINE

What was left of the tribe of artists regrouped, and changed location, guided by their dwindling masters. They moved on, they grieved. After the destruction there was a scattering of the tribe, its dream, its people and its art. They became etiolated, and slowly vanished in the mists of time. Then there was silence . . .

. . . and it was only after a century, on several other continents, that their fire was kindled again, in different forms . . .

But in the old land, after the silence of their ways, only standing stones and mysterious sculptures that endure the wrath of time's decay remain in enigmatic places in the forest, among wild plants and trees that have grown over their old habitation. Their shrine turned to dust and returned to the air. Their gods returned to the deepest realms of dreams.

CHAPTER TEN

The elders ruled for a while in the kingdom of the prince, and in the absence of the king. They ruled with unwisdom, and much dissension broke out amongst them, and the people distrusted and undermined them, and one by one they fell to each other's blades at night, or to secretly administered poisons by day. Their children were mostly lost to a terrible lassitude, others to a madness that took the form of incurable fits of fiendish laughter; and they laughed themselves into early graves. Then the gaps began to devour the kingdom. And then the full force of the white wind descended on them and wiped out great areas of the past, and wiped out memory, and dissolved many traditions. And then the white spirits came and the land lost the spring of its ways. Forgetfulness followed and new ways grew over the oblivion of the old ways. And those that came after were not heirs to those that went before, because of the great gaps, and the onslaught of the white wind that almost created a desert out of a flowering land.

CHAPTER ELEVEN

For a long time it did seem as if all was lost. But, after a century, a myth began again in the minds of historians and artists who sought an explanation of how such a rich artistic heritage came to be, and how or why the community that created it so suddenly and completely disappeared. Its legacy was now spread throughout the world, enriching the hearts and dreams of strangers and the secret children of the tribe all over the globe. The hidden masters maintain still that nothing is ever lost, but abides in the dreams of humanity, and in the infinite story, in the infinite book among the stars.

But in the land, with time's passing, only children playing in the dreamtime of their most innocent years, when spirits are as real to them as birds or trees, only such children would one day stumble on the monoliths and statues and enigmas in stone of the vanished people, and release ancient spells into new centuries.

It seemed that only their dreams given form remained, concealed. And when these works were discovered it would be surmised that they were created by masters from a distant planet, a more advanced civilisation . . . alien artists creating in solitude and homesickness for their magic constellation . . .

CHAPTER TWELVE

. . . and the prince had undergone his final test; as a slave he had endured his last crucifixion. Among the slaves he had spread dreams of freedom, dreams of illumination, which never perished. He was, by all accounts, a secret master who saw it all, suffered it all. It is whispered that this was his last time on the wheel, in the dust of living.

After the years of slavery, spreading a new message in the undergrowth of those who suffered, he returned, it is said, to the realm of his father, the laughing king; and served the kingdom in the highest way, among the stars and in the whispers of the soul.

CHAPTER THIRTEEN

The maiden's parents survived, as did their grandchild. The tribe did regroup from among those who scattered in the forest and among the hills; and quickly, leaving everything behind, they began their migration, never staying anywhere long enough to be noticed. Time passed and one day a mysterious deputation of wise men and women appeared amongst them and came to claim the grandchild as their future king. They brought great gifts. The masters of the tribe of artists recognised this act of destiny, and the maiden's parents acceded to this extraordinary claim. In ceremonial splendour the grandchild was led back to the palace of his paternal ancestors, led to the throne, and to his rightful inheritance. His coronation was as legendary as the mystery of his lineage. But the kingdom ever awaited the return of his father; and the laughter of the original father was heard again, in faint harmonies, growing in clarity, throughout the kingdom.

CHAPTER FOURTEEN

Though the tribe of artists had regrouped, it had only partially recovered; and its strength was no longer able to hold out against the dissolution wrought on it by the destruction of its old ways. The tribe survived long enough as a people to have one last stage of almost great flowering. It was the swan song of their golden age. It was the last days of their old dispensation before they vanished into the dust of time.

They must have felt acutely this last air of their days. An elegiac mood pervaded their works. They created with the terrifying intensity of a people who know they are dying and want to populate the world, to fertilise the universe, with the potent seeds of their invention, their creativity. These last years, before they succumbed to oblivion, were their most poignant. Everyone created, shaped, dreamt in stone, in wood, in non-durable material, on cloth, in songs as if turning their lives into forms that must endure and survive the passing of their flesh, their bodies, their hearts. Children created as intensely as the aged who were dying. Everywhere among the tribe they began to create their testimonies, their whimsies, fantasies, prophecies, and pure forms of no purpose other than to salute the mystery and the unappreciated joys of living.

The maiden's parents were very old now. Most of the masters had gone to join the ancestors. The Mamba and his followers had raged in the forest for a time, had marauded, and terrified surrounding peoples, had, some of them, been caught and bundled off to slavery, and others had grown old too, and were heard from no more. No one knew what became of the Mamba, though tradition has it that one day, following the legend of the gaps that led to a fabulous kingdom of gold and happiness, he had stumbled into one of the worst gaps of all, and had been seen spontaneously combusting into wild red and fiery green flames from which he could not be rescued. And such was the awesome nature of his fiery consummation that his followers, such as were left, were terrified by the sign and fled away from the forest, back to the open plains, and sought ways to redeem themselves among the living.

CHAPTER FIFTEEN

How did this tale come down to my mother, this tale that she began to tell me when I was a child?

Somebody has to create a myth. Somebody has to turn a life into legend. Someone has to project a story into the future. This is how a fragment of that legend came down to me.

Around the time of the swan song of the tribe in its elegiac stage, the maiden's father, now on the verge of death, and in great secrecy, invented a new kind of drama. He had long abandoned the art of sculpture, and had been silent as an artist since his daughter disappeared one night and was never found again. Out of his great silence, his great age, and the profound nature of his myth, he created a new form to add to the ritual and memory of the race. And so one day actors appeared near their new shrine and performed a new kind of story-telling theatre, and astonished the tribe in their dying years. The first act went something like this . . .

Griot (standing in a circle's centre): Memory is better than gold. And so listen to this legend as it is told. Now that there is little time left, this is the only way to tell it quickly. Listen wisely with your souls, and not your eyes or ears. Become this drama I am about to show you. Listen as if to the good ones dead, who have a light in your head.

Then silence. Then in the darkness different voices, interspersed with bells, drums, sighs, bird calls, flutes, koras, cowhorns, recite these lines.

Voice: If you enter through the magic gate, if you walk through the encampment of the tribe . . .

CHAPTER SIXTEEN

. . . You will find them carving at wood sculptures in open workshops, hammering at bronze, singing poignant songs in groups, in lovely harmonies. You will see children making new objects out of rejects, drawing pictures on the ground. You will see the women painting cloth in vivid colours, or creating new forms with jewels and cowries, practising new dances in the square. You will find the old at work, directing great projects, telling stories to the young, listening to the dreams of maidens.

You will see sculptures everywhere, in wood, in shining bronze, in copper, in stone. You will see sculpted shapes of animals imagined or dreamt, of visitants from the sky, of gods, ancestors, the unborn, of spirits, or the noble busts of sages. You will see images of harvests and beautiful women, and strong men, images of the future, shapes drawn on walls.

You will find a place alive with art in every corner, art in the square, art all around the shrines. You will find a place alive with constant creativity. Such was the place the prince encountered as he entered the encampment of the tribe, disguised as a humble man, according to his principle of the heron, in quest of a maiden.

He had for many years heard tales of gods who made love to maidens disguised as birds or gentle animals. He had understood from this that to get to the best woman the man must be simple as a swan. He had also taken from this that it is best not to frighten a special maiden with too much power. To be lowly, to be low, was the only way to gain her trust. The highest became the lowest to do their highest work. The seduction of the maidens by the gods he took to be a metaphor of enlightenment, of the penetration of the soul of humanity by the ecstasy of the godhead. The soul of man is a beautiful virgin; the god is the instrument of the great God. These thoughts he had toyed with in the forest as he journeyed onward. Now that he was of the tribe of artists, he was overwhelmed by the beauty of their way. More than anything, he felt at home there.

He made his way to the maiden's father, and offered to be his servant, for nothing, for no pay. The father saw the spirit of the prince in the guise of the beggar. The father set him seven tasks of art and love, and if he performed them he could be his apprentice.

When, that evening, the prince caught a glimpse of the maiden in moonlight, crowned in white light, he nearly died from concealed joy ...

This is how a fragment of that story came down to me, and haunted me.

CHAPTER SEVENTEEN

That was how it seemed before that cycle ended, before their golden age perished, before they passed away into the sands. The maiden's father died, and her mother passed on not long after. The tribe slowly disintegrated from loss of vision, vigour and guidance.

Where do all the sculptures go afterwards? And why was it that only minor works followed? That was the high point of its culture. It had no name then. Afterwards, during its descending ages, the works displayed were of rumours, of incest, of abominations, of men making love to animals, animals making love to women, images of alien colonisers, of big-bellied children.

The tragic nobility had left their art because when it spoke clearest, and with the greatest beauty and grandeur, the people did not listen, did not see, did not interpret clearly, did not prepare, did not heed the warnings in the golden light. And so their golden age died, and their true way died, and their world lost its axis. And it got set on a new course, at the low ebb of a new cycle, that may or may never again know the simple grandeur of its past.

CHAPTER EIGHTEEN

But all was not lost. It only seemed that way for a hundred years or so. In their disintegration the tribe of artists all but disappeared from the known spaces. They had finally learnt their lesson. They were forgotten, they became invisible, and yet their works continued to appear in the land, in the world, along trade routes, in marketplaces, in palaces, in the new centres of the changing world. They became the world's tradition and its future.

They had followed the fragments of the guidance of their secret masters and had moved often, till they dwelt in a place called no-place. There they thrived in quietness, responding to the needs of the world in art.

The decades passed, and as the world settled round the changing ideas of the new centuries, the tribe lost its taste for frequent migration, and slowly became visible again. But they were not the same as they had been. Their art had much diminished. Their golden age was long over and was now a whisper. They didn't even have a sense of connection with the art of the tribe that was all over the kingdom, mysteries in the forests or in caves. They were not heirs to themselves.

Their artistic creation was good enough to inspire delight among the uninitiated, but not astonishment among themselves. They are now a celebrated community in the land; and people from all over the world make long journeys to see their latest creations. If you walk into the town, down its main streets, you will see paintings and sculptures on display everywhere, but you will not see what was once a ...

CHAPTER NINETEEN

And yet somewhere, as yet undiscovered, among the images of prophecy and vision, in the vast storehouse of the tribe's hidden trove of artworks going back to its earliest times; among these works that foretold, in their images and codes, world wars, genocides, the destruction of great cities, turning points in the history of humanity, the assassination of world leaders, the death of whole tribes by unnamed diseases, the discovery of vehicles that can fly, the first publicly acknowledged encounter with alien beings from distant constellations, and the hint of the end of the world, which is really the beginning of true illumination; among these undiscovered works that hide underground, in deep forests, there is an image of haunting beauty and simplicity, made of pure lines, a heavenly light and an unaccountable pathos – the image of a dying prince.

And among those which were found was the image of a maiden as a princess, which was carried away from its home and stares mutely behind glass at the curious eyes of countless generations ...

CHAPTER TWENTY

The ways of time are indeed strange; and events are not what we think they are. Time and oblivion alchemise all things, even the greatest suffering.

CHAPTER TWENTY-ONE

All is not lost. Greater times are yet to be born. In the midst of the low tide of things, when all seems bleak, a gentle voice whispers in the air that the spirits of creativity wander the land, awaiting an invocation and the commanding force of masters to harness their powers again to noble tasks and luminous art unimagined.

They wander and they wonder at the unseeing eyes of men and women who dwell in the splendours and darkness all around them, in an unseen world.

CHAPTER TWENTY-TWO

What more is there to tell? Just fragments seen in the book of life. All stories lead to infinity. There is no end to them, as there was no beginning. Just an epic sensed in the unheard laughter of things. Just fragments seen in the murky mirror of mortality, when bright beings shine momentarily in the brief dream of living.